She was seeking revenge.

What she found was a vampire who swept her into the darkest depths of passion . . .

HIS HEAT AGAINST her still-naked back . . . the fresh soap scent of his skin. Aden's arm reached around her and lifted a flogger from its hook. It was leather, a light brown suede that gave its multiple tails a deceptively soft appearance.

Aden dragged the soft suede across her naked skin. Her breath grew uneven, and her heart was going a mile a minute. But she wasn't afraid.

Aden lowered his mouth to her ear. "Do you know what I thought when I laid eyes on you for the first time, Sidonie?"

Sid tried to come up with something clever, something to break the unbearable erotic tension that was freezing her in place. But she could only shake her head mutely.

"I thought how beautiful your pale skin would look under the lash," he crooned, trailing the flogger down her body.

Without warning, he snapped the flogger in the air, letting her feel the barest kiss of suede against her thigh. Aden closed the small distance between them until his body was flush with hers. She closed her eyes, letting her head fall back against his shoulder.

His lips closed over her neck, and she reached up, curving her fingers over the back of his head, caressing him, holding him against her.

"Let me show you, Sidonie." His voice was deep, compelling . . . irresistible.

"Yes," she breathed.

Other ImaJinn titles
by D.B. Reynolds

The Vampires in America Series

Raphael (Book One)

Jabril (Book Two)

Rajmund (Book Three)

Sophia (Book Four)

Duncan (Book Five)

Lucas (Book Six)

The Cyn & Raphael Novellas

Betrayed

Hunted

Aden

Book 7 of the
Vampires in America Series

by

D.B. Reynolds

ImaJinnBooks

This is a work of fiction. Names, characters, places and incidents are either the products of the author's imagination or are used fictitiously. Any resemblance to actual persons (living or dead), events or locations is entirely coincidental.

ImaJinnBooks, Inc.
PO BOX 300921
Memphis, TN 38130
Print ISBN: 978-1-61026-139-5

ImaJinnBooks is an Imprint of BelleBooks, Inc.

ImaJinn Books was founded by Linda Kichline.

We at ImaJinn Books enjoy hearing from readers. Visit our websites
ImaJinnBooks.com
BelleBooks.com
BellBridgeBooks.com.

10 9 8 7 6 5 4 3 2 1

Cover design: Debra Dixon
Interior design: Hank Smith
Photo/Art credits:
Cover Art © Pat Lazarus
Body photo © Yuri Arcurs-123rf
Head photo © Dmytro Konstantynov-Bigstock
Arabic background photo © Santosh Telkhede—Bigstock
Chicago skyline © Songquan Deng—Bigstock
Tattoo © Pat Lazarus

:Laqz:01:

Dedication

For Linda Kichline

Prologue

Chicago, IL

SIDONIE REID gripped the seatbelt tightly, the nylon digging into her fingers as the ambulance roared through an intersection to the sound of blaring horns and squealing tires. There was so much noise. The siren was a constant assault to her ears. The radio blatted voices—the dispatcher, other drivers, hospitals.

There were no windows, and even if there had been, she couldn't have made sense of it. She didn't even try. All of her energy was focused on the pale woman strapped to the gurney, struggling to live. She squeezed Janey's hand harder, willing her to fight, to know that she wasn't alone, that there was someone here who cared, who knew the truth of what had happened. Not what it looked like, but what it was.

"Ma'am, I need you to let go of her hand." The EMT's voice was brisk and businesslike. Janey was just another patient to him, one more casualty of the war on drugs. Lines in, needles out, pump up the cuff, write something down. He was in constant motion, and even though Sid knew he was working to save Janey's life, that he had to maintain that one emotional step away in order to do his job, she resented his detachment.

Janey wasn't just another junkie. She was dying because someone wanted her dead, and no one cared. No one but Sid, and who was she? She'd lied to the police and said she was family, but the truth was Sid didn't even know if Janey *had* a family. She didn't know her birthday, her favorite song, didn't know if Janey was even her real name. All Sid knew for sure was that someone had done this. Someone had stuck that needle in Janey's vein, had sent a lethal dose of pure heroin on a straight path to her heart. Someone wanted Janey out of the way, wanted her dead, and *that* was Sid's fault. That's what she had brought to her friend's life. Nothing but death.

"You have to let go," the EMT repeated, more strongly this time.

"I'm sorry," Sid said, letting Janey's limp fingers fall back to the gurney, bowing forward over her knees, getting as close as she could to her friend without touching. "I'm sorry, Janey," she whispered. She felt hot tears rolling down her cheeks and didn't try to stop them.

The EMT glanced up. "Is this her first OD? Do you know what drugs she was taking?"

"No drugs," Sid insisted.

The EMT gave her a pitying glance. "Look, lady. She's OD'ing on something, probably heroin, and I need to know if there's anything else in there. You're not doing her any good by pretending she's not a junkie."

"She's not. Someone did this."

Medical alarms blared, drowning out the wail of the siren as they pitched around another curve.

"Stay back," the EMT ordered tightly, then ripped the sheet off Janey's chest, baring her small, pale breasts, and oh, how her friend would have hated that. The smell of something burning filled Sid's nostrils as the EMT tried to jolt Janey's heart back to life, her back bowing off the gurney. The EMT swore as the monitor continued to show nothing but flat line, and then the ambulance doors banged open, and Janey was gone, whisked through the double doors, surrounded by men and women who probably saw cases like this every night. Just one more junkie overdose.

But Janey wasn't a junkie. Someone had killed her to send a message. Well, message received. But Sid wasn't backing off. She was going to find out who had done this, and she was going to make them pay.

Chapter One

Six months later

SID GAZED AROUND the crowded ballroom, fighting against the urge to pinch herself. She'd done it. She was actually standing in the midst of the most powerful vampires on the North American continent while they decided who would be the next Midwestern Vampire Lord.

She'd be the first to admit that she didn't know precisely what that meant, didn't know the boundaries of the territory, or what powers such a vampire possessed. But what she did know was enough. The winner of this competition—and she wasn't entirely clear on what sort of *competition* it was either—would rule Chicago. That meant he'd also be the one picking up the reins of the white slavery ring the old vampire lord, Klemens, had operated out of this city for nearly twenty years before his death. And that was something Sid did know about. She'd spent all the last year, and especially the six months since Janey's death, researching and writing the stories about Chicago's connection to sex trafficking.

Ostensibly, the series was for her hometown newspaper, the only piece of serious journalism in a paper that was better known for covering the high school basketball team's pancake breakfast. The town was a distant suburb of Chicago, an upscale community that did its best to resemble Mayberry in everything except its property values and fashion sense. Her stories often motivated little old ladies to stop her on the street and chastise her for reporting on the kind of ugliness they'd moved to suburbia to get away from. Couldn't she find something *nice* to write about? But Sid didn't care about nice. She wanted to make a difference, and since her father owned the paper . . . well, she might hate the idea of riding on the coattails of her daddy's money, but if that was the only way she could get the story told, then that's what she'd do.

Because Chicago wasn't simply a convenient marketplace for slaves. When it came to this particular trafficking ring, the city was *the* transit hub to the rest of the United States. Shut the Chicago operation down, take out the vampires operating it, and you would disrupt the entire supply chain. And that's what Sid wanted, to shut them down. She wasn't naïve enough to believe that would end the problem. As long as there was a demand for sex slaves, someone would come up with the supply. But shutting down the Chicago pipeline would deal a major blow to the traffickers, and that was a good first step.

It was also a very dangerous step. The traffickers would do almost anything to stop her from exposing their disgusting, but extremely profitable, business. She'd learned that the hard way, although it was Janey who'd paid the price. Janey had been one of those slaves, but she'd been luckier than most. When her owner had decided he had no more use for her, he'd given her a hundred dollars and dropped her on a corner.

But Janey hadn't stayed on that corner. She'd found a shelter and a program. She'd gotten off the streets, earned her GRE, and was working as a waitress when Sid happened to stop at her diner one night. And when she found out what Sid was investigating, Janey had offered to help. Which had gotten her dead.

The slavers hadn't dared go after Sid directly; her father had too much money, too much influence. Sid's death would have brought in the police and the press, would have triggered a real investigation. But not Janey's. Her death had gone all but unnoticed by everyone except Sid.

And while Janey's death hadn't changed Sid's mind about exposing the ugly truth, it had convinced her to try going to the cops. She'd called in every favor, had thrown her family name around, but eventually even the cops had stopped taking her calls and wouldn't return her messages. They had more important crimes to solve, crimes with American victims, monied victims, high-profile victims. The women caught in the slavers' web were nameless, faceless foreigners, and by the time they arrived in the US, most were hopelessly addicted to heroin. Their story was lumped in and buried beneath the overall problem of drugs, and nobody cared about one more heroin addict or how she got that way.

What Sid needed was a blowout story, something no one could ignore, and the vampire angle was it. She was determined to do whatever it took to get close to the big honcho vampire, to get her story from the inside. Vampires needed blood, and Sid had plenty of blood. She just needed to meet the right vampire. Past experience had taught her she could draw the attention of any man she set her sights on, and a male vampire couldn't be all that different from any other male, right?

A bit of research had led her to Claudia Dresner, a sociology professor at University of Illinois who was writing a book on vampires. Dresner had tenure and so couldn't be fired for her choice of subject, but that didn't mean her colleagues respected her work. Sid had provided a sympathetic and interested ear for the professor and in the process gleaned a wealth of information on vampires, including the existence of something called a blood house, a place where vamp groupies and wannabes went to mingle with the real thing and offer blood on the hoof, so to speak. There were several in a city the size of Chicago, but Professor Dresner had taken her to the one closest to the center of power, a club where she'd insisted Sid could meet the kind of vampire who could take her to the top. Dresner had only gone with her that first time, but she'd pointed out a couple of possibilities. Not the big guys themselves, but vampires who could get her *access* to the big guys, the vampires powerful enough to go all the way to the top.

Sid had been an excellent pupil, and her reward was the vampire standing next to her, the one who'd wrangled an invite for her to this highest of vampire galas. His name was Travis, and if she'd met him under any other circumstances, she'd have seen nothing more than an easy-going surfer dude who had somehow been displaced to Chicago. Just over six feet, he had the sleek, muscled body of a swimmer, with the sharp edges of a tribal tattoo visible below the right sleeve of the black T-shirt he wore like a uniform. And underneath the hustler attitude, he was a surprisingly sweet guy.

"Exciting, huh, babe?" Trav was standing too close, his body constantly brushing her ass as he fidgeted from side to side. If anyone was excited, it was Travis. He was like a little kid about to meet his superhero for the first time. Either that or a dog with a juicy piece of meat that he worried would be stolen by a much bigger dog at any moment. Unfortunately, that made Sid the meat. And she wasn't anyone's dinner, not yet anyway. She'd managed to avoid actually letting Travis drink from her, although she'd have been willing to go that far, if necessary. And she had a feeling that the next time she met him, Trav would be asking for payment for getting her in here tonight, but for now, at least, she was off the menu.

"So," Sid said, taking a sidling step away from Trav's nervous twitching. "Any idea who's going to win this thing?"

"Sure, no question. See the big guy over there?"

"I see a lot of big guys, Trav. Just point him out for me."

"Wow, great idea! These guys are pumping adrenaline like prize fighters on cocaine, but I'll just stick my finger at the baddest guy in the room for you. You can scoop up my ashes later."

"Don't be dramatic. Can you at least give me a clue?"

"He's the one standing alone over there, no drink in his hand."

Sid scanned the crowd in the direction Travis indicated and huffed an exasperated breath. For fuck's sake, *most* of the vampires here were standing alone. According to Travis in his less dramatic moments, tonight was about the contenders displaying their power, kind of like animals giving off aggression pheromones during the rut or something. She figured it wouldn't be long before one of these guys pulled out his dick and start spraying everything in sight. The mental image had her snickering, but her laughter died in her throat when her gaze fell on *him.*

Oh, yeah. Trav had been right. He *was* standing alone. But his aloneness was more than a physical separation, it was an invisible wall that kept anyone from getting too close, a force field of *get the fuck away from me.*

"What's his name?" she whispered, afraid he could hear her somehow from across the room.

"Aden," Travis supplied, and his voice was quiet and drenched in awe . . . and something else. Worship?

"Do you know him?"

He nodded. "Yeah. I mean, we're not buds or anything, but . . . he's the one."

"I want to meet him."

Travis laughed. "Right."

"I'm serious," she said, tugging on his hand. "Introduce me."

He shrugged. "Introduce yourself, babe. Just make sure you know what you're doing."

Sid tightened her hold on Travis's fingers, though whether it was to keep herself from moving or to drag him along with, she couldn't have said. Either way, it didn't matter, because Trav had a mind of his own, and he was a vampire. He wasn't going anywhere he didn't want to. He shook his fingers free.

"You're on your own for this one," he said, "but take a tip from someone who knows . . . be polite."

She scowled. "I'm always polite."

"Sid, what's your gut telling you right now? Be honest."

She glanced over at him in surprise. This was more serious than she'd ever seen Travis, and it made her swallow the clever response on her tongue and go with the truth instead. "My gut's afraid of him."

"You've got a smart gut. Talk to him if you want, but listen to your gut and watch what you say."

Sid flattened her lips in irritation, then quickly rolled them together, not wanting to ruin her lipstick. She hated using her looks instead of her brain, but first impressions mattered, and she'd use every weapon she had. She found herself considering a dash to the restroom for a quick makeup check and discarded that idea, seeing it for the act of cowardice it was. This was what she'd been waiting for, what she'd spent the last several months working toward, a chance to meet someone who could make a difference. And if this Aden really was going to be the next vampire lord, she couldn't afford to blow it.

She sucked in a breath and started across the room. She took a roundabout path, moving from cluster to cluster of gala goers, both human and vampire, stopping for a few minutes and pretending to join in the conversation, then moving on. And all the while she kept an eye on her target, studying him.

As she'd told Trav, there were a lot of big guys in the room. And not just big, but unusually good-looking. Professor Dresner had offered the theory that what she called the *vampire symbiote*—the thing that turned an ordinary human into a vampire—worked a lot of physiological changes on its host for its own survival. The most obvious changes were the new vampire's need for blood and an aversion to sunlight. But there were additional, more subtle, changes that happened over time, things that made vampires better hunters, made them more attractive to their human prey. The professor had suggested that vamps eventually became better looking, because the longer they were a vampire, the more time the symbiote had to work on them.

Sid didn't know if that was true or not, but she did know that there were a hell of a lot of gorgeous men here. Far too many for it to be random.

But even in a room filled with handsome men, Aden stood out. He was beautiful and wild, an untamed beast who'd donned a tuxedo for the night. It was a thin veneer of civility, and one that barely managed to contain his savagery as he scanned the gathering with a predator's gaze, a single breath away from ripping out someone's throat.

She glanced away, then back, and caught him watching her. She shifted her gaze quickly, but not before she saw that he hadn't bothered to do the same. He stared at her unabashedly, his eyes so dark that at first she'd thought they were black. But then the light caught them just right, and she realized they were the deepest dark blue, with thick, black lashes that flirted with his sharp cheekbones on every lazy blink. His wavy hair was as black as his lashes, a little too long and curling above the stiff white collar of his formal shirt. He had a sexy mouth, full and soft-looking, but saved from pure sensuality by a touch of cruelty that tilted his lips into a small smile as he eyed her approach.

Sid closed the final few steps between them and stopped, shocked, now that she was closer to him, at how big he really was. Not just tall, though he was well over six feet, but with broad shoulders and a deep chest that hinted at plenty of muscle mass underneath the designer tux.

She drew a breath and plunged ahead. "Lord Aden," she greeted him, going with a friendly but respectful approach.

He raised a single eyebrow in response. She waited for him to do more, to say something, anything. To ask how she knew his name, if nothing else. But the eyebrow was the only reaction she got.

Sid gave a careless shrug. "I do my homework like any other reporter," she said, pretending he'd actually asked the question. "I asked my sources which vampire was the most likely to win this . . . whatever you call it," she said, gesturing at the gathering of vampires. "And your name was the only one that came up."

He regarded her a moment longer before his gaze dropped in a typical male response and did a quick toe to chest scan, starting with her Louboutin peep-toe pumps—far too cold for a Chicago winter—raking up silk-clad legs, taking in her short, form-fitting silk sheath, with its bare shoulders and arms, and ending with a sneering glance at the mandarin neckline, which was so high that it nearly met her chin.

"What can I do for you, Ms. Reid?" he asked, his voice a deep growl of sound that had her heart kicking into high gear even before she'd processed what he'd said.

Her eyes flashed to his face. "How do you know—"

He laughed, and it wasn't a happy sound. "You played Travis for three weeks to get into this party. I *created* him three *decades* before you were born. Do you really think he'd bring a human around without my permission? I do *my* homework, too, sweetheart."

"I didn't know he was—"

"That much is obvious. So, why are you here? Not for the party, I'm guessing," he added, eyeing her unsubtle choice of neckwear.

"No," she said quickly. "I don't—" She was going to tell him she didn't play in vampire circles, that she was no one's *food*, but something in his eyes made her stop. She froze beneath that gaze, abruptly aware of every breath moving in and out of her lungs, of her heart pounding within her chest until she was sure he could see it thumping beneath the second skin of her tight dress. She bit her lip nervously, and Aden's hooded gaze grew heavier. God, he was beautiful. She wondered just for a moment what it would be like to bed someone like him. A powerful vampire. Sexy, savage, uncontrollable. An image flashed across her brain of a naked Aden lying beneath her, muscles flexing, strong hands locked on her hips, slamming deep between her thighs with every upward thrust as she thrashed helplessly above him.

And she realized her body was already responding to the vision. Heat was pooling between her thighs, right where she'd imagined him pounding into her, and she was afraid to look down for fear she'd find her nipples visibly swollen and demanding attention.

She shot a nervous glance at Aden and saw one corner of his sensuous mouth curve slowly upward, as if he knew what she was thinking, knew what her *body* was feeling. She pushed such thoughts forcibly out of her head. She had no intention of falling under any vampire's spell, much less one as dangerous as Aden.

"You were saying?" he prodded her smugly.

Sid wished viciously for a nice sharp stake.

"*If* you're the next vampire lord," she said intentionally, "then I'd like to meet with you. There are things going on in this city, crimes against humanity that you may not be aware of."

He frowned. "Such as?"

"This is not the place, Lord Aden. But know this: they enslaved and killed a friend of mine, and I intend to expose every—"

His gaze hardened, every bit of seduction vanishing in an instant. "You will come to my office tomorrow night." He reached into an inner pocket and produced a thick white business card, flipping it through his fingers as he held it out to her.

Sid didn't take well to orders, especially not from rude, but sexy, vampires. Her gut reaction was to tell him to shove it, but that would have been stupid. And stupidity was not one of her many faults. This was what she'd wanted—a private meeting with the next Midwestern Vampire Lord—and he was offering it to her. Okay, so he'd pretty much ordered her to show up, but she wasn't going to argue semantics when the inside track she needed was being offered up on a platter. Or, in this case, a business card.

She took the card. It held an address and phone number, nothing else.

"There's no name on this. How do I know whose office it is?"

He gave her the raised eyebrow again. "Because I just handed you the card," he said slowly, as if speaking to a nitwit. "Be there two hours after sunset tomorrow evening."

"What if I don't know when sunset is?" she asked, just to be obnoxious. She knew exactly when sunset was. She'd been checking it daily for the last several months, ever since she'd decided to try and get inside vampire society.

"Then check your father's newspaper," he said impatiently, proving that he knew far more about her than she did about him.

She was trying to think of an appropriate comeback when he abruptly shifted his gaze over her head and gave someone a curt nod. Sid spun, but whoever he'd been signaling was too far away for her to identify. She started to turn back and nearly crashed into Aden. He reached out to steady her, curving the fingers of one big hand over her hip.

Taking advantage, he leaned in and put his lips right next to her ear. "Do wear something more suitable tomorrow night, Ms. Reid. I'm rather fond of redheads."

Sid gasped at his temerity, but he was already gone, walking easily through the crowded room, a path clearing before him like magic. She watched him go, his height and size making him easy to follow until he joined a small group of men and women who stood apart from the rest. She stared until Travis sidled up next to her once again.

"Was I right?" he asked.

"Right about what?" she asked absently.

"About Aden. He's going to be the one, don't you think?"

She opened her mouth to tell him she had no idea, no basis to judge something like that. But then she frowned. "I don't know," she said honestly. "But I think you might be right."

Travis grinned proudly. "You see those guys over there?" he asked, nodding toward the small group which now included Aden. "The one in the back, looks like a rich Wall Street exec? That's Raphael, probably the most powerful vampire on the planet. The two closest to him are Lucas and Duncan, but all of them up there are vampire lords, Sidonie. The real deal."

"And the women?" she asked, noting in particular the tall, black-haired one who looked like a model in a long-sleeved Stella McCartney that covered everything, but still managed to look provocative as hell. She was greeting Aden with a big smile, and Sid experienced an unwelcome jolt of pure envy. She scowled at her own reaction. What did she care if Aden hustled some other woman? Hadn't she just persuaded herself that she wasn't interested in him or any other vampire?

"The short and curvy dark-haired one is actually Sophia. She's Lord of the Canadian Territories and the only female on the Council. The rest of the women are human. The one talking to Aden right now is Cynthia Leighton, Raphael's mate. Don't know the others' names, but they're all mated to the lords. So don't worry, they're way off limits to Aden."

Sid shot him a surprised look. "I don't care about that," she said, turning back to watch as Aden spoke to the Leighton woman. "This is simply business for me."

"Uh huh. Well, how about you and I do a little business of our own then?"

She glanced over and did a double take when she saw his fangs on full display.

"That's not my thing, Trav. I told you."

"Hey, don't knock it until—"

"Look, I appreciate you bringing me here and all, but it's not going to happen."

"Okay," he said agreeably. So agreeably that she suspected he'd been acting under Aden's orders all along, that he'd never really expected her to put out. The thought made her frown.

"Can't blame a guy for trying," Trav was saying. "But I'm going to mingle now. Plenty of willing flesh here tonight. See you around, babe."

She gave him a little wave, glad he was making it easy, even as she suspected she'd been manipulated. She took a final look across the ballroom, but Aden and the others were gone. She sighed and glanced down at the business card in her hand. She'd have to be careful with this one. Aden wasn't Travis, and she had a feeling he wouldn't be making anything easy for her.

ADEN GAVE Raphael a respectful bow, then turned and deliberately disappeared into the crowd. There'd been nothing untoward about his interaction with Raphael tonight, nothing to indicate that he or any of the lords favored Aden over the other candidates. But then, nothing was ever what it seemed with vampires, and he knew the rumor mill would already be rife with rumors about secret meetings with powerful vampire lords. He knew, because he'd been the one to make sure the rumors got started. Aden had no doubt he could defeat his opponents handily on his own, but it never hurt to pad the odds in his favor by making his enemies worry about powerful friends.

He faded back into the shadows to better watch the crowd. He was aware of his effect on people, even vampires. His size and attitude were intimidating even without the aura of power that his vampire nature granted him. It was something he often used to great effect, but there were times when he needed to disappear. And his vampire nature had gifted him with that, too: the power to wrap himself in darkness and hide in the shadows.

He caught the flash of copper-colored hair and watched with hooded eyes as Sidonie Reid wove her way through the crowded room. Her dress was tighter than she was probably used to. It made her stride unconsciously seductive, emphasizing the glide of silken thighs, the sway of her hips above nicely toned legs. More than one head turned to follow her progress, vampire nostrils flaring as she passed, scenting the bouquet of her blood beneath that delicate skin. She had a striking beauty, not classic, but unique, with crystal blue eyes and a curly mass of red hair that tumbled artfully down her back. She'd been raised with money and privilege, and it showed in the arrogant assumption that she was safe in this room full of predators.

The truth was that her blood would have been tasted long ago if he hadn't ordered otherwise. She was lucky that it had been Travis she'd approached seeking information in that blood bar. Trav could fake stupidity with the best of them, but there was a calculating mind behind that scruffy blond exterior. As soon as Trav had discovered who she was, he'd called Aden, and Sidonie Reid's fate had been set.

She made her way toward the exit, oblivious to the effect of her passage. Covetous eyes followed her, but turned away when Aden emerged from the shadows to lay claim. Sidonie had come here tonight to seduce him, thinking that would give her power. But she had a lot to learn. He smiled privately, anticipating his meeting with her the next night.

He did love redheads. Their pale skin marked so very prettily under the lash.

Chapter Two

ADEN STRODE swiftly through the halls of the hotel. His business tonight was finished. From here on out, the competition would be mostly guerilla-style ambush and attack, although some might go old-school and issue formal challenges. There was only one real rule, and that was no human audiences or casualties. As long as no bodies were left for the humans to find, there was little chance of accidental discovery, and in the event humans chanced upon a challenge battle, the participants were responsible for wiping the humans' memories. Anyone who failed in that responsibility would face the combined wrath of the Council, which was a far worse fate than any challenger could pose.

Aden's lieutenant, Sebastien, emerged from one of the side hallways, matching his pace as they headed for the exit. Bastien was nearly as tall as Aden and just as dark. He was a warrior in his blood and bone, a former officer in the French Foreign Legion who still wore the Legion's grenade and colors in a tattoo on his left forearm.

Aden had four vampires who called him Sire, but Bastien had been his first, turned before Aden ever left Europe. Aden's Mistress, the female who'd made him Vampire, had released him from her service decades earlier, but when he'd arrived in America and met Lucas, he'd known that this was a master he could willingly serve. So, Aden had sworn to Lucas, and Lucas had not only permitted Bastien to remain bound to Aden, he'd taken it a step further and encouraged Aden to make more children of his own. It was a gift that Aden would never forget, one that had demonstrated Lucas's confidence in Aden—that he was loyal and no threat to his master. But it had also been solid proof of Lucas's belief that Aden was meant for greater things. Because in order to achieve the lofty position of vampire lord, one needed children of one's own to rely on for both loyalty and raw power. If it came down to a duel between powerful vampires, the strength of one's children could sometimes make all the difference in the world.

"Any news?" Aden asked Sebastien.

"The usual rumblings, Sire. Lots of gossip floating around about

Magda and how she died, even though no one seems to have considered her a serious contender. My favorite rumor is that Lucas took her out to advance your cause."

"As if she was in my way."

"Exactly. I estimate half of those spreading that particular fantasy will be gone by morning."

"By choice?"

"Some. But others will suffer a more permanent departure. The weaker challengers are trying to boost their confidence by killing each other off."

"Fascinating. Anyone I need to worry about?"

"Not at that level. One moment, Sire." Bastien strode ahead of him and pushed open the heavy door leading to the loading docks, where their limo should be waiting.

Some of the other contenders went for glitz, arriving and departing under the porte-cochère of the hotel like some sort of rock star. Word had gotten out—or more likely some fool had intentionally pushed it out—that there was a big vampire gathering at the hotel, and there were actual paparazzi waiting out front. Aden shook his head. The last thing he wanted was his picture splashed across a gossip magazine.

"We're ready, Sire," Bastien said and held the door open.

Aden proceeded through to the loading dock without pause, welcoming the blast of cold air after the stuffy heat of the hotel corridors. The dock was empty this time of night, or rather morning. It was nearly 3:00 A.M., midday for vampires, but dead of the night for most humans. In a couple of hours the dock would be bustling, but for now it was quiet and, more importantly, private.

One of Aden's other children, Freddy, was driving the limo tonight. He'd just stepped out of the vehicle and opened the rear passenger door when two SUVs came roaring around the corner.

"Sire?" Bastien said, his voice urgent, but controlled as the SUVs moved to box them in.

"We fight," Aden said calmly, already probing the arriving vampires, weighing their strength against his . . . and finding them sorely lacking. "There's no one who can hurt us."

Bastien flashed him a vicious grin, in part because he'd detected the disappointment in his Sire's voice at what was bound to be an easy victory. But the other part of Bastien's grin was because he was a bloody-minded warrior who loved a good fight. Or any fight, really.

Freddy reached into the limo and tossed Bastien a Heckler & Koch

MP5 submachine gun with one hand, even as he came up shooting with the other, his MP5 spitting death and destruction before the attacking vampires had managed to do more than raise their weapons. He rolled over the hood of the limo to reach Aden's side, taking up a position in front of his Sire as he urged him into the protection of the limo's armored body.

"I can't believe they're going with guns, my lord," Freddy called, his joyous laugh piercing the gunfire, sounding like the cackle of a madman. Aden had a moment to ponder the fact that his two closest advisors were both what would have been called berserkers in the old country, but then the guns went silent, and the SUV's door opened to reveal a familiar figure.

"Stig Lakanen," Aden said, identifying the most powerful of this current batch of foes, although that wasn't saying much. Stig's presence explained the choice of weapons. Most vampires avoided using guns. They were noisy and drew the attention of human authorities. Of course, Stig's presence also explained the sudden lack of gunfire. He wouldn't want to risk getting killed by a stray bullet from one of his own. He'd probably hoped to catch Aden unawares by coming in guns blazing, hoped to weaken Aden by killing off his children with a surprise first strike.

Too bad that hadn't worked out for him.

"This won't take long," Aden told his vampires, never taking his eyes off of Stig. "Deal with these others however you please, but make it quick. I have more important things to do tonight."

Dual grins greeted his decision as Freddy and Bastien engaged their enemy with cheerful zeal, wading in with knives and fists, blood flying. Aden ignored their battle, confident in the abilities of his people to get the job done. He focused instead on the leader of this poorly-conceived ambush who was hiding back by one of the SUVs, looking more worried by the minute. Stig Lakanen was one of Lucas's children. His usual haunt was Minneapolis where he was a rank and file warrior at best. He had no chance in hell against Aden in a stand-up fight, and his wary stance indicated he knew it. Unfortunately, once a challenge was issued, there was no taking it back.

Aden strode over to confront the challenger, more interested in getting this done than wasting time on posturing bullshit. The two of them faced off, both seeming oblivious to the bloodshed behind them.

"What the hell, Stig?" Aden asked, eyeing the vampire's long, greasy hair. "Couldn't even shower for the big gala?"

"Fuck you," the blond vampire snarled. "Put up or shut up."

"Are you so eager to die?"

"Fuck you twice."

"You're really not my type, and I have places to be." Aden attacked without warning, using a slap of power to pin Stig to the SUV, letting a bare smile of satisfaction tilt his lips when Stig's eyes widened in surprise.

"I don't know who put you up to this, Stiggy," he said, using a nickname the other vampire hated. "But I'll find out. Tell me who it was, and I'll make this easy."

"Fu—"

Aden hit him with a second punch of power, slamming it into his chest with enough force to crush his ribcage. Stig gasped as he strained to draw breath with lungs that no longer worked. Aden could feel him struggling to gather his power, to fight back.

"One more chance, Stig. Save me some time, tell me who put you up to this, and I'll make it easy."

Stig's eyes were wide with disbelief, bloody with broken capillaries as he slowly suffocated. He stared at Aden, and Aden saw the first signs of pleading enter his expression. But Aden had no pity. Stig had known what the game was before he joined it. Or, he should have.

"The name, Stig."

The other vampire's mouth opened, his lips moving as they tried to form a word. Talking was difficult with no breath to drawn upon, but his teeth finally clenched around a hiss of air that was a name. "Silas."

Aden nodded, unsurprised. Stig clamped his fist around Aden's cuff in a last bid for mercy, but Aden had none to give. He'd promised to make it easy. He would do that much, but no more. Extending his right hand, he slammed his fist directly into Stig's chest and grasped his heart. The organ thumped once against his palm, and Aden smiled absently at the sensation before closing his fist and squeezing until muscle and blood slithered between his fingers.

Stig's final cry sang in his ears as he focused his power once more, and the heart burst into flame, becoming nothing more than ash snowing down to join the pile of clothes and dust that had been Stig Lakanen.

Aden brushed his hands together and shook his head in disgust. What a waste. Stig hadn't been the sharpest knife in the drawer, but he'd been a perfectly fine warrior. Silas had wound him up and set him on Aden's trail knowing full well Stig would die. Maybe hoping to at least do some damage. But had Silas really thought Stig Lakanen could weaken Aden in any meaningful way?

"Sire?"

He turned at the sound of Bastien's voice, becoming aware of the silence all around him. Lifting his gaze, he quickly located Freddy who gave him a jaunty salute despite the copious amount of blood staining his tux.

"Freddy?" Aden said, eyeing the blood.

"Most of it belonged to your enemies, Sire. I'll be healed by the time we reach the office."

Aden nodded. "Call someone to get rid of these trucks," he said, indicating the attackers' two SUVs.

"Already done," Bastien said from behind him. "We should leave now, my lord, just in case."

Aden knew what he meant. Stig had been used as Silas's sacrificial lamb, very possibly to weaken Aden in advance of a real attack which could come at any moment.

They all piled into the limousine for the short ride to the six-story building where Aden had set up his headquarters two months ago. It was an elegant structure of mixed use, with many of his fellow residents using the space for home offices. It also had excellent security, although Aden had augmented his top two floors with safety measures of his own, especially since he and his vamps spent their daylight hours in the living quarters adjacent to the offices.

Most importantly, the sixth floor penthouse couldn't be reached directly from the lobby. One took the main elevator to the fifth floor and a private elevator from there. None of Aden's offices or living quarters were on the fifth. It was occupied solely by his contingent of daylight guards, many of whom lived there.

Aden's limo was en route to his offices when the phone signaled an incoming call.

"My lord," Aden answered, recognizing Lucas's number.

"Not much longer, my friend," Lucas said, making a veiled reference to the challenge. "So . . . ," he continued. "Stig?"

"Yes. I'm sorry."

Lucas sighed audibly. "I chose him for his skill on the battlefield, not his IQ. I wouldn't have predicted he'd go for the territory, though."

"Someone charged him up and sent him off to die."

"Silas?"

"Most likely. He admitted as much before he died. Could have been part of the feint, I suppose, but I wouldn't credit Silas with *that* much influence."

"Stig was always willing to obey orders. It's part of what made him a good warrior."

"Why throw in with Silas, though?"

"Silas was his commanding officer back in the day. Good with a blade."

"Silas or Stig?"

"Both, actually, but I was thinking of Stig."

"Maybe he should have gone with his strengths then. His people came out firing MP5s."

"Stupid. Oh well, onward and upward. Stay alive, my friend. The real battle is ahead of us."

"I plan on it, my lord."

Aden tucked the phone back in his pocket thoughtfully. "Bastien, I'd like confirmation of Silas's involvement in this as soon as possible. I need to know if there's another player out there. If someone has enough cunning to use Stig against both of us, I need to know who it is before we end up as dead as Stig."

Chapter Three

"DO WEAR SOMETHING more suitable, Ms. Reid," Sidonie simpered, mocking Aden's parting words to her. She lowered her voice to better replicate the vampire's rumbling bass for the rest of it. "I'm rather fond of redheads." She frowned, wondering what the hell he'd meant by that last remark, her suspicious nature not letting her believe he'd simply been admiring her coloring.

Her frown deepened as she stared at the full-length mirror. Or not so much at the mirror, which was an antique and rather lovely, but at her own reflection which was . . . not. Her hair wasn't having a good day, flying everywhere, and she had circles under her eyes thanks to several weeks of night-owling with vampires. She wasn't exactly a morning person normally, more of a midday person, preferring to stay up late and sleep late. But there was a big difference between staying up late and staying up all damn night.

Not that she cared about her sleep-deprived looks, or not overmuch, anyway. Her blood would taste the same whether she was tired or not. Her scowl was aimed at the scooped neckline of the sweater she'd chosen for the evening. She wanted to seduce Aden, the overbearing jerk, but she didn't want to hang out an all-you-can-eat sign. Still, she'd chosen the sweater with seduction in mind, and it did fit perfectly. It accented the figure she worked hard to maintain, and the burnt-gold color brought out the copper highlights in her hair. Also, being cashmere, it wouldn't shed all over her black wool slacks. It was just that *neckline*.

Her phone rang, and she spun away from the mirror, grabbing it and checking caller ID, frowning when it wasn't the call she was waiting for. She answered anyway.

"Hi, Will," she said.

"Hey, Sid. Let's do dinner tomorrow."

"You'll be in town?" she asked, ignoring the obvious that, of course, he'd be in town, or why else would he be asking her to dinner?

"Driving up in the morning, staying until Saturday," Will said cheerfully. He didn't even call her on the stupid question, but then he wouldn't. William W. Englehart was a genuinely nice guy. The guy her parents assumed would be her husband someday. Once upon a time, Sid had thought so, too. He was handsome and charming and had outstanding career prospects. He was a considerate lover and an excellent dinner companion. All the checkmarks were in the right column on the perfect boyfriend list.

There was only one thing missing. Passion. Sid didn't love him. At least, not that way.

"I'm not sure about dinner," she told him now. "I'm doing a lot of work at night. How about lunch on Wednesday instead?"

"Still doing the big story?" From someone else, the question might have sounded mocking, but not from Will.

"Yeah. I'm making progress, though."

"Good for you. It's a date. Lunch Wednesday, and maybe I'll talk you into dinner later."

That was the other thing about Will. He didn't love *her* that way either, but he was more than willing to marry her, because he agreed with their parents. They would be an excellent match, and he bought into the whole dynastic marriage idea. In her more depressing moments, she sometimes envisioned their future together, with each of them discreetly finding the passion they desired outside their marriage, and neither one caring as long as the only children—and, of course, there would be children—were unquestionably from the marital bed.

Sid sighed. "Call me Wednesday morning. We'll set a place and time," she told him. Her phone beeped an incoming call. She checked the ID. *At last*, she thought to herself, and tried to keep the relief out of her voice when she told Will, "I've got to get that. I'll see you then, okay?"

"Righto. See you then."

Righto. That was Will in a nutshell.

Shoving aside all thoughts of Will and their parents' plans for a wedding, she clicked over to Professor Dresner's incoming call. She'd phoned the professor hours ago, hoping to get tips on how best to go about getting what she wanted from Aden tonight. She'd all but given up on getting a call back in time for her meeting with the big vampire.

"Professor Dresner," she answered the phone. "Thanks for calling back."

"I'm so sorry, Sidonie. I was at a wedding. They actually made an announcement before the ceremony, asking everyone to turn off their phones. Just like they do in the movies, although the wedding was far less entertaining, unfortunately. But what can I do for you?"

"I met Aden last night," she said excitedly. "He's one of those you told me about, right? The ones you think are most likely to win the entire challenge?"

"Aden, yes. He's one of half a dozen, but certainly in the running. So you met him?"

Sid nodded in her excitement. "We didn't have time to do much more than exchange numbers, but he's invited me to meet him at his office tonight. And that's why I called you. I need to know the best approach. Do I seduce him? Or go for a business approach? And what about clothes? I'm afraid if I show too much skin, he won't take me seriously. But if—"

"Sid, Sid," Dresner said, laughing. "You've overthinking this. First, I need to know how serious you are. How far are you willing to go?"

"I'll do what it takes," Sid said determinedly.

"All right, then. You need to go all in and dress for seduction. You have to understand that the only thing most vampires want or need from humans is blood. And that's doubly true for the really powerful ones, many of whom are so distanced from their human roots that they barely see us as sentient anymore."

Sid groaned.

"I did warn you about what might be necessary when you first set out on this path."

"I know," Sid sighed. "And don't worry. I'll do what it takes. I might hate it, but I'll do it."

"That's the spirit. I'm sorry, Sid, but if there's nothing else, my feet are killing me, and there's a hot bath calling my name."

"Oh, of course. Thank you so much for calling back and for the advice. I really do appreciate your time."

"I don't mind at all. This is one of the more interesting things I've done lately. Academics isn't *all* excitement and adventure, you know."

Sid laughed dutifully, though she had no idea what the woman meant by that. Was she suggesting that academics sometimes *was* exciting? That didn't seem likely, especially in sociology, but it took all kinds, she supposed.

"Okay," Sid said, avoiding the whole excitement issue. "Enjoy your bath, and I'll let you know how it turns out."

She tossed the phone onto the bed, then turned to face the reality staring back at her from the mirror. Was her outfit sexy enough? Damn.

She stepped out of her heels and unzipped the wool slacks, then stomped over to her closet, thinking all the while that she must be certifiable. It was fucking freezing outside, and here she was trading in her tights and wool slacks for silk stockings and a skirt.

She cursed as she smoothed the tight skirt over her hips, wishing her target could have been anyone but a vampire. She had to admit that the skirt looked better, though. And, in any other context, the sweater would have been considered modest. There was no cleavage. It was only her neck that was on full display. But then she was seducing a vampire, and if she wanted Aden's cooperation, she was going to have to play his game. Hadn't she just told Dresner that she'd do whatever it took to get revenge for Janey's death? Well, whatever it took had just become the necessity of flashing some skin.

And if it also meant letting Aden take a bite, as it almost certainly would?

She ignored the thrill of excitement that thought generated, telling herself that her nipples were peaking because there was a cold draft in the room. This was Chicago, after all, and the wind was a nearly constant buffeting against the windows.

"All right, that's it," she told her reflection. "Buck up, Sid."

But she still felt better once she'd pulled on her long, wool coat along with a warm scarf. Maybe it would be cold in Aden's office. Maybe she'd have an excuse to keep the scarf on.

"SIDONIE REID IS here, my lord."

Aden swung the chair around from his contemplation of the Chicago skyline and met Bastien's amused expression.

"She's wearing a scarf," Bastien explained.

"Show her in," Aden said. "And, Bastien," he added before his lieutenant could open the door. "Turn up the heat."

He grinned. "Right away, my lord."

Aden leaned back, not bothering to get up when Sidonie marched into his office. And that's what she did. She *marched*, determination furrowing her brow and tightening her full lips into a pinched pout. Did she realize that her resolve to resist his seduction only made her that much more irresistible? That her very defiance was a blatant challenge to his dominance as an apex predator? He smirked privately, thinking of the many ways he could deal with her deliberate provocation, and he *would* deal with it. But that didn't mean he couldn't play with her first.

"Ms. Reid," he said lazily, "you're late."

She blinked in surprise, and he wondered if she'd expected him to pounce on her the minute she walked through the door.

"It . . . I couldn't get a taxi, and it was too cold to walk. I had to wait—"

"You should have called. I would have sent my car."

Her pouty lips opened in a silent *oh* before she visibly gathered her wits and came closer to his desk. She surprised him by unwinding her scarf and shouldering out of her winter coat. So he surprised her in turn, using his vampire speed to get behind her and play the gentleman by helping her with the coat, then tossing it over the couch against the far wall.

She gasped in startlement, giving him a surprised look over her shoulder. A look that quickly reverted to irritation when she saw Aden's satisfied smile. But his smile only grew broader when he saw the elegant line of pale skin bared by the swooping neckline of her sweater.

Well played, Ms. Reid, he thought to himself. *Well played, indeed.*

"That's a lovely sweater," he commented, enjoying the flush of color the compliment brought to her cheeks. With skin like that, she'd be hard-pressed to conceal her emotions. Not that he needed visible proof of such things. Her fluttering pulse and pounding heart, her delightful scent, told him much more than her blush. But he appreciated the beauty of it all the same.

"Thank you," she said, showing the first sign of real nerves since she'd walked into the room. She eyed the chairs in front of his desk, but clearly didn't know if she should simply sit down or ask if he minded first.

Not wanting the desk between them, Aden walked over and gestured at the flat expanse of window where the Chicago skyline was now decorated by a few fitful flakes of snow being tossed wildly in the ever-present wind. "Do you live in Chicago, Ms. Reid?" He knew she was staying here, but didn't know if she considered this home, and he wanted to hear what she'd say.

"Call me Sidonie," she responded politely, coming to stand next to him by the window. "My family home is in the distant suburbs. So distant, it barely qualifies as such, but I've been living in the city for nearly a year while I research my latest story. But you probably know all of that."

Aden dipped his head in acknowledgment. "True, but you're a reporter, so you understand the polite fiction of pretending you haven't already investigated someone you're meeting for the first time."

She glanced over and gave him a half smile. The first real smile he'd gotten from her. "Touché," she said. "But you know far more about me than I do about you. You're a difficult man to vet, Lord Aden."

"Not a lord yet, Sidonie."

"No?"

He turned and gave her a patient look. "I did mention that Travis belonged to me? I'm quite certain he's explained the process to you. Because I told him to."

Her blue eyes widened. "You knew all along who I was?"

"Travis suspected something was up. You're not exactly the blood groupie type, and he's far smarter than he sometimes chooses to seem."

"Why let him invite me to the big shindig then?"

Aden shrugged. "You were very determined, and I was curious. What is it you really want, Sidonie?" He reached out to trace one finger along the delicate curve of her collarbone, leaning close enough to draw in the sweet bouquet of her blood. She shivered, and he scented her fear. She was excited, too, by him, or maybe simply by the thought of having a vampire drink from her. But there was fear there. And that was far more arousing to him than any sexual curiosity.

Still, it wouldn't do to play into her desires. This wasn't a blood bar, and he wasn't some lust-driven idiot on a blood-drunk.

He skimmed his finger sideways, as if he was about to tug her sweater down and bare her shoulder, but then lifted his hand and stepped deliberately away from her. She sucked in a breath, her face registering obvious dismay at his abrupt departure.

"You still haven't told me why you're here," he said absently, crossing over to sit behind his desk. He brushed idly at his pant leg and gave her an inquisitive look.

She was still over by the windows, her heart fluttering, her breathing rapid, as she stared at him. A spark of something lit her eyes suddenly—embarrassment maybe, or even anger that he'd left her standing there while he sat.

She blinked several times, then pressed a hand to her throat and said, "I think—" She coughed drily, and he gestured at the wet bar at the other end of the room.

"There's bottled water in the fridge."

She gave him a disbelieving look. A polite man would have gotten the water for her, would have ushered her to a chair as if she wasn't fully capable of planting herself there. But then, he was neither polite nor a man. Besides, he didn't trust himself not to taste her . . . and more . . . if he touched her again, so it was best that he keep his distance. He had other things on his mind tonight. Tomorrow was another matter entirely, however.

He watched her walk over to the bar, hips swaying in her tight skirt. She bent over to the small refrigerator, displaying a nicely heart-shaped ass. Oh, yeah. As Travis would have said, he was definitely going to tap that before this was all over.

She turned, bottle in hand, and he let her catch him watching. Her heart sped up again, and he smiled lazily, which only made her heart act up even more. A blush pinked her cheeks, and he pictured the same rush of blood coloring the imprint of his hand while she was bent over his desk, begging him prettily for release.

"Lord Aden," she chastised breathlessly, as if she knew what he was thinking. She took a sip of water, then pressed the cold bottle to her overheated face.

He gave her a smug look and gestured at the two chairs in front of his desk. "Have a seat, Sidonie. You seem overcome."

Her soft lips tightened in irritation, but only briefly. Whatever it was she wanted from him, it was important to her. Important enough that she'd sought him out, enough that she was willing to put up with his toying with her. And yet she hadn't told Travis anything at all, clearly not willing to give up her purpose until she had the right audience. Interesting.

She sat down, crossing her long legs with a slide of silk stockings. Aden gave her a blatant once-over, starting with her legs, traveling to her chest, and finally to her very annoyed expression.

"We have business in common," she said primly.

"And what business would that be?" he asked, letting his doubt, and his amusement, show.

"The late, and unlamented, Klemens was a drug dealer, and—"

"I'm aware."

"But that was the least—"

Aden's phone rang, interrupting the woman's discourse on Klemens's many dissolute ways. He was both relieved and disappointed at the same time. Relieved because he really wasn't up to a lecture on the evils of drugs in modern culture, and disappointed, because he'd expected better of Sidonie Reid. She'd gone to all this trouble only to tell him what he already knew? That Klemens had derived the bulk of his income from various illegal activities, including drugs? How very ordinary.

He picked up the phone. "Bastien, what is it?" he asked, hoping it was something worthwhile.

"We've found Silas, my lord."

"Tell the others. We're leaving immediately."

He'd expected disappointment, but Sidonie's look was more one of disbelief than anything else. "You're leaving?" she asked.

"Duty calls," he said abruptly, not feeling any particular need to explain himself. "I'll have my car—"

"No," she said quickly. "I'll get a cab. Is it the challenge?"

Aden was already halfway to the door, but her question made him stop and stare at her. "Why would you ask that?"

"Curiosity," she admitted, shrugging. "It's a rather unique process, one we know little about. And it's not exactly front page news."

"No, it's not," Aden said flatly. "And we intend to keep it that way."

She rolled her eyes. "I've no interest in writing an article on the inner workings of vampire politics. That's not why I'm here."

"Why *are* you here?"

"Because Klemens's dirty business got a friend of mine killed."

"Vengeance? Klemens is dead already. There's not much else you can do to him."

"But the others aren't, the ones who worked for him. I want to see them destroyed, too. Them and their whole network."

Aden nodded, only half-listening. His thoughts were already on the fight ahead. Silas was very possibly the strongest opponent he had in this challenge, and Aden couldn't afford to be distracted. "Be here tomorrow night," he told her, not because he cared about her personal war on drugs, but because he wanted *her*. And he always got what he wanted. "Same time," he added, not bothering to ask if the date and time were convenient for her.

He started to turn away, but then looked back and skimmed his gaze over the bare skin of her neck, the snug sweater and form-fitting skirt, the spike heels. And he bared his teeth in what some might call a smile. "I do like the sweater," he said, then strode out of the office without another word.

"THE MOST ARROGANT, high-handed, *rude* man I have ever—" Sid paused in her muttered imprecations against Aden long enough to flash a reassuring smile at the building's doorman and ask him politely to call her a cab. She'd been surprised initially that Aden's office was in Chicago's Loop District. It was an older building, although completely renovated, and the neighborhood was very expensive for a supposedly temporary office, especially when that office took up two entire floors. Not that she'd seen much of the fifth floor. It seemed to be little more than a transfer point for the private elevator.

She gave the doorman another smile and a generous tip, then climbed into the back seat of the cab and immediately pulled out her cell phone.

"Sidonie," Professor Dresner answered, her voice laced with surprise. "I didn't expect to hear from you tonight. Did Aden cancel your appointment?"

"No, I suppose you could call what we had a meeting, but a very unsatisfactory one. I've never dealt with such an arrogant—"

Dresner interrupted her with a laugh. "Oh, my dear. They're all like that, the more powerful the vampire, the more arrogant he'll be. And, yes, they can seem rude, though I'm not sure they see it that way. I think they simply have no time for the slow thought processes of a lesser species."

"Lesser . . . you mean us?"

"Humans, yes. You must have gathered by now that they don't consider themselves human anymore, but rather something superior, more evolved."

"And yet they need us lesser types to survive."

"As we need cows and chickens, my dear."

Sid scowled. She hadn't thought of it exactly that way and didn't particularly care to. "It would serve him right if I wrote an article on *him* instead of Klemens and his criminal network."

Dresner's response was instant and surprisingly prim. "I don't think—"

"Don't worry. I already got that lecture from Aden. No writing stories about secret vampire stuff, or at least not the challenge, which is the only thing I know about him."

"No," Dresner said, still sounding a bit stiff, but clearly trying not to. "I would imagine he wouldn't like that. Vampires are very secretive about their society. It's why I was so surprised you managed to get an invitation to their challenge gala. Although, as I said before, there are always a certain number of attractive humans invited to these things for obvious reasons."

"Yeah, there were a lot of those reasons going on in the corners by the time I left the party last night."

Dresner's mood swung to a delighted laugh so quickly, it made Sid's head spin. "I can imagine," she giggled, sounding far more girlish that she ever should.

That was one thing Sid found rather uncomfortable about the good professor. She didn't only study vampires, she seemed enamored of them. And though Dresner had never said as much, Sid was convinced that her vampire expert had "donated" blood on more than one occasion.

Sid winced as the professor's giggle finally trailed off. "Well," she said, feeling uncomfortable. "Anyway, as I was saying, I'd barely begun to tell Aden what I was there for, when he got a phone call from someone named Bastien. I think that must be his assistant, the guy who met me at the elevator."

"His lieutenant, you mean, and he's far more important than you might think. His full name is Sebastien Dufort. His friends call him Bastien."

"Lieutenant, gotcha. I don't know what he said, but Aden told him they were leaving immediately, then hustled me out of there."

Professor Dresner made a noise that sounded suspiciously like disappointment. Had she been hoping for tales of Sid's adventures in vampire debauchery? But when the professor spoke, it was to ask something else entirely. "He didn't say where he was going?"

"No," Sid responded drily. "He barely said good-bye. But I overheard one of the guys on the phone on my way out. Maybe Bastien, I don't know, but he was saying something about Silas. Whatever that is."

"Not a what, a who," Dresner said absently. There was a pause during which Sid could hear her shuffling something on the other end, then she said, "I'm sorry, dear, I've just received a message, and I have to respond to this. Different time zone, you understand."

"Oh, of course. I didn't mean to interrupt. By the way, Aden asked me to come back tomorrow night—ordered me actually, but—shall I call you?"

"Please do. I hate to rush, but I really must go."

"Okay, I'll talk—" But she was already gone. Sid frowned at the phone, then shrugged philosophically. Dresner was an odd duck, but a useful one. Sid tucked her cell phone away and wondered who Silas was to Aden that he went rushing off so suddenly. And the more she thought about it, she also wondered why Dresner's entire demeanor had changed when Sid mentioned the name Silas. The prof knew a lot more about local vampires than she'd been willing to tell, almost as if she worried that Sid would scoop her big story. In fact, the only way Sid had gotten her to tell as much as she did was by promising a quid pro quo. Sid would tell her everything that happened, everything she discovered, once she managed to meet the right vampire, and in exchange Dresner would tell her how to make that meeting possible.

Sid pondered the possibilities. Maybe Dresner knew where this Silas was. Maybe Silas was another challenger, and Dresner was rushing off to be there for the big showdown between the two powerful vampires.

For all of a minute, Sid considered calling Dresner back and asking to go along. But a minute was all it was. The prof might delight in the vampires' brutal natures, but Sid was more cautious. The little she'd learned about vamps told her a challenge at this level would be bloody. And Sid was more concerned about making sure that none of the blood flowing tonight was hers, than she was interested in watching a big, bloody vampire showdown.

Chapter Four

ADEN TRANSFERRED from the private to the main elevator along with his vampires. These four were his own, his children. Once he became a vampire lord, they would form the core of his command structure. He trusted them with his life and quite literally held *their* lives in his hands. He also loved them in a way it was difficult to admit, even to himself. He had sworn off caring about anyone so long ago that he'd have thought he'd forgotten what it felt like. The most shocking thing to him, when he'd created Sebastien more than a hundred years ago, was the powerful bond he'd felt toward the new vampire. Even then, he'd assumed it was only because Bastien was his first. But with every new child he brought into the world of Vampire, the bonds became tighter to all of them.

That reality had nearly dissuaded him from becoming a vampire lord, the idea of all those vampires, hundreds, maybe thousands, looking to him for their very lives. So many hearts beating in cadence with his own, so many ties binding him ever more tightly.

But it was in his nature to seek power. Whatever it was that had made him Vampire had gifted him with the power of a vampire lord, and he could no more resist the lure of that power than he could his thirst for blood. And tonight, he would take one more step toward that goal.

Silas was a child of Klemens's, one of the dead lord's favorites by all accounts. Many of Klemens's surviving vampires—ignoring the fact that they only continued to live because Lucas had offered them protection after their Sire's demise—now looked to Silas as their next lord. It made Aden's challenge even greater, and it meant he'd have to kill many more than just Silas before his rule was secure.

But Aden had never shied from death. Some people deserved to die. And others, like Silas, chose their own path, placing themselves in death's way. Or Aden's, which was usually the same thing.

"Bastien, do we have confirmation on Silas's whereabouts?"

"Yes, my lord. Our source called a second time to confirm that Silas is at the West Loop blood house."

Aden frowned. "That's a public club, isn't it? How many humans are we going to have to deal with?"

"The club has a private room, my lord," Travis supplied. "That's where we'll find Silas and whatever humans have been chosen for the night. Shouldn't be more than a few once we get past the main room."

"You know the layout of the club?"

"Yes, my lord. There's a rough sketch on your phone."

Aden pulled out his cell phone and checked the diagram. The club was in a former warehouse, and the layout was straightforward.

"All right, we go in the front and directly to the back room. Silas might have a watcher, but that won't matter. It's not like we can conceal our entry, anyway. Once in, it's take no prisoners. It's safe to assume Silas will have more fighters than the five of us, but power and skill count for more than numbers. We show no mercy, gentlemen. None of Silas's people are to leave that room alive. I'll handle Silas myself."

A chorus of murmured assents met his orders, and then the elevator hit the ground floor, and they flowed through the lobby and out onto the Chicago street. It was a cold night, and the few pedestrians who happened to be passing by shrank back as the five determined males pushed through the glass doors and into the long SUV waiting at the curb.

Aden took note of every single person in his vicinity, categorizing and dismissing them as he went. He'd been born a slave, but the warrior blood of his Scottish ancestors flowed in his veins. Those genetic gifts had been honed to perfection on behalf of his vampire Mistress, until he had become a superb fighter and a brilliant strategist, the most lethal weapon in her arsenal. And now those skills, that lethality, were about to make him the next vampire lord in North America.

The drive to the West Loop and the renovated warehouse was short. Klemens had established the warehouse as a blood house long before his death at Lucas's hands. Aden had to admire the strength and discipline it must be taking for Lucas to maintain control not only of his own territory, but all of Klemens's former territory as well. Especially when at least some of those vampires didn't welcome him as their new lord. Fortunately, his friend wouldn't have to carry that burden much longer.

Aden and his crew parked a short block away from the warehouse entrance. They were too big and too noticeable to approach unremarked upon, whether walking or driving, so Travis took the nearest parking spot that could handle the big SUV.

There was a line of customers waiting in front of the club, every one of them eager to donate blood to whatever vampire crooked a finger. Aden had been to plenty of blood houses over the years. He and Lucas had shut a few down back in the day. But it wasn't his choice of donor. He much preferred a private party for two with someone like Sidonie Reid. In fact, before too much longer, he and the lovely Sidonie would be having that party. But first . . . there was Silas.

The club was crowded inside. Being a warehouse, it had high ceilings, rough brick walls, and a floor that was cold concrete beneath his boots. But it was no more than 2,000 square feet, rectangular in shape, and with a brightly-lit bar running nearly the full length of the back wall.

Aden and the others shoved their way through the crowd, ignoring the delighted squeals of blood groupies and the occasional groping hand. A few vampires objected loudly to their sudden appearance, but quickly fell back when they got a good look at who the newcomers were. A path cleared before them rather quickly, as vampires faded into the crowd and took their human companions with them.

"The private room, Sire," Bastien said in his ear, nodding at a wide metal door to one side of the long bar. It was painted an unimaginative bright red, but at least the color made it easy to spot in the flickering light of the dark warehouse.

Trav reached the door first. It had an ordinary metal door knob, which he twisted experimentally, finding it unlocked. He shared a skeptical look with Aden. Where was the security on this supposedly private room?

"Is there an anteroom inside? A second door?" he asked Travis, needing to shout to be heard over the noise, despite their enhanced hearing.

"Not that I've seen, Sire," Trav shouted back.

Bastien came up on Aden's other side. "Something's not right here," Aden told him. "They're expecting us."

Bastien looked up and met his eyes. "You think our source was playing both sides?"

"Maybe. But it's too late now. This changes nothing, except that now we know they're waiting for us. Stupid of them. They should have left a guard on the door. Ready, gentlemen?"

His question was met by vicious grins and nods all around. "Let's do this."

Travis yanked the door open on his signal.

They were outnumbered four to one. No, Aden corrected, five to one. And Silas was nowhere to be found. Typical. First, the coward sent a team of incompetents to ambush him outside the hotel, and now this. Silas couldn't dredge up enough courage to face Aden one-on-one, but wanted to be the next Lord of the Midwest.

Not gonna happen, but that showdown would come later. Right now, Aden had to deal with the current threat, had to keep his own people alive. Because Silas or not, there were plenty of enemies here, all trying to kill him and his.

Aden waded into the crowd of hostile vampires, his power lashing left and right, thundering off the walls of the small room. There was a small bar against one wall, and the stench of alcohol permeated the air quickly as bottle after bottle shattered. Glasses rattled and fell from shelves, while the industrial lights overhead swayed alarmingly on their unadorned cables. Gradually, the air filled with a fine gray dust as vampire after vampire fell before the combined might of Aden and his cadre.

From the depths of Aden's power, a dark force lifted its head and scented death, demanding to be set free. Drawing on two centuries of discipline, Aden flexed his will and forced it down, unwilling to permit Silas's spies to carry word of his true abilities back to their master. But a taste of that dark cruelty must have shown in his gaze, in the midnight glow of his eyes, because Silas's followers took one look at Aden standing there covered in blood and saw their deaths. They broke for the exit, but Bastien and the others got there first. No mercy, Aden had told his people, and they granted none.

Finally, Aden stood in the middle of the room, smelling the dust and blood that were the inevitable remains of a vampire's battlefield, searching for an enemy among the shattered remains of tables and chairs, the pile of glass and wood that had once been an antique bar front. No one rose from the rubble to challenge him. No heart beat within the twenty-by-twenty confines of the private room, but for those four who were under Aden's care. And Aden himself.

He knew what he looked like. Knew the cold glow of his eyes, the curl of his fingers into claws, and the gleam of his fangs dripping blood. Even his own children hesitated to approach him with echoes of his power still bouncing off the walls. Only Sebastien knew what the night's work had cost him, the effort it took to contain the unique and gruesome ability that had come to him with his vampire blood. But he'd learned the necessity of rigid control as a child, a never-forgotten lesson that had stood him in good stead since he'd become Vampire. When he finally ran Silas to ground and forced a fight between them, he would hold nothing back, but the lesser vampires she'd left to die tonight had been more of her sacrificial lambs.

Silence slowly filled the room. The dust settled, and the last shattered bottle drained its contents onto the debris.

"Sire." It was Bastien, of course. Of all of them, it was his eldest who had the least fear of him, no matter the circumstances.

"Any humans?" Aden growled, barely able to form the word from the depths of his anger.

"There were none in this room, my lord. A small grace, but Silas must have cleared them out in anticipation of your arrival."

Aden clenched his jaw against the incontrovertible conclusion from that bit of information. Silas had known he was coming. But how?

"I'll want to speak directly to your source tomorrow, Bastien. Someone warned Silas we were coming, and I want to know who it was."

"Our action was unplanned, my lord," Bastien protested. "No one knew except—"

Aden turned sharply to regard him. "Except who?"

His lieutenant eyed him warily, then drew a deep breath and ventured, "Ms. Reid, Sire. I was on the phone when she walked past. She might have overheard."

Aden frowned. Was that the real reason Sidonie had approached him when she did? Was her story of a dead friend and drugs simply a cover to get her into his office, like a silk-clad Trojan horse? The thought made him so angry, he nearly choked on it. He wanted to storm over to her home and confront her, wanted to tear the truth from her mind until she begged for death.

But it was late, and he had others to protect.

"Sidonie will be joining us again tomorrow," he said coolly. "If it was she who betrayed us, I'll know it before the night is over."

Chapter Five

SID STOOD IN FRONT of the mirror, once again trying to decide what to wear for a meeting with Aden. She kept glancing at the clock. She didn't want to be late, didn't want to give him any reason to turn her away. She was determined not to be sidetracked tonight. She was going to confront Aden with what she knew about Klemens's sick enterprises and ask him what he planned to do about it. She was also curious, after her conversation with Dresner last night, about what had happened between Aden and Silas. She even admitted to being a little afraid that Aden had been defeated and that there'd be no one to meet with her when she arrived at his office. Or even worse, there'd be some strange vampire that she couldn't trust.

Not that she trusted Aden. She wasn't that naïve. But he seemed, if not honest, then at least businesslike. And maybe a little intrigued by her sexually. And, okay, maybe she was intrigued right back at him, which made her wonder at her own sanity. But she couldn't get the image out of her head of Aden's mouth on her neck, his breath warm as his fangs slowly emerged from his gums, as they pierced her vein . . .

Damn. She shook herself mentally. Was this why so many women, and men, too, lined up for those blood houses? Did the vamps exude some sort of pheromone that made regular humans lose every ounce of survival instinct?

"Snap out of it!" Sid told herself sharply, then laughed. She really was going nuts. She stepped into the green wool sheath she'd decided to wear tonight, pulling it up over her hips and reaching back to zip it before eyeing herself critically. It was a nice enough dress, but she'd chosen it for the neckline. Most of her winter clothes had turtlenecks, because they *were* winter clothes. This was Chicago, after all. The sweater she'd worn last night and this dress were probably the only exceptions in her closet.

She smoothed the soft wool over her hips, fighting the instinct to find a cardigan to cover the sweetheart neckline, which not only bared her neck, but also showed a fair amount of cleavage. With a deep sigh, she stepped into a pair of simple black pumps. Simple in that they were unadorned, but the heels were high and spiky, and there was a tiny bow on the back that transformed them from businesslike to sexy. Or so she thought. Hopefully, Aden would, too.

With another long-suffering sigh, she pulled on her warm coat and headed off to walk voluntarily into the lion's den once more.

ADEN STOOD BEHIND his desk as Sidonie Reid entered his office. Not for the first time, he wished his vampire gift had included a greater telepathic component, especially when it came to humans. He could work his will on them easily enough. If he'd wanted, he could have had Miss Reid stripping herself naked and on her knees before him in no time at all. He rarely did such things, however. He preferred seduction, drawing his victims in until they begged for the very thing he'd wanted from them all along, even when they'd denied him only moments before.

Some vampires used their ability to mesmerize humans to enrich themselves. But it was never money or gold that Aden wanted. He had plenty of both and could always get more. No, what he desired was sexual surrender. And he was a master at getting what he wanted.

Take Sidonie, for example. She wanted something from him and was willing to use her sexuality to get it. She probably had no intention of following through on her seductive advances. No doubt she was used to confusing men into giving her what she wanted and then dancing away without ever having to deliver. She and Aden were alike in their use of seduction, except that Aden *always* delivered. That was half the fun, after all.

She dropped her coat onto the sofa and turned with a polite smile. The dress was a dark green that flattered her hair and accented the pink hue of her pale skin, especially along the curve of her breasts which were showcased by the curved neckline. She wasn't quite comfortable with the dress. He could tell by her frequent, aborted attempts to tug the neckline higher. He smiled in amusement at her modesty, especially when contrasted with the fuck-me heels she was wearing.

He didn't say anything, just watched and waited, as an embarrassed flush crept up over her neck and face.

"Is something wrong?" she asked, managing to stop her hand halfway to another tug at her neckline.

"I don't know," he said smoothly. "Is there?"

She tried to cover her irritation, but two little crease lines appeared between her brows.

"Where did you go last night, Sidonie?" he asked. "After you left here."

The crease lines deepened into a scowl. "I went home. Why, what'd you do?" she demanded.

Aden's lips curved into a slight smile as he strolled over to face her. She stared up at him with wide eyes and started to take step back. But then she squared her shoulders and glared, her lips flattened defiantly.

"Sidonie," he purred and smoothed the back of his fingers down her silken cheek.

She blinked rapidly, her clear blue eyes meeting his, her heart pounding so loudly in his ears that she had to be hearing it herself. She swallowed and whispered, "Yes?"

"Oh, don't say *yes* too quickly, sweetheart," he murmured, letting his fingers continue downward, over the curve of her elegant neck, and down even farther to skim the swell of her breasts. He leaned forward until his lips were nearly touching her ear. "I like the dress even better than the sweater," he whispered.

She sucked in a startled breath, and he was standing so close that her breasts brushed against his chest. But rather than backing away, as a gentleman might have done, he stepped even closer and rested one hand on her hip.

"Have you ever been bitten, Sidonie?" he asked, his mouth hovering above hers as he slid his hand around to caress her lower back, just above the curve of her ass. It was a light touch, but enough to hold her in place, enough to let her know she was his to control.

She shook her head, her eyes wide, pupils dilated with desire. "No."

"Would you like to be? Is that why you're here?"

She seemed to have trouble coming up with an answer for that. Did she think she could lie to him? Impossible. A vampire of his power could detect all of the subtle changes that affected humans when they lied. But maybe she didn't know that. Her tongue darted out to moisten her lips.

"That's not—" She drew a deep breath, her breasts once again brushing against his chest, even more so this time. He was holding her so closely that he felt the scrape of her erect nipples and heard the soft hitch in her breath that she probably hadn't intended him to hear.

Aden's lip curled in pleasure. She wanted to feel the kiss of his fangs, but she didn't *want* to want it. This was what he loved. This was what made him hard. His cock swelled, thick and hot beneath the fine wool of his slacks, and he shifted slightly, letting her feel it.

She sucked in a breath. Her hand came up to press against his chest, her fingers curled slightly, as if she couldn't decide whether to stop him or drag him closer.

Aden dipped his head and drew in the scent of her, her arousal, her blood so close to the surface, rushing through the big vein beneath her ear, thick and warm. He trailed his tongue along the path of her jugular, then lifted his head and blew softly on the wet skin.

Sidonie shivered and made a little sound of pleasure, and Aden smiled.

"Where did you go last night?" he whispered.

She stiffened. "What?"

SID LAID HER HAND on Aden's chest and sighed with pleasure. He was so big, the muscles beneath her fingers like iron. And she was going to do this thing. He'd started in on her almost the minute she walked through the door tonight, crooning at her in that low, sexy, voice, his dark eyes caressing every curve of her body, every inhaled breath that plumped her breasts over the low-cut neckline. Maybe he was hungry, maybe whatever had happened last night had drained him, and he needed blood. Maybe that was why he was doing the full-court press right off the starting line. The part of her brain that was a writer chided her for the mixed metaphor, but she told it to shut the fuck up.

She shivered as Aden bent closer, his wet tongue gliding over the skin beneath her ear, his breath warm, just as she'd imagined it would be. She couldn't stop the tiny sound of pleasure that escaped her lips. Hadn't she known all along it would come to this? Hadn't she dressed this way to seduce him, to have his teeth on her neck? And what could it hurt? It was just a little bit of blood, after all.

"Where did you go last night?" he whispered.

Sid blinked, the unexpected question like a slap in the face. "What?" she asked, and shoved at his chest to no effect.

Aden straightened and stared down at her, every inch of him cold and arrogant, the seductive lover gone. "For whom are you working?"

She shoved harder and stumbled slightly on her spike heels when he abruptly let her go. "I'm not working for anyone, you ass," she snapped. "I've been trying to tell you for days why I'm here, but you've been so busy being Mr. Important that you haven't taken the time to listen."

Aden closed the space between them again, looming over her, his size suddenly more threatening than sexy. "What did you hear last night? And whom did you tell?"

Sidonie had grown up with two older brothers. She'd been dealing with bigger males all of her life. She rammed her shoulder against Aden's chest, trying to force him to move, but he only laughed, and she felt her anger boiling up. Most people never saw it, but she had a temper. She didn't hold grudges and she couldn't hold a mad for long, but when her anger finally bubbled to the surface, it came up hot.

"Move," she demanded.

He gave her a gloating smile and said, "No."

With a shriek of anger, Sidonie swung her hand back in a fist aimed at his smug face, just as she would have one of her brothers. But Aden caught her hand and glared down at her.

"You don't want to do that."

"Then let go of me."

"Who'd you talk to last night?"

"No one, damn it. I live alone. There's no one . . ." Her voice trailed off.

"What?" he demanded, correctly interpreting her hesitation.

Sid's thoughts were racing. Professor Dresner. It had to be. She remembered Dresner's reaction as soon as she'd mentioned Aden leaving, how she'd pumped Sid for information, then almost immediately cut off the conversation.

"What happened last night?" she whispered, looking up at him. "Did somebody die?"

He frowned, and she thought he wouldn't answer, but then he said, "A lot of vampires died. None of them were mine."

Sid nearly choked on the guilt clogging her throat. Had those vampires died because of her? "What about Silas?" she asked.

Aden's gaze narrowed dangerously. "What do you know about Silas?"

She shook her head. "Nothing. I heard the name when I was leaving last night. Bastien was on the phone."

"And you told someone. Who was it?"

Sid didn't want to say. Surely she owed Professor Dresner that much. They weren't exactly friends, and it sounded as if she'd betrayed Sid's trust, but they were both human. Didn't that count for something? Some shred of loyalty?

"Someone warned Silas last night," Aden growled. "You want to know who's really responsible for all those dead vampires? Look to your friend who sent word that we were coming, and to Silas who ran, knowing what I would do to the vampires left behind."

Sid nodded faintly. Somehow everything had gotten turned around. She'd started this to save lives, and now it seemed she'd cost them instead. Or Dresner had. But wasn't she responsible, too?

"I've been working with someone," she whispered. Aden's hand gripped her hip once more, his fingers tight. "She's sort of an expert on vampire behavior."

"A human?"

"Yes. She's a professor at the university. She's the one who told me about that bar where I met Travis."

"Her name?"

Sid frowned up at him worriedly. "What are you going to do if I tell you?"

"I'm going to talk to her."

"That's all?"

"Depends, doesn't it? What would you humans do to someone who'd set up an ambush that resulted in several deaths?"

"I guess she'd go to jail, conspiracy to murder or something."

Aden shrugged. "Vampire justice is somewhat less ambiguous."

"I'll tell you who she is, but only if you take me with you when you go talk to her."

"You're hardly in a position to make demands," he growled, tugging her closer until she was flush with his hard body. And he was *hard* . . . all over. Damn it.

"That's my offer," she said stubbornly. "Take it or leave it."

Aden regarded her silently, and Sid stared as his eyes seemed to glow, taking on a deep blue hue like moonlight on a cloudy winter night. His gaze skimmed her face, down to the swell of her breasts and back up again.

"Oh, I intend to take it," he crooned in that deep voice.

Chapter Six

SID SHIVERED. "That's not—" she whispered, then had to swallow on a dry throat. "That's not what I meant."

"I know," he said smugly. "I just wanted my intentions to be clear."

He stepped back abruptly, and the loss of his heat, of his strength, was sharp.

"So where are we going?" he asked.

"I'm not sure where she is. But she knew I was meeting you tonight, so she'll expect me to call. I can tell her I need to see her in person."

"All right. But watch what you say, Sidonie, because I'll be listening."

"Stop threatening me," she demanded. "I don't like it."

Aden laughed again, but it was genuine amusement this time, not like before. "Just make the call," he said. "And we'll see what your professor friend has to say for herself."

As Sid dug her cell phone out of her coat pocket and brought up Dresner's number, she considered the possibility that the professor wouldn't want to talk to her. If Dresner had tipped off Silas about Aden, and if she knew the plan had backfired—after all, Aden was still alive, which clearly hadn't been what Silas was hoping for—she might want to distance herself from Sid, at least for a time. But as it turned out, Dresner didn't seem troubled at all. She was either secure in assuming Sid didn't know anything about what was going on with the vamps, or she actually hadn't been the one who warned Silas that Aden was coming.

Sidonie was willing to consider both possibilities. Unlike Aden, she wasn't prepared to hang a guilty sign on Dresner just yet.

"Sidonie," she said, answering the phone. "I didn't expect your call until later. Was your meeting with Aden cancelled again?"

"No, just the opposite," Sid said, letting just a touch of anxiety flavor her words. She didn't want to overplay it, but there had to be a reason for her to insist on a face-to-face meeting. "I have some information for you, but it's . . . it's pretty explosive. I'd really like to meet you on this one."

"Of course, but are you all right? You sound shaken."

"I guess . . . I didn't expect it to be like this."

"Where are you? Can you come to my place?"

"I don't know where—"

"I'm in Wrigleyville, on Lakeview. I'll text you the address. How soon can you be here?"

Sid looked up and met Aden's dark stare. "I'd rather not take a cab this late. Is it okay if a friend drives me? We could be there in half an hour or so." Aden's sensuous lips curved slightly in what she supposed could be called a smile, if it hadn't been for the cold calculation in his eyes.

"A friend . . ." Dresner repeated hesitantly.

"He lives here in Chicago. We work together."

"Oh." She hesitated, and Sid thought maybe she'd overplayed it, but then Dresner continued. "I suppose that's all right. Don't ring the bell, though, just knock. The neighbors complain about my late-night visitors." She hung up without saying good-bye.

Aden took the phone from Sid's nerveless fingers and pressed the button to disconnect before saying, "Very good, Sidonie. Is lying one of the skills you learned as a journalist?"

"I didn't lie."

He didn't say anything to that, just raised a skeptical eyebrow. "Are you still determined to go along?"

"Yes."

"Then get your coat. We don't want to keep the good professor waiting."

IT TOOK EVEN less time than Sid had expected to get to Dresner's house. Aden's driver seemed to know where he was going, and this late at night—it was after midnight in the middle of the work week—there were few traffic tie-ups. Having a driver at one's disposal helped, too. No public transpo for Aden. Sid didn't worry about money, but she didn't have a private driver at her beck and call, either.

"Are all vampires rich?" she asked, sitting next to Aden and trying not to think about what was going to happen when they confronted Professor Dresner.

Her question seemed to amuse him. He stretched a powerful arm over the back of the seat behind her, dropping one finger down to toy with a lock of her hair. "An interesting question," he said. "Are all humans rich?"

"No, of course not."

"Then why would all vampires be?"

"I don't know," she said irritably. "But you've got this big truck—"

"A Chevy Suburban, hardly exotic."

"—and a private driver," she persisted, determined to make her point. "And your supposedly temporary office occupies two entire floors of some of the most expensive square footage in Chicago."

"One must make an impression."

"Only if one can afford it."

His smile widened into something almost genuine, but Sid found herself irked all the same. She didn't want him to be amused. She needed him to take her seriously if he was going to help her destroy Klemens's network.

"Just answer the question. Are all vamps rich?"

His smile vanished, replaced by a haughty stare. That wasn't a word she thought of often, but Aden did haughty really well. Maybe he'd been born to money back when he'd been human. Maybe he'd always been rich.

"Were you like a prince or something back in the day?" she asked and knew right away that she'd made a mistake. His fingers stopped toying with her hair, and his expression went cold and distant, the look in his eyes so far away that it was as if she was suddenly all alone in the back seat.

Morocco, 1756

ADEN RACED through the halls of the palace, bare feet slapping the cool marble floor as he dodged silk-clad ladies and ignored the frowns of overfed gentlemen. The former only tittered in annoyance, but the latter would have swatted him to the ground if they'd dared. His father owned this particular palace, although Aden was a bastard and would never inherit a single copper *falus*. Still, his mother was the favorite among his father's concubines, and one could never be certain what standing young Aden had on any given day.

That same uncertainty made Aden wary, however, and he made a point of avoiding the better-traveled corridors whenever possible. On this particular day, however, he'd been summoned to see his mother, which was unusual enough that he hadn't wanted to waste any time getting to her. Not that he didn't see his mother often. After all, he was still very much a child and so lived in the harem. But his time with her was heavily dependent on his father's presence in the palace and his taste for female companionship on a given day. Not to mention the considerable amount of time his mother spent on efforts to maintain her beauty and fitness in order to maintain a pleasing appearance.

Aden's mother was a rare flower in the harem. He'd heard her described that way by the harem's matron, and not without a certain amount of bitterness either. Which made him think it was true.

His father called his mother Aini, which meant flower in Arabic, but her real name was Aileen, and she was a slave. A pampered one to be sure, but a slave nonetheless. She'd told Aden the story of how she came to be living in this palace, how she ended up in a land where five-year-old Aden spoke the native tongue far better than she ever would.

Her father, Aden's grandfather, whose name was also Aden, had been a sea trader in a place called Scotland, which was far away from this palace in Morocco. But it wasn't so far that pirates couldn't raid there, and they did so regularly, looking mostly for slaves—sailors like his uncles and grandfather, and women like his mother. She'd been lucky, she'd told Aden—although he didn't see much luck in being stolen from her life and made a slave. But her pale skin and blond hair, not to mention her intact virginity, had caught the eye of the slave master who'd known his own master's tastes very well. He'd made a private bid, thus sparing her the indignity of being auctioned on the block.

Aileen had been sold into the harem of the wealthy merchant who called her Aini, and some months later Aden had been the result. She'd learned after that to use herbs to prevent pregnancy, which ensured her continued favor with her master.

As for his father, Aden never saw him at all, unless by accident, and had never spoken two words with the man. Bastards were frowned upon by wealthy men and their families. They complicated lines of succession and made wives—particularly wives who'd been unable to produce male heirs—unhappy.

Aden scooted past the harem guards. They were used to his comings and goings and barely registered his passage. Once inside, he slid along back hallways until he reached his mother's rooms. He ducked through the curtained doorway.

"Mama," he whispered excitedly and raced over to her. She held him off when he would have embraced her, and he swallowed the small pang of hurt. Sometimes she was already dressed and perfumed and couldn't risk his dirty little boy hands messing her up. She always kissed him on the cheek after telling him such things, so he knew she loved him.

"Sit, Aden," she said, touching his cheek and leaving behind her flowery scent.

He plopped down obediently at her feet and was surprised when she took one of his brown hands in her own pale fingers. He had his Scottish grandfather's name, but his Moroccan father's coloring. There seemed to be little of his mother's Scottish blood in him, except for his size, which already made him bigger than any other boy his age, and several of the older ones, too.

"Aden, *mah sweit son,* you love your mama, don't you?"

"More than anything, Mama," Aden said quickly, ignoring the little pang of unease that tightened his chest, despite her use of the endearment. She never asked him if he loved her. It was assumed. Of course he loved her. She was his world.

"You're young," she continued in her soft voice. "Probably too young to understand what I have to tell you, but I need you to understand."

Aden nodded, more alarmed than ever when he saw the tears blurring his mother's blue eyes.

"Your father . . ." She looked away, then down at their joined hands, brown against white. "He's given me a command. You're big for your age, much bigger than the other boys. Someday you'll be a big man, like my father and brothers, and I hope the fates are kinder to you than they were to them. But, Aden . . ." She sighed, still refusing to look at him directly. "I must choose. I can take you and leave the harem—"

Aden's heart swelled with excitement.

"—to become a common slave in some other household, or I can stay here as your father's favorite for as long as my beauty lasts—which is many years yet—and then perhaps become matron to the harem and serve him that way."

Aden frowned in confusion. Surely it would be better for them to remain here? Why should there be any question?

"But if I remain, then you must go." She lifted her head at last, and Aden saw her decision in the sadness of her eyes. "You will leave tonight to begin serving your new master."

Aden stared, not quite understanding what she was telling him. A new master? But . . . "When will I see you, Mama?"

"You won't," she said, firming her lips. "It is not unlike the fostering that my people used to do. Children were often sent to live with families far away, never seeing their parents again until they were grown."

"Will I see you when *I* am grown?"

"Perhaps."

Aden was no longer a baby. He knew what *perhaps* meant. He swallowed the knot in his throat and stood, pulling his fingers from his mother's soft grasp. Apparently, he'd gotten more than size from his Scotsman grandfather. He had his pride. She had chosen her master over her own flesh and blood. So be it.

"*Insha'Allah*, we will meet again," he said simply.

His mother glanced up at him in surprise. But whether it was due to the casting of his fate to Allah rather than the Christian god of her youth, or his quiet acceptance of her decision, he didn't know. He didn't care. All that mattered now was that he'd been sold, that he'd wake up tomorrow in a new household. He would no longer be the bastard son of anyone, whether rich or poor. He would be only a boy, a slave with no friends in the world.

Aden turned and left the way he'd come, taking the slaves' hallways, which was only appropriate, since that's all he was now. A slave.

Chicago, IL, present day

"SHALL I COME with you, my lord?"

Bastien's question brought Aden back to the present with a jolt. He'd never seen his mother again after that day. He hadn't even thought about her in a very long time, and it didn't please him that he was thinking about her now.

"Dresner's not expecting a crowd," he told Bastien. "And I'll need an invitation into the house. Sidonie and I will go alone."

"What if she recognizes you?" Sidonie asked, staring nervously at the brownstone they'd parked in front of. "She knows who you are."

"I'll stay to the shadows."

"She has a porch light."

Aden slanted a look at her. "Don't concern yourself," he said shortly. "Just get us in the door."

"Fine. No need to get snippy about it."

Aden reminded himself that he needed this woman to get close to Dresner, that Dresner was probably the one who'd betrayed him to Silas. He also promised himself that in the very near future, he would lay Sidonie Reid out on his bed and leave his mark on every inch of her pale skin. That alone made it worthwhile to put up with her disrespect.

The attitude was something he'd come to expect from modern women, something he didn't consider to be a change for the better. But he was also minded of Raphael's recent admonition, that *some* women had skills to contribute to an investigation, or, as in this case, information and contacts.

So, he didn't take Sidonie over his lap, pull up her skirt, and redden her ass like he wanted to. At least not yet.

SID SNUCK A sideways glance at Aden as they made their way up the walk. Wherever he'd gone during the last few miles of their drive here, he was fully back with her now. She could feel his awareness of their surroundings like a faint electrical charge in the cold night air. He fairly buzzed with energy as they stepped up onto the covered porch. It was like the static charge one got on a hot, dry day. She expected to see blue sparks shooting off of him. Plus, she didn't know how she was supposed to keep Dresner from seeing him once the porch light came on. It wasn't as if he could hide behind a potted plant, after all. He was nearly as big as the whole porch.

Okay, so that was an exaggeration, but knowing that didn't give her any better idea of how to conceal . . . oh.

She stared at the place where Aden used to be, seeing nothing but shadow, even though she could still *feel* the static electricity of his presence. Frowning, she reached out and touched a hard-muscled arm.

"Aden?" she whispered, her eyes straining to see what her fingers told her was there.

"Control yourself, Sidonie," he said drily. "Your friend is about to open her door."

Sid snatched her fingers away. He was such a jerk all the time. Well, maybe not *all* the time. He'd seemed almost human for a while back there in his office. Better than human, actually. She'd never met a human male who was as seductive as Aden, much less one whose seduction she'd so willingly succumbed to. But then he'd turned off the seduction like a switch, which made her think it had all been a pose, just a game he played to see if he could get away with it. She figured he must have lots of notches on his bedpost. Maybe hundreds if he was as old as she thought he had to be.

The porch light came on, and the door opened, forcing Sid's attention back to their current problem, which was Dresner. The prof was standing in her open doorway, giving Sid a curious look.

Remembering the ruse she'd used to arrange this late night visit, Sid painted a nervous smile on her face and said, "Professor, thank you for letting us come over so late."

"You seemed upset," Dresner said absently. She tilted her head and leaned to one side, trying to get a look through the screen door at Sid's supposed friend. But the shadows Aden had wrapped around himself were too thick, concealing him while appearing to be nothing more than the natural shadow thrown by the yellow porch light.

"Could we come in?" Sid asked, nudging Dresner cautiously.

"Of course," the professor said at once. "Where are my manners, leaving you out in the cold? Come in, both of you."

"Thank you," Sid murmured, trying not to show the depths of the relief she was feeling. What would have happened if Dresner had refused? Or if she'd phrased her welcome to include Sidonie only?

"Don't look for problems," Aden muttered against her ear. The concealing darkness dissipated as if it had never been more than a trick of the eye. He stepped up to her side, pulled open the screen door, and gestured for her to go ahead of him, looking all too pleased with himself.

Sid scowled over her shoulder. Had he read her mind? She knew that some vampires could do that.

"No, I didn't read your mind. Your concerns were written on your face."

"Stop that," she snapped. The asshole just grinned and stepped inside, closing the door behind them.

Dresner had backed up a few steps, making polite room for them as they came through the door. But once she got a good look at Aden, she backed all the way to the open archway leading to her living room, her knuckles going white as she gripped the elegant molding.

"Introduce us, Sidonie," Aden drawled, his dark eyes heavy-lidded as he watched the professor shrink away from him, her eyes wide.

"Professor Dresner," Sid said obediently. "This is Lord Aden."

"I know who you are," Dresner said, her words defiant, despite her obvious fear. "You think you're going to be the next Lord of the Midwest," she sneered.

"I don't think," Aden responded dismissively. "I know. No one, not even your precious Silas, will stop me."

"Arrogant bastard," Dresner hissed. "You're not fit to lick Lord Klemens's boots. He was a giant, a genius. And it won't be someone like *you* who takes his place, a masterless bastard from God-knows-where. Silas is his child and rightful heir."

"The same Silas who has run twice from a stand-up fight? Who sends minions to kill me, while waiting in safety? That Silas? Silas isn't fit to run a dockside blood house, much less a territory."

"You think you're so smart," Dresner persisted. "But you'll see."

Aden took a long step forward, until he was towering over her.

"You're right," he agreed. "I *will* see. You're going to show it to me."

She glared up at him. "I'll show you nothing. I'll *tell* you nothing."

Aden's sensuous lips curved up in a confident smile. "Wrong," he said softly. "You'll tell me everything."

Sid stared as Dresner's defiant stance softened into something almost dreamy. Her entire body relaxed, her lips tilting into a peaceful smile. "I'll tell you everything," she agreed happily. "Whatever you want."

"Did you warn Silas about me coming to the club the other night?"

"Yes," Dresner said, nodding eagerly. "When Sidonie mentioned Silas's name, I knew that's where you had to be going, so I called and warned them."

"And why won't Silas meet me directly?"

"You're so strong," she cooed. "Silas is afraid. If my master Lord Klemens was still—" She cut off her words with a wince.

"Who is your master, Claudia?" Aden demanded. And it took Sid a moment to remember that Dresner's first name was Claudia. She'd never called her anything but *Professor Dresner*.

"*You* are my master, Lord Aden," Dresner responded fervently.

Sid tuned out their voices as Aden continued his interrogation. She was more than a little creeped out by what he was doing and how Dresner was acting. Aden had somehow taken over Dresner's mind and was making her act against everything she believed in. He was quite literally making her a slave to his will. Would he do that to Sid, too, if she disagreed with him about something? Was this the vampire she'd thought would help her wipe out Klemens's old slave network?

"Stop it," she whispered, staring appalled at the simpering Dresner. Then more strongly, "Stop it."

Aden glanced over. "Stop what?" he asked distractedly.

"Stop what you're doing to her. You're . . . you're stealing her will, enslaving her."

Aden lifted a hand, halting the flow of information from Dresner. He gave Sid a sharp look.

"What did you say?"

"You're forcing her to do things she doesn't want to, things she'd never do willingly. That's slavery, and that's not why I brought you here, not why I sought you out in the first place. I wanted you to get rid of Klemens's old slave network, not create your own."

Aden crossed the room in three hard strides, until he was standing only inches away from Sid. He stared down at her, and Sid had to admit he was pretty intimidating with his size and dark glowering looks. But Sid wasn't the now pathetic Dresner, and she wasn't cowed. She glared wordlessly right back at him, getting up in his face.

"What do you know about slaves?" he demanded distinctly.

"I thought you knew," she said, her glare becoming a frown of confusion.

"What. Do. You. Know?" he growled.

Sid recoiled, realizing abruptly that he was way more than pissed off. If he'd been intimidating before, he was truly scary now. She hadn't gotten this far by scaring easily, but a little common sense wouldn't hurt, either, so she answered his question and didn't give him any attitude.

"Klemens used his drug network to bring slaves into the country," she said calmly. "Chicago was his hub, his distribution center."

"Claudia!" he barked, without looking away from Sid.

"Yes, my lord," Dresner said instantly.

"You will tell no one of our conversation. You will cease all communication with Silas, or any other vampire, other than myself, is that clear?"

"Yes, my lord. Thank you, my lord."

"Right. You," he said, locking gazes with Sid, "come with me."

Sid narrowed her eyes irritably and didn't move. "Where are we going?"

His scowl intensified. "What does it matter? You say you want

Klemens's slave network shut down. Then you will tell me what you know."

"That's not how this works. I'm going to expose his whole network for what it is, so they can't simply set up shop somewhere else. I want in on whatever you're going to do."

"Not gonna happen, sweetheart. I'll do what needs to be done, and when it's over, I'll tell you what you need to know. This is vampire business, not yours."

"Not—" Sid couldn't form the right words around the anger choking her throat. "The women they're kidnapping and selling are human, Lord Fucking Aden. That makes this *my* business. And you wouldn't have known *any* of this if I hadn't told you about it."

"Bullshit. I have my own sources. You just made it easier. Now, either tell me what you know, or go play reporter somewhere else."

Sid stared at him in disbelief. What a total asshole. She couldn't believe she'd been ready to let him . . . Fuck. She couldn't even think about what she'd almost let him do.

"Tell you what, Aden," she said pleasantly. "Go to hell." And with that, she spun on her heel and stormed out of the house.

Bastien was waiting on the porch, probably worried about his precious asshole of a vampire lord. He looked up questioningly when she banged open the screen door.

"He's fine. I'll see you later," she snapped, then almost growled out loud when she caught Bastien's quick look over her head. He was obviously checking with Aden to see if she was allowed to leave. She didn't wait to find out. She didn't need anyone's permission, no matter what these vampires seemed to think. Reaching the street, she looked both ways, calculating her best chance of catching a cab.

"Don't be an idiot, Sidonie," Aden said from right behind her.

She spun around, fighting the urge to jump, but knew she hadn't succeeded when she saw one side of his mouth curl up knowingly.

"I'll give you a ride back to your condo," he told her.

"No, thank you," she said primly. She turned away from him and started walking.

"Have it your way," he murmured. "But don't blame me if Silas finds you."

That stopped her. She spun to face him. "What?"

His thick shoulders moved in a careless shrug. "Dresner told Silas how she knew I was coming. Your name came up."

Well, wasn't that great? Sid pulled her cell out of her pocket. "I'll call a cab."

Aden strode forward until he was blocking the street light, and she was standing in his shadow. His deep voice curled around her. "Let me give you a ride, Sidonie."

Sid swayed closer, then realized what he was doing. "Don't you *dare* do that to me!" she gasped. "I am not some pathetic vampire groupie you can mesmerize into becoming your slave."

"Be careful," he warned her. "My patience is not unlimited."

"The truth hurts, Lord Aden. Good-bye." Sidonie turned her back on him and started off toward Clark and Wrightwood. There were a few clubs up there in Lincoln Park that had music seven days a week. She should be able to find a cab there, or at least she'd have other people to hang out with until one could arrive.

It was a short walk to the corner, and she felt Aden's stare against her back every step of the way. She kept waiting for his crooning voice to drift over her shoulder, for his big hand to wrap around her waist. But it never did. He let her go. And she told herself it didn't matter. That the disappointed ache she was feeling was only because she was losing a powerful ally in her efforts to close down Klemens's old network.

And she nearly believed it.

ADEN WATCHED Sidonie storm away down the street, as if she were in control. As if she could escape him. He let her go . . . for tonight. There were only a few hours before sunrise, and he had a lot to do before then. He'd pretty much drained Dresner of any useful information, but he wanted to pursue Sidonie's claims regarding Klemens. His vampire sources had hinted at the existence of a slave ring here in Chicago, something he found deeply troubling. He wasn't a total innocent. He knew many vampires indulged their darker natures and ignored human laws. Aden himself frequently bypassed the human legal system, considering it irrelevant to most vampire affairs.

But slavery was one thing he would never permit in his territory. He knew the emotional toll of being owned, of having one's very existence dependent on the whim of another. Sidonie thought he'd enslaved Dresner by capturing her mind and compelling her to tell him what she knew. But what he'd done to Dresner was temporary and harmless. He hadn't altered her memories, though he could have, and he hadn't stripped her mind bare, although he could have done that, too. Once he'd dealt with Silas permanently, Dresner could go back to her sad devotion to the dead Klemens, and Aden would have nothing more to do with her.

That wasn't slavery.

Sidonie Reid had no idea what it truly meant to be a slave.

Morocco, 1763

ADEN OPENED HIS eyes and shivered in the cold morning. It was raining. His master Hafiz would be in a foul mood again today. Hafiz hated the rain. He claimed it lowered his profits, and Aden supposed that must be true, since he doubted people would want to stand in the rain and bid on shivering, wet slaves. But what Aden knew for certain was that if business was slow, his master would take out his unhappiness on his own slaves, and that included Aden. Especially Aden. It was as if Hafiz derived particular pleasure in beating the bastard son of one of the wealthiest merchants in the city. More than once, Aden had wondered if his father had known the kind of treatment he'd receive at Hafiz's hand, and if he'd chosen the slave master for that very reason. Had his father wanted to punish him for being born? For taking even a small part of his mother's love? Though that love had obviously meant nothing to her. She'd sent him away willingly enough.

He poured freezing water from the cracked pitcher on the wooden table next to his bed, filling the crude pottery bowl. He no longer even thought about the elegant furnishings he'd left behind in his father's home, things like smooth pottery and fresh-smelling soaps. As the bastard son, Aden had made do with the lowest quality available in his father's palace, and yet they were still a thousand times better than what he had now. He splashed water on his face and washed his hands with the harsh soap. It hurt his skin, but he did it anyway, knowing it would earn him lashes if he failed to present a neat appearance. Not that he wouldn't be whipped anyway, but he'd discovered there were degrees of pain.

There was no need to change clothes. He had only the one set, and it had been too cold last night to sleep naked. The shirt was ragged and unhemmed, the pants torn and too short for his long legs, but they were the only ones he possessed. And even these were owned by his master. Aden owned nothing. He was nothing. He was a thing, a possession, easily discarded and of very little value.

"Aden!"

He heard his master's bellow and rushed from his room, drying his hands on his pants as he went.

Dropping to his knees at the open door to his master's morning room, he bent nearly in half, face to the floor, and shouted, "How may this useless one serve you, master?"

His master's laugh greeted his query. "Didn't I tell you?" Hafiz chortled. "Perfectly biddable."

"So you said," a woman's husky voice responded.

Aden didn't move from his prostrate position, but he was intrigued. His master didn't entertain many women. Boys were far more his style, and only the smallest, weakest ones at that. It was one thing Aden had to be grateful for, that his Scottish blood had made him too big to suit Hafiz's perverted taste in sexual amusement. Even at the age of five, when Hafiz had first purchased him from his father, Aden had been too strong, his attitude too arrogant. The arrogance had been beaten out of him quickly enough, but his size and strength were there to stay.

"Get in here, worm," Hafiz's hated voice called.

Aden lifted himself from the floor, and, keeping his head lowered, eyes downcast, he shuffled into his master's audience chamber, where he promptly prostrated himself once again.

"Master."

He felt the sharp end of Hafiz's cane dig into his shoulder and tensed, but then the woman intervened.

"No," she said sharply, and amazingly, Hafiz stopped his poking. "Stand up, boy," she commanded. "Let me see you."

Aden froze uncertainly. The woman had given him an order, but Hafiz had not. If he stood without his master's permission, he would be beaten. But if he ignored the command of his master's guest, he might very well be beaten, too. Though perhaps not as severely. So he remained prostrate.

"Do it, imbecile."

Aden stifled a sigh of relief, jumping to his feet at his master's order.

"Raise your head," the woman said. His mind told him the words were a command, but his gut felt it was a request. He chose not to obey either his brain or his gut, because the words didn't come in his master's voice.

Hafiz sighed deeply. "This is becoming tiresome. Do whatever she says, worm."

Aden lifted his head and tried not to stare. He barely managed not to meet the woman's eyes, which would have earned him far more than a lashing in punishment.

"You're right. He's very big for his age," the woman observed, standing suddenly and coming close to Aden. He fought the shiver that tried to race along his nerves at her nearness. No female had been this close to him since he'd bid his mother good-bye. Hafiz didn't own female slaves, didn't have a wife or a mistress. His entire staff was male.

"Take off your clothes," she said quietly, leaning close enough that he caught the flowery scent of her perfume. It confused him for a moment, because it reminded him again of the last time he'd seen his mother.

"Take off your clothes, boy."

Hafiz's harsh command broke through his confusion, and he jumped to obey. Slaves had no souls, but Aden had gained enough religion before being sold to know that it was unseemly for this woman to see him naked. But that didn't stop him. Modesty of any kind was something he'd lost long ago. He loosened the tie on his pants and let them fall to the floor as he tugged the rough garment that was his shirt over his head. Stepping out of the pants, he folded both pieces neatly and set them aside before standing straight once more, eyes cast downward.

The woman's delicate laugh tightened his gut with fear. Did she find his nakedness amusing? Was there some flaw that proved him unacceptable and would result in his punishment for embarrassing Hafiz?

"He's certainly tidy," she said over her laugh. "And very pretty, too."

Aden surrendered to the shudder that rolled through him as her soft hand stroked over his skin, starting at his back and caressing his buttocks, the trail of her fingers following her slow steps around to his chest. He fought against his body's instinctive reaction, but he was a twelve-year-old boy who'd never been touched by a woman like this. His abdomen clenched with an entirely different kind of fear as her slender fingers glided down to his belly and lower, finally grasping his erect cock with a boldness that shocked him. And terrified him.

"Lovely," she commented. "Though you've marked him more than once, Hafiz."

"Boys require discipline," Hafiz said casually, as if the beatings he subjected his slaves to were for their own good and nothing to remark upon.

"Fortunately," the woman said, "the marks will fade with proper treatment. It's a shame you don't appreciate true male beauty. Still, your loss is my gain. I'll take him."

"And the price?" Hafiz inquired in his oily voice.

"I'll meet your price," she said negligently. "But he goes with me this morning. I know you and your *discipline*. I'll not have you marking him out of spite. The last boy I bought from you couldn't work for nearly two weeks."

Aden listened to this exchange and wondered what it meant. Clearly, his master had sold him to this woman, and that was a good thing. Or so he hoped. Aden was untutored, but not stupid. As much as he despised Hafiz, he knew there were far worse fates that could be his. It seemed unlikely, however, that this woman ran a slave ship, or any of the other detestable positions he could find himself in, especially given her admonishment to Hafiz about not marking him. He took that as a good sign, but, in truth, he had no idea what it meant.

His head still lowered, Aden watched from the corner of his eye as the woman picked up his clothes and fingered them with distaste.

"Put these back on for now. The matron will clothe you more suitably later." She turned away dismissively as he began to dress. "Our business is complete, Hafiz. Come, boy."

And that easily, Aden's entire existence changed once more.

Chapter Seven

Chicago, IL, present day

SID WOKE THE next morning, feeling frustrated and angry. It wasn't supposed to have worked out this way. Dresner had assured her that vampires were horndogs, always looking for an easy conquest to score both blood and sex. Unfortunately, she was now forced to question everything Dresner had told her, because it seemed the prof had been working for Silas all along. Dresner had all but admitted setting Sid up as bait for Aden, purely so she could help Silas win control over the territory. And now, because Sid had visited Aden's office once or twice—with Dresner's encouragement—she was in the crosshairs of this Silas, a vampire she'd never even heard of before last night.

Sid didn't even *care* who won the territory. The only reason she'd approached Aden in the first place was because Dresner said he was the guy most likely to win, and therefore the guy most likely to help her fulfill her crusade to shut down Klemens's old slave trade.

Granted, that was before she'd actually *met* Aden, the overbearing asshole. And now that she had, she *really* didn't care who won. Or so she'd told herself all through her long walk in the dark last night, from Dresner's house to a busy club where she'd caught a cab. And ever since she woke up this morning, too. Unfortunately, she wasn't having much luck convincing herself that it was true. Somehow that infuriating, chauvinistic, high-handed . . . gorgeous, powerful, and intensely masculine hunk of vampire had gotten under her skin. And wasn't that a bitch? Because as long as she was listing things that frustrated her, Aden had to be at the very top. One minute he was seducing her, and the next, like a switch being thrown, he was all business, all *don't get in my way, little human, the big bad vampire will handle everything.*

"Fuck that," she muttered and stormed over to her computer. Hadn't she been working this story for months? She knew more about Klemens and his sleazy businesses than Aden did. He hadn't even been sure there *was* a slave network until she'd told him. He'd seemed upset once he found out, though. She'd give him that. Of course, then he'd immediately gone all high-handed me-Tarzan and shuffled the little lady off to the tree house where she'd be safe. Well, *double* fuck that. She'd worked this story alone so far, and she could keep doing it. She didn't need almighty Aden's permission to do her job.

Checking her calendar, she saw it was the eleventh of the month, and the slavers maintained a surprisingly strict schedule, for bloodsucking bottom feeders. The newest shipment of girls would have come in last night. They'd be penned up in one of several holding houses, awaiting the next online auction, which would be on the thirteenth. The number of women to be auctioned varied. It could be as few as five or as many as twenty. It just depended on the gleaners and how much *merchandise* they could round up. Sid's problem would be determining which of the houses the women were being held in. If she could figure that out, she could do some recon and maybe gather enough evidence to take to the police. If she could only persuade them to conduct a raid while the women were still being held prisoner, they'd have no choice but to open a wider investigation. Granted, she'd brought the police evidence before, and they'd never moved on it. She suspected they'd been bought off, though she'd never been able to prove it. But she kept trying, and maybe this time her report would fall to someone who wasn't in the slavers' pay, someone who would follow up on her information.

And if that went against Aden's preferences for keeping the human authorities out of it, then too bad. If he'd listened to her, it never would have come to this.

Sid settled down to work. Because the slavers were so organized in other things, she'd been working on a system for figuring out which house they'd use in any given month. It wasn't perfect, but so far, she'd been right about sixty percent of the time. Eventually, her odds would go up, but with any luck they'd be shut down before that happened.

She'd calculated her best guess and was gathering her stuff for a little field trip when her phone rang. She almost didn't answer, too focused on her plans for the afternoon to be interrupted, but then she caught Will's name on the caller ID.

"Fuck," she whispered. Was it Wednesday already? She briefly considered letting it go to voice mail, but decided that was just too cowardly, so she picked up the phone with a breathless, "Hi, Will."

"Hey, sweetheart. Everything okay?"

"Yeah, sure, why?"

"You sound out of breath."

"Oh, that. I dropped a file and was crawling around under my desk," she explained, appalled at the ease with which the lie tripped off her tongue.

"Can we make it an early lunch today? I've got a meeting."

It was the perfect excuse to cancel, but she couldn't do it. She didn't have many friends since moving to Chicago. Or rather, she had them, mostly from college, but they were spread all over the globe. Will was one of the few who always made an effort to stay in touch, something she herself was woefully remiss in. Besides, who knew? Maybe they *would* get married someday.

Sid contemplated that last thought and shook her head. Nope. She just couldn't see herself settling into her mother's routine for the rest of her life. And that's what life with Will would be. Not a bad life, but not the one Sid wanted, either.

"You there, Sid?"

"Yeah, sorry. My brain took a short trip without me. Early lunch is fine. Where and when?"

"I reserved 11:30 at Naha. That work?"

Sid checked the time on her computer. It would be tight, but she could do it. And she'd still have plenty of time this afternoon to check out the slavers' house.

"Works great. I'll see you there."

"Looking forward to it."

She disconnected, smiling at Will's sign-off. No brooding, alpha male bullshit from Will. He was beta all the way. Had she ever seen him angry? Did he ever *get* angry? He must, right? Everyone did eventually. She sighed and slumped back to her bedroom to change clothes. Ripped Levi's and scuffed Chucks weren't going to cut it at Naha.

SID TOOK A BIG bite of her Naha "famous" half-pound burger and chewed with great relish. She caught Will watching her with a lopsided grin.

"What?" she demanded.

"How a bitty thing like you manages to chow down the way you do—"

"First, I'm not a bitty thing. I'm nearly five-eight, as you well know. Second, no woman wants to be told she *chows down*. As for the rest of it, there's no reason you couldn't have ordered a burger if you'd wanted one, so stop looking at my lunch like a starving dog, and eat your damn halibut."

"Testy. But I had steak yesterday, and I'm trying to cut back on red meat, now that I'm getting older."

"Oh for God's sake, you're going to be thirty, not sixty. Get over it."

"Wait 'til it's your turn. Speaking of birthdays, I assume you're heading home this weekend for your dad's big bash?"

Sid blanked for a moment. Her father's birthday party was . . . oh, God, *this* weekend? She was mortified and feeling more than a little guilty that she'd forgotten.

"You forgot, didn't you?"

"Of course not," she insisted, thinking that she and Will knew each other entirely too well. "It's on my calendar."

"And you forgot anyway."

"I'd have picked it up tomorrow. My alert's set for two days before."

"You have a present yet?"

"Bought it last month, Mister Know-It-All, so there."

"Want to drive out there with me? I'm staying over at my parents' 'til Sunday."

Sid thought about the significance of that last part. It didn't occur to either of them to stay in a hotel together, because there was no *passion*. Will would stay at his parents' house, and, if she stayed over at all, it would be in her old room at *her* parents' house. She found the reminder depressing.

"Sure," she said to his invitation. At a minimum, he'd be good company for the drive, and if it turned out she didn't want to stay over, she could always take the train back.

"Good deal. I'll pick you up around ten. Gives you time to get gorgeous before the party."

"Mmm," Sid agreed, but her mind was hung up on the unfairness of it all. That a smug, chauvinist bastard of a vampire could rock her world, while a great guy like Will was relegated to the friends department. What did that say about her? Nothing good, that was for sure.

Will's cell phone vibrated discreetly. He stole a glance at it and signaled the waiter for the check.

"Hope you don't mind, Sid. But I can't be late for this meeting."

"Of course not."

"Your brother said to say *hi*, by the way."

"Tell him *hi* back." Her oldest brother, Jameson Reid III, was Will's best friend and a partner at the same law firm. Which was why Will saw her brother far more often than Sid did. She'd come by her obsessive work ethic naturally. It ran in the family.

Ten minutes later, Will gave her a brotherly kiss good-bye and slipped into a cab.

"You sure you don't want to share?" he asked, before closing the door.

Sid shook her head. "It's the opposite direction, and I don't want you to be late. I'll take the next one."

"See you Saturday morning, then."

She watched the cab carry him away, staring at the traffic until the doorman drew her attention with a polite, "Do you required a cab, miss?"

Sid regarded him blankly, considering. She felt like walking, but it was already late, and she'd have to take the train to her destination later. "Yes, please. Thank you."

The cab ride was longer than she'd hoped. She'd forgotten how bad lunchtime traffic could be and could probably have walked faster. But it was too late for that. She rushed into the elevator and down the hall, kicking off her heels as she walked into her condo, pulling off her black cashmere sweater and charcoal pencil skirt and tossing them on the bed. She took the time to wash her face of makeup and confine her hair in a long braid, but before she got dressed, she added something she only wore during these nighttime recons of hers, and that was a bellyband holster along with a 9mm Glock 26 Gen4 with a ten capacity mag.

Sid wasn't all that fond of guns and had never fired one before moving to Chicago. But she *was* fond of her life, and some of the places she'd had to venture in pursuit of this story were unsavory at best and flat-out dangerous at worst. She hadn't really taken the danger seriously before Janey had been killed, but afterwards, one of the first things she'd done was buy a gun and learn how to shoot it. She now went to the range every week and fired a couple hundred rounds. Her first few times there had been laughable. She'd flinched so hard, she'd barely hit the target. But she'd stuck with it, and now, while she'd never be a sharpshooter, she was confident she could at least hold her own long enough to get away. Unless her enemy was a vampire. But in that case, she figured nothing would save her anyway.

She racked the slide, putting a round in the chamber, then dropped the magazine and filled it, giving her a total of eleven rounds. She replaced the mag with a hard slap, just as she'd been taught, then slipped it into the bellyband. Once she'd yanked on her clothes—a pair of torn jeans, a heavy, long-sleeved T-shirt, and a dark gray fleece hoodie, along with the black Chucks she'd had on earlier—the small 9mm was undetectable to anything but a pat-down.

Other than the gun, she didn't take much with her on these recon forays. A notebook and pen, her ID and transit pass, and enough money for a cab, just in case, plus a small bottle of water and an energy bar. Experience had taught her that she could sometimes be stuck somewhere a long time, unable to move without giving her position away. She shoved it all into a small backpack, then checked the time again. Nearly 2:00 P.M. It was later than she liked, but there was still plenty of time.

She'd discovered early on that her best chances for sneaking up on the holding pens was during the day when the vamps were sound asleep. They hired human guards, but the humans had clearly been told that their job was to keep the women *in* rather than everyone else *out*, so they paid very little attention to what was happening on their own perimeter.

Besides, Sid had become quite proficient at blending into her environment. She could put on a sexy dress and high heels to seduce Aden, or she could pull on a pair of raggedy jeans and some scuffed Chucks to become just another teenager making her way in a rough neighborhood. She took the train, tucking her braid of red hair down the back of her sweatshirt, pulling up the hood, and adding a baseball cap to better conceal herself before disembarking. She'd been enough of a thorn in the slavers' sides that at least some of them would know her on sight.

The house she was headed to was in Woodlawn not far from Jackson Park, and only a short distance from Lake Michigan. She actually knew of at least one shipment of slaves that had been moved by boat. She didn't know where they'd gone after that, because she'd had little luck tracking any of the captive women beyond Chicago. She only knew for sure that her suppositions about the extended network were correct because of Janey's personal experience.

Keeping her head down as she got off the train, Sid made her way to the street she needed. Her target was a fifties era, single-story house, with a broad, covered porch. She walked by the first time without slowing, continued down two full blocks, then crossed the street and did a second pass on the opposite side of the street. Most of the houses in this neighborhood had been replaced by large apartment buildings, which was a bit of good luck. She couldn't hang around too long without the wrong people noticing her, but there was enough tenant turnover in the surrounding apartments that it gave her a little bit of cover.

Her initial walk-by told her the house she wanted was being guarded by two thuggish-looking guys. They didn't do much, just sat on the porch, chairs kicked back, and watched the street. It said something about the neighborhood that no one gave them a second look, even though they were obviously armed and didn't try to hide it. Holding her cell phone and pretending to carry on a conversation, she snapped several pictures of the guards, including a few that zoomed in on their guns, just for the record. Illinois had some of the strictest gun laws in the country, but that didn't mean no one ever broke them. The police would be no more interested in the guns than the neighbors were, which meant not at all.

She kept walking. This was the hardest part, when her back was to the guards. It would look too suspicious for her to keep glancing over her shoulder, but she was always waiting for the attack to come. For a hard hand to grab her shoulder or a shot to ring out.

She reached the end of the block with a sigh of relief. There wasn't much traffic, but she looked both ways, and as she did, she saw a third guard appear from the back of the house. He walked down the cracked concrete driveway, exchanged a few words with the porch sitters, and then exchanged places with one of them, who then disappeared into the back.

A total of three guards. That was doable, especially since Sid wasn't planning on being a hero. There'd be no breaking and entering, no sneaking in to free the prisoners, and sure as hell no big shootout in the middle of the day. But she wasn't going to limit herself to standing across the street, either. Today's trip was all about recon, which meant she had to get close enough to verify that there really were captives inside the house.

She'd made that mistake early on, rushing off to report her findings to the police, only to have them discover an empty house and no sign that anyone had ever been there. Sid had been sure she had the right house, but it had been nothing but a decoy. She'd later learned that this was the slavers' *modus operandi*. But that incident was part of the reason why the police didn't give much credence to her reports anymore.

For the next phase of her recon, she circled around the block and cut through a second apartment complex that stood behind the small house. This late in the day, the sunlight barely penetrated the narrow space between the several buildings. With her dark gray hoodie, she had plenty of cover to stand and observe the slavers' back yard. The third guard was there, sitting on a battered aluminum lawn chair and looking bored out of his mind. At one point, she was pretty sure his eyes drifted closed, but she didn't make her move until he got up and cruised back around the left side of the house to rotate guard duty with his buddies on the porch.

Moving quickly, Sid slipped over the ancient and drooping chain-link fence bordering the property, and hurried across the mostly dirt yard and up to the right side of the house, which was covered in prickly and neglected holly bushes. She remained still until the new guard was settled on the lawn chair, forcing herself to wait even longer, until there was a good chance he'd grown complacent and bored. And then, hugging the right side of the house, trying to avoid getting her clothes snagged on half-dead holly branches, she moved from window to window. She always hoped for a torn window shade, or a gap in the curtain, something to give her a glimpse inside, but that rarely happened. And today, as usual, the house was buttoned up tight.

She'd never been inside this house, but real estate websites were full of information, if one knew what to look for. She knew the house had three bedrooms, two on the side where she was now, and a third at the end of a short hallway. The windows on the other bedroom faced the back yard which made them too dangerous to sneak a look at. The lawn-chair guard was absent during the changeover, but walking up to the house in plain sight was too much risk for too little payoff. Sid had no doubt what they'd do to her if she was caught. These were the people who'd killed Janey, and although her father's name protected her from the vampires at the top, their street thug guards might not check her credentials before killing her.

Hopefully, she'd find what she was looking for in one of the two bedrooms above the holly bushes. She paused beneath the window closest to the front of the house. She couldn't see what was inside, but people were rarely silent. She listened intently, but there was nothing. Not the scrape of a foot, not a single whimper or cry. Sighing, she crept through the prickly bushes to the second bedroom and stood up just enough to see that this window, too, was sealed off tightly. It was as if they didn't want any bit of sunlight to creep in, as if . . . She froze as a horrible thought occurred to her. What if there weren't slaves in the house at all? What if it was nothing but vampires?

Her heartbeat kicked into panic mode as she checked her watch.

Nearly 4:00 P.M., and this was December. Days were short, nights were long. She'd actually counted on the early darkness to help her slip away after her little recon. But if those were vampires in there, she had to make like the birds and get the fucking flock out of there right now.

Sid forced herself to move carefully, ignoring the old fight-or-flight instinct that was telling her to *Run! Now!* She kept telling herself she had time. Sunset had to be at least half an hour away, and if the vamps were at all like people, they wouldn't jump up and be ready. Didn't they have to pee like everyone else? Brush their teeth or something? She rolled her eyes and concentrated on the important stuff, like remembering how long she'd been lurking in the bushes, and how long since the guards had made their last switch. Glancing toward the front of the house, she considered slipping out through the front yard instead. The covered porch where the guards sat had an old railing around the open sides and more of the unruly holly bushes. It was just possible she could sneak past them and blend into the shade of the big apartment building next door. That was certainly a better alternative than risking a dash across the wide-open back yard with the guard sitting right there and nothing moving but her.

The weak winter sun was fading fast, the shadows growing deeper. And the more she thought about slinking through the front yard, the better it sounded.

She shrugged out of her hoodie, put the ball cap in her backpack, then tightened the straps until it lay flush with her back. Donning the hoodie once more, she zipped it fully and yanked the hood up over her hair, with her braid tucked inside. Then she got down on the ground and crawled along the base of the house until she reached the edge of the porch. On this side of the house there was an open lattice along the base of the porch that let her see the underside of it. It was dark in there, and it smelled wet and rotten, not like something recently dead, but maybe something long-ago dead that was taking its time to decay completely. She briefly thought about hiding in there, but realized that the noise she'd make breaking through the latticework would alert everyone to her presence. She shuddered in relief, then froze when she heard the guards talking.

"What time's the sun go down?"

"Hell if I know. When it's dark."

"Do we wait 'til they come out? I ain't sure I wanna hang around that long. What if they wake up hungry, man?"

The guard snorted. "You rather they hunt you down for not doing the job they paid you for? You don't want these fuckers coming after you, bro. Besides, they like the women better."

"Yeah, the women. Think they'll share?"

"You ask too many questions. Better you sit there and shut up."

Sid heard all of this with a mixture of fear and triumph. She shivered at the idea that some of Klemens's old vampires were sleeping only a few feet away. But at the same time, there was a zing of vindication in discovering she'd been right about the slaves being held here.

Now, if only she could persuade the police to do something before the vamps and their captives were long gone. She sighed in frustration, then had a sudden thought. She'd seen the flash of rage in Aden's dark eyes when she'd told him about Klemens's slave trade. She hadn't imagined that. He might not want her involved, but his reaction had been real.

On a whim, she pulled out her phone and dashed a quick text message off to Aden. He'd probably ignore her, but just maybe he'd be interested enough to check it out, or at least have one of his guys do a drive-by.

She tucked her phone back into her pocket and looked around. The shadows had grown much deeper in just the few minutes since the guards had started talking. The apartment building next door towered four stories over the small house, casting a long shadow this late in the afternoon. The street lights had flicked on a moment earlier, but they were dim, and it was probably no coincidence that the light closest to the vamps' house was dark, the lens sporting a star-shaped bullet hole.

It was now or never.

Checking her gear one last time, Sid turned off her cell phone and shoved it as deep into her pocket as it would go. She drew a long breath, closed her eyes, and whispered a prayer to whatever universal forces might be listening, then rose into a bent-over crouch and made a dash for it.

She nearly made it. A few minutes sooner, and she'd have disappeared into the shadows with no one the wiser.

But those gods she'd whispered to obviously had a twisted sense of humor, because just as she made her dash for safety, the third guard came around the corner from the back and caught her movement. He gave a wordless shout, alerting the other two guards, and suddenly she had three armed thugs coming after her.

She ran for it anyway, but the guard nearest to her position, the talkative one who'd asked all the questions, hopped directly over the porch railing and landed only a few feet away from her. Sid was fast, but he had the advantage of height and caught her in three strides. He grabbed the back of her hoodie and twisted, nearly yanking her off her feet.

"What you doin', fucker?" he growled and hauled her back against his thick chest. Her hood fell back, revealing her braided hair, and the guard grunted. "Well, fuck me, we got us a real live girl," he crowed and dragged her kicking and fighting back to where his buddies waited at the foot of the stairs.

"Fuck." Sid recognized the other guard's voice, the one who'd been the voice of reason. "This ain't good. Where'd she come from?"

"Side of the house there. She didn't see nothin'." Her captor shook her, his big hand gripping her hoodie so that it dug into her throat. "You didn't see nothin', did you, bitch?"

"I gotta tell the boss—" the reasonable one started to say.

"Fuck that. She's ours."

"Let go of me, you asshole," Sid hissed and kicked backwards, hitting him in the shin hard enough that he howled. Unfortunately, the howl was mostly anger. He shifted his grip to her hair, grabbing her braid like a rope and yanking her back against his chest.

"You're gonna be sorry for that, bitch."

"What's this?"

The thug holding on to her turned sharply toward the porch, jerking Sid with him. What she saw there didn't make her feel any better. A man stood in the open doorway. He was average height, slender, with dark hair and . . . eyes that flashed red when he stepped out into the faint light of the porch. He was a vampire, and his gaze scanned the three guards before moving to her and staying there.

"Who's this?"

"Caught her sneaking around the back, sir," the more reasonable thug said. "We'll take care of—"

His words ended in an unmanly squeak of surprise as the vampire was suddenly standing right in front of them, his hand reaching for Sid. He lifted her chin to the meager light and studied her face.

"Let go of her," he ordered quietly.

"Aw, she ain't nothin' but—"

Sid fell to her knees, her captor's grip suddenly going lax as the vamp wrapped long fingers around the man's throat and lifted him off his feet.

"That wasn't a request, human," the vampire said. He threw the gasping thug several feet to land choking and coughing on the hard ground.

She looked up as a hand appeared in front of her face. "Come," he said, and mindful of his reaction to the thug's insolence, she chose the path of least resistance and took his hand.

He pulled her effortlessly to her feet. "Jordan will pay you," he told the others, then hustled her over to the driveway where a late model Audi sedan was parked.

Once in the car, he backed onto the street with a squeal of tires and then immediately got on his cell phone and punched a number.

"I have something that belongs to your master," he told whoever answered, then laughed cynically. "It's red, and he had it with him at the party the other night." He nodded. "Ten minutes."

"Look," Sid started, "I don't know who you just called, but—"

"Save it," the vamp said tersely. "Just sit there and shut up. And be grateful about it."

"Grateful?" Sid gave him a disbelieving look, for all the good it did, which was none, because he didn't even glance at her, much less acknowledge her.

Sid sat in silence for a few blocks, then slanted a sideways glance at her vampire companion. Now that he had her, he seemed to be ignoring her. Taking a chance, she slipped her fingers into her pocket and withdrew her cell phone. She wasn't sure exactly whom she'd call, but—

"Whatever you doing," the vamp said, almost wearily, "don't bother. It won't—" He glanced over and amended whatever he'd been about to say. "A cell phone? Please. Who're you going to call? Buffy?"

Sid glared back at him, refusing to admit she hadn't had a plan to call anyone. But she'd no sooner had the thought than the vamp was pulling up in front of a familiar building. She leaned forward to scowl through the windshield as the car came to a sliding stop, but before she could voice a protest, she was swinging around as someone pulled her door open.

"Babe," Trav said, grinning as he took her arm and half pulled, half lifted her out of the car. "You've been a very bad girl."

Sid tried to slap his hand away. "Let go of me."

He held onto her as he leaned down to talk to the other vampire. "Thanks for this, Elias. Anything else?"

Elias shook his head. "I've gotta get back. Tell Lord Aden I should know more after tonight."

"Will do. You be careful," Trav said, then straightened up and slammed the car door. He watched the Audi drive away, then gave Sid a reproachful look.

"Sid, Sid," he chided. "What did you think you were doing out there tonight?" He was careful not to hurt her, but he didn't let go, either.

"What I was doing long before I met you," she retorted. "Besides," she admitted grudgingly, "I meant to be gone before it got dark, but I got stuck, and suddenly it was too late."

"Good planning." He started toward the front doors, taking her with him, but she dug in her heels. Trav had the strength to force her, but not without making a scene, and she counted on him not wanting to draw that kind of attention.

"I don't want to go in there," she insisted.

"Babe, you stuck your nose where it doesn't belong, and now—"

"What do you mean *where it doesn't belong*? I've spent months doing exactly what I was doing tonight. This is *my* investigation, not yours. And—Wait a minute. You already knew about the slaves, didn't you?"

It hit her then how stupid she'd been. Why had she thought Aden would be any different than Klemens? Why had she assumed he'd be willing to let go of Klemens's very profitable businesses, regardless of whether they were moral? Or even legal?

"Let go of me, or I'll scream," she said quietly.

Travis let go of her arm, but not before giving her a truly offended look. "Jesus, Sid. You really think we'd have anything to do with that crap tonight? That *I* would?"

"I don't know. I don't really know any of you, do I? But tell me, Trav, why else did that vamp know who I was, and why'd he bring me *here*? And why does Aden shut me down every time I try to talk about it?"

"Maybe because it's none of your damn business," Trav snarled, then glanced around. "We're not discussing this here. If you want to talk, you come upstairs."

Sid frowned at him unhappily. She didn't want to go upstairs, but she *did* want answers.

"Fine. But only long enough—"

Trav didn't wait for her to finish, just hooked her arm again and started walking, not saying anything until they were in the elevator alone. He let go of her arm and said, "You're a pain in the ass, Sid, but Aden insisted—"

"Wait, Aden's upstairs? Let me out of here." She started punching all of the floor buttons. Trav caught her hand.

"Stop that. Fuck! What's wrong with you?" He grabbed her again, wrapping his arms around her and trapping her back against his chest.

Sid fumed, but stopped struggling, feeling a little stupid when she saw the row of lighted floor buttons. Fortunately, it wasn't a very tall building. The elevator stopped at the next floor, and the one after that, the doors opening and closing without anyone getting on or off. Trav made a disgusted noise, but Sid fought back a grin.

When they transferred past the guards to the private elevator on the fifth floor, she stopped grinning. She reached up automatically to check her hair and discovered her braid was beginning to unravel. With a guilty glance at Travis, she tugged the coated elastic off the end and forked her fingers into the mess, trying to restore some semblance of . . . well, attractiveness was out of the question, but sanity would be nice.

Travis chuckled. "Don't worry. You look fine."

Sid bit back a retort, knowing whatever she said would only add to his amusement. Flattening her lips, she remembered she didn't have an ounce of makeup on. She'd been trying to look ordinary. Unfortunately, she'd succeeded. Digging around in the small backpack which she'd removed from underneath her hoodie, she found a sample tube of pale pink lip gloss. It wasn't her best color, but it was better than nothing. Not even trying to conceal her actions from Trav, she unscrewed the cap from the rollerball end and smoothed it on her dry lips. Trav made a rude noise anyway, but she ignored him, too busy slicking her tongue over her teeth and remembering how many hours it had been since she'd brushed. *Note to self: add an emergency kit to backpack with all of the basic necessities.* Basic necessities being defined as those things necessary to look good after a couple of hours spent lurking in the bushes and spying on criminals.

The elevator dinged, and the doors opened on the sixth floor penthouse. Travis started to take her arm, but she jerked away, unwilling to be dragged into the great Aden's presence.

The elevator opened onto a small foyer, with a marble floor and a lovely Chippendale table against the opposite wall. A wide hallway opened off to the right, delineated only by the change from marble floor to carpeting, and the door to the offices was about twenty feet down. At the end of the hall beyond the offices was a set of double doors, deep red and highly lacquered. She'd noticed them on her earlier visit, mostly because she was absolutely certain that they weren't standard issue in the building. They were far too expensive for that, and, in her view, it said something about the man behind those doors that he'd been willing to put forth the money and the effort on a set of doors that most people would never see.

As she and Trav neared the door to the office suite, Sid started to turn, expecting him to lead her into Aden's office, like before. But he touched her arm lightly, steering her instead down the hall to the red lacquered doors she'd admired. This close, she could see that while they appeared to be nothing more than decorative, they were in fact security doors of some sort. There was a keypad entry, which Trav accessed, and when the doors closed behind them, it was with a solid thunk of sound, like the noise a big refrigerator door would make, or maybe a bank vault.

What greeted them wasn't a vault, though. The corridor continued, but everything else was different. The carpet was deeper, and the walls were painted a warm, sandy beige. There were no more harsh fluorescents. Wall sconces lined the corridor, incandescent and lovely, casting a soft light that illuminated without being garish. Closed doors lined the walls, three to a side, and at the very end of the hallway, a final door stood open slightly.

Travis guided her to the open door and paused, giving her scruffy athletic shoes a meaningful look. "Shoes off, Sid."

She looked at him in surprise, but complied readily enough. Sid was well-traveled enough to know that it wasn't uncommon to encounter cultures, or simple personal preferences, where one was expected to leave shoes at the door. She bent over and untied her Chucks before toeing out of them, scowling when she realized it cost her an inch of height. In her previous meetings with Aden, she'd worn high heels. With her feet bare, he would tower over her even more than he usually did.

She set her shoes neatly side by side on a small, elegant rug to one side of the door, which had obviously been placed there for that purpose. She couldn't help but note that hers were the only shoes there, and that Travis hadn't removed his loafers.

She gave him a questioning look, and he grinned. "It's just you and Lord Aden, babe. Just what you always wanted."

Without any further warning, he tapped lightly on the door. No one answered, but Trav made a sweeping gesture with his hand, indicating she should go on in. Sid frowned unhappily, but then gave a resigned sigh and pushed the door open.

She took two steps inside and paused, letting her eyes adjust to the muted light. There were no overhead lights, no wall sconces, not even the elegant ones that had lined the hallway. As her eyes adjusted, she realized this was someone's—probably Aden's—personal suite. It was decorated in rich colors of burgundy and gold, with an occasional streak of brilliant blue. An intricate silk hanging covered one entire wall, drawing Sid like a siren's song, offering her a rare glimpse of ancient history. It was incredibly well-preserved, the threads gleaming with color, and those gold strands were the real thing. Their color was too warm, too deep to be anything else.

Sid's mother was a weaver. Her pieces were much smaller than this, but they hung in small galleries and wealthy homes all across the Northeast. As her only daughter, Sid had been dragged to every decorative arts collection in museums all over the world. Sid knew fabric and weaving. And this hanging was as fine as any she'd ever seen. Even better.

She stared at the magnificent piece of art, completely taken in by the decadent and bloody scene it depicted. Eastern lords—she couldn't have said which country, only that it wasn't the western hemisphere—rode into battle, their horses' hooves sharp and deadly, their teeth bared and eyes sharp, their swords dripping blood. And at the other end of the hanging, an elegant palace where ladies in dresses of striking color reclined in indulgent splendor while servants bowed and scraped.

Feeling grubby after her recent crawl through the dirt and bushes, Sid shoved her hands into the pockets of her hoodie to resist touching the tapestry and wished she could turn up the light just a little to see it better.

She was so engrossed that she didn't realize someone else was in the room until a deep, smooth voice drawled, "Sidonie."

She spun around, chagrined at her own rudeness, irritated that he'd managed to startle her. She glared at him as if it was all his fault.

Aden sat in a deep, upholstered chair on the other side of the room. The chair was covered in short-napped velvet, its burgundy color rich with gold deep in its threads. A standing lamp was just over his left shoulder, casting a circle of warm light over him, sparking red highlights in his black hair and blazing off his olive gold skin, while leaving his eyes dark and gleaming.

Just sitting there, he took her breath away. She tried to focus on something else, anything but the way her foolish body was reacting to the mere sight of him, and her gaze fixed on what he was holding. A pile of paperwork sat on the table to his right, and he was holding a multiple-page document, the top pages flipped over as if she'd caught him in the middle of reading it.

Aden made a noise like an abbreviated chuckle, and Sid's eyes flashed up to meet his lazy stare. He did a quick head to toe scan before meeting her glare with a small smile of amusement. He gestured with one hand at the matching loveseat opposite his chair, and his smile only grew broader when she stubbornly remained standing.

"Sidonie," he repeated, his voice flowing over her skin like the finest silk. "I wouldn't have thought criminal activity was your thing."

"Very funny," she said, feeling the blush to the roots of her messy hair. "But as long as we're talking criminals, I wouldn't have thought slavery was *your* thing."

Something changed behind his eyes. Every shred of humor was gone in an instant, replaced by something much colder and angrier. He dropped the papers to the table and stood, towering over her just as she'd known he would despite the fact his feet, too, were bare.

He reached out and twisted a lock of her hair around one long finger, then leaned in close, as if to share a secret.

"You don't know me, Sidonie Reid," he purred. "So I will forgive you this once. But never again accuse me of tolerating slavery. I won't forgive it a second time." He tugged her hair until the curl slipped away from his fingers, and started to turn away. But then he stopped. As if it was an afterthought—although she doubted Aden did anything without thinking about it first—he said, "And for the record, I don't need you or anyone else to tell me what's going on in my city."

"*Your* city?" she managed to say.

Aden's lip curled into a crooked smile. "My city. My territory. It's only a matter of time. And not much more of that."

Sid thought privately that his arrogance knew no bounds, but she kept that to herself, saying instead, "So, that vampire Elias, the one who brought me here, he's one of yours?"

Aden regarded her skeptically, clearly deciding whether to answer her question or not. "Elias belonged to Klemens," he said, still studying her as if trying to figure out what angle she was working. "Klemens's people now belong to no one, other than Lucas who holds their lives until a new lord claims the territory. Elias knows who's going to win this battle and is being useful in hopes of gaining favor. Eventually, he will be mine."

"You already knew about the slaves when I talked to you the other night, didn't you?"

"I suspected, which is why Elias was there tonight. Fortunately for you."

"Why didn't you saying something? You know how important this is to me."

"Do I?" he asked archly.

She felt suddenly foolish in having assumed he would have found out about Janey, and that he'd know what she'd been doing since her friend's death and why. "I've spent the last several months trying to—"

"I know what you've been doing."

She glared at him angrily. Why couldn't he ever be up front with her? Why was he always with the games? "You're an asshole, you know that?"

Aden gave her a devastating smile. "That may be," he said, closing the fingers of one hand over her hip and drawing her closer. "But you want me." He glanced over her head, and she started to turn, thinking someone was there, but then she heard the door close and lock with a quiet snick of sound. She looked up and met his eyes in surprise.

"Magic," he whispered against her ear, his breath a fan of warm air against her skin.

"I don't want you," she insisted. "I only—"

"Do you know," he began, depositing a row of butterfly soft kisses along her brow and down to her cheek, "that when you lie, your heart beats faster?"

Sid's heart was pounding against her ribs.

"Your pulse speeds up."

Her pulse was throbbing like a tiny creature trapped inside her artery.

"Your breathing grows shallow."

She was going to faint if she didn't manage to draw more oxygen soon.

"And you sweat." Sid's gaze flashed up to meet his. "Just a tiny bit," he amended, and his tongue darted out to taste her skin.

"Altogether—" He kissed each corner of her mouth, then touched his lips to hers. "It tells me you just lied when you said you don't want me."

Sid swallowed hard. "Okay," she said, still fighting for breath, "you're attractive, maybe unusually so, but I don't *want* to want you, and that means—"

His arm slipped around her waist, pulling her flush against his hard body. And, oh God, it was so *very* hard. Everywhere. Her hands ached to touch, to stroke her fingers over the ridges of muscle she could feel pressed against her stomach, to squeeze the thick pads of his chest and shoulders that were straining the soft cotton of the long-sleeved black T-shirt he was wearing. She bit her lower lip, her eyes closing of their own volition as she imagined slipping her hand beneath the zipper of his low-slung jeans, her fingers wrapping around the solid length of him, imagined the velvet glide of his skin as she pumped—

"Some women," he murmured, his dark voice a burr of sound that rubbed along her every nerve, "want what's not good for them."

"I don't—"

"Sidonie," he growled in warning.

She looked up at him and found his nearly-black eyes limned in deep blue, the color more of a light than a tint. They were so beautiful, and his face was so very handsome, that she reached up without thinking and touched his cheek. It was softer than she'd expected. Rough where his beard was already stubbled, but silky smooth above that. He blinked slowly, long, black lashes coming down to shadow his eyes.

"Why me?" she whispered. "You could have any woman in the city. Why me?"

His eyes filled with heat and something else . . . victory. "I like redheads."

Sidonie started to pull away, pissed that her only attraction to him was something so shallow. He laughed at her efforts, holding her fast and not letting go.

"You don't like that?" he asked. "Then answer the same question. Why me?"

Sid looked up at him in surprise. This arrogant, confident, powerful creature . . . and he needed to ask her that? She stared at his perfect face with its sensuous mouth and chiseled cheekbones. His extraordinary eyes.

"You're beautiful," she said honestly.

"And so are you," he crooned, and then he was kissing her. There were no more teasing brushes of his lips. His mouth came down hard, crushing her lips against his. It was passionate and sensuous, a demand and a claiming all at once. Sid lost herself for a moment in the force of that kiss. She clung to him, her fingers clenched in the fabric of his T-shirt, and she felt . . . things. Emotions and desires she'd never experienced with any other man. Things she'd read about, but never thought to feel for herself.

His hand slipped from her waist to cup the curve of her butt, lifting her up until the thick bulge of his erection was nestled in the vee of her thighs, taunting her with its presence so close to where she wanted him, where she needed him. Sid moaned softly, rubbing the unaccustomed ache between her legs against the temptation of his cock.

As if her soft moan had been the trigger he was waiting for, Aden swung her up into his arms, and, holding her tightly, his fingers tangled in her hair and tugging her head back to make her mouth available to his kiss, he strode across the room to a closed door she hadn't noticed before.

She felt the magic this time—maybe because he was holding her so close to his chest—but she felt the frisson of energy as he exerted his will, as the door swung open at his command. He walked through without stopping, the door slamming behind them, sealing her inside with this dangerous, sexy vampire. Sid shivered in equal parts fear and excitement, her eyes going wide when Aden looked down at her with fangs bared for the first time since she'd met him.

"Are you afraid of me, Sidonie?" he asked, though he didn't seem bothered by the prospect.

She nodded, not admitting that what she felt was nothing as simple as fear.

"Excellent," he growled. "Now tell me the rest."

Sid closed her eyes, unwilling to admit she was more aroused than she'd ever been in her life. He was already too damn arrogant by half. He didn't need any more ego stroking. But then he bent his head and kissed her once again, his tongue exploring every inch of her mouth. She couldn't stifle the groan of desire that started somewhere in her gut and rolled out of her throat. She'd never wanted anyone as much as she wanted him.

"Tell me," he demanded, nipping at her lower lip sharply enough that she was certain he'd drawn blood. "Or I'll take you back out there and tell Trav to drive you home."

Her eyes flashed open. He wouldn't. But his expression said very clearly that he most certainly would.

Sid wrapped her fingers around the back of his neck and tugged hard on the ends of his hair, trying to gain some small measure of control. He bared his teeth at her in a snarl and started to turn back toward the door to the sitting room.

"I want you!" she said before she could stop herself and felt her entire body heat with embarrassment. At least the parts that weren't already burning up with lust. "I want . . ." Sid didn't know how to say what she wanted him to do to her, or couldn't say it out loud. "I want you," she repeated.

Aden tugged her head back, baring her neck. He lowered his head, and his lips skimmed along the curve of her jaw and lower, until she felt the kiss of his teeth on her neck, his breath warm and moist, his voice a rumble of sound when he said, "I'm going to fuck you."

Sid felt herself falling then gasped in surprise when he dropped her onto a bed she hadn't even noticed. She sat up, trying to take it all in, when Aden yanked off his T-shirt, and she suddenly couldn't look at anything else. There was nothing in this room, nothing in her lifetime of experience, that was more beautiful than the magnificent male standing in front of her and stripping away his clothes.

He tossed his T-shirt to one side, and Sid could only stare at the play of smooth muscle over his chest, the power of his shoulders and arms. She saw with some surprise that he had identical tattoos on both arms, dark bands that circled the thick muscles of his biceps. He started on the buttons of his 501s, and her gaze lowered, taking in the rippled abs and flat belly, the line of silky hair arrowing down to . . . The blood left her brain when he slipped the last button and shoved his pants down past narrow hips. Her imagination hadn't done him justice. His cock was long and thick and hard, proudly jutting upward as he stalked toward the bed, his eyes lit with that blue-moon glow again, his fangs white and gleaming.

Sid tried to scoot back, but he struck with snakelike speed, grabbing her ankle and drawing her closer before climbing onto the bed and straddling her still fully-clothed body. He didn't bother taking off her hoodie; he simply yanked the two sides open, breaking the zipper, then gripped her heavy T-shirt in both hands and, with a powerful flex of his arms, tore it down the middle. He paused briefly then, his hot gaze taking in her blue satin bra and the curve of her breasts pushing out of the top. A strange little smile crossed his face as he slipped a finger under one of the straps and tugged it over her shoulder, then shoved the bra cup down until her nipple was exposed, flushed and hard. His eyes lifted to meet hers, his look smoldering and heavy lidded at this undeniable evidence of her arousal. Heavy lashes came down to cover his eyes as he leaned over and took the traitorous nipple into his mouth, swirling his tongue around in a wet caress. Sid's moan of pleasure turned into a startled gasp when his teeth closed over the swollen bud, biting down until she could feel the sharp edge of his fangs. She looked down, scraping her nails through the back of his hair, and found him watching her over the curve of her breast, his gaze filled with something wicked, something out of control that dared her to stop him.

Sid could only moan, too overwhelmed by sensation to think rationally. She wanted to grab him by the hair and yank him away from her breasts, to pull her torn clothes together and run for her life. But even more than that, she wanted him to suckle the other breast in its lonely cocoon of blue satin, wanted to know what it would be like just once to make love to a man, a vampire, who could make her feel such intense pleasure with nothing but his mouth. Her brain couldn't begin to conjure what the rest of him could do to her.

With a final swirl of his tongue, Aden released her breast and sat back, reaching for the zipper to her pants. Fearful that he'd destroy them the way he had her T-shirt, she grabbed for the zipper herself. But he pushed her hands away with an evil-sounding chuckle, and taking slow, exaggerated care—so slow that she began to wish he'd simply rip them off—he slid the zipper down and stripped her jeans away, exposing the blue satin thong that matched the bra.

Aden eyed the tiny blue triangle briefly before hooking his fingers into the narrow bands to either side and snapping them like thread. Sid's entire body blushed when he fisted the now useless piece of blue satin and tossed it over his shoulder before running his big hands up the insides of her thighs and pushing her legs apart, baring her aching sex to his hot stare. She moaned, uncomfortable with such unaccustomed exposure, and tried to close her legs. Aden gave a warning growl and bent her knees toward her chest, pushing her thighs wider apart and opening her even further to his scrutiny. Fixing her with a scorching stare, he dipped one thick finger between the swollen lips of her pussy and found her slick with arousal. His sensuous lips curved with satisfaction as he slid his finger up and down, smearing her wetness over and around her clit, tormenting her with slight touches that had her thrusting against his fingers, her hands gripping his forearms as she cried for more. And then, as if to torture her, he took his hand away altogether, and while Sid was still trembling, while her clit was still begging for his touch, he brought his finger to his mouth, and, holding her captive with his hot gaze, he tasted the proof of her arousal, sucking his finger as if to get every last drop.

Sid closed her eyes against the sight, her head thrashing from side to side as she swore in frustration. He moved in close once more, and she felt the hard brush of his cock over her wetness. Her eyes flashed open, her thighs closing around his hips as she reached for him, certain he'd fuck her at last. But instead, without saying a word, and without releasing her from his stare, the sadistic bastard reached down, grasped his cock, and began pumping it slowly.

Sid groaned at the sight of this beautiful male, golden skin stretched over sweeps of elegant muscle, dark hair tangled and messy, his eyes no longer the blue of moonlight, but the searing blue of lightning before it strikes. There he sat between her thighs, stroking himself, the very picture of masculine perfection.

And she wanted him like she'd never wanted anything or anyone in her life.

"What do you want, *habibi?*" he crooned

Sid nearly sobbed with relief at the question. "You," she whispered.

Aden's sexy mouth curled into a satisfied smile. "Say it."

"I want you."

He tilted his head curiously. "What do you want me to do?"

Sid mewed a wordless protest. He *knew* what she wanted, but he was still waiting, watching her with that smug look on his face, while all the while his strong fingers stroked up and down his shaft, the muscles in his arm bunching and releasing . . .

"I want you to fuck me," she muttered, knowing that's what he wanted her to say, that he wouldn't settle for some pretty euphemism.

"Mmm," Aden moaned, eyes closed, head thrown back as he pumped himself.

"Damn it. Fuck me!" she demanded loudly, worried that he was mulish enough to jerk himself off right in front of her, just to make his point. But she needn't have worried.

He was on her before she'd finished speaking, pressing her against the bed, his hips spreading her thighs wide apart, and his cock plunging balls-deep into her slick sex. He fucked her fast and hard, giving her no time to come to grips with his size, no slow buildup to the overwhelming thrill of his thick shaft filling her beyond what she'd thought possible. He pumped in and out, forcing the quivering tissues of her inner walls to accommodate him, taking her just to the point of discomfort before pulling out and starting all over again. And all the while, his eyes were locked with hers, keeping himself propped up, his arms straight, gorgeous muscles straining as his hips pumped between her thighs.

Sid grasped his arms, holding on for dear life, swamped by such desire, such *need*, that she knew she'd drown in a maelstrom of wild emotions if she let go of him. Every nerve ending was firing at once, her skin so hyper-sensitized she feared she'd come if he so much as kissed her shoulder, her arm, any part of her. Her breasts were swollen and aching, the smooth fabric of her bra feeling like a shimmering electrical charge rubbing all over her, instead of the silky satin it was.

And Aden just kept fucking her, until she was so wet that her thighs were slick and sticky, until the friction of his smooth cock going in and out was so hot that it was a brand, marking her as belonging to him and no one else.

She felt the orgasm begin in her belly, a spasm of pleasure, a shivering ripple of sensation that spread in every direction, until she felt it in her fingers and toes, her breasts, even her nipples which longed to feel his mouth again. The wave of desire rolled through her, growing higher and hotter, until it stole her breath beneath her racing heart, until her clit was a pulsing nub of carnal heat.

"Aden," she gasped and flexed her hips upward to meet his thrusts, rubbing herself against him, desperate to relieve the terrible aching need, to release the orgasm that he was denying her.

"Sidonie," he growled, and she looked up to see his fangs pressing against the fullness of his lower lip.

Sid's eyes widened as she struggled to think. Sex equaled blood for a vampire. How many times had she been warned about that? Her breathing grew choppy, her pulse dancing counterpoint to her clit. She thought about those sharp fangs slicing through her skin and into her vein, about her blood rushing down Aden's throat, the strong column of his neck as he swallowed, his head thrown back, eyes closed in ecstasy. And she nearly came just from thinking it.

A small part of her brain tried to say there was something wrong with her. That Aden was right, and she was one of those women who wanted what was bad for her. But good or bad, she wanted *him*. And she meant to have him . . . now. She'd waited long enough.

Sid wrapped her arms around his powerful shoulders and dug her fingers into the muscle.

"Kiss me," she demanded.

Aden gave her a hooded look, as if to say he'd kiss her when he was ready. But then he lowered himself slowly, his weight crushing her into the mattress, his heat enveloping her. He kissed her mouth, her jaw, and over to the soft skin in front of her ear. His fangs were a smooth, sharp glide as he scraped them over the swell of her jugular. His lips opened, and she braced herself for his bite, but he sucked at the skin of her neck instead, his mouth warm and wet. Sid cried softly, her fingers tangling in his hair as she pulled him closer, as the shiver of erotic sensation grew. She moaned at the first prick of his fangs, cried out as he sliced into her vein. And then the euphoric contained in his bite jolted through her like an electric shock, sizzling along every nerve and fiber, bowing her back while her womb contracted and her sheath clenched around his cock.

His fangs were still buried in her vein when her inner muscles began a fierce ripple along his length. Aden groaned, and the sound vibrated in her bones as he fought to keep pumping in and out of her heated sex, to keep slamming his cock deep inside her, their bodies slapping wetly against each other. He lifted his head to stare at her, her blood dripping from his fangs, his throat working as he swallowed. He held her gaze as he licked his lips, letting her watch as he savored every drop. And then he dipped his head and kissed her, and she tasted her own blood on his tongue as he began pumping harder, faster, until finally he tore his mouth away from hers, threw his head back, and came with the triumphant snarl of a predator who has claimed his prey.

ADEN ROLLED ONTO his back, savoring the last few drops of Sidonie's blood as they slid down his throat. The energizing effect of what he'd already taken from her was like a hot liquid in his veins, warming his muscles and sparking fire in his nerves. He stretched his arms above his head, savoring the burn. Sidonie took that as an invitation and curled up next to him, her head on his shoulder, one slender arm thrown across his chest.

Aden frowned and moved only his eyes to look down at her curiously. He could see the pile of curls on top of her head and the pale stripe of her arm against his own much darker skin. He didn't do post-coital cuddling. Women were a source of sex and blood, obtained through a process that was enjoyable for all.

On the other hand, he discovered to his surprise that he wanted more of Sidonie Reid. Tonight had been like the appetizer before the meal, and he had every intention of savoring the main course. Probably more than once.

He dropped a heavy arm over her back, drawing her in closer and feeling her relax infinitesimally. For all her appearance of ease when she'd cuddled in next to him, she'd been tense, waiting to see what he'd do. She was not a woman who fucked casually. That he'd managed to draw her in so easily was partly attributable to his skill in the art of seduction, but that wasn't the whole story. She was curious about him and what he represented. Sidonie wanted to know what it was like to walk on the wild side. She'd been a good girl all her life, and he was the forbidden fruit.

Aden hugged her close with a private smile. He was more than ready to introduce Sidonie to the sort of things done in the dark of night. He only hoped she was ready for just how dark he could get.

Chapter Eight

SID OPENED HER eyes without moving. She knew where she was, but she wasn't sure about anything else. Okay, that wasn't quite true. She also knew she just had the best sex and made the worst mistake of her life all at the same time. She'd fucked a vampire. What was even worse, she'd fucked a vampire lord and let him take her blood. She groaned out loud, and then froze, hoping he wasn't close enough to hear her. Although, given his penchant for playing games, he'd probably fuck her again just to prove she wanted it. Which she did, because, yeah, it was the best damn sex of her entire life.

Not that she had all that much to compare it to. She hadn't even lost her virginity until college, and she'd always dated proper young men of good families. The kind she could bring home to Mom and Dad. The kind who knew which fork to use at all of those charity fundraisers. They were nice, they were considerate, and they always made sure she came during sex.

Aden? Well, one out of three wasn't bad, right? Who was she kidding? She was doomed.

She sat up slowly, figuring that since he hadn't reacted to her groan, he wasn't in the room. She looked around, taking in all the details she'd been too overcome to notice before. The bed was a big four-poster, king-size or better, with damask silk draperies the color of a fine ruby cabernet. Rich, but dark. Kind of like Aden himself. Beautiful and strokable on the outside, but with a soul as black as coal. It made her wonder about his history, about where he'd come from and what had made him the way he was. Just thinking about it made her sad and she gave herself a mental shake. She wasn't here to psychoanalyze Aden or to soothe his tortured soul. They'd had sex, great sex, but it would be a mistake for her to romanticize it into anything else. Aden was a consummate lover, but she had a feeling he'd be a demanding boyfriend.

And speaking of Aden, where was his moody self? She listened carefully, but didn't hear any noise except her own breathing. No shower running, no voices. Thinking about showers made her realize she needed one. There was a door cracked open on the wall opposite the one they'd come in earlier; at least, she was pretty sure that was where they'd come in. She'd been somewhat preoccupied at the time.

Scooting off the bed, she gathered her clothes—what was left of them. Her T-shirt was almost useless, but it was the only top she had, so she grabbed it along with her underwear, which was . . . darn, also ruined. She remembered him snapping the sides of her thong, remembered the way the muscles in his arms had bunched up . . . and found herself getting warm and sticky simply thinking about it.

"Gah!" She considered leaving her destroyed underwear on the floor for the big, bad vampire to pick up—after all, he was the one who'd ruined it—but she really liked that blue satin, and the bra was fine. Maybe the thong could be repaired. Clutching the clothes she still had, she located the bathroom and cleaned herself up. What she really wanted was a shower, but she didn't want to be standing there naked and soapy when Aden showed up. She entertained a brief fantasy of him stripping down to skin and joining her in the steamy enclosure. She could feel the glide of his wet skin against hers, imagined the play of his muscles as he lifted her against the tile . . .

"Stop that!" she scolded. This wasn't like her. She didn't moon over men, and she certainly didn't entertain private fantasies while standing in a strange man's bathroom. Maybe Aden had done something to her brain, put thoughts in her head that shouldn't be there.

That was the easiest explanation, but she wasn't willing to let herself off the hook so easily. She'd known Aden was seducing her, and she'd wanted what he was offering. She couldn't blame him now that it proved to be more than she could handle.

She put her bra on, realizing only belatedly that she'd have to go commando under her jeans. It wouldn't be comfortable, but at least she still had pants to wear, and socks. She frowned in dismay at the broken zipper on her hoodie, but did the best she could with what she had, putting her T-shirt on backwards and her hoodie over that. And then she caught something in the mirror that had her leaning forward in dismay. Yep, she had the mother of all hickeys, although, given her fair skin and what she remembered of his bite, she was surprised it wasn't worse. She knew vamps sealed the puncture wounds with a lick after they bit someone. Maybe that same chemical in their saliva healed the wound faster, too.

Well, at least it was winter and she could wear turtlenecks without anyone wondering about it.

Once she was as dressed as she could get, Sid walked out into the sitting room with its gorgeous silk hanging. She looked around for her backpack, but it wasn't there. That didn't make her happy, because the key to her condo was in there, along with her ID, her cell phone, her notes.

She walked over and opened the door to the hallway. Her shoes were on the small rug where she'd left them, so she sat down and pulled them back on.

Feeling more or less prepared, she headed down the hallway toward the red doors, thinking she'd find Aden in his office. Or, if not, at least find her backpack, so she could go home.

As it turned out, she didn't have to go looking, because as soon as she opened the door to the hallway with the elevator, Travis popped out of the office entrance.

"Sid," he said cheerfully, although without any of the flirting that had been his usual attitude toward her. "Lord Aden's in here."

She smiled, feeling a little embarrassed. She was holding her hoodie closed, her arms across her chest, but it had to be obvious what had happened in Aden's bedroom.

"I just need to get my stuff," she said.

"Right," Trav said agreeably and repeated, "Lord Aden's in here."

Knowing she wasn't going to get anything else out of him—it was obvious that Aden had given him orders of some sort—she followed him back into the office where she'd wanted to go anyway.

Aden was on the phone when she walked in, but his eyes blazed as he gave her a long, slow head-to-toe perusal, the kind that said *I know what you look like under those clothes.* Sid flashed back to a naked Aden staring at her fully exposed sex, her thighs spread wantonly, and a shiver of arousal skated over her entire body. Her breasts swelled, and an aching warmth began to build between her legs.

Aden gave her a knowing little wink.

Her face heating with embarrassment, Sid busied herself with a quick perusal of the office, looking for her backpack. If she could only find that, she'd be gone. Then, at least, she could enjoy her fantasies in private.

"Keep looking," Aden said. Sid jerked around to stare at him in surprise, but realized he wasn't speaking to her, but to whoever was on the other end of the line. He hung up without saying good-bye, and Sid thought it was nice to know he was rude to everyone, not just to her.

"How are you feeling?" he asked, his voice a sexy rumble of sound.

"Great," she said, hearing herself and knowing she sounded way too chipper.

"Come here."

"Oh, I don't think that's—"

"Come here, Sidonie," he growled, giving her a dark look from under those lush lashes.

Sid knew she should tell him to fuck off, that she didn't go for the whole me Tarzan, you Jane routine. But that was her brain talking. Her body was going all melty and warm, her nipples hard as rocks, her pussy, which had always been so well-behaved, was wet and hungry, yearning to be filled. Her *body* wanted him. And her body won.

She managed to walk slowly, trying to look reluctant, but the end was the same. She rounded the desk to stand before him, getting close enough that their legs were touching.

Aden stroked his big hand up the back of her thigh and left it there.

"Be here at seven tonight, and wear a dress. I like those better."

Sid frowned. "But you said Elias works for you. Aren't you going to follow up on the slave thing? If their guards follow the pattern, those women will be gone by tomorrow night, and we'll never find them."

"I'll take care of it. You'll only get hurt."

His dismissal cut through the lust fogging her senses. "Fuck that," she snapped. "I've been following this for months. I know the routes, the holding houses, I know the people involved. I know way more than *you* do about it."

"This is vampire business, Sidonie. I don't want you involved."

"I'm already involved, and I don't care about your super-secret vampire business. You either take me with you, or I'll follow you there. Actually forget that, I'll get there before you."

Aden released her leg and stood abruptly, doing that towering-over-her thing that he did so well. She thought for sure that he was going to snarl at her and forbid her from going after the slavers. For all the good it would do him.

But he surprised her by saying, "Fine. You want to see how the game is played, you can come along. Just remember, *habibi*, human law does not apply here. There will be no Miranda warnings, no worrying about civil rights. The only law that will matter is *mine*."

"I'm not some delicate flower to be afraid of a little bloodshed, Aden. And I don't give a damn what happens to those animals."

She didn't quite trust the smile he gave her, but he nodded his head and said, "Then be here an hour after sunset. You can wear similar clothes," he added, glancing down at her jeans dismissively. "But bring a dress for later."

"I don't know why I need to bring—"

"Because I like skirts. They make you more accessible."

"More accessible?" she repeated, frowning. "What does that—Oh," she said, suddenly understanding what he meant. A skirt made it easier for him to fuck her. Part of her was outraged at the very idea of him saying something like that to her. But then a suddenly vivid image flashed through her brain, a picture of him bending her over his desk, his big hand shoving up her skirt . . . Lust punched her in the chest, and she shuddered uncontrollably. Clearly, her brain was going with her body on this one.

Aden's hand on her hip startled her back to awareness. His fingers tightened, and he pulled her flush against his body. "You should sleep today," he crooned. "Because you won't be sleeping much tonight."

Sid's mouth went dry. "You mean, because we'll be raiding the holding house tonight?"

"Of course," he said, a smile playing around his lips. "Did you think I meant something else?"

His hand slid down to the curve of her butt before he lowered his head and kissed her, a sensuous tangle of his tongue and lips, slow and seductive. Sid sighed into his mouth, reluctant to let the kiss end.

"Tonight, *habibi*," he said against her lips.

And Sid didn't know if it was a promise or a threat.

Chapter Nine

SID FINALLY KNEW what it meant when people said they were on pins and needles. That's what it felt like to her, as if every inch of her skin was being pricked by tiny little pins . . . from the inside. She sat with Aden in the back seat of his big SUV. Bastien was in the front passenger seat, and Travis drove as they raced through the streets of Chicago, going at what were surely illegal speeds, and definitely reckless. This wasn't some wide open highway. This was Chicago. Even at midnight on a weekday, there was traffic. But Travis had reflexes worthy of the Indy 500, and apparently no fear of death or dismemberment. She only wished she could say the same. Tonight was going to test every inch of her resolve, every ounce of her courage. She'd never confronted the slavers directly before, had always settled for doing recon, gathering information. That was the sensible thing. She was a journalist, after all, not a soldier or a cop.

But tonight was Aden's show, and he and his vampires were definitely ready for a fight. Assuming she survived the trip to the house where the slaves were being held, there would be a showdown between Aden and his guys and whoever was in charge at the house. And she doubted they'd go down easily.

Even more than the impending violence, though, she was worried that the slaves had already been moved. That the vamps had somehow gotten word they were coming and spirited the women away. But Aden's man on the inside, Elias, had reported that tonight was the night.

Despite her trepidation, the inevitable violence, and everything that could go wrong, Sid was jumping with excitement, exhilarated by the prospect of finally doing something real to stop the slavers and avenge Janey's death.

And if that wasn't enough to leave her taut as a bowstring, there was the vampire sitting next to her. The vampire who only a few hours ago had been balls-deep inside her. Every time he moved, every time he spoke, she was reminded of what it had felt like to make love to him, to have him murmuring her name as he thrust between her thighs. She was almost embarrassed to find herself sighing dreamily, wondering how long it would be before he did it again.

"Heavy thoughts, Sidonie?" Aden's midnight voice had chills skating over her skin, his words like warm honey sliding into her ear and down her throat into her belly.

She shook her head sharply. "Just . . . I've worked so hard on this and now . . . it might all be over."

He chuckled and let his arm, which had been stretched across the seat behind her, fall heavily onto her shoulders. His hand dropped to her chest where his fingers began to play idly along the swell of her breast. Sid wanted to roll her eyes at her own pathetic response to him, her heart racing, her skin heating to his touch. Aden leaned close and pressed his lips to the side of her face. She felt the wet touch of his tongue as he tasted her skin. It was a not-so-subtle reminder that he could sense her reactions to him.

She didn't even have to look to know he'd have a smug expression on his face, and she'd have loved to smack that look away. But, one, she'd already established that she wasn't exactly qualified to smack anything off of anyone, much less a vampire lord, and, two, he'd stop her before she even got close. And then either there'd be hell to pay, or he'd find the whole thing oh-so-amusing. Neither of which appealed to her.

"What's the plan?" she asked, trying to think of anything other than sex.

"The plan is simple. We go in two teams, front and back, and kill every vampire present."

"What about the women?"

"The van will transport them to a safe location," he said, referring to the second vehicle following behind them. She'd been surprised when they'd started out to see the plain, full-size passenger van in their mini-convoy. "Any injuries among the women will be treated," Aden continued, "and they will have the option of returning to their homes, or being settled in this country. Either way, they will be well cared for."

Sid blinked in surprise. She hadn't expected that. In fact, she'd been prepared to put up a fight, to demand something close to those very arrangements.

"You seem surprised," Aden murmured.

"No, it's just—"

He licked her face again. Not a delicate taste, but a blatant doglike lick.

"Fine," she admitted, rubbing her wet cheek. "I'm surprised."

"I've no tolerance for slavery."

"I see that." And she did. It was the second time he'd made that point very strongly, and it made her wonder again about his background. She'd assumed he'd been born rich, simply because he *was* rich. She'd told him as much. But what if he hadn't been? According to Dresner—assuming anything that bitch had said was true—the powerful vampires were all extraordinarily old by human standards. Not because age equaled power, but because those who gained power as a result of their transition to Vampire won every challenge as they took their time learning to use their newfound power. So, Aden could be old. Old enough that he'd been born in a time when slavery was common.

She remembered the fantastic silk wall hanging in his sitting room. Her mother would have known instantly where and when it was from, but Sid could only guess. Maybe she could get a picture for her mom next time she was in Aden's room. She smiled ruefully. Might as well call it what it was, the next time they had sex. And please let there be a next time, her body was begging silently.

"This is it, my lord," Bastien said from the front seat. "White house, fourth one down on the right, broken street light."

Sid was jerked out of her lust-filled thoughts by his announcement. She looked around and found herself back in the same Woodlawn neighborhood where she'd been skulking around . . . was it only the night before? So much had happened, it seemed longer ago.

"There's an apartment house in the back," she told them. "You can sneak in through—"

"There'll be no sneaking," Aden said, cutting her off. "Trav, Bastien," he continued, "we'll take the front."

They parked two houses away. Sid climbed out after Aden, listening as he conferred with Freddy and Kage, the final two members of his inner circle who'd traveled in the van, telling them to come in from the back. She watched them slip away into the shadows, thinking about her own clumsy spying and wishing she could move with even a fraction of their stealth. Bastien and Trav had already started up the walk. She pushed away from the truck, intending to follow them, but Aden wrapped his fingers around her arm, pulling her to a stop.

"Sidonie, this will not be civilized by your standards. You may want to wait—"

"I'm going in with you," she insisted stubbornly.

He eyed her steadily, and she thought she saw a glimmer of

approval in his dark eyes before he nodded sharply and said, "As you wish. But you will go in last and remain by the door. I wouldn't want to kill you by accident."

Sid scowled, pretty sure he was joking about that last. But she hung back when the vampires climbed the stairs, not wanting to chance it. Her main objective tonight was to be there for the captives afterward.

Bastien reached the door first, and Sid waited to see if they'd knock and then rush the entry, or—

One kick, and the door flew inward.

Okay, well, that worked, too.

ADEN WOULD HAVE entered first, but Bastien shoved his way through the door ahead of him. It went against Aden's nature to let someone else take a risk for him, but he was gradually coming to terms with the necessity. If he was going to rule a territory, he'd have to surrender to the requirements of security. Not for his own sake, but for the sake of those whose lives he would hold in his hands.

Once inside, however, all bets were off. There were half a dozen vampires in the living room as they came through the door, with more rushing in from other rooms in response to the noise. His inside man had told him to expect ten or more fighters, all vampires. The slavers were moving their captives tonight, and that meant the entire crew would be present. Which was what made this night perfect. Aden could wipe out the entire filthy operation with one blow.

His power lashed out, cutting through vampires like a barbed whip, saturating the air and spraying the walls with blood. Vampires screamed and died, and dust joined the bloody miasma filling the shabby room. Some of the slavers seemed to recognize him then, or at least recognize the brutal nature of his ability and the strength behind it, but even here he didn't draw on the full depths of his power. He didn't need it for vermin like these. And like vermin, they scurried for the back of the house, thinking to escape, but Freddy and Kage came roaring in through the kitchen door, and the fight was all but over. The slavers went down with disappointing ease. This wasn't like the challenge battles that Aden would fight in the coming days, including the inevitable showdown with Silas. Tonight's encounter was a bloodbath. None of these vampires had the juice to offer him even a semblance of a challenge. They were puffed-up line vamps who wouldn't be alive if not for Lucas's willingness to step in and keep their hearts beating after Klemens died.

The last slaver made a dash for the hallway where the captives were being kept, intent either on escape or mayhem. Aden was across the room and on top of the coward before he'd gone five feet down the hallway. Grabbing the vampire by the throat, he lifted him off his feet, watching dispassionately as his face first flushed with blood, then began to purple with a lack of air.

"Mercy, my lord," he managed to gasp.

Aden bared his fangs. "Shall I show you the same mercy you gave these women? I know masters who will pay to own a gelded vampire. One whose will has been burned out, but who still walks and talks. Is that the mercy you'd have of me?"

The vampire's eyes went wide in shock and fear, and he struggled to shake his head in denial. "Please," he ground out.

Aden studied the vampire, not bothering to conceal his disgust. "I think not." With a quick twist, he broke the vampire's neck and dropped him to the floor, then, wielding his power with a fine control, he carved into the vamp's chest and destroyed his heart.

"Aden, what—" Sidonie's voice cut off mid-sentence. He could feel her behind him, but the violence storming through his veins was so great that he didn't dare turn to face her.

"I told you to wait," he growled.

"I did wait," she retorted, or at least she tried to. Her bluster failed her on the last word, betraying the fear he could sense making her heart pound, a fear that he drew in like the sweetest air. It made his fangs emerge; it made his dick hard. He wanted to take her right there, to put her up against a wall and pound into her with the blood and ash of his enemies still fresh around him.

"Aden?" she asked, her voice still a little shaky.

It was too much. He spun around and snagged her by the waist, slamming her against the wall and holding her there with the full length and weight of his body. His cock was a hard bulge against her belly, and he saw her pupils flare the moment she felt it.

"I told you to wait," he murmured, his lips right against her ear. Cupping her ass in one hand, he lifted her high enough that his cock fit neatly where it belonged.

"Is this what"—she swallowed before continuing—"is this what happens when you fight someone?"

He grinned, letting her see the length of his fangs. "Only when I kill them, *habibi*. Only when I drain their blood."

"Oh." Her tongue darted out nervously, and Aden caught it,

covering her mouth with his, sucking on her tongue and closing his teeth over her tender lower lip.

"Sire, there are sirens."

Aden kept his gaze on Sidonie's flushed face. "Tell the others to load the women into the van. I want everyone gone in five minutes."

"Yes, my lord."

"Let me help," Sidonie said, her voice steady as she met his gaze. "Please. At least let me talk to the women and tell them what's going to happen next. They probably don't speak English, but I know Spanish."

Aden regarded her silently, then nodded his head once, letting her slide down the wall until she was standing on her own. "You have the same five minutes, and then you're coming with me."

Rising up onto her toes with a little smile, she lifted her mouth to his and kissed him. "Thank you," she whispered, then slipped away down the hall. She went directly to the second bedroom and opened the door. A chorus of hysterical cries greeted her, and he heard her soothing the women in Spanish, telling them it was all right, that they were safe. Freddy and Kage hurried past, and Sidonie reassured the women again, embracing a very young girl, telling her not to be afraid, gripping the hand of another woman as she repeated that these men were here to help, that they'd take them to a safe place.

Aden stared at her, feeling something in that moment that he hadn't felt for a woman in . . . He struggled to remember how long it had been. Centuries. Not since his mother had chosen her luxuries over the life of her only child. Not even when he'd met his vampire Mistress, the woman who'd changed his life forever.

Chapter Ten

Morocco, 1778

ADEN LAY BACK on the pillow-strewn bed and watched the Lady Na'ima finish dressing. He wasn't supposed to know her name, wasn't supposed to know that she was married to the second wealthiest man in the province. But Aden's owner, Zaahira, was a smart woman, and this was her brothel. Whorehouses were one of the few businesses that a woman was allowed to own outright, and they were allowed that only because no man would sully himself with providing such a service. That didn't stop those same men from *using* the service. Although if they knew how many of their *wives* made use of it, if any of them understood that Aden was far more than the bodyguard they thought him to be, those fine gentlemen might have been far more motivated to shut down Zaahira's operation.

As it was, however, Aden's particular set of skills was very profitable for Zaahira. She'd trained him personally, beginning on the day she'd bought him from Hafiz. For three years, she'd kept him as her personal toy, teaching him all the ways to please a woman. By the time he turned fifteen, Zaahira's female customers had begun to inquire about him, and his mistress was nothing if not a businesswoman. She'd presented the idea to Aden with honeyed promises of money and gifts, but they'd both known if he'd refused, she would have simply ordered him to fuck whomever she'd wanted, and he'd have had no choice. He was a slave. Zaahira's personal slave, perhaps, maybe even her favorite, but still a slave. The tattooed bands on both his biceps announced his status to the world, including the expensively-dressed ladies who showed up in the afternoons looking for the kind of attention they were never going to get from their husbands.

Zaahira knew the true identity of all of her carefully-veiled female customers. She made sure of it before she permitted them into Aden's bed. Not because she cared that much about Aden, but because she cared that much about her business. Blackmail was the best kind of insurance for a woman like her to have.

Aden didn't need Zaahira's files to tell him who the women were, or even why they came to his bed. Half their time with him was spent complaining about their husbands' many infidelities with both women and men.

Zaahira had never offered Aden to her male customers. It was mostly because he was too big, his looks too masculine, even when he was younger. Customers who came seeking that particular entertainment generally preferred pretty, delicate boys, ones who couldn't fight back. But it was also true that Zaahira had a woman's appreciation of Aden's beauty—or so she'd always told him—and wouldn't see him ruined by the kind of brutality those men favored.

Besides, from the very beginning, he'd been more than busy enough with his rich ladies . . . like the lovely Lady Na'ima. Soft-skinned and doe-eyed, she'd been married at fourteen, and now, barely nineteen years old, she had already been dismissed from her husband's bed.

Na'ima finished dressing, pulling a heavy veil over her face before turning to him with a smile in her eyes, the only part of her face he could see. It seemed a ridiculous conceit, since he'd been buried between her tender thighs only a short time earlier, but if his ladies wanted to believe this candlelit room was too dark for him to distinguish their faces, who was he to deprive them of that?

For his part, Aden made no effort to cover his nakedness or to conceal his arousal. Lady Na'ima ducked her head in embarrassment, which only made him harder. He loved the power he had over his women, loved that he, a lowly slave, could reduce such fine ladies to begging for his touch.

He gave Lady Na'ima a wide, inviting smile, and he could almost feel the heat of her blush from across the room. She was the youngest of his customers, sweet and eager, and so very compliant. Tearing her gaze away from his body, she pulled her veil even higher and opened the door slowly, checking the hallway before hurrying out and leaving his door open.

Aden took his time getting up, unbothered by the open door. Living in a brothel made one very casual about nudity. He pulled on a pair of linen pants, tying them loosely and letting them hang down on his hips. Na'ima was his last client for the day. Afternoons were his busy time, his evenings almost always free. The female whores—and that's what they all were, what *he* was, a slave and a whore—saw most of their business in the evening, when the fine gentlemen had finished with work and family.

They came to the brothel seeking to entertain themselves with women who couldn't say *no*, especially if their desire was to explore the more perverse practices. Zaahira gave her clients a wide berth when it came to such perversions. As long as the whore wasn't left too scarred or too damaged to work, it was allowed . . . for a suitable fee, of course.

Aden changed his mind abruptly and stripped off the linen pants. He needed to get out of the brothel for a few hours, needed to feel like a man instead of a whore. By law, he was required to keep his arms bare, his slave bands in view at all times. But he was the son of a free man, the grandson of two free men. And on occasion, he chose to live as a free man. If only for a few hours.

He pulled on his finest clothing, which was very fine, indeed. On top of whatever they paid Zaahira, his ladies always left him a generous gift, and that money was his to do with as he chose. It was the only money that was his, since he received no compensation at all from Zaahira. She owned him; his labor belonged to her.

Dressed for the evening, Aden closed the door to his room and headed toward the stairs. He was almost to the door, had in fact lifted his foot to take the last downward step, when he heard the scream. He would often think of that moment later in his long life, would contemplate what might have happened if he'd left a few minutes sooner. But as it was, he heard a woman's terrified scream and knew instantly who it was.

He spun on his heel and raced back up the stairs and down the hallway, passing the startled faces of both whores and customers peering curiously from half-open doors. The door to the small room at the very end remained closed, however. Sana's room. Sana had been sold to Zaahira as a small child and had practically grown up in the brothel. She'd been a pleasing little girl and everyone's pet, but there was no room for sentiment in Zaahira's world. When the child had become a woman, she'd become a commodity. Thirteen years old and not even a month past her first bleeding, her virginity had been a rare prize and brought a high price for Zaahira. But Aden knew Sana's fee remained high. She was very pretty and small and delicate in build. She appealed to men who were looking for someone weaker, someone to dominate and sometimes to destroy.

Aden threw the door open. He found Sana quickly enough. She was curled in a corner, sobbing and naked, her back bruised and welted, small drops of blood visible in the welts.

"You," a man's voice bellowed. "Get out of here. She's taken."

Aden's head turned slowly. A fat man stood on the other side of the bed. He was completely naked, and in his hand was a thin-tailed whip, stained dark with blood.

Aden saw that whip, and a haze as red as Sana's blood obscured his vision. He leapt over the bed and grabbed the fat man, wrenching the whip out of his hand before shoving him to the floor. Lifting the whip, he brought it down with brutal intention, intending to do to this monster far worse than what he'd dared do to Sana. The fat man screamed, but it wasn't his cry that stopped Aden. It was Zaahira's voice, her command carrying every ounce of her authority as the mistress of the brothel, as his lover and friend . . . as his owner.

"Stop!"

Aden managed to halt his downward swing before it landed on the useless bundle of flesh cringing on the floor before him. One thin lash touched the man's pudgy thigh, making him scream as if he'd lost the leg instead.

"Out," Zaahira snapped. Aden met her angry gaze with one of his own, and for a few brief seconds, he wasn't sure he was going to obey. But then Sana whimpered, and he rushed to pick her up instead, dragging the sheet from the bed and covering her before taking her out into the hallway where all those prying eyes waited. He took her down the stairs to Isabel, an older slave who worked as Zaahira's housekeeper and cook.

That's where Zaahira found him, helping Isabel apply a soothing balm to Sana's poor back, holding the girl's hand against the pain.

"Aden." Zaahira spoke from the doorway, as if afraid she'd catch something if she came too close. He shouldn't have been surprised, but he was. He'd thought if the brothel owner had feelings for anyone, it would be Sana, a child reared in her own house. But instead, she gazed at the scene with distaste, as if calculating how much money she was going to lose while Sana healed.

"Leave that," his mistress said sharply when he continued to help Isabel. "Come."

His anger was so great it threatened to burn him alive. Isabel must have sensed his rebellion, because she reached out and laid her hand over his, drawing his eyes up to meet hers.

"Go," she said, her gaze filled with warning. "I'll take care of her."

His jaw clenched, but he gave her a short nod and stood to his considerable full height, drawing a small measure of satisfaction from the quick flash of fear on Zaahira's face.

"My office," she ordered, then marched down the hall, assuming he'd follow. Which he did. Anger still simmered deep in his gut, but he'd lived with that particular fire for so long, he'd long ago learned to swallow it and take on a suitable mask of compliance.

Zaahira stormed into her office with a swirl of silk and perfume. There'd been a time Aden had lived and breathed for the privilege of enjoying that scent. A time when pleasing Zaahira had been his only reason for waking every morning. But whatever charm she'd once held for him had been lost on the day she'd chosen to rent his body to others for money. Aden had been devastated, even as he'd scorned himself as a fool for believing in the affection and honor of yet another woman.

After all, if one couldn't count on one's mother, why would one ever trust the good intentions of a whoremonger, no matter how prettily she wrapped herself?

Zaahira poured herself a cup of mint tea, then sat and sipped feverishly, as if she needed the beverage's calming effect. Since she was ignoring him, he strode over and slumped into the chair opposite hers without being invited. She shot him an angry glance but didn't say anything, simply continued her zealous tea consumption until the cup was empty.

"You put me in a bad position," she said tightly, setting the empty cup on a nearby table. "Rasim Ahmad is demanding recompense for the injury you caused him."

"Injury," Aden sneered. "It was a scratch. Did you see Sana's back? He deserves—"

"You forget your place, slave," she said. Her voice was cold, her eyes hard and uncompromising, and Aden was reminded that this woman was not his lover, not his friend. He was a useful piece of flesh to her, nothing more.

"Consider yourself fortunate," she continued. "He could have demanded your life, but I persuaded him you had other . . . *uses*."

Aden froze. Zaahira had never ordered him to service a man. He honestly didn't know what he'd do if she ordered it now. Was his life so worthless that he'd rather surrender it than permit himself to be used that way?

"Rasim Ahmad is waiting for you in the black room," Zaahira told him with a dismissive wave.

And Aden forgot how to breathe.

Chicago, IL, present day

SIDONIE WATCHED the van's red taillights disappear as she hurried to the blacked-out Suburban idling at the curb. Aden was already in the back seat, the door standing open in invitation. Or command. One could read it either way.

Her steps slowed as she drew closer. On the face of it, this moment didn't seem like much, but it was the point of no return for her. She'd seen what Aden could do, seen the exhilaration in his face when he'd killed those other vampires. Not that she had any sorrow that they were dead. They'd been the lowest of the low, selling human beings for profit.

But a small voice inside her head kept telling her she should be horrified by the violence she'd witnessed inside that house. And she had been at first. Maybe if the vampires being so brutally slaughtered hadn't been the merchants of misery they'd been, if they hadn't been responsible for kidnapping and selling human women and girls. And who was to say it was only human women they sold? Maybe they tossed a female vampire or two into the mix, vamps too weak to defend themselves.

But as she'd stood there watching in horrified fascination as Aden and his team systematically annihilated the very slavers she'd spent months trying to get *someone* to pay attention to, her overriding emotion had been one of vengeance met. And it had felt good.

Besides, there'd been more than violence in there tonight. Aden and his vampires had treated the freed women with kindness and infinite patience. There they'd been: five big, terrifying, capable warriors, and they'd cared for those frightened women as if they were their own sisters and cousins. It had forced Sid to view Aden in a different light. Not as a violent criminal, but as a protector. A powerful male who wreaked vengeance on those who would enslave others.

Even as she'd had the thought, she'd known she was once again romanticizing the situation. After all, Aden's competitors for the territory probably weren't evil people, not all of them anyway, and he'd just as happily destroy them, too. He was a scary guy, a total alpha male who asked for no one's approval for what he did. He was nothing but trouble, and a very special *kind* of trouble, a vampire. And she was probably going to end up dead if she hung around him too long.

But that didn't stop her heart from racing at the memory of his naked beauty, or the hunger that twisted her gut every time she looked at him. She told herself it was just one more night. That she was tired of being a good girl, and she wanted one more night in Aden's bed. She wanted him fresh from the fight, bloody and victorious. She wanted more.

She stepped up into the Suburban without a word. Aden's fingers closed briefly around her thigh, supporting her as she crossed in front of him to sit behind the driver. His fingers dipped to her inner thigh when she sat down, sliding up until she was sure he could feel the growing heat between her legs. She found herself hoping he'd touch her, that he'd ease some of the ache. But his fingers stopped a hairsbreadth away from touching her cleft where it strained beneath the tight shield of her jeans.

With a soft chuckle, Aden leaned down and kissed her temple, and she felt the wet touch of his tongue. The bastard was toying with her again. Sid stiffened in annoyance and would have put the short distance available to her between them. But Aden growled a warning when she started to move, lifting his arm and pulling her tightly against his side.

"Be good, Sidonie," he murmured.

Her lips tightened, but she couldn't hold on to the irritation. A satisfied grin wiped it away, leaving nothing but anticipation behind. She'd wanted an alpha male, and that's what she'd gotten. She only hoped she survived the night.

Chapter Eleven

ADEN WAS RUNNING on pure adrenaline. The blood of his enemies was soaking the battlefield, while he and his people were unharmed. It didn't matter that the battlefield was a run-down house in a crime-riddled neighborhood of Chicago. This was the time in which he lived; these were the enemies he faced. And defeated. And this was only the beginning.

He glanced at Sidonie sitting next to him. He'd felt the heat between her thighs, the way she'd lifted herself to his fingers, probably without even knowing she was doing it. His good girl wanted to be very bad tonight, and he was going to make her wish come true.

He reached up and pulled the elastic band from her hair, catching her curls as they tumbled over his hand. Grabbing a fistful, he tugged her head backward and took her mouth in a hard, hungry kiss. She stiffened in surprise, but then opened her mouth eagerly, her tongue tangling with his until she snagged on one of his emerging fangs. A drop of her blood swelled from the tiny pinprick, and Aden sucked it up, pulling her even more tightly against him. He was consumed by the taste of her, by the heat of her mouth and the passion of her response. He would have forgotten himself and fucked her right there in the back seat had they not arrived at his building in that moment.

He held her hand across the lobby and into the elevator, through the transfer to the private elevator, and down the hall and into his personal suite. But once the door was closed and they were alone, he grabbed the front of her jacket and pulled her to him, crushing his mouth against her tender lips in a fervor of teeth and tongues. Wrapping an arm around her waist, he swung her around and pressed her against the wall. Ripping open her jeans, he jammed his fingers between her thighs, finding her hot and wet, cursing as the tight pants kept him from getting to her.

"I told you to wear a skirt, damn it," he growled.

"I can't wear a skirt to a fight," she said breathlessly, struggling to get her hands under his T-shirt.

"Fuck this." He swung her up into his arms, strode across the sitting room, and shoved the bedroom door open with a punch of power.

SID WANTED TO laugh for joy when Aden dropped her on the bed and stripped off her clothes. There was no sexy striptease, no slow peeling away of layers. Her clothes were in the way, and he got rid of them. But if she'd thought this was any indicator of his intentions for how the rest of the night would go, if she thought he'd be on her and in her as quickly as she'd hoped . . . she was mistaken.

He dragged off his own clothes and prowled up and onto the bed, his body a study in lethal grace, muscles bunching and releasing in an elegant dance of perfection. His shaft hung between his legs, hard and thick, dragging along her thighs and belly in a trail of velvet heat as he made his way up her body, until his powerful thighs pinned her hips to the mattress, his cock so close to her yearning pussy, but so very far away. He leaned forward and clasped her wrists in one huge hand, stretching her arms above her head and holding them there as he kissed her.

Sid had thought she was ready for this, ready for whatever Aden would do tonight. She'd expected him to take her hard and fast, goaded by battle-driven adrenaline, expected his kisses to be a demand for surrender. But what he did was far more diabolical. His kiss was a whispered seduction, a hint of things to come that left her weak with wanting. His lips caressed, his tongue danced, stroking her teeth and gums until every inch of her mouth felt branded by his touch.

And that was only the beginning. He moved on to her cheeks, her forehead, every inch of her skin, tasting and kissing his way to her neck, lingering at her taut jugular until she was trembling with anticipation, aching for the sweet release of his bite. But instead of biting her, he lifted his head and smiled. At least, she supposed one could call that a smile. It was wicked and charming, a warning and an invitation. And before Sid could figure out what he intended, he'd captured her wrists in something soft and tied them to the headboard.

Her eyes went wide. She twisted around, looking above her head to see that the soft something was a bright silk scarf. Sneaky vampire. He must have had it there all the time. She tugged on the scarf and realized two things—the binding was loose enough that she could slip the binding if she wanted, and she really didn't want to. She lowered her head and met Aden's hot gaze, and she knew this was a test. She could escape, but she'd be leaving behind far more than the silk binding. She'd be leaving Aden.

His eyes held hers, asking the silent question. Sid's pulse was throbbing in time to her racing heart. She was scared. Of what he had planned, yes, but also of what it said about *her* that she'd never been so aroused in her life, and that she wanted to stay. She licked her lips nervously, and his eyes snapped to the sweep of her tongue before coming back to meet her gaze with that same challenging look.

Damn it. With a soft sigh, she surrendered. Consciously relaxing her body, she went soft beneath him, letting him feel her submission.

Aden's eyes lit up, glowing so brightly that she could see the blue shadow limning her breasts, her jutting nipples. With a rumbling growl, he lowered his mouth to her neck once more, and Sid felt a zing of lust that sank from her breasts to her belly and below. A rush of wet heat made her groan aloud, and she struggled against his pinning thighs, needing to spread her legs, to open herself to his cock where it lay on her belly, taunting her with its heavy presence.

She flexed her hips in silent demand, and Aden snarled a warning, a rustle of sound along the overheated skin of her neck. The blunt backs of his fangs slid beneath her jaw, and she panted eagerly, waiting for the sting of his bite. But he kept going downward, teasing her with feathering kisses on her shoulders, her chest, finally biting her, closing his teeth over the taut tendon between neck and shoulder. But it was only his teeth, not his fangs, and she moaned a protest, her eyes closed, her head thrashing back and forth as she tugged on the silk bindings, wanting to bury her fingers in his hair and force his fangs back to her neck.

Aden ignored her wordless pleas as his hot mouth closed over a nipple. He sucked and tormented, his tongue scraping around and around until her nipple was hard and swollen. And then he moved on to her other breast, thrumming the abandoned nipple between finger and thumb as his mouth sucked and teased again until both nipples were aching and puffy. Sid moaned, the rush of sensation from her breasts adding to her growing arousal until she thought she would come right there, just from his tongue.

He took his mouth away, and she nearly cried, thinking he was leaving her on the edge again. But then she felt the scrape of his fangs along the soft swell of her breast, and she held her breath, waiting for the thrill of his bite, swallowing the cry of need that wanted to escape her throat. She looked down and saw two lines of pinprick blood droplets following the path of his fangs along the curve of her breast. And she saw something else. Aden's back was tattooed, something big that flowed up his broad back and stretched to his shoulders. She raised her head from the pillow, straining to see what it was, but Aden lifted his gaze at that moment, his eyes gleaming their midnight blue as they met and held her stare.

Sid froze, mesmerized by the erotic sight of Aden in all his magnificence, thighs bracketing her hips, muscles like banded iron as he held himself above her, his eyes never leaving hers as his tongue slowly stroked her breast, licking up the tiny crimson drops of blood, letting her see as he savored the taste of her, as he rolled the small amount of blood over his tongue, drawing every nuance, every subtle flavor, like a man tasting a fine wine. His gaze was raw with desire, and she thought for sure he was finally going to give her what she wanted. He'd taken her blood, and he was blatantly, gloriously ready, his cock brushing against her thighs whenever he moved, smooth, hot skin over the taut steel of his shaft.

But he wasn't finished with his erotic torture yet. The cool air hit her nipples, leaving them to crave the heat of his mouth, as he abandoned their tight peaks to kiss and lick his way downward, his tongue tasting her abdomen and belly, lingering at the neat triangle of red curls on her mound. Without raising his head, he bent her knees upward, then spread her thighs with his strong fingers, and slid his thumbs into the slit between her swollen lips, baring her completely to his burning gaze. He was so close to her pussy that she could feel the heat of his breath on her aroused flesh. She squirmed in embarrassment, then jerked in surprise when Aden growled and gave her ass a sharp slap of warning, quickly followed by a soothing caress of his big hand.

Sid blinked in confusion, but not because he'd spanked her—and what else could she call what he'd done? It had been little more than a sting of his palm on her butt cheek, just enough to pink her fair skin. But what confused her was the zing of pleasure she'd felt when he did it. As if the slight sting of the spanking had instantly become a jolt of exquisite pleasure, one she felt over her entire body, a shiver of sensation that seemed to skate along her nerves until it concentrated directly in her clit. She groaned almost unwillingly, struggling through a haze of arousal to figure out what it all meant.

But then Aden put his mouth to her pussy, and all rational thought fled, swamped by a tidal wave of erotic sensation that literally stole her sight, a curtain of white lightning suddenly filling her vision as if every synapse in her brain had fired at the same time.

She bucked against Aden's mouth, her orgasm building, soaring to unstoppable heights, her womb clenching as muscles contracted, her skin so perfectly sensitive that every touch felt like a caress directly to her clit. Aden's tongue scraped roughly over the swollen nub, and she cried out, her hands fisted around the scarf that still held her, her thighs spasming as they squeezed Aden's broad shoulders.

And then he stopped.

Sid panted, disoriented by the abrupt shift, blinking in disbelief. Her climax, which had been building so sweetly, so surely, eased back and flowed away, and she wanted to scream. She looked down between her thighs and found Aden watching her, a knowing smile playing around his sensuous mouth as he licked his lips slowly, lasciviously, tasting her wetness on his mouth, savoring it as he had her blood only moments before.

She did scream then, a wordless shout of anger and frustration.

And Aden laughed. He laughed! And then he dipped his head and nipped gently at her inner thigh before covering her body with his, sliding up inch by inch, letting her feel the firm glide of every muscle, his fingers dancing over her skin, kneading her breasts and rolling her nipples, until his mouth was on hers, and she was tasting herself on his lips.

Sid moaned into his kiss, pleading, desperate for the release he'd stolen from her, but overwhelmed by the sheer sensuality of his kiss.

"Please," she whispered. "Please let me—"

He didn't let her finish, shushing her before covering her mouth with his, swallowing her words as his warm hands swept down her body, his fingers dipping between her thighs, skimming over her clit without ever touching it, disregarding her eager thrusting against his hand as she tried to force him to give her what she needed. He ignored that as he had everything else, intent on his own diabolical torment as he slid first one finger, and then two, into the slick opening of her sex, pumping in and out, fucking her with his fingers, adding a third when her pussy proved so wet, so ready for him, that she was almost embarrassed at this proof of her wantonness.

But Aden didn't seem to notice, or didn't care. Maybe that was what he'd wanted all along, to prove to her that she was shameless in her desire for him. Without warning, his thumb grazed her engorged clit, and she cried out eagerly, her back bowed until she was lifted nearly off the bed. She panted his name, a breathless litany of prayer, hoping he meant it this time, that he was finished with his teasing, that her release was near. His fingers continued to pump in and out, his thumb circling the swollen bud of nerves without ever touching it.

He lowered his mouth to her neck. She felt the hard press of his fangs and sucked in a rasping breath. His hips maneuvered between her thighs, spreading them wide until she could feel the rigid length of his cock sliding back and forth between the swollen lips of her sex, bathing in her wetness. Sid wrapped her legs around his back, trapping him there, wanting to feel his thick erection plunging inside her at last, his fangs slicing into her vein.

He kissed her neck, and his tongue scraped over her jugular . . . but he didn't bite her, and he still didn't fuck her.

Hot tears filled her eyes. "Aden," she whispered.

"What do you want, *habibi?*" he crooned, the length of his cock still sliding up and down between the slick folds of her sex.

"I want," she gasped, "I *need* you inside me. I need to come."

"Are you mine then?" he whispered, dropping tasting kisses on her forehead, her cheeks, closing his teeth over her lower lip with a playful bite that was just short of pain.

Sid nodded. "Yes. Yours," she said, though she would have agreed to anything at that point, and Aden seemed to know it.

One half of his mouth curved into a slight smile as he reached up and tugged away the silk scarf that bound her wrists. Sid had time to frown, worried that he was going to release her without ever bringing her to orgasm . . . but then he was turning her over, pulling her hips up until her knees were braced on the bed, and her ass was in the air.

Grabbing her long hair, he pulled it to one side, baring her back as his strong fingers dug in, massaging her neck, stroking up along the delicate slope of her spine, until he reached her ass where it was pressed against his groin. He lifted his hand and brought it down in a sharp smack against her butt cheek. Sidonie cried out, but once again, it was more pleasure than pain as the sting of his hand sent a jolt of carnal delight directly to her over-sensitized clit, stabbing into her womb until her entire abdomen clenched with desire. She rocked back against his hips, feeling the velvet heat of his erection against her ass.

"Do you want this, *habibi?*" he growled, grasping her hips and grinding against her.

"Yes," she said, more of a demand than an answer.

Aden bent over her back and reached beneath her to caress her breasts, sliding his hands along her torso to her belly and burying his fingers in her pussy. Sid moaned her bliss, twisting her hips from side to side and rubbing her ass against him. He slapped her other butt cheek, then leaned forward and murmured, "I like a matched pair."

Sid threw her head back, feeling the same zing of sensation from his slap, overwhelmed by all of the things she was feeling—his fingers in her pussy, his hard length in the crease of her butt, the unexplainable shock of sexual pleasure that touched every nerve in her body when he spanked her. His thumb skimmed over her clit, and she sucked in a breath, waiting for him to steal her orgasm once again, to wait until she was pleading for release, and then cruelly abandon her. But then he stroked her clit again, and she couldn't help the cry that escaped her lips as she rocked against him, her heart pounding, her breath rasping in and out of her lungs.

"Tell me what you want, Sidonie," he growled.

"You," she nearly sobbed. "I want you."

She felt a smooth drizzle of liquid, felt its cool touch as it rolled down between her butt cheeks to caress her overheated sex. She had a heartbeat to realize what he was going to do, to think that she'd never done that before . . . and then he was pinching her clit, and she was coming harder than she'd ever come in her entire life, and his cock was pushing into her ass, filling her in a way she'd never known, filling her so completely . . . He pulled her onto her knees, her back to his chest, his fingers still fucking her pussy, his cock buried in her ass. He gripped her chin with his other hand, turning her mouth to his kiss before he bared her neck and lowered his head, his lips just brushing the skin below her ear before his fangs sliced into her vein with a sting of sensation, his mouth hot as he sucked her blood, the euphoric in his bite lighting up every nerve in her body with exquisite, unimaginable pleasure.

And it was too much. Sidonie screamed as every part of her body crashed instantly into orgasm, muscles clenching, nerves firing with an ecstasy she'd never known before. She thrashed in his grip, his strong fingers holding her steady as he took her blood, his hips thrusting his cock into her ass, his fingers easing their caress of her clit, as if he knew that the engorged nub could take only so much before intense pleasure crossed into pain. His own climax struck as he held her, his fangs still buried in her neck, his groan rolling through her body as she felt the hot rush of his release filling her, pumping deep inside her until she was limp, and the only thing holding her up was Aden.

ADEN PULLED OUT of Sidonie's sweet ass. She'd been so tight, as he'd known she would be, like a warm velvet glove around his cock. Holding her closely, he eased them both down onto the bed, cradling her limp body in the curve of his much greater strength. Her eyes were closed, and she seemed half-asleep as she smiled and snuggled closer to him. Aden stared down at her, a foreign sensation squeezing his heart. He cared for this woman. She was strong and passionate, innocent in a way that was at complete odds with her fearless persistence in pursuing the slavers who'd murdered her friend.

And for some reason, she seemed to trust *him*.

He let her sleep, drifting into a half doze that let his thoughts go their own way. Vampires didn't sleep, not the way humans did. Their daytime sleep was far deeper and more restful than human sleep and inescapable because of their vampire blood. But he sometimes found this sort of half sleep to be useful, letting his mind drift over problems and solutions.

Such as who was left to challenge him, and when would they strike? Silas was the most obvious contender, his only real competition in the field. But there were others whom he couldn't disregard. His opponent's chance luck could be as fatal as superior strength. He'd have to meet with Bastien and the others first thing tomorrow night. Maybe the time had come to attack, rather than sit back and wait.

"What are you thinking?" Sidonie's voice was the lazy drawl of a satisfied woman, and he couldn't help his own smug smile.

"I don't trust that smile," she murmured, snuggling closer.

He kissed her forehead. "I'm not allowed to smile?"

She made a dismissive noise, then kissed the side of his neck, a liberty he allowed no one, but that he somehow allowed her.

"So what were you thinking about so fiercely?" she asked, drawing his thoughts away from his own confusing emotions.

He shrugged. "The challenge. What happened tonight needed to be done, but it doesn't change anything. The challenge continues."

Sidonie stroked a hand over his bicep, her fingers pausing to rub the line of his slave band.

"What is this?" she asked. "And the other arm, too. It's like you covered the original tattoos with something different."

"Because I did."

"What did they used to be?"

"Are you always this chatty after a hard orgasm?"

He felt the heat of her blush before she answered. "I don't know," she said softly, not looking at him. "I've never climaxed that hard before."

Aden felt a rush of concentrated pleasure at her words. It was almost like the sensation he got after defeating an enemy, the exhilarating high of victory. But it was a new experience in this context. He knew he was a skilled lover; he'd had hundreds of years to improve on what he'd learned about a woman's body during his time in Zaahira's brothel. But he'd always taken the satisfaction of his lovers for granted. He always got them off, but it didn't matter. It was simply a by-product of his need for sex and blood.

But not with Sidonie. For some reason, she mattered. She was *his*. He didn't know how long this new sensation would last, but he knew that he'd kill anyone who came near her. He blinked in surprise at the intensity of that thought. Huh.

"They're slave bands," he told her abruptly, not wanting to pursue his previous line of thought any further, and certainly not with her.

Her brow wrinkled. "Slave bands," she repeated, clearly troubled by the concept.

"Yes," he said, before she could ask the question. "I was a slave a very long time ago."

Sidonie pushed herself up so she could meet his eyes. "Were you born that way?" she asked, her eyes full of a compassion he didn't want.

"No," he said simply, watching her reaction. "I was sold when I was five."

"Sold. How can . . . by whom?"

He stared at her, trying to decide if he'd answer truthfully or not. "My father," he said simply.

"Oh, Aden," she breathed and hugged him tightly, her soft breasts crushed against his chest.

"It was a long time ago, *habibi*," he said, stroking his hand down her back, feeling the need to comfort her, despite the fact that it was his story.

"But still . . . What about your mother? Where was she?"

"You have a lot of questions."

"And you're avoiding the answer," she said, but then caught her breath. "Never mind. I'm sorry. I'm prying. It's a bad habit. It comes with the territory . . . investigative reporter and all. I'll be quiet now."

Aden continued to rub his hand idly up and down the elegant curve of her spine. What would she think if he told her about his mother? That she'd given him up, because she preferred playing the whore for his father over caring for her own child. Would Sidonie hate his mother for him? Did he want her to?

Seeming to sense his reluctance, or maybe his indecision, she crawled up onto his chest and propped her chin on her hands, so she could smile into his eyes. "What about the tattoo on your back?" she asked, changing the subject for him.

He slid his hand down to cup her delicious ass, smiling when he saw her wince in anticipation of another spanking, catching the relief on her face when he only rubbed her firm little butt cheek fondly.

"The back tattoo is mine. It's a phoenix and all it represents."

"Why do it on your back? Is that significant?"

"I offended a wealthy man once, when I was still a slave. That particular man liked to inflict pain on those who couldn't fight back. His preferred victims were very young women. I objected . . . forcefully to his torture of someone. He demanded satisfaction, and my mistress gave me to him in recompense. He had no interest in fucking me, he couldn't even get an erection, a fact that I'm certain disappointed him. But there are other ways to humiliate a man, and there was always the whip.

"He had free use of me for three days and nights. I received no medical assistance and only enough water and bread to keep me alive and able to feel pain. My mistress wouldn't let him blemish my face or genitals, but my back was so damaged it took weeks to recover. And even then, the scars were so numerous and so thick that I was in constant pain even after I healed."

Tears shone in her eyes, but she swallowed hard and said, "But . . . there aren't any scars now." She touched her fingers to the back of his shoulder where he knew the tip of one wing could be seen.

"When I became Vampire, the scars began to heal. It took time, but eventually they vanished completely. Sometime later, I got the tattoo to make a point. My body is mine, and no one else's."

"What a bitch," she muttered, presumably about Zaahira. "I hope she died old and ugly."

Aden smiled in fond remembrance of Zaahira's death. But that was a story for another time. "I do believe Zaahira—she was my whore mistress—eventually regretted the whipping. Not because she cared about me, you understand, but because I was unable to fuck her other clients while I recovered, and even then . . . it was never the same. Any pleasure I'd taken in the seduction of rich women was gone. I never again forgot that I was nothing but a slave, no matter whom I fucked."

She frowned in concentration. "Wait. You said you were unable to fuck clients, that means—"

"It means I was a sex slave," he said harshly, watching for her reaction. "A whore, just like my mother." He pushed the words out, trying to conceal the anger they hid, daring her to judge him for his past. But, of course, she didn't. Sidonie didn't judge people on the actions of others. She rescued them instead.

"That's why you hunted the slavers tonight, why it was important enough that you took time out from the challenge to see it done."

He nodded slightly.

She ran a soft finger down over his shoulder, to his arm, and along the black line of his slave band. "I didn't know vampires could be tattooed. I thought your bodies repaired everything."

"It works as long as we mix our own blood with the ink. It takes considerable skill and patience. Kage is my tattoo artist."

"Kage is the one with the buzz cut, right? With all the piercings?" She indicated her left eyebrow where Kage wore a titanium bar. He also had a tongue stud, although Sid had no way of knowing that.

Aden nodded in response to her question. "Kage is the youngest of my vampires, though not young by human standards. He's been the go-to guy for some time for all the vamps in Lucas's territory who wanted tats, but he's mine, so he goes where I go. Lucas will just have to find his own artist now."

"I always wanted a tattoo, but I never got up the nerve."

"I like your skin the way it is. Leave it."

"Says the guy who covered his back to prove it was his."

"Says the guy who will spank this sweet ass if you go against me on this," he growled, cupping her butt cheek.

She shivered, but that wasn't fear in her eyes, it was remembered pleasure, and he smiled.

"It's not like I was planning on doing it," she grumbled.

Aden laughed and rolled her beneath him. "How's that slick pussy of yours, Sidonie?" he murmured, rubbing his hardening cock against her belly.

Her eyes went wide in surprise, but then she wrapped her legs around his hips, tightening her hold possessively. "Are you going to tease me again?" she asked with mock severity.

"No," he said thoughtfully. "I'm just going to fuck you until you scream."

SIDONIE LAY BONELESSLY across Aden's chest, exhausted, drained, completely washed-out. Aden had been true to his word . . . several times. She found it interesting that the Vampire virus, or whatever it was, left a male capable of getting an erection over and over again, and yet incapable of actually producing offspring. It was an interesting evolutionary twist, but one her mind was too exhausted to ponder overmuch right at that moment. For now, she'd simply count her blessings that she not only had a vampire lover, but one who had apparently learned the art of lovemaking from the best . . . even if the bitch had enslaved him to do it. She frowned, not liking that part.

"Why are you scowling?" Aden's chest rumbled beneath her ear, making her smile.

"I love your chest," she said, cracking a huge yawn. "It's very resonant."

"Resonant," he repeated drily.

"It's big and deep and so very strong, oh wonderful one."

He squeezed her butt cheek in warning.

"You're entirely too obsessed with my ass."

"I love your ass," he said, smacking it lightly. "It's very resonant."

Sid laughed, sitting up to stare down at him in surprise. "You made a joke."

"Call the press. Oh, wait. You are the press."

"It'll be front page news," she said, yawning again as she stretched her arms over her head and cracked her neck from side to side. "What time is it?" she asked, glancing around for a clock.

"Nearly dawn."

"What time is . . . Oh. Do I need to get out of here?"

He hesitated, then nodded. "The suite will lock down, so will the elevator entrance. No one comes or goes until sunset. And I won't exactly be a sterling conversationalist in the meantime."

"Oh," she repeated stupidly. She should have thought about that. Aden and all his guys would be sleeping helplessly, while she . . . she could probably do anything she wanted. She could kill them all, and they'd never know. She stared at Aden in sudden alarm. If she could get to them, maybe someone else could, too. "Do you have security? Like guards or something to be sure no one sneaks in here?"

"We have guards," he assured her, reaching up to brush tangled curls away from her face. "And our sleeping quarters are very secure. We've been doing this a century or two."

She nodded, her throat suddenly too clogged with emotion to

permit words. She was overcome by the brutal image of Aden lying helplessly asleep, his muscular body stretched out naked, one arm thrown over his face in complete abandon, while a faceless form, dark and malevolent, crept through the shadows and . . .

She shook her head to clear the horrifying picture and felt tears threatening. She turned away so Aden wouldn't see and was struck by another terrible thought. *Oh, no. No, no, no.* She could *not* be falling for him. She wasn't that stupid, was she? This was supposed to be a bad boy fling, not an affair almost guaranteed to break her heart.

She climbed off the big bed and began gathering her clothes.

"Sidonie?"

"I'll be out of here in a minute," she said, without looking at him. "It won't take me long to get dressed. I can shower—" She squeaked in surprise when he was suddenly right there in front of her, forcing her to look at him. He was so beautiful. Evolution had gotten that much right, at least. Beautiful and deadly, the perfect combination for a predator.

Aden was studying her curiously. He ran a thumb under her eye, catching a lone tear with a gentleness that was surprising in a creature capable of the kind of violence she'd witnessed earlier.

"You'll come back later," he told her. There wasn't even a hint of a question in there. He was either completely self-assured, or just plain bossy. Unfortunately, either way she didn't have the strength to turn him down. Not yet. She wanted to keep her bad boy a little longer.

"I will," she agreed. "Any particular time?"

"The usual."

She looked up from where she'd sat down to tie her shoes and was distracted for a moment by the view of a very naked Aden from this perspective. It took her a moment to remember what she wanted to say.

"Do we have a usual?" she managed, then laughed at his flat look of disapproval. She stood, going up on tiptoes to kiss his scowling face, her arms circling his neck. "There's the no-nonsense Aden I'm used to. I'll be here."

"See that you are," he said, walking her to the door. And then he kissed her good-bye. A full-body kiss, deep and slow and promising all sorts of dark, erotic pleasures.

When he finally let her go, she had to hang onto him for a bit, her legs were so wobbly. Yeah, she definitely needed more of *that* before she gave up her bad boy fling.

She waved as she walked down the hallway, hearing his door close behind her with a very solid thunk of sound. The red doors were equally substantial, and when she turned to make sure they'd closed completely, she found they had already locked behind her. Down the hall, the elevator was open and waiting. She took it down to the fifth floor and was nodding a somewhat embarrassed hello to the guards when one of the men approached as if he'd been waiting for her. He was slightly older, maybe mid-forties and had an air of authority.

"Ms. Reid?"

"Yes?" she responded, wondering if she'd triggered some sort of alarm by coming down in the elevator when she did.

"My name's Earl Hamilton. I'm chief of Lord Aden's daylight security team. Lord Aden said I should introduce myself."

Sid smiled. Bad boy, schmad boy. How could you not love a guy who thought about you like that?

"Thank you, Mister Hamilton."

"Oh, call me Earl. Everyone does."

"Earl. It's a pleasure, thank you. I'll just—" A thought occurred to her. "Let me give you my cell number, Earl, just in case I can ever help out."

Numbers exchanged—she got Earl's number, too—Sid made her way to the street and climbed into the taxi which Earl had summoned for her. The ride was thankfully short. At her own building, she rode up to her condo, went directly to the shower, and then to bed. She was nearly asleep before she realized there'd been something . . . or rather, some*one* very important who'd been absent from the night's bloodbath at the slavers' holding house.

She reached for her cell phone automatically and called Aden, not remembering until she got his voice mail that he wouldn't get the message until later, and she simply could have waited until she saw him. But as long as she had him, or at least his so-abrupt-it-was-almost-rude voicemail response, she left a message.

"Hey, it's me. We'll talk later, and you probably know this, but . . . we didn't get everyone at that house tonight. You know that, right?"

She barely managed to disconnect before she was sound asleep.

Chapter Twelve

"WHAT DO YOU mean we didn't get everyone?"

"And good evening to you, my lord," Sid said. She dropped her backpack and walked right up to Aden, smiling up at him expectantly.

He stared down at her, his eyes sparking blue fire and promising all sorts of retribution, but he fisted a big hand in her jacket, yanked her closer, and then he kissed her, starting out hard and dutiful, but quickly turning seductive and ending with a sensuous flourish of his tongue that left her breathless.

"We'll continue that later," he murmured directly into her ear, and she wiggled happily.

"Now, what did you mean by your message?" he demanded.

Sid pressed a hand to her chest, still trying to catch her breath. She glanced up to let him know an answer was coming and found him regarding her with a smug look that said he knew exactly why she was having trouble breathing. She rolled her eyes, but he only winked back at her.

"Okay," she said, taking a full breath. "I didn't see everyone you killed last night, because—"

"Because some of them died before you made it through the door," Aden interrupted impatiently. "What's your point?"

"I'm getting there," she admonished him. "I think you missed someone. The slave business was Klemens's operation, but he didn't do the grunt work. There was another vampire who ran the whole thing, drugs and slaves both. I got the impression he did other stuff, too, because he wasn't around much, but he was definitely in charge. His name was Carl Pinto."

Aden glanced over her head, and she turned to see Bastien coming through the door to the office where they stood. Bastien was the most buttoned-up of Aden's vampires, always dressed in black, his hair a neat razor cut. He moved with an economy of motion that Sid thought must indicate military training, maybe Special Forces or something.

"Pinto," Bastien repeated, then shared a look with Aden before asking Sid, "When was the last time you saw him?"

She grabbed the notebook out of her bag and thumbed through it, looking for Pinto's name. "It was just before the big gala," she said, half to herself, then found the note she was looking for. "Yep. Eight days, to be precise. He was at their place in Fuller Park. It's kind of a drug clearinghouse for them."

Both vampires were looking at her oddly.

"What?" she asked.

"I don't want you lurking around drug houses anymore," Aden said flatly. "Especially not in Fuller Park."

She shrugged. "I'm careful. And that's where they do their business. It's hard to keep track of them if I don't go where they go. Duh."

"Sidonie."

For the first time, she registered how intent he was. How angry. At her? Why would he be angry at her?

"What?" she asked, confused and a little irritated that he was giving her attitude for doing her job.

"I understand your need for revenge for your friend's murder," Aden told her, clearly trying not to be patronizing and failing miserably. "But this has to end. If Pinto is still alive—"

"He is."

"—we will take care of it. These people are too dangerous for you to continue this surveillance on your own. It's only dumb luck that you haven't been seriously harmed before this."

Did he just say dumb luck?

"If not for me," she pointed out with admirable patience, "you'd still believe Pinto was dead. I think there's a little more to what I do than dumb luck."

"We're getting off the subject," he said, shutting her down. "Bastien, if Pinto's alive—and it seems he is," he added, before Sid could do more than open her mouth to protest. "I want him found. Get Elias on it immediately."

Bastien nodded, turned on his heel, and left the office, leaving Sid alone with Aden.

"You," he snarled, closing his fingers around the front of her jacket again, pulling her against his body and up onto her toes, and holding her there as he lowered his mouth to hers. But Sid wasn't ready to kiss and make up. She bit his lip angrily and pulled back.

"Look," she said, trying without success to push him away. "I get the whole alpha male, vampire lord-of-all-he-surveys thing, okay? I kind of even like it in the bedroom. But out in the real world, you are *not* the boss of me. I don't forfeit my brain just because we have sex. And I'll do whatever I think is necessary to get my story. And it's not like most of what I do is that dangerous. I'm not aiming for Woodward and Bernstein. But I'm not stupid either. I don't take unnecessary risks, and I'm careful with the risks I do take."

Aden was eyeing her with very little expression on his face, which made it difficult to tell how he was receiving her liberated woman speech. Whatever his reaction was, however, it didn't extend to his body, which was ready to fuck, and no question about it.

"Kind of like it?" he asked finally, one corner of his mouth curling upward with amusement as he focused on the one part of her speech that she'd thought he'd have no problem with. "I think I can do better than that."

Sid's first thought was that she wouldn't survive if sex between them got any better than what they'd done last night. But she didn't tell him that.

"I'm serious," she insisted, trying to keep from smiling back at him.

"So am I," he insisted.

"Aden—" she began, but Bastien chose that moment to return.

"My lord," he said. "Elias is here."

Aden glanced at her, but anticipating his vampires-only speech, she said, "I'll sit in the outer office. I want to check some things anyway, and I've got my laptop with me. You all have Wi-Fi?"

"Of course," Bastien assured her. "The code's above the keypad on the phone."

"Good enough," she said. She looped her backpack over her shoulder, but then she paused, pretending a thought had just occurred to her, and said, "Don't forget to engage your cone of silence device."

Aden rolled his eyes, but still managed to give her butt a firm swat as she walked away. What was it with him and her ass?

She sat down at the desk, pulled out her laptop, and went to work as Bastien and Elias disappeared into Aden's office and closed the door. What she'd told Aden about her last sighting of Carl Pinto was correct as far as it went, but her full notes, going all the way back to the beginning of her investigation, had all been transferred into her laptop. She had a system that let her track the individual players over time. And just as she'd been able to predict which house the slavers would use for this month's transfer, she'd be able to see the pattern in Pinto's movements that would help Aden track the vamp down and get rid of him once and for all.

She was still hunched over her notes when the office door opened and Elias walked by sometime later. She nodded at him and waited to see if Aden would call her back in. When he didn't, she wasn't particularly concerned. Figuring he and Bastien were still conspiring, she flexed her fingers, ready to go back to her own work, but then realized Elias had left the door partway open, and she could hear Aden and Bastien talking. Eavesdropping shamelessly—she was a reporter, after all—she stopped working and leaned toward the open door, listening.

". . . a concern, my lord." She caught the tail end of Bastien's sentence.

Aden laughed dismissively. "You know me better than that, Bastien. When have I ever let a woman get in my way?"

The two males laughed, and Bastien said something she didn't catch, but she did hear Aden's reply.

"It's all about blood, my friend," he growled. "But don't worry. She won't be around much longer."

Sid blinked, surprised at how much his words stung. She wasn't even sure they were talking about her, but she couldn't shake the sense that they *were*. That Bastien had been concerned she would get in the way of their plans to seize the territory, and that hers was the blood Aden had dismissed so readily.

It shouldn't have bothered her. After all, it was no more than she'd been telling herself all along, that this thing between them was temporary. Her bad boy fling. So why did it hurt so much to hear him say it?

She stood and gathered her things. There was no more reason for her to stay. Aden didn't need her—he'd made that abundantly clear—and her reason for being here in the first place was done. She'd wanted justice for Janey, and she'd gotten that. Or close enough. Carl Pinto was still out there somewhere, but she had the tools to find him. Better tools than Aden had. After all, she was the one who'd found the house last night. She'd find Pinto, and, despite what Aden seemed to think, she wouldn't be stupid about it either. She'd find him and pass on the information to Aden via telephone. During the day, when she could simply leave a voice mail message. And that would be it as far as Aden was concerned. There'd be no need to humiliate herself further, no need to pretend that there was something besides sex going on between them. Because he clearly wasn't feeling anything at all.

Time to let go of her bad boy and go back to her real life.

The phone rang as she closed her laptop and slipped it into her backpack. Someone picked it up before it rang a second time. Not that she would have answered it anyway. She wanted no more part in vampire business. She'd already gotten in deeper than she'd ever intended.

Stepping over to the office, she spied Aden and Bastien deep in conversation. Whatever they were discussing now, they'd gone back to their secret vampire voices. Maybe something to do with the phone call. Not that she cared, she reminded herself.

Aden looked up the moment she appeared in the doorway. A few minutes ago, she'd have interpreted that to mean they had a connection. Now, she just figured he wanted to make sure she didn't overhear whatever he and Bastien were plotting.

"I can see you guys are busy," she said, with false cheer. "And if I'm going to finish this, I'll need my old notebooks, which are back at my condo. I'll head over there now, and if I come up with anything, I'll give you a call."

Bastien smiled, but she could tell by his quick glance at Aden that he was waiting for the boss to react before he said anything.

Aden just studied her silently, as if waiting for her to say more. But there wasn't anything else. She was going home.

ADEN WATCHED Sidonie as she stood there in his office doorway and fed him a huge steaming pile of bullshit that she apparently expected him to take at face value.

"I'll give you a call," she said, and turned away without so much as a wave.

He stared at the empty doorway until he heard the ding of the elevator, followed by the sound of the doors closing. Then he glanced at Bastien. "Put Kage on her. And tell Hamilton I want her tailed during the day."

Something had put a bug up her ass. He didn't know what it was, but he intended to find out. If she thought she could dismiss him with a lame excuse and walk away, she had a lot to learn. And he was going to enjoy teaching it to her.

But not tonight. That phone call had been formal notification of a challenge. Not from Silas, which might have been expected, but from a vampire named Ramiro Salvador. Aden didn't know much about Salvador. He was from Mexico, which made him one of Lord Enrique's people, and he'd been at the gathering on Sunday which had officially launched the challenge. Officially being the operative word, since the maneuvering, and the killing, had begun days before . . . as Aden had reason to know.

But other than those few bits of information, Salvador was a cipher to Aden, which was never a good thing going into a challenge. Bastien was working their contacts here in the Midwest and elsewhere trying to find out what he could, but they didn't have much time. The challenge was set to take place an hour from now in Washington Park. Not the neighborhood, but the actual park. It was a big public space on Chicago's South Side, consisting of several hundred acres, most of it grass and trees, and largely deserted at this time of night. A public park wasn't the place Aden would have chosen for a challenge battle, but then he had private properties of his own within the city that he could use. He'd been building his network here for some time, well before Lucas had finally offed Klemens. Lucas had tapped Aden to run his Kansas City operation several decades ago, which had put him only a short flight away from Chicago.

On the other hand, this was probably the first time Salvador had spent any time in the city. Notwithstanding the significant drug trade Klemens had been carrying on with certain interests in Mexico, there wasn't much in the way of cross-border dealings between vampire territories. Raphael was trying to change that, trying to get the North American territories talking to each other in order to fight a common enemy.

But that was in the future. For tonight, it meant there'd been no opportunity for Salvador to check out the battleground or set up any kind of headquarters in advance. Even if Klemens had allowed the foreign vampire to visit his city, Enrique probably wouldn't have agreed. The Lord of Mexico was said to be very old school with his vampires and saw the rivalry between the territories as a good thing.

All of which meant that Salvador's choice of Washington Park was a smart one.

"Sire," Bastien said, interrupting his contemplation of tonight's opponent. "I spoke to Lord Raphael's lieutenant, Jared. We had some dealings last year before his promotion, when he was still troubleshooting for Lord Raphael."

Aden nodded his understanding. The long explanation wasn't really necessary, but Bastien's caution was understandable. Vampires were hugely territorial, and a different master might have wondered why his lieutenant had a relationship with a high-ranking vampire in another territory. But Aden wasn't that insecure, nor did he view Raphael as an enemy. Especially not with what he'd recently learned about the threat from Europe.

"Jared put me in touch with a vampire named Jaclyn who is Raphael's representative in the Southern territory. She's been helping Lord Anthony rule the South—"

"More like ruling the South herself," Aden observed. "But I'll play along. What does Jaclyn have to say about Salvador?"

Bastien shot Aden a quick grin. Everyone knew that Anthony couldn't hold the South without Raphael's support. But then, based on what Aden had learned recently about who really killed Jabril, the previous Lord of the South, it was Raphael's *mate* who had a better claim to the territory than anyone else, no matter whose ass currently occupied the seat of power.

"Jaclyn knows Ramiro Salvador reasonably well," Bastien continued. "With all the cartel violence in Mexico lately, there have been multiple issues related to territorial security, and she's met him several times. In her opinion, Salvador's strong enough to hold a territory, although she was unaware that he had any designs on the Midwest. She's never met you, my lord, and so had no direct comparison, but she did say Salvador was on a par with Jared. And Jared is more than commonly powerful."

"He wouldn't be a member of Raphael's inner circle if he wasn't. Has Salvador fought anyone else in the current challenge, or is he jumping right to the top?"

"A few minor skirmishes during the gala, picking off easy targets. No death matches."

"Guess I'll be his first then. Let's get going. Don't want to make him wait for his own funeral."

Chapter Thirteen

ADEN AND HIS team parked very close to the house where they'd wiped out what was left of Klemens's slave trade the previous night. Or so they'd thought. If Sidonie was right, there was still at least one significant outlier left to kill.

The neighborhood they walked through wasn't bad, especially compared to Fuller Park where Sidonie had staked out Carl Pinto's drug house. But it wasn't somewhere Aden had ever anticipated visiting so frequently, either. He'd left behind this kind of poverty long ago. Contrary to Sidonie's assumptions, not all vampires were wealthy, but most of them were at least financially secure. When one lived for centuries, one had a different view of life and necessity. And what vampires couldn't earn for themselves, they *persuaded* others to give them. Once upon a time, they had simply taken what they needed and killed anyone in their way. Modern life demanded greater subtlety, but there were still ways of acquiring whatever one needed, or wanted. And a vampire's life span put a whole new spin on long-term investment.

Freddy and Travis roamed ahead as they crossed into the park and entered the shadows beneath the trees, while Bastien walked at Aden's side. Kage would probably be upset at missing the fight, but he was sitting on Sidonie, who, by all reports, had gone home and stayed there. But concerns about Sidonie were a distraction Aden couldn't afford, not if Salvador was as powerful as reported, so he put her out of his thoughts. He hadn't come this far to be undone by a female, not even one he actually cared for. There would be time for Sidonie tomorrow. Tonight, he had a challenge to survive.

Ramiro Salvador had been somewhat vague, when he called earlier, about the specifics of where they'd meet within the park. Aden assumed the Mexican vampire had scouted the area ahead of time and chosen ground that favored him, but they'd walked nearly all the way to the Hyde Park side before he finally felt the first twinges of the challenger's presence.

Aden pulled Freddy and Travis back, wanting all three of his vamps close at hand before the fighting broke out. It was a common tactic to pick off an opponent's vampire children in an effort to weaken him before the battle. Aden didn't want the distraction, but he also didn't want to lose any of his vampires. He loved them, if not as children, then as brothers. Never having had either, he couldn't say which it was, but he knew their deaths would pain him greatly.

"Tighten your shields," he warned all of them.

"Sire." Three voices answered as one.

Bastien's low-voiced warning presaged Salvador's appearance from the darkness on the other side of a small clearing. Not that Aden needed the warning. To his vampiric sight, the Mexican vampire shone like a beacon, his power every bit as strong as reported. Maybe stronger.

"Ramiro Salvador, I presume," he called out.

"And you are the great Aden," Salvador responded with a sneer. "Your name was everywhere in the ballroom on Sunday. The fools are all saying you'll be the next Lord of the Midwest."

Aden dipped his head in acknowledgement, already bored with the theatrics.

"I even saw you kissing Raphael's ass, making nice with his woman, for all the good it will do you. It's not Raphael who will decide this."

"Perhaps not," Aden conceded, unconcerned. "But you're a fool if you think he can't affect the outcome."

Salvador bristled at the sideways insult, just as Aden had intended. The Mexican's power was lapping across the clearing in big looping waves, as if he was making no attempt to conceal it. It was as if he hoped that broadcasting his aggression would dissuade Aden from the challenge altogether.

Or perhaps he was more clever than that. Perhaps he thought that by making himself seem undisciplined and unable to control his own power leakage, Aden would assume he was weaker than he really was.

But Salvador was badly underestimating Aden, if he thought to fool him that easily.

For his part, Aden kept his power under a tight leash as always. Even knowing that Salvador might be only playing the fool, it was simply bad form to permit one's power to slop all over like that. Besides, it would be much more fun to see the shock on his opponent's face when he realized who, and what, he was really up against.

Salvador stalked out from under the trees and into the moonlight. He was of better than average height, with a wiry build, and his posture was stiff with hostility. His hands were clenched at his sides, his body leaning forward slightly, leading with his jaw.

Aden watched him come, then dropped a comforting hand on Bastien's shoulder and strolled into the light himself. He let a mocking smile drift over his face and said, "Last chance, Salvador. You can still go home alive."

"You should heed your own warning, *cabron*. Only one of us will be walking out of here tonight."

Aden's amusement fled. He liked to think, after more than 250 years, that he'd gotten over the fact of his illegitimate birth. But that didn't mean he had to accept the insult from the likes of Ramiro Salvador.

He loosened the hold on his power just a little, letting it waft around the clearing like a gentle breeze, still only the smallest hint of his true strength.

Salvador grinned, putting his fangs on full display. "That all you got? One more chance, big man. Walk out of here."

Aden bared his own teeth in a blatant challenge. "Too late."

He released his power in a flood, his eyes hooded with satisfaction as he took in the wide-eyed realization on Salvador's face. Deep inside Aden, the part of his Vampire gift that he rarely tapped and that very few knew existed came alive. It reached out, rolling in the scent of the Mexican's fear, like a dog in something dead, drinking it in, drawing strength from it. The more rational part of Aden's brain waited to see if Salvador would surrender, half-hoping he would. But that deep part of him, the part that was chortling with pleasure at his enemy's dread, that part hoped Salvador would stand and fight . . . and die.

And that's what he did.

Once Salvador had stepped into the clearing, there had been little chance of anything else. If he'd made the challenge and then surrendered without fighting, he'd never have been able to go back home, never have been able to face his Sire. For all Aden knew, Enrique was the kind of Sire who would execute his own child for embarrassing him.

But after his initial shock, Salvador stood his ground. He stopped playing games and immediately tightened his power around himself, creating a nearly impenetrable shield.

Aden had fought many challengers over the years, had seen his opponents' power take the form of a variety of shields and weapons. But Salvador's was something new. Most shields were either constantly in motion, or solidly immovable. Salvador's was like a series of overlapping plates that were constantly changing, shifting position, freezing fractionally, then shifting again. It was a particularly difficult shield to overcome. One had to figure out when the shield was weakest, when it was moving or when it was realigning itself, and then time the shifts in order to anticipate a vulnerability. But, its very complexity made Aden wonder why the Mexican vampire hadn't fought and won enough duels to make a name for himself. There had to be a weakness, a fatal flaw.

Aden didn't have time to consider that, though, as Salvador launched the first salvo, clearly having decided his best bet lay in striking hard and fast. Aden absorbed the initial attack—shields pulled tight around his body, fixed and secure—not even trying to deflect. He wanted to feel the weight of Salvador's power, feel its heat through his shields. He was still learning his opponent, still gathering intel.

What Salvador saw, however, was the slight give of Aden's shield under his attack. Misunderstanding its cause, the Mexican vampire grinned viciously.

Aden grinned back, and the Mexican's pleasure faltered.

While Salvador was still figuring out what had happened, Aden attacked, his power whipping out in a long, flexible curve of energy, wrapping around Salvador and tightening like a noose, but a noose made of edged steel rather than rope. Salvador's shield slid, trying to slip away from the grasp of Aden's assault, trying to cut through the whip-thin band of energy. Aden felt the pressure and pulled his power back, once again letting the Mexican vampire grin in victory. But this time, Aden kept his own expression carefully blank. The Mexican's grin only widened.

Aden now knew at least one of his challenger's weaknesses— arrogance, which some mistook for confidence. Confidence was good. Arrogance would get you killed.

Salvador struck again, and the fight truly began. Power lanced back and forth without halt, singeing the trees overhead, starting little fires that were quickly doused when the next blast of energy sucked all the oxygen out of the air. Aden unleashed the full weight of his power, slamming it outward in a concussive wave that knocked Salvador back several steps and sent one of the Mexican's minions crashing into a tree. The vampire minion yelped in pain, and Salvador leapt back into the fray, his fists raised then slammed into each other, creating a vibrating roll of energy that bombarded Aden's shields with sound and fury, pounding against his eardrums and setting up a cacophony in his head that was badly disorienting. Aden was forced to retreat within his own shields, using his power to push back, interrupting the energy waves and stopping the noise.

Salvador had clearly been waiting for just that reaction. He attacked again, a pinpoint shaft of power this time. It burrowed through Aden's shield, digging into his arm, burning through flesh and into bone.

It was an agonizing pain. But Aden had learned at a very tender age to set aside the worst pain imaginable, to keep working regardless of blood or torment. He flexed the muscles of his wounded arm, choosing his own pain, using the agony to fuel his rage, channeling that rage into a whirlwind of razor-edge flails, hammering and slashing at Salvador's shields, slipping through to slash at his face, to batter his body.

Blood ran freely from every inch of Salvador's exposed skin, from the rips and tears in his clothing. But still he fought, using Aden's attack against him, taking advantage of his focused distraction to strike at his legs, narrow beams of power cutting through his flesh like tiny lasers.

Aden nearly staggered, but would not grant himself that weakness. With a snarl of pure fury, he doubled his attack, shifting from the pounding force of a flail to the knife-edge slice of the thinnest of whips, the kind of whip that could fillet a man as neatly as a fish, could slice the flesh from his bones so quickly he wouldn't even know until he'd fallen that he was dead.

Salvador's answering howl carried more rage than pain, his head thrown back, his clothes almost gone, no longer able to hold form. Bloody strips of flesh hung from every inch of his body, white bone showing through, his face barely more than a skull. His teeth were bared, his eyes wild and gleaming a ruby-tinged gold as he pinned Aden with a furious stare and launched one final salvo.

And Aden saw it. The weakness in the Mexican's shields. For the space of a long breath, the constantly shifting plates of Salvador's shield froze completely as he drew upon every ounce of his remaining strength, draining the shield's power.

Aden pounced. Channeling his own power into a single whippet of energy, he slashed out, wrapping the thin beam around the Mexican's neck, letting the whip curl around and around like a snake, and then giving a single sharp tug.

Ramiro Salvador's eyes met Aden's in an instant of shocked disbelief, and in that moment, something passed between them, an understanding, a recognition of mutual respect. And then his head separated from his body, and he died.

Aden fell to his knees, his head thrown back as that hidden aspect of his power came roaring to the fore. It drank in the energy of

Salvador's death, as if by dying he released his power for Aden to draw upon. Distantly, Aden heard the screams of Salvador's minions as they followed their Sire into death, too newly made to survive the trauma of his ending, and Aden drank in their deaths, too. He didn't like this gift of his Vampire nature, but he used it. It was a morbid and dark power, but it was also a tremendous secret weapon. And he was a warrior. A warrior used whatever weapons were available to him. Aden's ability to draw strength from the death of other vampires made it possible for him to recharge in the middle of a fight. And it meant that when the battle was over, he was not so weakened by blood loss that he was vulnerable.

Aden became aware of Bastien at his side. He turned and saw the worry shadowing his lieutenant's face. He reached out mentally to Bastien and the others and felt their loyalty tinged with genuine fear for his safety, because they . . . loved him. His breath caught in his throat. Had anyone ever loved him before? Not like this.

He gripped Bastien's arm in thanks and pushed back, stopping his vampire children from offering their own power to aid his healing. He didn't need it, and they weren't home free from this challenge yet. What if Silas had learned of the challenge and was waiting for the victor to emerge, thinking he would be weakened and vulnerable in the aftermath?

"We must leave, my lord," Bastien told him. "Freddy has gone for the truck."

Aden nodded and stood, feeling an ache in his right leg, which he was fairly certain had been broken a moment ago, the bone sliced through by Salvador's last attack.

"The Mexican was a worthy opponent," he said.

"Not worthy enough," Bastien replied loyally.

Aden's lip curled in a half smile, but he privately wondered what the situation was in Mexico, that a powerful vampire like Ramiro Salvador had come this far north in search of territory. But then, wasn't that precisely the situation Raphael had described as happening in Europe? Powerful younger vampires forced to extreme measures to find territories to rule?

It was something to consider, but Aden set the thought aside. That was the battle for another day, *after* he was Lord of the Midwest. For tonight, he had to get himself and his vampires home safely. He briefly considered paying a visit to Sidonie. He knew where she lived, of course, and could easily bypass her doorman. And while the energy infusion from his unique ability was useful, there was nothing like blood, warm, fresh, and velvety. Like Sidonie's.

Unfortunately, he was in no mood to deal with whatever had sent her off in a huff earlier.

"Make sure Hamilton knows I want a daylight tail on Sidonie tomorrow," Aden said as they returned to their SUVs. "And tell Kage to take over the watch after sunset."

Tomorrow would be soon enough to find out what bug was up her ass. He'd get his answers first.

And then he'd get his blood.

Chapter Fourteen

SID HOVERED NEAR the edge of the crowd, drink in hand, pretending she was having a great time at her dad's birthday party. Everyone else was. But she was just . . . sad. Not weepy, put-on-a-cowboy-love-song sad, it was more of a stare-out-the-window-at-nothing sad. She knew where the blame belonged for this particular sadness, though. He was tall, dark, and handsome, and he sucked blood. Although if she was being perfectly honest, it wasn't Aden's fault, either. The fault rested with her naïve assumption that she could ever be anything to him besides a quick drink and a lay. Dresner had warned her about vampires, about their preference for short-term hookups and no commitment. Blood and sex. Wasn't that what she'd said? And Sidonie had been certain she was prepared, that her goals were clear, and she didn't want or need anything else.

"Hey, Sid."

She turned with a smile for Will Englehart. They'd driven up together, and she'd been a terrible companion, silent and staring out the window. He was looking very handsome in his tuxedo, and she was about to tell him so when she noticed the woman holding his hand. She was blond, petite, and curvy, and the look she was giving Sid held just a hint of challenge.

"Sid, this is Jennifer Lascher. Jenny, Sidonie Reid."

Sid shook the woman's hand, trying to keep the curiosity out of her voice and expression, and settled for the ever reliable, "Nice to meet you."

Jenny murmured something polite but didn't bother to conceal either her own curiosity or the little bit of hostility that lingered in her eyes.

Amenities done with, Sid gave Will a look that said, "What now?"

Will grinned back at her, but when he spoke it was to Jenny. Draping an arm around her shoulders, he pulled her close and brushed a kiss across her forehead. "Give us a few minutes, okay? I'll meet you back at the table."

Sid studied Will as he stared after Jenny's retreating back. He turned and caught her watching him.

"New girlfriend?" she teased, knowing full well it was more than that. She might not want to marry Will, but she'd known him all her life.

He smiled back at her, and Sid knew she was right. "Let's talk," he said.

"I think this one needs privacy," Sid commented, slipping her hand through his arm. "The patio's empty."

The blast of cold air when they opened the French doors told them exactly why the patio was empty, but her parents—or their party planner—had set up heaters for the few hardy souls who were willing to brave the cold in order to grab a quick cigarette break. There was no one out here now, however, so Sid and Will had the patio to themselves.

"Is it serious?" she asked him, glad she'd worn a sweater over her dress. The heaters could only do so much.

"You could say that," he said, looking out at the sloping yard. "We're engaged."

Sid drew back in quickly-concealed surprise, thankful that Will had been admiring her parents' perfect landscaping instead of looking at her.

"But—"

"I know. I should have told you, but . . . it's not like you and I were really going to get married, Sid." He looked at her then, his pretty brown eyes solemn and sincere.

She smiled to let him know it was okay. "Will," she said soothingly, "I'm not upset. I'm just surprised that you didn't say anything before this. How can you be engaged when I didn't even know you were dating someone?"

"It happened kind of fast. We worked a case together a few months ago, one of those multiple plaintiff deals. Anyway, we just . . . clicked. She loves me, Sid. It's like . . . I walk into the room, and her whole face lights up. Like I matter."

Sid slapped his arm playfully. "Of course, you matter, you idiot. You always have. Do you love her?"

"More than I ever thought possible," he said with a dreamy sigh that would have done a teenaged girl proud.

"Well, I'm happy for you. For you both. Do your parents know?"

"We're telling them this weekend. Tomorrow actually, brunch at the club, both families at the same time."

"Brave man."

He laughed. "Nah, my parents will love her, plus they kind of know each other, since it turns out her parents are members, too. But, Sid," he added, going serious. "I wanted to tell you first."

She went up on her toes and kissed his cheek. "That's sweet, thank you. But I'm not upset, so don't worry. Will I be invited to the wedding?"

"Of course! Won't be for a while yet. At least a year. Jenny wants the whole catastrophe, and I'm told these things take time to plan."

"So I've heard," Sid murmured. She didn't tell him she'd heard it from her own mother at least once a year for the last several years, and always in reference to her own wedding . . . to Will. "You should find Jenny now," she said, pushing him toward the door. "She'll be wondering what we're doing out here."

"Right. Thanks, Sid. I still love you, you know."

"And I love you, just—"

"—not that way," he chorused along with her, laughing. "Are you going back inside?"

"I think I'll hang out here a bit longer. It's kind of stuffy in there."

"Not too long, though, okay? You're not dressed for this weather."

"Got it," she said, fighting a grin. She watched as he opened the patio doors and was quickly lost in the crowd of partygoers, then watched a little longer. All those people, laughing and talking. There were even a few couples dancing now, including her parents. They were an attractive couple. Her mom pretty and trim, despite her three children, two of whom—Sid's brothers—had been enormous babies. And then there was her dad. Tall, slender, and handsome in a classic all-American way, the reddish-gold hair he'd passed on to his only daughter now threaded with silver.

Sid knew that all children wanted to believe their parents were in love, but she was convinced that her parents really were. And that's what she wanted. She didn't want a marriage of convenience or dynasty. She wanted passion. She wanted . . . Fuck. She wanted Aden.

Stupid, stupid Sidonie.

A sudden cheer drew her back inside as she saw her parents making their way to the front of the room where the DJ was set up. Her brothers were already there, and her dad was searching the room, looking for her. His face lit up in a smile when he found her, and Sid hurried to join them, knowing they'd hold everything waiting for her.

"A toast," her older brother, Jamie, called out, slinging an arm around her shoulders. "To our dad on his—"

"Now, now," her father shouted, stopping Jamie before he could say the number. "No need for that."

"—birthday," Jamie finished, laughing. "Happy day, Dad. We love you."

The crowd cheered, and everybody drank. More toasts were shouted out from friends, and everybody drank some more . . . and so it went, until her parents slipped out of the room, disappearing into a back hallway, where their suitcases were all ready to go, with a town car idling in the driveway.

They didn't linger after that. Quick kisses all around, admonitions to take care while they were off on a month-long European vacation, and they were gone. But the party was just getting started.

Sid told her brothers she wanted to change clothes and headed upstairs to the same room where she'd slept since grade school. Thankfully, her mother had updated the décor over the years. Sid didn't want to think about sleeping under the picture of Eminem that had been taped to her ceiling in high school, although she supposed that was better than the Backstreet Boys poster she'd hidden on the back of her closet door.

She opened her laptop, then stood and changed clothes while it found her parents' Wi-Fi and logged on. She hung her dress in the closet and pulled on the turtleneck sweater and well-worn jeans she'd worn for the drive up. Still barefoot, she settled in front of her laptop and brought up the train schedule back to Chicago. There was one more departure tonight—she checked the time—and she could just make it, if she hurried.

She yanked on socks and boots, then tapped out a quick e-mail to her brothers. She called a cab using her cell phone, then turned it off. Hopefully, her brothers would be too busy to pick up her e-mail before morning, but just in case, she didn't want them nagging her about her abrupt departure. She'd done her duty; she'd come to the big party and mingled. But now she was going home, which had somehow become Chicago instead of this pretty suburb. She'd always told herself she'd return here when the story was finished, and maybe she'd really planned on doing that back when she first moved away. But not anymore. Her home was in Chicago, and so, unfortunately, was her heart.

There wasn't anything to pack. Her party clothes could stay. All she really needed was her laptop, her purse, and her jacket.

Grabbing all three, she ran down the back stairs and made her getaway the same way her parents had. Half an hour later, she was racing through the train station. Half an hour after that, she was sitting on a train, heading for Chicago, and contemplating the dismal state of her love life.

She wasn't happy with the way she'd ended things with Aden. It wasn't like her to slink away. If he was an asshole, then she needed to tell him that. And if not, they could at least say a civil good-bye, nice having sex with you, have a good life.

"You heading to the city?"

Sid jerked in surprise. She'd been so caught up in planning for what she would do when she saw Aden next that she hadn't realized someone had sat down across the aisle from her. She'd reserved a seat in business class and had found the car mostly empty when she'd arrived. She looked up and down the aisle and saw that that was still the case. There was one couple at the other end of the car, and then there was her new and unwanted friend.

"I am," she said pleasantly, then immediately pulled out her book and pretended to read.

"Me, too. Had one of those family things tonight. Grandparents' anniversary. Their fiftieth, so I had to be there."

Sid barely glanced over and made a noncommittal noise, hoping he'd take the hint. No such luck.

"Morning after brunch tomorrow, too, but you know how it is. I didn't want stay over," Mister Chatty Cathy continued.

She smiled politely and kept reading.

"So . . . you from around here?"

She put her book down, letting him see a little bit of polite irritation. Maybe if she let him talk a minute or two, he'd get it out of his system.

"What do you do in the city?" she asked. Unwilling to give him any tidbit of information about herself, she switched the questions back on him.

"Commodities trader," he said with a sly smile, clearly expecting her to be impressed.

"Must be interesting," she said, thinking to herself that she had no interest in the subject at all.

"Definitely," he enthused, and proceeded to tell her in mind-numbing detail about every pork belly and soybean he'd ever sold. She knew in principle what was involved in commodities, but this was far more than she'd ever cared to learn.

As he regaled her with the wonders of his job, she studied him. He wasn't bad looking. Medium build, dark brown hair, medium height—although it was difficult to tell the latter with him sitting down.

On another day in another year, she might have been interested. Maybe. But not tonight.

"I'm Vasco, by the way," he said, offering his hand. "Richard Vasco."

"Sidonie," she said, not giving up her last name.

"Would you like a coffee, Sidonie? Or maybe something cold?" He stood as he offered, and she saw she'd been right about his height. He was a couple of inches over her own five foot seven and a half.

"No, thank you," she said pleasantly.

He shot her a quick, "Be right back," and moved down the aisle.

Once he was gone, Sid checked the time on her cell phone and realized she'd never turned it back on after leaving her parents' house. Figuring she was well away from her brothers, who by now were either sound asleep or so drunk that they'd forgotten her, she turned the phone back on. Then she draped her jacket over herself like a blanket and pretended to fall asleep. It was cowardly, and she was deeply ashamed . . . okay, so she wasn't ashamed at all. She simply wanted a quiet ride back to the city. Was that too much to ask?

She heard Vasco return, felt him standing in the aisle studying her, maybe trying to figure out if she was faking it or not. But Sid was made of sterner stuff. She kept her eyes closed and her breathing steady and eventually dozed off for real.

ADEN OPENED YET another file on his computer, this one a long windy financials report, when a simple one-page accounting would have done the job just as well. It made him long for another bloody fight to the death. He'd been at his desk for hours, but business didn't stop just because the challenge was underway. Lucas was still his master for now. He knew Aden was in Chicago and why, but that didn't mean they could ignore what was happening in Kansas City. Reports still came in and so did a thousand requests. Some vampires couldn't make the simplest decision without seeking advice or permission. Aden knew these vampires were as necessary to the race as he was, but sometimes their timidity drove him to distraction. They were *vampires,* damn it. Why couldn't they act like it?

He sighed, knowing the answer to his own question. If every vampire was as aggressive and driven as he was, they'd have wiped themselves out long ago.

He looked up when Bastien entered the office, hoping for a

distraction. But one look at his lieutenant's face, and he knew it wasn't good news.

Aden did a quick mental check of his vampire children, and finding them all well and alive, he asked the question he wasn't sure he wanted answered. "What is it?"

"Earl Hamilton called. They've lost Sidonie Reid."

Aden grew very still. "Lost her? What does that mean?"

"She left the city this morning in the company of"—Bastien checked some scribbled notes—"William Englehart. We don't know much about him yet, other than he's a lawyer from her hometown. Hamilton's guy said—"

"She left the city," Aden repeated flatly.

Bastien studied Aden carefully. "Yes, my lord. Englehart picked her up this morning in his personal vehicle."

Aden slapped his laptop closed, fighting against the urge to do something violent. Had Sidonie dared to continue seeing a human lover after being with Aden? Was she really that stupid?

"What else?"

"Hamilton's man said they seemed friendly." Bastien looked down, reading from his notes. "She had no luggage other than her computer and a garment bag, and they—" He broke off with an uneasy glance at Aden who was sitting perfectly still, his hands flat on the desk.

"Continue," he said.

"They kissed when she got in the car."

Aden's jaw was so tight, he thought the bones would break. He was surprised at the intensity of his own reaction, but she was *his*. Maybe not forever. He didn't do forever. But for as long as he wanted her, and he fucking did not share.

"What else?" he demanded.

"They drove to her parents' home together, although it's not clear whether Englehart stayed at the house with her, or went elsewhere. Reid didn't leave the house the rest of the day. There was a party, starting late this afternoon and going into the evening. It looked like the party was winding down when Reid suddenly jumped in a cab and hit the train station. By the time our guy parked and got inside, she was gone."

"So we don't know where she is," Aden observed coldly. "What about Englehart? Where's he?"

Bastien blinked and immediately grabbed the phone.

"And tell Hamilton I want his guy fired."

"Yes, my lord," Bastien said, then conveyed the orders to Hamilton with a few terse words before disconnecting.

"Sidonie has a cell phone," Aden growled. "Get someone tracking it."

"Already done, my lord. It's turned off right now, but the minute it comes back on, we'll pick up the ping and start tracking her."

Sidonie's phone was off. Aden could think of many reasons why a woman would turn her phone off, and he didn't like any of them. He was trying to think of what else they could do when the phone rang. Bastien answered, his posture radiating tension. Intellectually, Aden knew none of this was Bastien's fault, but he wasn't inclined to let him off the hook. If Aden had to suffer, Bastien could damn well suffer with him.

"Sire," his lieutenant said, disconnecting the phone once more, but keeping it in his hand. "Englehart is at his parents' home."

"But Sidonie isn't there."

"Definitely not, my lord."

"So where the fuck is she?"

The phone rang again. Bastien glanced at him, but Aden waved a hand, telling him to answer the fucking thing. Another terse conversation, and Aden saw Bastien's entire demeanor change, becoming if not relaxed, then at least less tense.

"Ms. Reid's phone just pinged, my lord. She's on a train," Bastien reported, seeming puzzled by this latest news. "Fortunately, at this time of night, there aren't many trains moving. We're fairly certain she's on her way back here, to Union station. We won't know for sure until the phone switches cell—"

"She's going home," Aden interrupted. "Let's greet her, shall we?"

SID WOKE WHEN the train slowed to enter Union Station. She slitted one eye open carefully. No Vasco. Sighing in relief, she gathered her things, thinking she'd take a cab home.

But as she made her way through the station toward the cab stand, Vasco appeared at her side.

"I have a town car," he said, taking her elbow. "I'll give you a ride home."

Sid felt a trickle of unease. It was one thing to flirt on the train, but something else entirely to stalk her through the station and touch her uninvited. She jerked her arm away from him.

"That's all right," she said firmly, "I'll take a cab."

"Don't be silly," he insisted, his eyes going flat as his fingers closed around her arm. "It's far too late for that."

Unease turned to genuine alarm, and Sid stared around, looking for help. The station was busy, but no one was paying attention to them.

"Look," she said, trying to remain calm. "I appreciate the offer, really. But I don't know you, and I'd really rather—"

"Sid!"

Sidonie looked up at the sound of her name and saw Kage striding toward her, a big smile on his face and one arm raised in greeting, as if they were long-lost friends. Next to her, she felt Vasco stiffen. His grip tightened enough to leave bruises, and she thought for a moment that he was going to make a break for it and drag her with him.

But then Kage was there, flashing a hint of fang as his fingers gripped Vasco's wrist and forced him to release Sid's arm. Kage wrapped an arm around Sid, placing himself between her and Vasco, who backed away with a hissed curse.

"This isn't over, vampire."

Kage grinned. "Bring it on, human," he said dismissively, then guided Sid toward the exit.

"Thanks," she said breathlessly, trying to keep up with his long strides. "That guy was a jerk."

"He was more than a jerk. He knew who you were."

She glanced up at him as they left the station and climbed into the SUV Kage had left parked illegally.

"He knew you were a vampire," she said in sudden understanding.

"Right."

"How would he know that?"

"I couldn't guess."

"You mean you won't."

His gaze cut over to her. "Same thing."

"Not really. How'd you know I was on that train?"

"You should ask Lord Aden."

Sid rolled her head back against the seat. She could push for answers, but there was no point. The one thing she'd learned about vampires was that they were completely loyal to their Sires. That loyalty could be compromised, according to Dresner, if a vampire was strong enough to break away. But Sid's impression of Aden and his people was something closer to a brick wall. They were solid.

If Aden didn't want Kage to talk to her, he wouldn't talk.

She looked up in surprise when Kage pulled the SUV up in front of her building and stopped, clearly waiting for her to get out. She'd expected him to take her to Aden and had to stifle the surprisingly strong surge of disappointment.

"Thanks," she said, forcing a smile. "For rescuing me." Although she still wondered what exactly she'd been rescued *from*.

"No problem," he said, giving her a quick sideways smile. "See you around, Sid."

She made a beeline for the elevator, giving her doorman a wave as she went by. She was beyond tired and imagined she could hear her bed calling to her with its down comforter and soft sheets. Her hallway was empty as she unlocked her door and stepped into the quiet darkness of her condo. Closing the door behind her, she leaned against it with a sigh of relief, then pushed away and was already stripping off her jacket when she made her way down the short hall to her sparsely-furnished living room. Her bedroom was on the other side of that open space, and she could see the white of her comforter gleaming in the moonlight from a window she rarely covered. That was her only goal for tonight. Bed.

But then a light clicked on, and her heart nearly stopped.

"Good evening, Sidonie," Aden's deep voice purred.

Sid clutched a hand to her heart, feeling it bouncing so hard behind her breastbone that her ribs rattled.

"Aden, damn it," she swore, hanging on to one of the tall stools lined up at the bar between her kitchen and living room. "You scared me half to death. What are you doing here? And how did you get in?"

Aden stood to his full height. He remained still for a moment, as if inviting her to admire him, and damn it, she did. He looked good. He wasn't wearing a jacket, just a black long-sleeved T-shirt and a pair of black jeans that showed off the length of his legs, the powerful muscles of his thighs, and cupped the rest of him lovingly. Sid blinked, honest enough to admit that she wouldn't mind cupping him herself. She raised her gaze to his face, and his knowing smile told her he was aware of the effect he had on her.

Sid gave him a narrow look and opened her mouth to tell him to take his beautiful self right out of her home, but then he moved, and she was caught up in the pure, lethal elegance of him. He didn't so much walk across the room as he prowled—long graceful strides, loose hips rolling like those of a big cat, his dark eyes limned in blue.

She looked up at him, suddenly right on top of her.

"Where have you been, Sidonie? And more to the point, whom have you been with?"

Sid blinked, the spell of his beauty broken by her sudden anger. What right did he have to ask her such things?

"None of your business," she snapped and tried to push past him. It was like trying to push a ton of brick.

"*You're* my business," he snarled.

"Is that so? Don't you have better things to do? Winning the challenge, world domination? Don't let me get in your way. Isn't that what you said, that you'd never let a *woman*"—she added a sneer to the word, just as he had the other night—"get in your way? Well, I'm officially taking myself out of your fucking way. So you can leave now."

She pushed at him again to no avail, but this time he bracketed her arms with his big hands.

"World domination?" he repeated, smirking.

"Whatever."

"Where have you been, Sidonie?" he repeated implacably. He was like a stone statue, immoveable and unmoved by anything she said.

"Fine. It's my father's birthday. We had a party for him. I went. Happy now?"

"And who's William Englehart?"

Sid's mouth dropped open in surprise. "How do you know about Will?"

"So it's true," he snarled, stepping even closer until she was backed up against the bar.

"What's true?" she asked in confusion. "And what about Will?"

"What is he to you?"

"He's a friend."

"Did you fuck him?"

"What?" Sid glanced around. She didn't see any of Aden's vamps, but there was no way he'd come here alone.

"We're alone," Aden said, accurately reading her concerns. "Bastien's in the lobby by now. He started down when you started up."

"How did you . . . Kage," she realized. "He must have called you from the car."

"Must have," he said. "Did you fuck Englehart?"

Sid glared at him. "You know what? Go to hell. And how did you get in here anyway? I thought you guys needed an invitation, like at Dresner's house the other day."

"Your doorman let me in."

Sid scowled. "Why would he do that?"

"I persuaded him you were missing. He was very concerned and invited me to search your condo."

"I thought you needed *my* permission."

"Not really, just an invitation from someone with the right of entry. Your doorman has that."

"Not for long. And I'm going to hang garlic over the threshold."

Aden laughed. "That won't do anything but smell up your home, and I don't like the scent. Don't do it."

"Stop giving me orders."

"Then tell me the truth. Did you fuck Will Englehart?"

Sid was on the verge of telling him to go hell again, but she saw something in his eyes, a hint of vulnerability in that otherwise tightly-controlled face. Too many people bought into Aden's hard-ass exterior and never looked beneath the surface, probably because he didn't let them. But for some reason, after a long lifetime of protecting himself, he'd let her in. He'd trusted her, and she couldn't imagine what it must have cost him to do so. She wouldn't betray that.

"No," she admitted softly. "Will and I dated, but we haven't been lovers in years. Our families are close, and he's a very old friend, but that's it." She flattened her palm against his chest, feeling his muscles bunch beneath her fingers. "I haven't fucked anyone but you lately."

"Define lately."

"Jesus, you're a pain in the ass."

"Answer the question."

"No, *you* answer the question. How long's it been since *you* fucked someone?"

"Other than you?"

She gave him an impatient look.

"A couple of weeks," he admitted. "Not since I came to Chicago for the challenge."

Sid's breath ran out in a rush. A couple of weeks?

"They meant nothing, Sidonie," he murmured, cupping her cheek in his warm hand.

Weren't vampires supposed to be cold? Aden never was. Wait. *They?*

"They?" she said out loud.

He shrugged carelessly. "Until you, I never bothered to stick with anyone."

Well, that was sweet in a man-slutty sort of way. "But you told Bastien—" she started, but couldn't finish. She didn't want to sound like a clingy, needy *woman.*

His eyes lit with understanding. "So that's what this is all about. You eavesdropped, and as is often the case when one listens to a conversation that is none of one's business, you misunderstood."

"What you said was pretty clear, Aden," she said, wondering if he enjoyed his little lectures as much as she *hated* them.

"I'm sure it was, but it had absolutely nothing to do with you."

"If not me, then who? Who's the woman who's getting in the way of your grand plans?"

He gave her a quizzical look, as if there was some obvious truth she was missing. "Silas, of course," he said.

Sid stared at him. "Silas is a woman?"

"To be accurate, Silas is a female vampire."

"I just assumed—"

"You assumed she was male," he tsked. "Not terribly liberated, Sidonie."

"Hey, most of you guys are . . . well, *guys.*"

"Silas is most assuredly not a guy. She's quite beautiful if one cares for the type."

"What type?" Sid asked, feeling a twinge of jealousy.

"The type who will cut off your balls without remorse if the mood strikes her. And I'm not speaking figuratively."

Sid stared at him. "You mean she's actually—"

"I'm told she has a collection."

She wrinkled her nose. "That's disgusting. You should definitely kill her."

"I plan on it, but not in search of some cosmic justice for males everywhere. She's in my way, so she has to go."

His hand, which had been stroking her cheek, dropped to her neck and grabbed a handful of hair, tugging her head back so she had to look up at him.

"Why didn't you tell me you were leaving town?"

"I didn't think you'd care. Besides, you knew anyway. Your cover was pretty much blown when Kage rescued me at the train station. Thank you for that, by the way."

Aden's hand clenched almost painfully in her hair, and he went preternaturally still, his eyes gleaming as if lit from behind. "Rescued you from what?"

"Some guy," Sid told him. "He sat near me on the train, but I brushed him off. I thought that was it, but then in the station he got really pushy about giving me a ride. Kage showed up just in time."

"What did he look like?" he demanded.

But before she could answer, there was a knock on her door. Aden glanced down the hallway, and the next thing she knew her front door lock was gliding open, and Bastien was standing at the entrance to her living room, his dark hair slicked back and shining in the moonlight, his eyes fixed on Aden.

"Kage just reported in," Bastien said. "Sidonie was approached this evening."

"I just heard," Aden agreed. "Did Kage know him?"

"No, my lord. But the assailant most definitely knew Kage."

Aden drew Sid against him in a protective gesture, even though there was no one in the room except Bastien. He cupped her chin, tilting her head back until she was looking at him.

"What did he look like, Sidonie?"

She took his hand and turned in his embrace, leaning against his side with his arm heavy over her shoulders. "Nothing about him stood out. He was a little bit taller than I am, brown hair, brown eyes, fit, but on the slender side. He said his name was Vasco."

Aden spoke over her head, addressing Bastien. "Sound familiar?"

"Was he human?" Bastien asked, his eyes eerily intent as his gaze cut to her.

"I think so. It was after dark when I got on the train, but he'd have to be human, wouldn't he? I mean, I didn't go to my parents' place until this morning, so how could he have . . ."

Her voice trailed off, because neither vampire was paying any attention to her.

"Silas, you think, my lord? The description could fit Balderas."

"Who's Balderas?" Sid asked.

"Silas's daylight security chief," Aden growled. "One of two."

"She has two security chiefs?"

"*Daylight* security. And Silas likes to surround herself with men, especially human men. They're her favorite food source. Unfortunately for them, her idea of post-coital relations all too frequently resembles that of a black widow spider. Balderas must not be her type, because he's been around long enough to be noticeable. What did he say to you?"

Sid hadn't paid much attention to what he'd said. Her focus had been on getting rid of him. "*If* it was Balderas," she qualified, then paused when Bastien shoved a cell phone under her nose with a picture of . . . "Okay, fine. That's him. Mostly he talked about himself and commodities trading. What kind of security chief is hung up on commodities trading?"

"One who was a trader before he was convicted of fraud and did a stint in federal prison."

"Oh. He *was* a little intense."

Aden took her by the shoulders and turned her in the direction of her bedroom. "Pack some things. You're coming home with me."

She spun back around. "What? Why?"

He gave her a droll look. "You don't want to go home with me?"

Sid's heart leapt at the heated look in his eyes. A look that said *going home* implied a lot more than sleeping in a guest room.

"Fine," she agreed and, ignoring his confident smirk, went off to pack.

ADEN SPRAWLED lazily on his bed, still fully clothed, his back against the headboard as he watched Sidonie unpack the few things she'd grudgingly brought with her. It wasn't much. He didn't know if she didn't want to intrude, or, more likely, if she was unwilling to surrender her independence enough to stay with him longer than she had to. But whichever it was, she was here, and here she was staying. She just didn't know it yet.

"You can use all of the drawers in that dresser," he said, pointing. "It's empty."

"You don't use it?"

"I use the one in the closet. That one's art."

She ran her hand over the delicate flower motif and mother-of-pearl inlays on the chest of drawers. "This is beautiful. Is it, um, original?"

"Is that a delicate way of asking if it's an antique, something from my past? I'm not worried about my age, Sidonie. But, yes, that's an original fifteenth century Ottoman, and no, I only purchased it a few years ago."

"All right," she said, turning to give him a gimlet stare. "So, how old *are* you?"

He laughed, something he'd done much more frequently since meeting her. "I was born in 1753. This body"—he touched a hand to his T-shirted chest and noted with satisfaction that her gaze followed the gesture appreciatively—"reflects more or less my age when my Mistress acquired me and made me Vampire. I was close to twenty-seven years old at the time, although I could be off by a year or two. I was a bastard and a slave. What records existed were hardly precise."

Sidonie had crossed the room while he spoke, and she now climbed up onto the bed to straddle his thighs. Her eyes were soft and sad, and he knew it was because of what he'd told her about his early life. She pretended to be tough, but his Sidonie was tender-hearted, the toughness only a thin shell that protected her from the carelessness of others.

Whoa. *His* Sidonie? He did a mental double take at that thought. When had she become *his*? And not in the way of previous lovers whom he'd only claimed for a day or two until he was done with them, and even then only because he didn't like to share. Sidonie was his in a way he'd never considered before, a way that would last a hell of a lot longer than a day or two. A way that said he didn't plan on sharing her *ever*.

She leaned forward, gentle hands cupping his cheeks, her full breasts barely touching his chest as she brushed a kiss over his mouth. He wanted more. His arms banded around her back as he rolled her beneath him and took what he needed. His mouth was hard on her soft lips, his tongue plundering as she opened to him, her hungry moan telling him he wasn't the only one who needed more.

He shoved his hand under her sweater and palmed her breast through the lace of her bra, feeling her nipple poke at his fingers. With a growl, he yanked on the delicate fabric, hearing it tear and not caring. He'd buy her a new bra. He'd buy her a hundred. Right now, he needed her naked, and the bra was in the way. Lifting slightly, he pushed her sweater up over her breasts and released the front clasp on the torn bra with a deft twist of his fingers. Her breasts spilled out heavy and full, her nipples flushed a deep rose against her pale skin.

Unable to resist their temptation, Aden took one of the plump morsels in his mouth, sucking until the pink rose became a succulent cherry, so hard and engorged with blood that he could smell it, so rich that it made his fangs elongate with hunger. Beneath him, Sidonie was making eager little noises, her breaths choppy, her fingers tunneling through his hair, holding him against her breast, almost begging him to bite, to taste her blood. But he wasn't ready to release her to an orgasm just yet. He wanted her hot and begging.

He bit down until he knew she could feel the sting of his teeth, heard her suck in a breath and hold it in anticipation of his bite, but he didn't let his teeth sink in, he didn't draw blood. Lifting his mouth from her flesh, he switched to the other breast, smiling against her hot skin at the sound of her groan, her hand fisted against his back, pounding once in frustration.

Stroking his hand down over her hip, he cupped the curve of her ass, then slapped her once, smartly. She jumped, but it only seemed to heighten her arousal, as he'd known it would. Aden would never beat a woman, he'd never beat *anyone* who was weaker than he was, but he was a master at understanding the sensuous pleasure to be found in the right kind of pain.

Sucking her second breast into his mouth, he lavished it as he had the first, sliding his tongue over her nipple, feeling the blood pulse, sucking harder until the entire tip of her breast was between his teeth. He bit down again, knowing there'd be marks on her delicate flesh tomorrow and taking pleasure in the knowledge. He'd mark every inch of her before he was through.

"Aden," she gasped, her breath warm and wet against his ear.

"Not yet, *habibi*. Not for a long time."

She growled angrily, making him smile. Until she thumped his back again in her anger.

"Not nice, Sidonie love. You'll pay for that one."

"Big talk," she muttered, then cried out in surprise when he whipped her sweater over her head and used it to tie her hands to the headboard. She tugged on the stretchy material, but his binding held fast. Of course.

"This is what happens when you hit," he told her solemnly, breaking into a grin when she narrowed her eyes at him, lips pursed in annoyance.

Unable to resist, he leaned forward and took that pretty mouth in a kiss, her lips softening beneath his at once, her tongue twisting over and around his tongue and teeth, her body straining upward, undulating against him as she tried to get closer.

But Aden had other plans. Ignoring her wordless protest, he lifted his mouth from hers and kissed his way along her jaw, then down to her neck where he teased with quick flicks of his tongue, and lower, to her shoulder. He closed his teeth over the delicate bone of her clavicle, letting her feel the edge of his fangs, before moving to her chest once more. Sidonie thrust her breasts upward, and he took a moment to admire their lush beauty, the plush nipples and pink areolas, the bright red brand of his teeth marks.

"Aden!" Sidonie demanded, bucking impatiently, obviously wanting him to do more than admire.

He gave her a single flat look of warning. She huffed in frustration and favored him with a scowl, but then lay quietly beneath his hand where it rested against her abdomen.

Leaning down, he brushed a kiss over the soft skin of her belly, then began stripping away the rest of her clothes. He unfastened her jeans and dragged them down her legs, hooking his thumbs in the lacy edges of her panties and taking those, too, until she was completely naked beneath him. He sat back and admired his work, his lovely Sidonie.

"How come I'm always naked and you're not?" she asked sulkily.

Aden stroked a hand down her bare leg, starting at her thigh and continuing down to cup her calf behind him.

"Because I like you this way." He closed his fingers around her calf and pulled her leg up, bending her knee and pushing outward until he could see the first rosy blush of her pussy.

"I like you naked, too," she said, somewhat more breathless than she had been.

"But this is my bed," he said patiently, sliding his fingers under her other thigh and bending that leg as well, until she was completely open to him.

"I hate it when you . . . oh, God," she gasped as he slid a single finger into the wet heat between her swollen folds.

"What were you saying?" he asked mildly, as his finger played in the slick moisture which gave lie to her words.

"Don't stop," she moaned, eyes closed as she fairly rippled under his hand.

"I don't think that's what you said."

Her eyes flashed open to glare at him.

"Oh, fine, I'll stop." He wiped his fingers on her thigh and stood next to the bed, laughing as she snarled a furious protest. Until he began removing his clothes.

She grew silent as she watched him undress, her eyes hot and hungry, her tongue darting out to lick her lips when he yanked his T-shirt over his head and tossed it aside. She was such an erotic sight—tied to his bed, her pale skin flushed, damp with a fine sheen of sweat, his teeth marks on her breasts, her thighs wet with her own arousal. His cock strained at the heavy fabric of his jeans, so tight it was almost painful. Slipping the buttons one at a time, he reached inside and fisted himself as his heavy shaft sprang free, pumping his hand slowly up and down as he ate in the sight of her.

"Aden," she said urgently, her breath coming in pants, her gaze fixed on his cock as he stroked himself.

"Spread your legs for me, Sidonie," he crooned.

She obeyed readily, bending her knees even closer to her chest and spreading her legs until he could see the slick opening to her sex, her vaginal lips flushed and swollen in invitation.

Captivated by the sight, Aden released his cock and climbed onto the bed to kneel between her thighs.

"You have the prettiest, pink pussy," he murmured, then leaned over to taste, his tongue dipping inside her, then out again, swirling over and around the hard pearl of her clit. He lifted his head enough to meet her hungry eyes. "Sweet, too."

She made a noise very much like a sob, but though he saw her stomach muscles flexing with the effort, she remained still beneath his hands. Such discipline deserved a reward.

Bending his head once more, he inhaled the scent of her arousal, taking it in, feeling the sizzle as it sped along his nerves and over his skin, his cock jerking with the need to bury itself inside her hot little body. But first he closed his lips over the hot bundle of nerves that was her clit, kissing and sucking, his fangs aching with the need to taste more than her wetness.

He scraped the edge of one fang along her clit, and then the other. Her heart was pumping, her muscles taut as she writhed against the binding of her hands, as she strained to keep her thighs open against the need to clasp them around his head.

He teased her, lifting his lips away with a soft kiss, a gentle nip to the tender skin of her inner thigh. She did sob then, the emotion of the moment too much for her to hold in, her need for him warring with her desire to remain still, to please him. He blew softly on the wet flesh between her thighs before rasping his tongue the full length of her slit, stimulating her clit until it was hard with arousal.

And then he truly tasted her, tasted the sweetest blood a woman's body could offer. His teeth closed over the pulsing pearl of her clit, and Sidonie screamed, her back bowed as the orgasm swept through her body, her sex flooding with juices, pulsing with hunger as it searched for something to fill its emptiness.

Aden gripped her hips, holding her to the bed, keeping her legs open and her pussy available to him as he lapped up the cream of her climax like a sweet topping to the richness of her blood. He sipped and tasted until she began to calm down, until the first throes of orgasm had passed and her breathing was beginning to slow, her heart to cease its racing.

And then he rose up between her thighs and, positioning his cock at her slick and swollen opening, he leaned over her and thrust his hips forward, slamming his cock deep into her tight body, feeling the trembling flesh of her sheath spreading to accommodate his intrusion. Sidonie gasped, then moaned in pleasure, as her legs closed over his back, ankles locked to hold him there.

Aden chuckled at her possessiveness, loving the clasp of her thighs around his hips, the way she arched her back to rub her nipples over his skin. Wanting to feel her arms around him, he reached up and freed her hands from their sweater binding. She responded immediately, curling her arms over his back, her nails scratching along his spine hard enough that he knew she'd drawn blood.

He growled his satisfaction as he pumped in and out of her hot embrace, as her inner muscles began to clench around his cock, her breath gasping in his ear, her heart pounding against his chest. He crushed his mouth against hers, letting her taste herself on his tongue, their teeth clashing until both were bleeding.

Aden lifted his mouth and howled in triumph as Sidonie had her first taste of his blood, as she jolted in surprise at the electric shock of it, shuddering as it exploded directly into her brain like a shot of liquid lust. She began lifting her hips in time with his thrusts, their hips slapping together, her teeth closing over the skin of his neck as if seeking to taste more of him.

Aden snarled and lowered his mouth to her jugular. He could hear the rush of her blood through her veins, the pounding of her pulse. Her scent was overwhelming. His gums ached as his fangs emerged, as Sidonie twisted her head, baring her neck in invitation.

She screamed when he bit her, when the euphoric in his bite raced through her already-electrified bloodstream, lighting up every nerve ending, every pleasure center in her body. Her pussy squeezed around him like a fist even as her blood rolled down his throat, fragrant and rich, thick and sweet. And he felt his own orgasm building, felt his sac stretched tight around his balls, until with a shout of triumph, his climax rolled over and through him, his release roaring down his cock and into her body, filling her with his heat, marking her body and claiming her soul.

Sidonie was his. And he'd kill anyone, man or woman, who touched her.

Chapter Fifteen

SIDONIE DIDN'T know if she could move. She lay on top of Aden, every bone in her body turned to Jell-O, her muscles to mush. He had that effect on her, and she didn't think it was only his vampire blood. Although that stuff should be bottled and sold as an aphrodisiac. Fuck little blue pills. The vamps could make a fortune selling their blood. There must be a reason they hadn't done so, she mused. She'd have to ask Aden about it. Although there was a hell of a lot more to sex with Aden than a sip of his blood. He had moves. The things he could do with his tongue . . . A delicious ripple of memory rolled through her body, her fingers digging into his chest as she shivered in a mini-orgasm.

Aden slid his arm around her, his big hand drifting down to cup her ass possessively. He didn't say a word, and she wasn't looking at his face. But she just *knew* he'd have that smug smile going on. She could hardly blame him, but it wasn't like she was the *only* one who'd gotten her rocks off. Pleasure had been had all around, hadn't it?

She propped herself up on his broad chest. He gazed down at her, his eyes all but hidden behind the veil of his lashes.

"Maybe next time I'll tie *you* up," she muttered thoughtfully, not even sure if she meant him to hear it.

But he did hear it, and his reaction was instantaneous.

"No one ties me up, Sidonie." His voice was hard, his hand on her ass suddenly unyielding. "Not ever."

He moved abruptly, lifting her off his chest as if she weighed nothing and vaulting off the bed with a flex of smooth muscle. He was careful with her, but he didn't linger. Sid sat up into a cross-legged position, watching as he strode across the room and disappeared into the bathroom. A minute later, the shower came on, and she sighed.

She'd been an idiot. Of course, he wouldn't want to be tied up. Hadn't he confided his history to her? It couldn't have been easy for a powerful male like Aden to admit to her that he'd been a slave in his former life, that he'd been forced to submit to people much weaker than he was—both men and women—that he'd been bought and sold, used like a piece of property.

Idiot wasn't harsh enough. She was an ass. She crawled off the big bed, determined to fix this somehow. She was a writer, damn it. Words were supposed to be her forte. She shuffled over to the bureau where her few clothes were stashed and realized she'd have to shower first. She was sticky with sweat and . . . other things. The shower was still running, and her brain had no problem conjuring up images of Aden's big, powerful, *naked* body, steam filling the glass enclosure, hot water flowing lovingly over every inch of smooth muscle and skin . . .

She shook herself out of the fantasy. He hadn't invited her to join him. Quite the opposite, in fact. He'd even closed the door.

Ass, she cursed herself again.

But she still couldn't put clean clothes on over her stinky, sticky body. She also didn't feel like being naked when Aden finally emerged from the bathroom. Sure, he'd seen, and probably licked, every inch of her, but that was then. This was now, and if he was pissed at her, she didn't want to face him at her most vulnerable.

She glanced around. Aden had been wearing a long-sleeved T-shirt earlier. She could pull that on until . . . She frowned, realizing he'd picked up all of his clothes on his way to the shower. Just her luck. She'd fallen for a neat freak. Casting around for a solution, expecting the shower to turn off at any moment, her eye fell on an antique armoire against the far wall. Maybe there was something in there she could put on, a robe or another shirt.

She crossed over to the tall closet-like piece of furniture. It was similar in design to the dresser, with latticework cutouts in a floral motif, but the inlays were tortoise shell and sliced so thin that when she pulled open the door, the light shone through in rich gold and chocolate brown. She stroked her fingers over the beautiful workmanship as she pushed the door fully open . . . and then she could only stare at what she'd found.

There wasn't a robe, wasn't a shirt, hanging inside. But what there was aroused so many different feelings that she couldn't process them all. She'd known Aden was dominant and had suspected his dominance was more than simply an alpha male personality, but this . . . this was whips and chains, handcuffs and arm restraints, collars and blindfolds, and other things she could only guess at.

She didn't hear the bathroom door open, didn't know Aden was there until she felt his heat against her still-naked back and smelled the fresh soap scent of his skin. His arm reached around her and lifted a flogger from its hook. It was leather, a light brown suede that gave its multiple tails a deceptively soft appearance.

Aden dragged the soft suede across her naked breast, and Sidonie felt every one of the multiple tails as they slid over her engorged nipple until it ached. Her breath grew uneven, and her heart was going a mile a minute. But she wasn't afraid. She was exquisitely aroused, with wet heat dripping between her still sticky thighs.

Aden lowered his mouth to her ear. "Do you know what I thought when I laid eyes on you for the first time, Sidonie?"

Sid tried to come up with something clever, something to break the unbearable erotic tension that was freezing her in place. But she could only shake her head mutely.

"I thought how beautiful your pale skin would look under the lash," he purred, trailing the flogger down over the curve of her breasts to her belly. He lingered above her swollen pussy lips, switching the flogger around and stroking the hard handle between her thighs, before snaking the multiple tails over her hip and down to her leg.

Without warning, he snapped the flogger in the air, letting her feel the barest kiss of suede against her thigh. Sid shivered, her nipples hard points of desire, her pussy drenched in heat. Aden closed the small distance between them until his body was flush with hers, his cock a heavy length against the curve of her butt. She closed her eyes, letting her head fall back against his shoulder.

His lips closed over her neck, and she reached up, curling her fingers over the back of his head, caressing him, holding him against her.

"Shall I show you, Sidonie? Would you like to see how pretty your skin would look?"

Sid trembled, afraid to admit her own desires. "I want you to fuck me," she said in a whisper so soft that she wasn't certain he'd heard until his arm came around her waist and she was spinning around. Before she could draw a breath of surprise, Sid found herself bent over the bed, her butt in the air, her legs spread wide as Aden nudged her feet apart.

His thick fingers dipped between her legs, spreading her lips, testing her wetness and finding her slippery with arousal. "You're soaking wet, *habibi*," he chided. "Such a wicked girl."

His hand stroked the full length of her slit, gathering moisture and dragging it over the skin of her butt, as if to demonstrate how very wet she was.

"Ask nicely," he murmured, his voice a rumbling burr of sound. "And I'll give you what you want. What you need."

"Aden," she whispered, the words scraping against her dry throat. "Go fuck yourself."

His chuckle in response was far too happy. As if he'd hoped she'd defy him.

"Bad girl," he hissed directly into her ear.

She heard the swish of the flogger before she felt the sting of its kiss. Her pussy clenched, and she could only groan, her back arching as she offered herself, her body begging for what her brain refused to admit.

"Pink and pretty," Aden crooned, and then the whip swished again, on her other butt cheek. "Mmm," he said appreciatively. "Lovely."

"Aden," she said, trying not to whine.

"Yes, Sidonie?"

Sid swallowed the knot of desire choking her throat, every nerve in her body stretched thin, hanging on the precipice and screaming for release. "I really need—"

She didn't have a chance to finish her sentence. One of Aden's strong hands flattened on her lower back, holding her in place, and then his cock was slamming into her, a long hard thrust that went deeper than she would have thought possible. She felt him all the way to her womb, all the way to her heart, as he thrust in and out in a steady rhythm, as she pressed her chest into the bed and arched her back, inviting him to go deeper still.

Aden fisted a hand in her long hair, wrapping it around his fingers as he bent low over her back and tugged her head backwards, bearing her neck.

"Mine," he growled against her hot skin. And that was all the warning she got before his fangs bit into her vein, and her entire body convulsed in orgasm. She buried her scream in the bed covering, her hips bucking against him as his fingers slipped under her body and deep between her thighs, delving into her wetness until he found her clit, then stroking and pinching until Sid thought she'd die as wave after wave of sensation rolled through her body, scorching her nerves, winding her muscles so tightly she could no longer move, only feel, as Aden's thick cock continued to pound into her, as his snarl of possession shivered against her skin.

He lifted his head, his fangs sliding free of her vein, his breath a silken brush over the flushed skin of her neck.

"Say it," he demanded, his tongue roughly licking her wounds closed.

Sid had trouble making sense of his words, her mind fogged with bliss, her synapses overwhelmed with sensation.

Aden's hand came down sharply on her ass, and she moaned.

"Say it," he repeated.

She thought hard, then finally realized what he wanted.

"Yours," she agreed, panting. "I'm yours."

Aden's roar of climax sounded like a shout of victory, his hot release filling her, setting off a final orgasm that left her overcome by too many emotions, too many feelings all crowding together, all demanding that she feel at the same time.

Aden collapsed over her sweaty back, breathing deeply as he sucked in oxygen, one arm braced to her side, the other stroking her face tenderly.

"Breathe, *habibi*," he murmured, his tongue brushing her cheek, tasting her tears.

Sid nodded and tried to concentrate on just that. Breathing. Inhale, exhale. Slow and steady.

"What does that mean?" she managed to ask, then drew in another lungful of air. "That word you call me."

"It has different meanings, but for you, it means *sweetheart*."

"*Habibi,*" she repeated, testing the syllables.

"Hmm," he agreed. Sliding a muscled arm around her waist, he dragged them both farther up onto the bed, settling against the pillows with her a limp weight against his side.

"I want you to stay here today," he told her. "It's not safe for you out there."

"You mean because Silas sent that guy on the train, but I don't get it," Sid said fretfully. "What would she want with me?"

"I've never kept a woman around before. Maybe she thinks I like you."

"So, I'm the only one?"

"Stop fishing, Sidonie. What do you need to know?"

Sid found enough energy to drape herself over his chest, so that their eyes were more or less even, his expression filled with a patient humor that made her want to bite something, *him* for starters. She blinked at the thought. She'd never been a biter before she met Aden. Come to think of it, she'd never done a lot of things before she met Aden. This bad boy fling was turning out to be a lot more than she thought. The question was, what did *Aden* think it was, and was Sidonie about to get her heart broken?

"Okay," she said, hoping she looked more alert than she felt. "I like you. Probably more than I should, given your . . . dangerous profession."

Aden laughed out loud. "Is that what we're calling it? My *dangerous profession?*"

Sid slapped his chest. "Don't make fun. What would you like me to call it?"

"I'm a vampire, Sidonie. Violence is in my nature. If that makes me dangerous—and it fucking well does—I make no apologies."

"I don't want an apology. I like you the way you are."

"You like the violence. You're as bloody-minded as I am. It's an unexpected bonus in such a wholesome all-American girl."

"Most people would consider it sick, not a bonus."

"I'm not most people."

"That's for sure. So what is this, then? Am I the flavor of the month?"

"Oh, surely longer than that. At least six weeks."

"Aden!" she protested. "I'm being serious here."

"So you are." He stroked his hand over her face, lifting the heavy weight of her sweaty hair and brushing it back over her shoulder. "I don't think in forever terms, *habibi*. Forever is a very long time for a vampire. But I find myself uncommonly attached to you. And when I think about some other man so much as touching your hand, I want to rip his heart out. Will that do?"

Sid smiled happily, then stretched up to kiss his mouth. She intended it to be quick, but as always Aden had his own plans. One hand on the nape of her neck, he wrapped the other around her back and held her in place, taking the kiss deeper, his tongue twisting around hers, tasting every inch of her mouth until Sid felt an impossibly powerful desire rising once again. She moaned as Aden closed his teeth over her lower lip.

"It's late," he murmured. "The sun is nearly here."

Sid voiced a wordless protest. She didn't want to give him up to the sun or anything else.

Aden rolled her beneath him with a rumbling growl, his fingers going unerringly to her drenched pussy. Sid flexed her hips, thrusting against his hand in a silent demand, spreading her legs wider when his clever fingers dipped into her sex, his thumb circling the tight bud of her clit. She started to grab his hand, although whether it was to crush him against her vulnerable flesh or to pull him away, she couldn't have said.

It didn't matter, because Aden bit down on her lip with a snarled warning.

Sid cried out in protest, but slid her hand along his powerful arm, stroking the smooth muscle up to this thick shoulder, before threading her fingers through his hair. Their kiss became deeper, more frantic as he continued to stroke her, as her pussy began to tighten around his fingers. Her clit was unbearably sensitive, every caress of his thumb sending a fresh jolt of pleasure, turning her nipples into hard pearls of exquisite sensation as they rubbed against the rough hair on his chest.

The orgasm rolled over her like a wave, unstoppable even if she'd tried. Aden's fingers continued to fuck her, his thumb a constant pressure against her clit, until the wave crashed, and she screamed into his mouth, her back bowing off the bed with the force of her climax, his weight the only thing keeping her from thrashing off the bed.

Aden kissed her, swallowing her screams, and when her screams turned to tears because it was all too much—too much sensation, too much love, damn it—he swallowed her cries, too, kissing away her tears as she held on to him, not wanting to let go.

He held her as she drowsed in his arms, until in the distance, from down the long hallway, she heard the distinctive trilling of the elevator bell as the doors closed, and the car dropped to the fifth floor for the day.

Aden brushed the sweaty mess of her hair away from her face. "This room will lock soon, Sidonie."

Her eyes struggled to open. "Will I be stuck here?" she mumbled, half asleep.

"No," he said, laughing a little. "You can stay here as long as you want. You can shower . . ."

Her eyes flashed open to see if he was being snarky with the shower comment. He winked at her, which could have meant almost anything, but she was too tired to figure it out and way too tired to do anything about it anyway.

"Take your time," he continued. "But once you leave my suite, you won't be able to get back in until sunset. So be certain you have everything you need."

"Mmkay," she murmured, ready to go back to sleep.

"Sidonie, are you listening? Open your eyes."

She forced her eyelids up and stared at him.

He didn't even pretend not to laugh this time, which told her how she must look. She scowled at him, and his expression became deadly serious, but she didn't think it had anything to do with her scowl.

"This is important," he said, holding her chin in his fingers and forcing her to meet his eyes. "Don't leave the office. You can use the computers, the phones, whatever you like. Hamilton and his security team will be manning the fifth floor, so you'll be safe up here. Do you understand?"

She nodded.

"Say it."

"I understand," she said grumpily, jerking her chin away from his fingers. "You haven't *completely* fucked my brains out, you know."

"Not yet," he murmured, smiling. "It's time, *habibi*. Kiss me good night."

She wrapped her arms around his neck and kissed him, soft and seductive, putting everything she was feeling, everything she couldn't say out loud, into the kiss. "Good night, Aden," she whispered, then jumped in surprise as the shields came down over the door in the next room.

She laughed nervously, feeling silly for reacting, but Aden only smiled. He pulled the covers out from underneath them, until they were both lying on the clean sheets of the bed, and then he settled back against the pillows and closed his eyes.

Between one breath and the next, she knew he was . . . gone. Not dead. Just no longer there.

Sid watched him for a long time. He was still breathing, although not as deeply, nor as often. She put her ear to his chest and heard his heart beating very slowly, but with a steady, strong rhythm.

Somewhere out there, the sun was shining, trapping their enemies in their holes. But she and Aden and the others were here. And they were safe, for one more day.

She believed that. She really did.

Chapter Sixteen

SID KICKED BACK on the leather couch in front of the TV, laptop in front of her, a bottle of cold water and an energy bar close at hand. One thing Aden hadn't thought of, when telling her she should stay here for the day, was the food selection in the office. Human food, that was.

There was plenty of booze to be had. Apparently vampires drank like fish. Who knew?

There was also an entire shelf of bottled water in the big refrigerator which took up most of the floor space in the office's tiny kitchen. The rest of the shelves were stacked with bags of blood, the kind you'd find in a blood bank. Sid wondered what their supply chain was. Dresner had told her that people volunteered at the nightclub-like blood houses, partying with vamps and letting them drink from the vein. But where'd the rest of this come from? She pictured a special room in every vampire-owned nightclub, with a staff of trained phlebotomists always ready, just waiting for donations. Cookies and orange juice available.

Sid chuckled. It was kind of funny, but also probably not far from the truth. Come to think of it, she wouldn't have minded some of those cookies and orange juice right about now. She'd found a lone bag of stale chips that must have been left behind by someone months ago.

Thank God for her backpack and its supply of energy bars, but by the time sunset rolled around, she'd be making a beeline to the nearest restaurant and some real food.

In the meantime, she was making do. She'd showered and changed, feeling every strained muscle, every bit of deliciously tender flesh. There was a unique soreness to a woman's body after sex, muscles used, secret places rubbed and invaded. Sid wasn't an innocent; she had prior experience of that soreness. But never like this. Sex with Aden was like nothing she'd ever known before, nothing she'd ever thought existed. And she could hardly wait to do it all over again.

She smiled to herself, wishing she could be there when Aden woke, imagining his eyes opening, his broad chest expanding as his lungs drew their first deep breath of the night. And then he'd roll over and wrap her in his big arms, tucking her beneath his body, one thigh slipping between hers, the weight of his cock against her thigh . . .

She sucked in a deep breath of her own. She felt herself growing wet, her pussy aching as she remembered the feel of Aden's thick shaft sliding in and out.

"Jesus, Sid, get a grip," she muttered and forced her attention back to her computer screen and the article she was writing about hidden slavery in America. That was a splash of cold water on any arousal she'd been feeling. This was the reason she was here. Meeting Aden had been an amazing bit of luck all around, but her purpose in getting inside the world of vampires had been to expose their illicit business practices.

Had been being the operative words there. She'd had every intention of rousing the peasants with their torches and pitchforks, of dragging Klemens into the light and letting him burn. But now it was Aden she'd be exposing, and that wasn't going to happen. Whatever sins he might be guilty of, selling women into slavery definitely wasn't one of them. He'd been ruthless the other night in killing every one of the slavers, but when it came to the slaves themselves, he'd shown tremendous care. Knowing his background, it made sense to her, but not everyone would have come out of his horrific experience with compassion for others. Studies had shown over and over again that some of the worst abusers had been abused themselves. It spoke to Aden's strength of character that he chose to protect the weak instead.

But Sid's story still needed to be told. Americans needed to know what was going on under their noses. Maybe she could play down the vampire angle. The fact that the slave ring had been controlled by vampires wasn't that important in the overall scheme of things. There had been plenty of humans down the food chain, too.

Her cell phone rang, and she glanced over. It was her oldest brother again. He'd been calling ever since the weekend, wanting to know what was up with her, why she'd left not just the party but the whole town so suddenly. She wondered what he'd say if she told him the truth, that she was shacked up with a vampire, and not just any vampire, but the next Lord of the Midwest. He'd probably send the men with their white jackets after her.

Sid touched the side of her neck. It was tender, but the wounds were almost gone. If she hadn't been so pale, there'd probably be nothing left to see, no evidence of a vampire's bite at all.

Her phone was still ringing. Two more rings, and it would go to voice mail. She should really answer this time. If her brother Jamie didn't hear her voice soon, he'd get someone to knock on her condo door. And when no one answered the door, he'd get the super involved. Jamie took his responsibilities as the oldest child very seriously. Particularly when it came to his baby sister.

She exhaled a long-suffering sigh and took the call.

"Hey, Jamie."

"About damn time," he shouted. "You disappear from the party and then don't even bother to answer the phone?"

"I'm sorry. Didn't you get my e-mail?"

"Seriously, Sid? I've been calling for two days."

"I'm sorry," she repeated. "You know how I get when I'm finishing a story."

He grunted wordlessly, but said, "So the slave story's almost done?"

"Almost," she agreed.

"You'll be coming back home then?"

That had been Sid's plan all along. Her move to Chicago was supposed to be temporary. A few months to write a story about drugs and violence, then back home to the suburbs. But the drug story had become a slavery story, and then Janey had died, and the slavery story had become a crusade to shut the whole ugly thing down. And now it was almost two years since she'd left her parents' safe and cozy suburb for the wilds of the big city.

If Jamie had asked her that same question two weeks ago, she'd have told him, *yes*, that she was leaving Chicago and coming home soon. Her condo lease was up in a month, and she'd have been more than ready to get out of the big city and back to the quiet comfort of her parents' suburb. There'd been nothing keeping her here.

But now that she'd met Aden, the idea of leaving Chicago made her chest hurt, because it meant leaving *him*. And she didn't know if she could do that.

"I don't know," she answered Jamie's question honestly.

"Mom misses you, you know. So does Dad, but Mom especially."

"I know, and I'm sorry. But . . . I haven't decided yet."

"Hmm. I hear Will's getting married," he ventured carefully, as if testing the waters.

"That's not the reason I'm staying in Chicago, Jamie," she told him patiently. "Will and I haven't been a couple for a long time."

"Just thought I'd check. I'd hate to break the guy's bones, but you know I would if he hurt you."

"Will would never hurt me." She didn't add that that was part of the problem, that Will was simply too *nice,* just like every other man she'd met until now. She hadn't realized it herself until she'd met Aden. Apparently, she needed a man with an edge.

"Okay, well . . . I'll be in town next week," Jamie told her. "We can do lunch, or dinner. You can cook for me."

Sid made a dismissive noise. "Yeah, right. You can take me *out,* how's that?"

"How're you ever going to get a husband if you don't cook, baby girl?"

"Who says I'm looking for one?"

"Mom wants grandbabies."

"Mom's got two perfectly good sons who can pop them out for her." She paused. "Unless you've got something to tell me? Maybe the popping doesn't work so well?"

"Fuck you."

"Now that's just sick."

"Jesus, Sid, that's disgusting. You've been hanging around the wrong class of people for too long."

"Maybe."

"Look, I've got to go, but we'll definitely get together next week, okay?"

"Sure. Call me when you get here, we'll work something out."

"Love you."

"Love you, too." Sid disconnected, then put her computer aside and sat up, feeling suddenly restless. Maybe it was the call from her brother, trying to drag her back within the circled wagons. If it were up to her family, Sid would never leave the suburbs. She'd get married and have a few grandchildren for her mom to spoil, if not with Will, then with someone equally suitable. Suitable meaning one of their own—white, educated, and moneyed. She didn't know how much formal education Aden had, but he clearly had plenty of money. On the other hand, she was pretty sure *suitable* didn't include a vampire, no matter what.

Needing to stretch some of her sex-sore muscles, and desperate to think of something besides her immediate future, she grabbed a bottle of water and headed for the hallway. Aden's office was one of three interconnected rooms, with the receptionist area the only one with a door to the hallway. The other two rooms opened off the receptionist area, with Aden's office the largest of the three and the only one with windows. The lounging area where she'd been hanging out was the other room, with its small kitchen area and man-cave ambience.

Walking out into the hallway, Sid paused and glanced in both directions. Aden's suite, and what she assumed were the apartments of his other vampires, were all to her right, secured behind the heavy red doors. At the other end, to Sid's left was the elevator, and that was it. As she stood there, she was abruptly struck by the nearly total silence. No phones rang, no music played. There was the quiet rush of air that was the heating system, but nothing else.

She felt suddenly very alone. And very vulnerable. Not simply for her own sake, but for Aden and the other vampires. There was a war of sorts going on in this city. Call it a challenge or a competition, but vampires were dying left and right. What if one of Aden's enemies decided to play dirty and attack during the day? Did the vampire culture have rules about these things? This was the sort of question she might have asked Professor Dresner not long ago. But for now, she had to rely on her own judgment, and her head was telling her that if, by some chance, any enemies managed to get to this floor, Aden had no one but her standing between him and disaster.

She spun around and headed for her backpack, which she'd left in the lounge area. She hadn't told Aden about her gun, thinking he wouldn't have approved. Besides, he'd only have insisted he didn't need her protection, because his security measures would hold, what with Earl Hamilton guarding the fifth floor and the private elevator locked down. But empires had been lost because the loser believed himself invulnerable, and Sid had studied enough to know that *no one* was perfectly safe. If the attackers were willing to die, anybody could be gotten to. And if Sid had learned one thing about vampires, it was that their followers would do *anything* for their vampire master . . . or mistress.

Crossing to her backpack, she pulled out her subcompact 9mm Glock. It didn't look like much compared to the big Glocks, but it was enough to stop a human, and since the sun was high in the sky, that was all she'd have to worry about. After dark, Aden didn't need her little firepower. He was more than capable of defending himself.

Shoving her shirt up and her jeans down, she wrapped the bellyband around her waist, then pulled everything back into place. She'd originally chosen the bellyband holster because she didn't want to advertise the fact that she was armed. With the lower edge of the bellyband tucked beneath the waistband of her pants, and her usual fleece hoodie adding another layer of concealment, no one would know she was carrying unless they took the time to pat her down. And if someone had enough control over her that they were patting her down, the fight was probably already over.

Checking the ten-round magazine, she slammed it home, then worked the slide, chambering a round. Going *hot* was what her firearms instructor had called it. It saved a few seconds on the first round, and a few seconds, he'd emphasized, might be all she had.

Sliding the Glock into the elastic, and putting her spare mag into its own special pocket, she pulled her long-sleeved T-shirt over it, but left her hoodie unzipped for now. Feeling slightly gunfighterish, she paced back to the hallway and down to the elevator, where she spent a few minutes staring up at the floor display, until the steadily lit number "1" began to flicker in her sight. She blinked rapidly and decided it wasn't going to change. No one was storming the battlements, at least not while she stood there waiting. And besides, she was getting hungry again, and she'd left her pitiful allotment of energy bars on the coffee table in the lounge area.

Grabbing a fresh bottle of the water from the fridge, she settled back on the big leather couch and squirmed around a bit, before finally finding a position where the gun didn't dig into her belly or scrape against her hip bone. She unwrapped the first energy bar, flipped on the TV, and felt her eyes begin to droop almost immediately. She hadn't gotten more than an hour's sleep last night. Setting aside the tasteless energy bar, she settled into the thick pillows and let sleep take her.

Sid came awake with a jolt, her heart racing as she stared at the unfamiliar room, taking in the giant TV screen which currently showed a bunch of hyperactive game show contestants celebrating mutely. Aden's office, she remembered. She was in Aden's office, and something had woken her. She sat up and checked the time on her cell phone. It was barely noon. Long hours stretched ahead of her, and she was beginning to hate the isolation of being locked in here.

She was reaching for her bottle of water, her fingers not yet touching the plastic, when she heard the very last sound she'd expected to hear. The elevator dinged faintly, as if the car was on its way up and she was hearing its progress through the lower floors. Was that what had woken her? It was so quiet in here that the smallest noise would seem loud.

She stood, listening. And heard it again. Maybe the elevator was simply moving up and down between the lower floors. Maybe she'd misunderstood what Aden had said about the car being locked down. Or maybe Earl Hamilton was coming up for some reason. Yes, that was probably it. Maybe he knew she was here and was checking on her.

Smoothing her T-shirt down and patting the gun for reassurance, she walked softly through the receptionist area and back to the hallway, where she paused. Sticking just her head through the doorway, she peeked down at the elevator and waited.

Nothing. Not even the earlier dinging she'd heard. That was good, right?

Feeling somewhat cowardly hanging back in the office, she ventured out into the corridor. Sticking close to the wall with the elevator on it, one hand running along the smooth surface, she approached the elevator cautiously. She could hear the hum of the car's movement, the rumbling slide of the thick cables.

Standing there next to the elevator, she cursed herself for an idiot. She should have called Hamilton from the office. He was probably on speed dial, or if not, she had his number stored in her cell from the other morning.

She was just turning to head back for the office when the thunk of an arriving car froze her in her tracks. She backed away, staring, afraid to breathe as she watched the elevator doors slide almost soundlessly open.

Men poured out of the elevator, their faces and clothes bloodied, guns much bigger than hers already in their hands. She screamed, her hand going to the flat bulge of her gun, but it was too little, too late. One of them swung a closed fist, striking her hard enough that she spun around and slammed face-first into the wall just outside the elevator. She tasted blood in the back of her throat and felt her nose swelling shut from the force of the blow. Behind her, someone grabbed her by the hair and yanked, torqueing her neck as he pulled her back to her feet and held her upright. Someone else wrenched her hands behind her back and zipped a plastic tie around her wrists, jerking it so tight that the plastic band cut into her skin. She barely had a chance to cry out before a wet cloth was pressed against her mouth. Unable to breathe through her swollen nose, Sid sucked in a breath through her mouth and nearly choked on the sharp, acrid taste, fighting not to throw up. Primitive instinct had her drawing a second breath, and stars dotted the blackness behind her eyelids.

Her last thought was that they wanted her alive, and that was a good thing. But she couldn't remember why.

Chapter Seventeen

ADEN WOKE TO a rare fury. His eyes opened, and he leapt from the bed, swallowing his howl of rage as he scanned the empty room, searching for whatever danger had his fangs splitting his gums, his fingers curling into claws. Nothing. The room was dark and silent. Searching farther, he sought out and found all four of his offspring, each just beginning to wake as the sun dropped deeper below the horizon.

He straightened from his defensive crouch, his heartbeat slowing to normal and his breathing evening out as the adrenaline drained away. He glanced over at the empty bed and thought of Sidonie. Reaching out again, he exerted his power in a search of the offices beyond the safety of his rooms, seeking the frail beat of her human heart.

She wasn't there. Or she wasn't alive.

Grabbing a pair of sweats on the fly, he ran for the door and input the release code, pulling the pants on as the shutters retracted slowly, as the bolts slid into the wall with the heavy thunk of solid steel. He didn't wait, but ducked under the still-moving shutters as soon as the bolts were clear and the door could open.

The smell of blood hit him like a cudgel, knocking him back half a step before he raced down the hall and slammed through the security doors, following a scent he knew well. He'd taken Sidonie's blood. It flowed through his veins, it pulsed in his heart. Her scent drew him not to the office as he expected but all the way to the end of the hallway, to the closed doors of the elevator and the smear of her blood on the wall.

The phone started ringing as he crouched down. Sidonie's blood was in the carpet, too, and it wasn't alone. There was other blood there. Human blood, and more than one person. But the scent was too faint to tell him who or even how many, as if they'd carried the blood on their clothes and lost only trace amounts when they struggled . . . with Sidonie.

He closed his eyes and tried to reconstruct what had happened, using only what his nose could tell him.

The phone stopped ringing. He heard an authoritative voice leaving a message, but didn't bother to listen to the words. Nearly silent footsteps and the unique awareness of his offspring informed him that Bastien was awake and functioning and now stood in the office doorway, listening to the message.

That same awareness told him a moment later that his lieutenant had come into the hallway and was waiting.

"What is it, Bastien?" Aden asked quietly, as he dipped his fingers in Sidonie's blood.

"That was the police, Sire. The caller didn't say so, but the lobby doorman is dead. I heard someone else discussing it in the background. They're interviewing tenants and are very unhappy that they cannot access our two penthouse floors."

"Where's Hamilton?" Kage asked, loping down the hall in time to hear Bastien's statement.

That was the question, Aden thought to himself. Where was his daylight security chief, and why wasn't he the one who'd called to report instead of the police?

"The invaders were here," Aden said, standing and eyeing the blood smeared on his fingers. "They took Sidonie."

He turned to face his people, all four of whom now stood in the hallway, watching him with identical expressions—puzzlement and anger, but no fear, he was proud to see. They had confidence in him, in his ability to protect them and to kill whoever had dared orchestrate this brazen attack. Vampires didn't send minions to attack in daylight. It was one of their few taboos. And to do it during a territorial competition was unheard of.

"We need to check on Hamilton and the others," he told them.

"And the police?" Bastien asked.

"For all they know, we haven't risen yet. Let them wait. Let's go."

They took the stairs down the single flight to the floor where Aden's daylight security people bunked when on duty. Travis went through the door first, shoving it open hard enough to crash into the wall and rushing through in a burst of vampire speed. The one thing that was certain was that the invaders had been human. If any had still been lurking, waiting to catch Aden and his people unawares, they would have been unable to track Travis's movement.

But there was no one there. Aden knew that as soon as the door opened. The scent of blood had grown stronger with every step he took. And now, he was nearly blown back by the stench. It was more than blood. It was a smell he hadn't experienced in more than a hundred years, the reek of a human battlefield—sweat and blood, and over it all the stink of bowels gutted or released in death.

"Spread out," Aden ordered. "Save anyone you can, and don't forget to wipe their memories after. Yell if you need me. And find Hamilton."

He followed his own orders, going from man to man, rendering aid, slicing his wrist and dripping blood into their mouths to accelerate healing where possible. Closing their eyes and offering a word to whatever gods were listening when it was too late for anything else.

"My lord!" Kage called. "I've got Hamilton."

Aden strode down the hallway to the control room, where video feeds showed him the lobby and every door in the building. Earl Hamilton lay on the floor against the far wall. Kage stood, making room for Aden at the injured man's side. It was obvious that Hamilton had taken the brunt of the attackers' rage. He'd been the only one with access to the sixth floor during daylight—the elevator and stairs having separate but equally complex codes—and the invaders had tortured him to get it. Every finger was broken, the joints swollen and bloodied where they'd used something like a hammer to do the breaking. Hamilton's face was so badly beaten, he was barely recognizable, and they'd stabbed him multiple times, as if they'd tried to kill him once they had what they wanted.

"Earl," Aden said, stroking a hand over the human's forehead and using his power over human minds to ease the man's agony. It took all of Aden's considerable control to kneel there, sending waves of reassurance and calm, while a part of him kept imagining Sidonie's pale skin and delicate bones, her lovely face. Kept imagining her at the mercy of men who were capable of this kind of brutality.

He wanted to rage to the heavens, to hunt down whoever had done this and to do to them a hundredfold what they'd done to Hamilton and the others. And he desperately wanted to find Sidonie and bring her back to safety.

But first he owed a debt to Earl Hamilton. Using his fangs, he sliced his wrist open and put it against Hamilton's mouth, urging the man to drink his fill.

"My lord," Bastien cautioned. "Let me give him my blood. If Silas is behind this, she may use the confusion to challenge—"

Aden gave him a cold look. "Every one of these men offered his life in my defense. If I can help them, my blood is theirs."

"Of course, my lord."

"See to the others, Bastien. No one else dies."

"And those who are already dead?"

Aden closed his eyes against the unexpected pain. He'd employed guards for decades, but he'd always considered daylight security to be more for appearances than necessity. He'd trusted his electronic locks and his vault doors to keep him safe. He'd never considered the possibility that any of his daylight guards would need to die on his behalf.

"We treat them with honor. Call the funeral home, you know which one. And notify their families. We'll cover all expenses—"

"Their employment contracts cover that, my lord, as well as compensation to the families."

"For all the good it will do them," Aden muttered.

"Forgive me, my lord, but you need to speak to the police."

Aden gazed down at Hamilton. The healing benefits of Aden's blood were already obvious. It would take days for the man to heal, but he was breathing more easily, and his color was improving. If Aden had been willing to give him even more blood, he would have healed in hours rather than days. But Bastien was right. Whoever had done this wasn't finished. And if the perpetrator was Silas, she could be planning to challenge him while he was weak or distracted.

Aden stood. Silas didn't know him very well, if she thought this was enough to weaken him.

"Bastien, you're with me. We'll talk to the police." They walked out into the main room. "The rest of you, clean this up. I'll make sure the police remain downstairs"—another way of saying he'd nudge the human investigators' minds in the right direction—"but I want these men moved to their bunks to recover. The bodies can be put in one of the side rooms for now, until the funeral home picks them up. And, Trav, get the appropriate cleaning crew in here. Make sure they arrive after the police are gone. And someone start checking the video feed of the lobby."

He looked down at the sweatpants which was all he had on. They were covered in blood and wholly unsuitable.

"I need to change clothes." He glanced at Bastien who was similarly half-dressed. "You, too. We need to make an impression. We will assure them that our security was never breached, and that we will, of course, cooperate fully."

Aden raced up the stairs with Bastien in his wake, forcing himself to focus on the details of what needed to be done right now in order to protect himself and his vampires. Entering his suite, he shoved aside the rage that was eating him alive, ignored the images of Sidonie's fair skin covered in blood, her face filled with terror. It wouldn't do her any good for him to storm all over the city in a fruitless search. He'd taken enough of her blood that if he got close enough, he could track her.

But Chicago was a big city, and her abductors could be hiding her anywhere. She might not even be in the city any longer. He didn't know when the attack had occurred, didn't know how many hours they'd had to spirit her away, to torment her . . .

He picked up a heavy brass sculpture and threw it at the wall with such force that it hung there embedded in the plaster. He stared, not seeing it, his fists clenched with the need to hit something, some*one*. When he found whoever was behind this, their life would become nothing but pain. They would live a very long time, and every moment of it would be spent learning what it meant to defy a vampire lord, to take from him the only woman in his entire long life that he'd ever cared for. The only woman who'd ever honestly cared for *him*.

Turning away from the destroyed wall, he dressed quickly, pausing only to eye his reflection in the mirror, to straighten his tie and button the double-breasted jacket. The police were expecting a vampire, fangs and all. He'd give them a solid citizen, a businessman who was shocked at the intrusion of violence into his ordered life.

And if they didn't believe that, he'd wipe their minds until they couldn't remember what they'd had for breakfast. He didn't have time for this shit. Someone had broken every rule of vampire society, someone had *taken his Sidonie*, and they would pay before the sun rose in the morning.

SIDONIE TWISTED and yanked at the plastic ties binding her wrists until her skin was slick with blood, but she couldn't get them off. Maybe if she'd had something sharp to cut them with, some edge she could use, but there was nothing. They'd tossed her into the trunk of a car, closed the lid, and taken off. The trunk was airless and reeked of exhaust fumes and something dead. The smell was nauseating, and she was fighting a constant battle against the urge to vomit, which could be fatal since her mouth was taped over, and she'd watched enough crime shows to know she would choke to death.

She didn't know how long she'd been stuck in this damn trunk. She'd faded out more than once, maybe from the fumes, or maybe from the blow to her head when they'd first taken her. But it left her unsure as to how long they'd been traveling. She only knew it was long enough for her to wonder where she'd gone wrong, how she'd found herself tied up and in the trunk of a car.

She sighed. It would be easy to blame Aden, but it wasn't his fault. Her current predicament was the multiplied effect of so many choices made over the years, beginning with her decision to forego the usual hometown stories of pancake breakfasts and basketball heroes in favor of pursuing what she considered serious journalism. Stories that could make a difference. She'd made a difference all right. Janey was dead, and she was probably going to join her before the night was over.

Was it even night yet? It had been full daylight when they'd taken her. She'd been half out of it from whatever had been on the wet rag they'd slapped over her face, but she remembered that much. The sun had still been shining when they'd dragged her out a back door and into the alley behind Aden's building.

Her heart lurched in a sudden burst of fresh fear. Aden. She had to believe he was okay, that the intruders had never made it past the last, and most hardened, layers of his security. She didn't think they'd had time, and besides, why take her if they had Aden?

But what would he think when he woke and found her gone? Would he find her blood on the wall where she'd hit her face? Or had her abductors cleaned that up, leaving him to wonder what had happened? Would he think she'd run? That she'd left him? Tears filled her eyes at the thought. Every woman in his life had betrayed him. But Sid hadn't. She wouldn't. Did he understand that?

Sid swallowed her tears, forced herself to think with her brain instead of her heart. She didn't think Aden would believe she'd run. And even if he did, he'd find her. Aden wasn't the kind of man a woman walked out on—he was the kind of man who made sure *he* did the walking. So, he'd come looking for her, even if it was only to dump her.

A new horrible thought struck her. What if that was what her abductors wanted? What if she was bait for a trap to catch Aden? She couldn't let that happen. She *wouldn't* let that happen.

She sighed, or she tried to. It was difficult with tape over her mouth and a nose that was so swollen she could barely breathe. Still, big words from the little lady all tied up in the trunk. She shifted awkwardly, but there was no comfortable way to lie scrunched up in this small space with her hands bound behind her back. They could have at least kidnapped her in a bigger car. Her head throbbed, her shoulders ached, and there was a hard something digging into the side of her belly. She tried moving again, but the hard thing kept digging . . . Sid froze. The hard thing was her gun! They must not have searched her, or at least not very well. The knowledge made her more determined than ever to get her hands free, but it didn't make it easier. The more she struggled, the deeper the plastic seemed to bury itself in her skin.

She made a frustrated sound behind the thick tape then forced herself to calm down, to think rationally. Her gun was useless if she couldn't get to it. She still needed her hands free, but it wasn't serving any purpose for her to thrash about. She had to think smart, and that meant planning ahead. Eventually, they'd have to open the trunk and get her out of here. Even if the plan was to use her as bait, they'd have to have a place to lure Aden to, someplace better than this car. There was no way to predict where that would be, though. So, the only thing she could do for now was be ready to take advantage of whatever opportunity presented itself. As impossible as it seemed, what she needed to do now was to rest, to turn off her head and sleep.

Good luck with that, she thought. But she closed her eyes and focused on relaxing one muscle at a time, feeling the dregs of the drug still in her system, letting the exhaustion take her . . .

She jerked awake when someone pounded on the trunk lid, surprised to realize she'd actually managed to sleep. The pounding came again, simply to scare her, she thought, because a moment later a key scraped in the lock, and the lid popped open. Her first reaction was surprise that it was nearly as dark outside the trunk as it had been inside. She must have been stuck in there for hours. But her next reaction was pure relief as cold, fresh air washed over her face, and she drew a strained breath that didn't reek of fumes and death.

Her relief was short-lived as one of two men staring down at her grabbed her upper arm and dragged her from the trunk, jerking her shoulder and whacking her ankle painfully against some sort of trailer hitch on the back of the car. Her legs, cramped from too long in a small space, couldn't hold her when she tried to stand, but her abductor didn't even try to catch her. He let her fall onto an asphalt driveway, and her elbow cracked against the hard surface. Her cry of pain was muffled by the tape still covering her mouth, but at the same time she registered the fact that the tape was no longer as tight as it had been. The heat and stress of hours in the small space had left her sweaty, her face tear-streaked, and all of that had combined to loosen the tape a little. The knowledge didn't do much to free her, but it made her feel better somehow. It gave her hope.

The man gripped her arm once more, and every muscle shrieked in protest as she stumbled upright. She closed her eyes, shutting out the sight of her abductors, wishing she could shut out the whole experience as easily. Everything hurt, from her swollen nose to her right ankle and everything in between.

"Walk, bitch. I ain't carrying you."

Sid really looked at her guards for the first time. She couldn't be positive—everything had happened so fast—but she didn't think either one of these two had been among her abductors this morning. Maybe that was what had taken so long. Maybe they'd driven her around until these two could pick her up. Or maybe they'd been parked somewhere while she slept. Or, hell, maybe she was simply mistaken about who'd been in on the original kidnapping. One thing she felt sure of . . . whoever was behind all of this was waiting for her in the small clapboard house at the end of this driveway.

She swiveled her head around as much as she could. The neighborhood was familiar in a way that told her she'd either been here before, or, equally possible, she'd been to someplace just like it. Badly run-down houses were squeezed onto tiny lots and surrounded by apartment buildings in even worse shape. Cars lined both sides of the street, some up on blocks and all of them old and badly used. The street was dark, lit mostly by the light of the half moon, the street lights either shot or burned out. And it struck her. This was the same neighborhood where she'd staked out some of Klemens's drug dealers. Not *this* house, but it was close enough that it worried her.

Her captor caught her looking around and shook her like a rag doll.

"Don't be looking at my 'hood, bitch. This place got nothin' to do with you."

Black splotches swam in her vision, but Sid fought them away, determined to remain conscious. She needed to see as much as she could in order to plan her escape. Some people might consider thoughts of escape ridiculous in her current situation, but that didn't stop Sid. Situations could change. People could grow lazy or complacent and give her an opening. She wouldn't need much. Although, she thought, frowning, she *would* need to get her hands free.

That thought had a deflating effect, and for the first time since her abduction, she felt the full weight of her predicament. Her shoulders slumped dejectedly. Her captors saw and laughed as they dragged her through the side door and into the house.

The sturdy door and elaborate lock confirmed that this wasn't an ordinary house, that it was probably used by drug dealers. But Sid couldn't imagine what they'd want with her. She'd done an article or two on the drug culture in Chicago, but that had been more than a year ago, and the stories hadn't garnered enough attention to inconvenience anyone, much less do real damage.

As they hustled her through a filthy kitchen smelling of grease and old trash, however, she had a second, chilling thought. Aden had wiped out the heart of the slave network, but he hadn't caught the one vampire Sid was absolutely sure had been the driver behind the whole thing. Carl Pinto. And Klemens's slave trade had always been closely tied to his drug dealings.

She felt a tremor that started in her stomach and radiated outward, shaking her entire body before it was finished. She wanted to attribute it to the drugs they'd given her, or to the adrenaline overload, but it was fear, pure and simple. She'd seen what Pinto was capable of, his cruelty and callousness. The women he'd trafficked had been nothing but meat to him. Objects to be bought and sold, and if they weren't profitable, they were crushed and thrown away.

"That's right, bitch," her captor said, reacting to her trembling. "The man's lookin' forward to takin' care of *you*."

Sid couldn't have responded to the taunt if she'd wanted to, not with the tape still covering her mouth. As it was, however, she was too busy trying to stay on her feet, trying to come up with a scenario that didn't end up with her dead or shipped off as a slave. She was pretty sure she'd rather be dead.

"Sidonie Reid," someone growled, and she looked up to find the very vampire she'd most feared. Carl Pinto sat in a big leather chair, the only piece of furniture in the room that wasn't falling apart.

Sid swallowed hard, her heart pounding so violently that it felt like it was crawling up her throat and had to be forced back to where it belonged.

"You've caused me a lot of trouble, little girl. A lot of trouble," he repeated thoughtfully, almost as if he was talking to himself. "But no matter. I've got you now." He nodded to the guard holding her arm, and she was shoved forward and to her knees, so that she had to look up at Pinto as the tape was ripped off her mouth.

"That's better," he said, gazing down at her with cold eyes. "That's where you belong, where *all* of you belong."

"All of us," Sid croaked, ignoring the voice inside her head that was telling her to shut up. She knew that it would be smarter, but if she was going to die, she was going to go down fighting, even if all she had to fight with were her words. "You mean all of us humans, or all of us women? You have a problem with women, Pinto?"

She saw the rage fill his face seconds before he leaned over and backhanded her hard enough to spin her around and slam her to the floor. He'd used his open hand, which was the only reason she was still alive. He was a vampire. She'd have to remember that. His strength was several times that of a human. A casual slap could break her jaw. And that had been no casual slap. Her ears were still ringing, and she was having trouble seeing straight.

"Watch your mouth, whore, or I'll put it to better use."

Sid lay on the floor, blinking, trying to come up with the energy, the desire, to force herself upright, to confront this monster with whatever dignity she had left.

"Get up," Pinto demanded.

Sid made the effort, but she'd been hit twice today, both times hard enough to have her seeing stars, and it was taking longer for her to recover. That her hands were still bound behind her back didn't exactly make it any easier, either. She made a show of trying to drag herself off the floor and nearly made it before falling to her side, unable to catch herself with her hands tied.

"I like seeing you like this," Pinto said, chuckling. "Rich bitch Sidonie Reid crawling on the floor."

Sid felt the heavy weight of his booted foot against her side, digging into her ribs hard enough to hurt as he shoved her back and forth, almost idly.

"Where's your daddy's money now, bitch? It wasn't my idea to let you live, you know. That was Klemens. Didn't want to rattle the moneyed class. They're willing to overlook almost anything as long as none of theirs gets hurt. He let me take that little whore friend of yours, though. What was her name . . ." His voice trailed off, as if he was trying to remember.

Sid knew he was playing with her, but she couldn't help it. She didn't want Janey's name on this monster's lips. "Janey," she said, shocked at the raw sound of her own voice. "Her name was Janey, and you killed her."

"Didn't stop you, though, did it? You just kept coming and coming, and still Klemens wouldn't let me kill you."

She heard the squeak of leather as he rose from the chair, the scuff of his boots on the rough carpet, and then he was crouched right next to her, cruel eyes staring at her out of a face that was too handsome to be so evil.

"But Klemens is dead now, princess. And you're all mine."

Sid croaked a wordless protest, and he laughed.

"Tell you what. I'm going to do you a favor. You care so damn much about my slaves, you can fucking well join them. You're a bit older than my usual merchandise, but that red hair's worth something, and you're white. That's always a selling point. You'll fetch a nice price."

Sid saw the kick coming, but there was nothing she could do to stop his boot before it slammed into her ribs. She sucked in a shocked breath and knew he'd cracked a rib or two.

"You," he said over her head. "Take care of her. You know what to do."

"Get up," her guard ordered. He grabbed one of her bound arms and pulled her to her feet.

Sid nearly screamed with the pain, but bit her tongue to stop the sound from escaping her mouth. She wouldn't give him the satisfaction of knowing he'd hurt her.

As the guard shuffled her from the room, Pinto spoke up from behind her. "Cut the ties on her hands before you lock the door. I don't want to damage the merchandise any more than necessary, but make sure she stays put."

The guard grunted an acknowledgment as he pulled a key ring from his pocket and unlocked one of the bedroom doors. Several women were already inside, and they looked up as the door opened, their faces wearing identical expressions of fear. Sid had enough time to register their presence before she was shoved hard, just managing to keep her face from slamming into the floor as she fell. The guard snorted a laugh as he knelt next to her, one heavy hand gripping her thigh, pinching it as if testing for tenderness. She tried to roll away from him, feeling something close to horror at the idea that he might rape her, knowing she'd fight with everything she had to stop him, and knowing it might not be enough. The guard grinned, as if her pitiful efforts amused him. Rolling her onto her stomach, he shoved her face into the rough carpet and held her there with a knee in the middle of her back. There was a tug on her bound wrists, and then, with a snap of released plastic, her hands were suddenly free.

Sid couldn't stop a cry of misery as blood flowed back into her hands and fingers, as strained muscles struggled to return to their rightful configuration. She lay on her side, gasping for breath, her sore hands curled protectively against her chest, her entire body shrieking with pain. But despite it all, a surge of adrenaline whipped through her system, making her heart pound with triumph.

She had her gun. And her hands were finally free. Things were looking up.

BEFORE THE ELEVATOR doors opened onto the lobby, Aden smelled more blood. It was nowhere near the slaughter that had greeted him upstairs. This was one man. He knew that before he saw the police gathered around the doorman's body in its dark blue blazer. Humans swarmed the scene, technicians gathering every bit of evidence they could find. It wouldn't do them any good, Aden thought. Whichever vampire had set this in motion would see to it that no one survived to testify to the event.

"Mister Aden?" A human male wearing a suit that cost less than the shirt and tie Aden was wearing approached him warily. He met Aden's eyes only briefly before quickly looking away. Many humans believed a vampire could only influence a mind if they met the person's eyes. That might be true of a lesser vampire, one who needed the contact to reinforce his control. But it was definitely not true of one with Aden's power and ability. He didn't correct the detective, however. The mistaken belief served vampire interests well.

"I am Aden," he acknowledged, scanning the scene. "How did he die?" he asked, although he already knew. He could smell the gunpowder.

The detective didn't answer his question, but posed one of his own instead, intent on taking charge of the conversation. "Where were you between ten and noon this morning?"

Aden gave the man a patient look. "I am a vampire, Detective . . ."

"Trevisani," the man supplied.

"Detective Trevisani. I assure you that I and my staff were quite incapable of rising from our beds when this was happening." He could feel Bastien's growing tension, his aggression simmering just under the surface, heightened by the blood here and upstairs, and by what he perceived as a threat to his Sire. He was a good lieutenant, disciplined and highly skilled. But having his Sire's territory invaded while they'd slept unknowing only yards away, and now with this human policeman all but accusing Aden of the crime . . . it was enough to strain the mettle of the most restrained of vampires.

To his credit, Trevisani had the grace to look embarrassed at his gaffe. Obviously, a vampire hadn't killed the doorman. That didn't mean a vampire hadn't been behind it, however, and the good detective was both smart enough to know that and confident enough not to be cowed by his initial mistake.

"Granted," he said, nodding. "But you own the top two floors of this building."

"I do."

"And my sources tell me there's some big vampire meeting in the city this week."

Well, that was interesting, Aden thought. The Vampire Council didn't exactly maintain secrecy about their affairs. It would have been impossible given the sheer number of participants staying in town, not to mention the gala itself, which had drawn some attention. But the detective's comment made Aden suspect that it went beyond idle curiosity, that perhaps the Chicago police had spies within vampire society in the city. He'd have to remember that when he became Lord of the Midwest.

"That's true," Aden said, agreeing without providing details.

Trevisani grunted. "I'm thinking maybe this attack had something to do with you personally."

"It was not a vampire who did this," Aden said confidently. "It clearly happened in full daylight—"

"Could be a hit team hired by a vamp," Trevisani interrupted to say.

Aden smiled patiently. "As I was saying . . . vampires do not attack each other in daylight. It's forbidden by custom, and the repercussions for any vampire who dared would be significant."

"So who hates you enough to pay the price?"

Aden huffed a humorless laugh. "I have many enemies, Detective, but I do not believe this was aimed at me. There was no attempt to breach my security."

"The elevator was open when we got here, and there's blood inside."

Aden didn't say anything to that. There had been no question posed, and it was always better, when dealing with authorities of any kind, not to volunteer information. Besides, what could he say? That he didn't need anyone to tell him there was blood, that he could smell it for himself? He doubted the detective would find that reassuring.

Trevisani waited, studying Aden's face for any indication of guilt.

Aden gazed back unflinchingly. He'd faced down far more dangerous opponents than this human detective.

"All right," Trevisani conceded. "We're just about done here." He gestured at two men who were cloaking the body in a black body bag and zipping it up. "This building's a co-op, isn't it? You'll want to hire a special team to clean this up. If you call the district, they can give you a referral." He tucked away the small memo pad and pen he'd been using for notes. "In the meantime, I'll need your contact information in case something comes up."

Aden reached into his jacket pocket and handed over one of his business cards.

The detective read it carefully, then nodded his acceptance, not understanding that his thoughts were no longer his own, that Aden had been slowly, unobtrusively, working his way into the detective's mind.

"I'll send you a copy of my report in the morning," Trevisani said. "I have to say, though, my gut's telling me this was a hate crime. You're just lucky they didn't make it upstairs."

Aden held back his smile. The detective had proven to be quite strong-willed, but Aden supposed that was to be expected given his line of work. The challenge, as always, had been taking over the man's mind without him sensing the intrusion. He could have achieved the same result much more quickly, if he hadn't cared about leaving the mind intact.

Normally, Aden would have relished the challenge of manipulating such a strong-willed human, but tonight it had taken all of his considerable self-control to hold back his impatience. He didn't want to be here bandying words with a human police detective. He wanted to be out there hunting down whoever had been so brazen as to attack Aden's lair in broad daylight, and so stupid that he'd left behind a body for the human authorities to find. It wasn't only Aden who would come down on the instigator for this, the entire Vampire Council would crush him.

"We'll talk, Detective Trevisani," Aden said, then dismissed him from his mind as the human gathered up his remaining crew and hustled them out the door. Aden let his power fill the lobby, nudging the humans into doing what their hindbrains were already telling them. To get the hell out as quickly as possible.

"All right," he said, watching as the last of the humans drove away. "Bastien, lock those doors until we can get a guard to man the lobby. Make it two guards, and be sure they're suitably armed and armored. And call—"

He stopped as the elevator opened behind him, and the rest of his vampires flowed into the lobby, taking up positions around him until they formed a defensive square. Even knowing that Aden was far more powerful than all of them combined, they stood ready to defend him. The bond between a Sire and his children knew no reason, only instinct.

"Trav, is that clean-up crew on the way?"

"Yes, my lord. They should be here any minute."

"What about the video?"

"One human did the shooting, the rest came in after. All of them were masked."

"Damn. All right. Bastien, we need—" Aden's attention was drawn to the front door where a wide-eyed vampire was tugging on the big brass handle and frowning when it wouldn't open. He lifted his gaze to find Aden staring at him, and his eyes grew even wider.

"Do you recognize him?" Aden asked no one in particular.

Bastien stared at their visitor. "Goodwin something. One of Silas's."

"Goodwin Pierce," Travis provided, blatantly placing himself between Aden and the front door. "Fairly low on Silas's org chart and apparently, tonight, her messenger boy."

"Or her sacrifice," Kage growled. "Give the word, my lord, and we'll send her a message of our own. It had to be Silas who took Sid. She already tried and failed once before."

Aden tended to agree, but it wouldn't help to kill the messenger. "Let him in."

Freddy and Kage moved to flank the front door. Freddy glanced back briefly, then unlocked the door and pulled it open, immediately grabbing Goodwin and slamming him to his knees.

Aden studied the young vampire. And he was definitely *young*, no more than ten years turned, if that. Either Silas truly didn't care whether he returned from this mission alive, or she'd chosen him precisely because he was so inoffensive that no one would bother killing him.

One thing was certain, the vamp hadn't known what he was walking into. His nostrils were flaring at the smell of blood, his pupils so blown with fear that his eyes were almost completely black. He didn't even seem aware that his fangs had emerged, an aggressive display that was almost a guaranteed death sentence in front of a powerful vampire like Aden.

Aden stepped out from behind Travis and Bastien. The night he needed to be protected from *Goodwin* was the night he'd stake *himself*.

"Who sent you?" he demanded.

Goodwin jerked, losing what little color he had as he stared up at Aden. He opened his mouth as if to speak, then seemed to realize his fangs were in the way. He retracted his fangs with a grimace of concentration and tried again. "The Lady Silas sent me, my lord," he said earnestly. "She wanted me to give you this."

He reached into his jacket and was immediately grabbed by Freddy, who immobilized him before he could produce whatever he'd been reaching for. Freddy, who was twice as big as Goodwin, kept him locked in a choke hold, while Kage carefully lifted the messenger's jacket and extracted a rolled parchment.

"It's a message, my lord," Goodwin gasped out. "Nothing else."

"Bring it here. And don't kill him, Freddy," he added, amused by the resignation on his vampire's face, despite their grim situation. "Let's see what Silas has to say for herself."

Aden took the scroll from Kage and had to fight the urge to drop it in disgust. His lip curled, and he felt unclean the instant he touched it. He glanced up and found Kage watching him.

"What is that, my lord? I've never felt anything like it."

"Human skin," Aden growled, turning to glower at the unfortunate Goodwin who only squeaked his denial. Forcing himself to unroll the thing, Aden saw it was a formal challenge. Handwritten in the old way, using human blood and skin for the message.

"What the fuck is that bitch thinking?" he snarled. "She's not old enough to have been around when we did this kind of crap."

Goodwin remained silent in the face of Aden's slur against his mistress's character, proving he was smarter than his current predicament indicated.

"Silas is challenging me to a duel," he explained to his vampires. "No surprise there," he added, but then frowned. The challenge was straightforward enough, despite the archaic delivery. There was no mention of Sidonie, but then, the obvious play would be to spring Sidonie as a surprise weapon at an opportune time, inducing Aden to concede the challenge to save his lover's life.

But that strategy would only succeed in leaving an unhappy Aden alive to challenge Silas another time. Something only a fool would do. And for all her failings, Silas was not that big a fool.

"Sire?" Bastien said quietly, clearly following the troubled direction of Aden's thoughts.

"Something's not adding up," Aden said. "The Vampire Council will not forgive this display. Silas would know that. So, what does she gain by it?"

"You don't think it was Silas," Bastien intuited.

"I don't know. Taking Sidonie is the kind of thing she would do, but this public mess . . . I don't know."

"But they're clearly connected."

"It would seem so," Aden agreed.

"Could Silas be hoping you'll forfeit the duel by going after Sidonie instead of meeting her tonight?"

"Perhaps. On the other hand, what's to stop me from killing her quickly and then going after Sidonie?"

"Maybe her intent was to split your forces. She knows you have only the four of us. If you send one or more of us after Sid, you'll be facing her without full back-up."

"We're assuming it was Silas who took Sidonie. What if wasn't? What if this is nothing more than coincidence?"

"I'm not sure I believe in such a coincidence."

Aden frowned. He wouldn't have believed such a thing before tonight, either. But what if Silas *wasn't* behind the kidnapping? Then where the hell was Sidonie? His jaw clenched, his gut telling him to drop everything and go after her. Fuck Silas, fuck the damn Council and their rules. But then his gaze roamed over the lobby, touching on each of his vampire children in turn. To a man, they were utterly loyal to him, and they trusted him to repay that loyalty with a care for their lives. If Aden lost the challenge to Silas, whether by forfeit or weakness, his children would be the first to suffer, perhaps even die.

But even more than that, he had an obligation to the larger vampire community to maintain the discretion that permitted them to live in peace among humans. Which meant dealing with the human police over the bloody spectacle that someone had left in his lobby. That was what it meant to be a vampire lord. It wasn't the wealth or the prestige, though those were nice enough. But at its core, being a lord meant taking care of those whose lives were entrusted to you. And as much as it grated on him to accept it, more lives than Sidonie's were at stake tonight.

Whoever had taken Sidonie had done so for reasons involving him. He was certain of that much. They'd taken her from *his* stronghold, after all—a bold move meant to make a point. If the power behind the kidnapping turned out to be Silas, then she would die tonight and Sidonie would be safe. But if it *wasn't* Silas? He sighed unhappily. Then whoever it was would contact him soon enough, and in the meantime, they would keep Sidonie alive. It was a bad bargain, but the only one he had.

His attention was drawn to a black panel van that had pulled up out front.

"Trav?"

"That's the vamp cleaning crew, my lord," Travis confirmed.

"All right, let them handle this and the scene upstairs. Freddy, I want you to reach out to our local sources, everyone we know. If anyone's heard word of Sidonie's whereabouts, I want to know about it, no matter how doubtful the information. In the meantime, we have to mop up this clusterfuck someone left on our doorstep. Silas may not care about creating a spectacle of our affairs, but I must.

"And when we've finished with that . . . I'm going to go kill Silas and bring Sidonie back home."

Chapter Eighteen

IT WAS LATE BY the time Aden finished cleaning up the mess the assassins had left behind, although most of his personal involvement was along the lines of wiping memories and dealing with the police. Apparently the doorman's uncle was high in the police chain of command. He'd raised holy hell with Detective Trevisani and had insisted on a personal interview with Aden. The initial demand had been for Aden to present himself at the station house, which he'd refused outright. They'd tried the usual bluster, threatening to arrest him, but Aden knew his rights and, more importantly, his power. Let them try to arrest him. They wouldn't make it two steps into the building before they forgot why they were there. The uncle had finally settled for a personal visit to the scene which Aden had been more than willing to accommodate.

But by the time the uncle departed with his thoughts suitably altered, Aden was seething. Silas, or whoever had engineered this clusterfuck, had been so wrapped up in their own needs that they'd disregarded one of the main tenets of vampire society. Vampires did not go around leaving piles of bodies for the human authorities to find, not even in the guise of human violence. Only the quick action of Aden and his people had ensured that there was nothing to tie vampire interests to the doorman's death. Aden's residence in the building became nothing more than a coincidence, with the police convinced that he and his people were innocent and had no specific knowledge of the day's tragedy.

But if Aden *hadn't* succeeded in cleaning up the disaster on the fifth floor before the police got wind of it, if he *hadn't* gotten to Detective Trevisani in time to steer the investigation along the desired path, it could have proved disastrous. Not just for Aden, but for vampires everywhere, especially given the high profile visitors in the city for the territorial challenge.

But then perhaps that had been Silas's goal. She'd never been one to risk her own life when someone else's life would do. She was no different than every other woman in Aden's life before he'd become Vampire. Always willing to let him bleed to ensure their own safety and comfort. That wasn't to suggest that women hadn't tried to use him since he'd been turned, only that they hadn't succeeded. The lone exception in a lifetime of bitter experience with women was Sidonie, and now someone was threatening to kill her. Aden's vision filled with blood as he contemplated the pain her abductors were going to suffer when he got a hold of them.

The first step toward that goal was meeting Silas. Aden's two SUVs pulled up in front of the warehouse near the Chicago River where Silas had set the formal challenge. The building appeared abandoned, its brick walls pockmarked and blackened with age, the windows old and thick, dull as they reflected the distant light of the waning half-moon.

Many of the buildings in this area had been given historical landmark status, a shining memory of another age. Sadly, this warehouse was not one of them. It was clearly abandoned, although on this particular night, there were a fair number of vampires clustered inside. Aden wondered if Silas had purchased the building for her own use during the challenge, or if she was simply squatting. It was also possible that this was one of Klemens's old buildings, since Silas had been close to Klemens and would know about his properties. If it *had* belonged to Klemens, it would be Aden's before the night was over, along with everything else Klemens had owned. Assuming it was still standing after Aden killed Silas.

The area around the building was oddly suited to tonight's activities. The streets were dark and narrow, with only a few lights along the river more than a block away. At first glance it seemed deserted, but it wasn't. There were people in the shadows, human predators drawn out by the unexpected activity and by the expensive vehicles which were out of place on these shadowy streets in the middle of a Sunday night.

Travis and Kage got out of the first vehicle and immediately dropped back to Aden's SUV, taking up positions front and back. In the front seat, Freddy and Bastien opened their doors simultaneously and joined them, leaving Aden alone until Bastien stepped back to open his door.

Aden slid out of the SUV, standing still for a moment as he surveyed the surrounding buildings, the alleys and streets. His power swelled, riding the edge of his anger, the midnight blue of his eyes gleaming from beneath half-closed lids. He sensed the heightened aggression of the human watchers at this invasion of their territory, felt their shock as his power reached out like a physical thing, a rolling wave of energy that buffeted each of them, shoving them back into the shadows. He smiled grimly at the sound of their hearts racing with unaccustomed fear, at the sweat-scented waves of dread rolling off of them as they slunk away. They were not predators this night, they were prey.

Aden turned his back, dismissing the humans from his mind, as he studied the old warehouse. Other than theirs, there were no vehicles in front and no other vehicles in sight, but for a few older cars parked along the curb, none of which Silas would have used. She was too vain to sink so low, even for purposes of subterfuge. She must have arrived earlier. This was her choice of battlefield, after all, so she'd want to prepare it to her best advantage, to deploy her people. He had no illusions about whether this meeting was meant to be a trap. He assumed it was.

He also knew the trap wouldn't be an explosion, because there was no question that Silas and her minions were inside the warehouse. The presence of so many vampires was as impossible to fake as it was to miss. They hummed like a bad fluorescent tube on the inside of his skull, and if he concentrated he could detect Silas buzzing louder than any of them. She was definitely in there this time.

He glanced around at the four vampires he'd brought with him. They were dressed as he was, in all black—a long-sleeved T-shirt, combat style pants tucked into ATAC boots. Freddy and Kage were conventionally armed, and there were several additional Heckler & Koch MP5 submachine guns within easy reach inside each of the trucks. It wasn't usual to bring human weapons to a challenge fight; the combatants were expected to rely on their vampire abilities and nothing else. But Aden didn't trust Silas. For all the old-time formality of her blood-scribed parchment, she'd proven her willingness to play dirty at every step. There had been Stig Lakanen's attack that first night, when Silas had goaded the much weaker Stig into going after Aden, even though she'd known he would fail. Then, she'd worked with Professor Dresner to maneuver Sidonie into Aden's camp, using her to set up the ambush at the club—an ambush which Silas had fled, leaving her minions to bleed and die in her wake. And now she'd likely taken Sidonie hostage, probably hoping to blackmail Aden into conceding the fight. As if he were too stupid to understand that she'd kill him anyway, the first time his back was turned.

Not that Aden had any intention of conceding anything to Silas.

The territorial challenges were supposed to be one-on-one, vampire vs. vampire. The kind of petty wrangling that Silas had engaged in—using humans as tools, letting others die in her place—only underscored her weakness. A weakness that would see the Midwest drowning in chaos if she became lord, as vampire after vampire challenged her from inside and out, nibbling away at the territory, breaking off chunks until it was fractured and vulnerable.

That wasn't going to happen. Even if Aden hadn't been certain of his superiority, confident in his ability to destroy Silas and every other challenger, he knew Raphael would never have permitted Silas to rule. The Western Lord would take her out himself first, letting Lucas continue to hold the territory until a more suitable candidate stepped up. Perhaps alone among the contenders, Aden had no illusions about Raphael's role in choosing Klemens's successor, nor his cold-blooded willingness to do whatever it took to ensure his vision of a secure North America. And now that Aden understood the threat from Europe, he wholeheartedly embraced that vision and would see to it that the Midwest did its part.

Silas clearly didn't understand any of it—not the looming threat and certainly not Raphael's role in deciding who would rule. And she just as clearly had deluded herself into believing she could win. Whether it was because Klemens had favored her, letting her believe it was her own power rather than his that fed her rise in his ranks, or if she was simply that stupid, Aden didn't know. But he did know that one of the reasons she'd remained loyal to Klemens was because he'd let her play her cruel little games, permitted her to take weaker vampires and torment them, to kill humans for the fun of it. Never mind that Klemens was sworn to protect the very vampires Silas had tormented, or that he bred instability by permitting her to prey on humans. The now-dead vampire lord had probably found her games amusing. It wasn't uncommon for a vampire's children to be reflections of himself. And Klemens had been one sick fucker of a vampire.

Regardless of why Silas was the way she was, it was too late for her. If she'd come to Aden at the beginning, if she'd stepped aside in recognition of his greater strength and pledged her fealty, he would have rewarded her, even given her a city of her own. Not a major city, but something suitably profitable.

But after everything that had happened, he wouldn't trust her out of his sight, and he didn't like her well enough to keep her *in* his sight. If she walked out that door right now and came to him on bended knee, it would only make it more convenient when he chopped off her head.

Aden did a final check of his vampires, receiving a quick nod from Bastien. Gathering his strength, he sent out a wave of power, searching the warehouse, wanting to know exactly what waited for them inside. True to form, Silas had brought so many of her minions that it was difficult to get an accurate count. He didn't bother trying. It wasn't worth the expenditure of energy.

"She's brought more than I can easily count, so stick close and expect trickery," Aden told his vampires, then glanced over at Freddy, who stood closest to the entrance, and nodded.

The big vampire pulled back the heavy door on its sliding track, entering first when Aden would have done so. Aden had to smile at that. It was vampire instinct to protect one's master. He would have done the same thing for Lucas.

Aden entered the warehouse and immediately stepped to one side, clearing the entrance for the rest of his vampires. There were no lights inside. The only illumination came from moonlight through the dirty windows, but darkness was hardly an impediment for a vampire.

Silas's people waited for him, spread out across the back of the warehouse in disorganized rows, their aggression palpable, raising whatever power they had in preparation for the fight to come. For the most part, their eyes gleamed red, betraying their lack of significant power. Silas stood in the very last row, surrounded by the buffer of her minions. She was a petite woman, so short that he only knew she was there because of the dirty-penny shine of her eyes in the dark warehouse.

"This is your party, Silas," he called out to her. "You and your pretentious invitation. We haven't used human blood for such things in a century or more," he added derisively, pricking her temper and reminding her that he was far older and more experienced than she was. He raked the assembled vampires with a sneering glance, ending with his gaze directly on Silas. "But all I see are underlings. Are you refusing to fight? Again?"

"At least I *have* minions," Silas responded, her soprano voice echoing in an odd way that told him she was enhancing it somehow. Probably making it louder, and what a waste of energy that was. "Unlike your pathetic four," she continued. "If they do nothing else, my many children prove my fitness to rule."

"Silas, Silas," Aden chided. "They do no such thing. Your *need* for them, and a sorry lot they are, proves nothing but your weakness."

Silas snarled angrily. "Kill him!" she ordered shrilly. "Kill them all!"

Aden engaged Silas's vampires without mercy, disgusted by the nature of the battle. He despised having to kill so many vampires, but he was in this battle to win, and so he fought with everything he had.

He and his four attacked as a team, his vampires feeding him their energy, while at the same time drawing strength from his staunch defense, from his willingness to die for them.

The attacking vamps swarmed Aden, trying to isolate him from his people, thinking to take him down by sheer strength of numbers. They were like yappy dogs nipping at a lion, but even dogs can do damage if there are enough of them. None of Silas's minions were powerful enough by themselves to kill him, but as Aden fought them off, as they managed to strike the rare lucky blow that left him bleeding, he knew her true objective was for them to weaken him for her. She didn't want them to kill Aden, she needed to do that herself, needed that notch on her belt if she was going to come out of the challenge with any honor. But that didn't mean she couldn't have her minions diminish him, leave him injured and bleeding, unable or unwilling to use his dwindling energy to heal himself.

That was how Silas saw the situation. Aden had other plans.

Aden let Silas's people wound him, let them draw blood thinking they'd beat him. He heard her victorious howl, felt the sudden surge of power that told him she believed her triumph was at hand. And still he waited. Until they were gathered around him like rats, their eyes ruby sparks in the darkness, their defenses lowered, confident he was bested. And then he killed them, mowing them down like a scythe through wheat, his power a sharp-edged blade that cut through their bodies with ease.

And deep within Aden, the dark half of his vampire gift stirred, roused by the blood soaking the ash-covered floor, by the scent of the air which had become a red-tinted miasma of death. But this time, Aden didn't fight it. This time he opened his arms and let it come.

He laughed with joy as the bindings broke, unleashing this darkest aspect of his power. It was an erotic rush, as if he'd been the one imprisoned, as if he was finally freed. Black flame raged through his muscles and blood, expanding his power, reaching outward, seeking victims, seeking . . . food. He roared his pleasure as the gruesome power which was so much a part of him sought out and drank the energy of the dying, sucking up their life force, growing stronger with every death, not caring whether the vampire died beneath his hand or another's.

Silas's minions gazed upon him with horror, no longer struggling to be the first to attack him, but shoving to escape instead. They trampled each other in their panic, ignoring the shrieked demands of their mistress ordering them to attack, far more willing to face her anger than the hunger of this monster who had suddenly manifested among them.

But none escaped. Aden wouldn't permit it. His loyal four wouldn't permit it. As the last of his attackers died, as the screams of disbelief still echoed off the brick walls, Aden reined in his most deadly power. It went willingly, like a satiated child, weary from its efforts and too full to protest. Aden closed his eyes briefly, then opened them and took stock. He glanced left and right, drinking in the sight of his four vampire children, bloodied but still standing staunchly by his side.

He caught movement in the dim recesses of the warehouse. There was a door in the back, and a sliver of faint light flashing as Silas tried to worm away once more.

Aden raised his power and slammed the door shut before it could open more than an inch or two. Silas spun to stare at him, her eyes going wide with fear and surprise.

"Not this time, Silas," Aden growled.

He stalked across the wide open space, taking his time, taunting her with his confident swagger. "A smart warrior knows his enemy," he lectured deliberately. "You didn't even bother to discover the true nature of my power. Klemens knew. Why do you think he refused to take the field if I was there?"

He came within five feet of her and stopped, the blue gleam of his eyes casting her in foggy color. "You thought your slavish minions would guarantee my defeat, but the only defeat tonight will be yours."

Her eyes narrowed in rage, their copper-penny glow making her look sallow and sickly. But for all her glare of defiance, she was afraid of him. She kept rubbing her arms, as if trying to scrape away the clinging webs of his power, kept reaching with her mind for her dead minions, becoming frantic all over again when she discovered they were gone.

She didn't even try to surrender, seemed to understand at last that she had come too far, had caused too much bloodshed for him to accept her submission.

But she was still a vampire, still driven by the power of her blood. She made a final, desperate bid for survival, marshaling all of her remaining strength into a single knife-blade of energy. With a gesture far more disciplined that Aden would have credited her with, she thrust it at Aden, a killing blow aimed at his heart.

Aden was not so easily taken in. He'd been fighting vampire challenges a century before Silas had even been born. He'd sensed her desperation, felt her gathering power. When she launched her surprise attack, he was ready for her. With a gesture, he deflected her conjured knife blade, turning all of that energy back on her and blasting her across the floor to slam against the far wall while she wailed in both anger and pain.

Aden was silent as he crossed the few feet to where Silas lay choking on her own blood, her power drained, her body damaged beyond her current ability to heal. Had Aden been willing, he could have saved her.

But he wasn't willing. Silas needed to die. The only question was how much pain she would endure first.

Sinking to one knee, he studied her dispassionately. She'd known the risk she was taking and had taken it freely. She wasn't the first vampire to die this way, and she wouldn't be the last. It was the lot of those who were made Vampire, especially those who were driven to climb the ladder of power.

Reaching down almost idly, he stroked his fingers over her chest where her heart still beat frantically. In another context, the gesture could have been sexual. But there was nothing sexual about this.

"One way or another, Silas," he murmured, "you're going to die tonight." He shrugged. "I can make it easy, or—" He bent his fingers slightly, and his power squeezed her heart. Silas cried out, her eyes going wide with shock at the intense pain"—I can make it very painful," he finished.

She blinked up at him, her breathing reduced to harsh gasps for oxygen.

"Tell me where Sidonie is," he said, his voice hard and uncompromising, "and I'll make it quick."

"I don't," she began breathlessly, struggling for enough air to speak. Her head rolled from side to side in denial. "I don't know what you mean."

Aden's gaze went flat, and his eyes lit up, bathing her in their cool glow.

"Wrong answer," he growled.

She shrieked as he ripped her mind apart, as he dug for knowledge of Sidonie's kidnapping and found nothing. And when he was finished, he dug his fingers into her chest and squeezed her heart like an overripe tomato, feeling the bloody flesh squish through his fingers like some gruesome puree.

When it was all over, when Silas had become part of the bloody mud on the floor of the warehouse, Aden stood. If she'd had any power left, he'd have absorbed it willingly, but by the time he'd killed her, she'd been drained of every ounce. He closed his eyes against the inevitable adrenaline crash and felt Bastien and the others gathering around him, offering their protection and their strength.

"She didn't know anything about Sidonie's kidnapping," Aden said quietly.

Bastien gave him a worried look. "Then where is she?"

"I don't know."

"We should go, my lord. There will be enough light through the windows in the morning to burn away this mess, and we can leave her vehicles out back. Local scavengers will strip them far more efficiently than we could."

Aden glanced around the nearly empty warehouse. "If any of her minions—" He didn't bother finishing the sentence. There'd been no one left to survive Silas's death.

"It's late, my lord," Bastien reminded him. It *was* late, much later than he'd planned. The business with the dead doorman and its follow-up had taken far too much of his time. And he wondered if someone had planned it that way, someone who had Sidonie in his clutches even now.

It did no good to curse the rising sun and its implacable effect on his vampire nature, but he did it anyway, swearing long and fluently. Sidonie was out there somewhere. Alone or worse. She wasn't dead. He'd taken enough of her blood that he'd have known if she died. Unfortunately, there were far worse fates than death. He had experienced many of them personally.

Did she know he was looking for her? That he wouldn't stop until he found her?

He drew a deep breath as they exited back onto the street, grateful for the fresh air. As cold and wet as it was, it was an improvement over the warehouse, which had become oppressive with the stink of drying blood and ash.

"Is it over, my lord?" Bastien asked, pausing to look at Aden as he opened the SUV's door.

His lieutenant was asking if the night's battle concluded the challenge. If Aden was now Lord of the Midwest.

Aden nodded, but waited until they were in the SUV and on their way home before going into detail. "Silas was the last major challenger that I know of. It's possible some unknown contender is out there waiting in the wings for the rest of us to kill each other off, but I haven't heard of any."

"But then, how do you claim the—"

"That's Lucas's call. He's the current Lord of the Midwest in fact, if not in spirit. I'll notify him of my intention to claim the territory. He has the option of fighting me for it, but I think we both know he won't do that. Although," he added thoughtfully, "if Silas had tried to claim the victory, he would have made *her* fight for it."

"Or simply sicced Raphael on her," Bastien muttered.

Aden chuckled. "You've met Raphael, Bastien. Does he strike you as a vampire who can be *sicced* on anybody?"

Bastien's face brightened in a rare grin as he looked over the seat at Aden. "I think Cyn could get away with it."

They shared a tired laugh, and Bastien said, "So, you inform Lucas, and then what?"

"Then we travel to that godforsaken ranch of his in the middle of nowhere, and he formally transfers the Midwest to me. We spend a night in drunken revelry, and then we come back to Chicago and start working. But before we do any of that, I need to find Sidonie. It wasn't Silas who kidnapped her, so who was it? And what do they want?"

"Could it be that unknown challenger you talked about?"

Aden frowned, shaking his head. "Maybe. It doesn't sound right, though. It took manpower to take Hamilton and his people down that way. If there was a challenger in town with the numbers to do that, I'd have heard about it. Damn it!" he swore, pounding the armrest in frustration, feeling the rippling heat inside his skull that warned him the rising sun was nearly to the horizon.

"I can have some our daylight people put out feelers tomorrow, my lord. It will give us a head start in the search for her."

Aden nodded, his mood grim. "He used humans for the assault, and humans talk. They can't seem to help themselves. Someone will be bragging about taking down a vampire, even though that's not what happened. We simply have to root him out."

"We'll find her, my lord."

Aden agreed silently. He would find Sidonie. He only hoped he wouldn't be too late.

Chapter Nineteen

THE NEXT NIGHT, Aden opened his eyes to the knowledge that he was Lord of the Midwest. He'd told Bastien they had to contact Lucas, had to go through the formalities first. But that was just the paperwork. He felt the victory in his bones and blood. He knew there was no vampire in Chicago who could stand against him, and if he stretched his awareness even farther, he detected no one within the entire territory, *his* territory, who could.

He would have to pay Lucas a personal visit anyway, in order to receive the full power and *burden* of his lordship. Every vampire within the Midwest would soon look to him for his next breath, for the next beat of his heart. Aden tried to imagine the weight of it. The lives of his four vampire children seemed heavy enough. What would it be like to have thousands weighing on him every minute of every day? He'd probably come to *welcome* the daily rising of the sun for the rest it would bring him.

He sat up, pulling his awareness in and narrowing his focus. Lucas would have to wait. Aden's *first* priority was to find Sidonie. She was somewhere in this city, a city he now owned. Somewhere out there was a vampire who knew something, who'd seen something, that would lead Aden to whoever had attacked his guards and taken Sidonie from him. He didn't need someone to point out the house, they only had to get him close. Her blood would tell him the rest.

Throwing aside the covers, he climbed from the bed and strode to the shower. He sensed his vampires waking up in their secure rooms down the hall. And then he blinked in surprise, his step nearly faltering as he felt something more, something only a lord would sense . . . vampires waking all over the city. Good. He'd put them all to work.

ADEN WAS SURPRISED to find Earl Hamilton waiting when he strode into his office. The human had been pacing the receptionist area and turned when Aden rounded the corner. He was wearing full combat gear, including a military-grade chest plate, with a MP5 hanging round his neck on a sling. His hands rested on the weapon as he faced Aden.

"Hamilton," Aden said in surprise.

"My lord," the human said, dipping his head respectively. "I heard . . . forgive me, my lord, but I heard Ms. Reid had been kidnapped. Is this true?"

"Unfortunately," Aden confirmed grimly.

The man's face was a study in regret. "I must tender my resignation, my lord. I failed you, and Ms. Reid paid the price."

Aden rested his hands on his hips and studied the human. He understood the man's dismay, but didn't see how resigning helped anyone.

"I don't accept that," he said finally. "I need you now more than ever. And if you insist on feeling responsible, then Sidonie needs you, too. As for whether or not you failed me, you offered your life in the defense of me and mine. Some of your men *gave* their lives in that defense. I would be a foolish lord indeed if I rewarded such loyalty by firing you."

Tears shone in Hamilton's eyes when he spoke next. "Thank you, my lord. I am honored to serve you in whatever way I can."

"Then help me find her."

"I will. We've had people out scouring the streets, listening to gossip mostly. And the phones have finally started ringing. Everyone knows we're looking, and we've offered a reward."

"Good idea. Double it for information leading to her rescue, and triple if they give us the exact location."

"Yes, my lord." Hamilton nodded respectfully and headed for the elevator, as Aden's four vampires made their way down the hall toward him.

"Travis," Aden called without turning, "the vampire who found Sidonie snooping around that slave house the first time, what was his name?"

"Elias, my lord," Travis supplied as he came even with Aden.

"Right. Call him. If it wasn't Silas, then someone associated with the slave network is the most likely culprit. Sidonie caused a lot of trouble there and cut off a nice flow of cash."

"And she insisted we'd missed the top vampire in the operation, too."

Aden nodded. "Carl Pinto," he confirmed, the knowledge like a light going on in his brain. "Find him."

The phone rang, and Bastien crossed to the desk to answer it. He spoke briefly, then held the phone out to Travis. "Speak of the devil."

Travis shared a quick look with Aden and took the phone from Bastien. "Elias?"

"Rumor has it your boss is the new lord." Aden could hear both halves of the conversation with ease.

"Rumor travels fast," Travis said. "I'm barely awake."

"Even faster than you think. I heard that particular bit of news in the last hour before the sun rose this morning. Is it true?"

"Looks like."

"In that case, I've another tidbit for you."

"I'm listening."

"You know that item I returned to you before?"

Travis lifted his gaze to meet Aden's. "Yeah?"

"Not everyone was happy with Lord Aden's interference in their business."

"Is that what the cool kids are calling slaves these days?"

"Don't fuck with me, Trav. You know—" Elias didn't get any further, because Aden yanked the phone from Travis.

"Enough bullshit," he demanded. "Where is she?"

"My lord," Elias breathed, and Aden could hear both shock and fear in those two words. This was what it was like to be a vampire lord. Only a day ago, he'd been Aden, just another powerful vampire. Now he was Lord Aden, with the power to reach out and stop a vampire's heart from beating.

"Talk," Aden ordered.

"Carl Pinto, my lord. He was Klemens's man at the head of the slave ring. Drugs, too, but he really liked the idea of owning those women."

"Where?" Aden's jaw was clenched so tightly, he had trouble forcing out the single word. If Pinto had touched Sidonie, he was going to die. Actually, he was going to die either way, but if he'd dared to harm her, his death was going to be slow and excruciating.

"I can give you the address, my lord, but it would be easier to show you."

"Fine." Aden handed the phone over to Travis. "Set up a meet. We leave in five minutes."

SID REGAINED awareness slowly, feeling sluggish and tired, fighting her brain's insistence that she wake up. She wanted to go back to sleep, and there was no reason she couldn't. She was a freelance reporter. It wasn't as if she had a set schedule, and if she'd had an appointment, her phone would have dinged by now. Smiling, she rolled over, jerking in pain when something dug into her hip bone, something hard and . . . Her eyes popped open as she remembered where she was. What the *thing* digging into her hip was.

She sat up too fast, making her head spin dizzily as she eyed the other women in the room, her fellow captives. Except that they obviously didn't view *her* as a fellow anything. There was very little light, only a bare, yellowed bulb overhead, but enough for her to count seven other women huddled as far away from her as the small room and their chains would permit. Distrust of her was plain on their faces, layered on top of a weary sort of horror at their predicament.

Pushing her hair away from her face, Sid scooted back until she could lean against the wall, easing her muscles after what felt like several hours spent lying twisted on the gritty wooden floor. She closed her eyes and tried to remember, to piece together the events that had led to her waking in this filthy room. She didn't remember falling asleep, but her body told her that hours had passed. The window was barred on the inside and boarded over outside, but she could see enough to know it was nighttime, and she doubted it was the same night as when she'd been kidnapped.

She remembered talking to the vampire, Carl Pinto, remembered his human henchman shoving her into this room and cutting her hands free. She'd felt excitement, because finally she'd be able to reach her gun. And then . . . nothing until she'd woken up just now. But something was wrong, something more than the obvious, because she shouldn't have been able to sleep at all. She should have been wide awake and terrified. Those bastards must have drugged her again, but how? She hadn't eaten or drunk anything. In fact, she was as thirsty as if she'd just run a few miles on a hot day without water. The thought had her looking around idly for water and not finding any. Not a surprise.

She pressed her back against the wall, then reached down and began to work the muscles of her legs, which were sore and aching from being crammed into the trunk for so long, then sleeping on the floor. Bending first one leg, then the other, she brought each knee to her chest and back down several times, massaging her calves, her thighs . . . She frowned, running her fingers over her right thigh. It was more than sore. It was tender, with a hard knot that was so feverish she could feel it through the heavy denim of her jeans. Under other circumstances, she wouldn't have thought much about it. She bruised easily and badly, and she frequently had no memory of what caused any particular mark. But this was more than a bruise. This was more like when she'd gotten vaccinations before going to South America that time, and she'd had a negative reaction to . . .

Shit. The guard hadn't been pinching her thigh last night. Or, rather he had, but he hadn't been sizing her up for rape, he'd given her a shot of some drug. She'd been so relieved when he'd cut her hands free, but he'd only done it because he knew she'd be out. Jesus, what had he given her? What if it was something addictive? What if the needle hadn't been clean?

She forestalled a full-blown panic attack by reminding herself that she had a much bigger and more immediate problem. She was being held prisoner by a vampire who wanted her dead, whose most optimistic plan called for her to be sold into slavery. A drug addiction she could deal with, a disease she could fight. Later. When she was free.

What she needed to focus on now was getting out of here and taking all of these women with her.

"*Por favor,*" Sid said, speaking to the oldest of the women, who was still several years younger than Sid herself. Sid's Spanish was good. Her mother's cook, who had been Sid's nanny when she was younger, was Puerto Rican and had used nothing but Spanish when speaking to Sid.

"How long have I been here?" she asked, continuing in Spanish. "How long was I asleep?"

"Many hours," the woman replied. "They brought you here last night, and you slept all through the day."

"But only one," Sid clarified. "One day."

The woman nodded. "They will come soon," she warned. "But at least they will bring food and water."

Sid nodded. That made sense. They wouldn't spend any more than necessary keeping the women healthy, but they did need them alive. You couldn't sell a dead slave.

"How many men, when they bring the food?" Sid asked.

"Two." The woman shrugged. "Sometimes only one."

"How long have you been here?" Sid asked curiously. With Aden wiping out the other house, she would have expected Pinto to move the women in and out as quickly as possible.

"Six days, I think," the woman said. "They chained us together after one night, and they told us we are leaving, but then . . ." She shrugged again. "They went away and didn't come back. I thought they would leave us to die. But then *he* came, and now we wait again."

"You mean the vampire."

One of the younger women, a girl really, chimed in, nodding. "The pretty one," she said, "with the cruel eyes."

Carl Pinto had meant to move these women with the others, Sid realized, the ones Aden had freed with his raid on the house Sid had discovered. But Pinto had been forced to change his plans. And now he sat here in this house with his few captives, probably afraid to move them for fear of getting caught, but not willing to lose the profit by freeing them either. Maybe he thought whoever won the challenge would let him return to his slave running. It was definitely profitable, if one didn't mind where the profit came from.

Sid, on the other hand, was convinced that Aden would be the ultimate victor. And that meant Carl Pinto's days were numbered.

Unfortunately, she couldn't wait that long. She stood and continued stretching, running through various escape scenarios in her head as she did so. On the one hand, she felt confident that Aden would look for her. He wouldn't believe that she'd left him. She hadn't been thinking straight before. There had to have been some evidence of her capture. Earl Hamilton and his entire security team had been on duty only one floor below. She frowned, wondering what had happened to Hamilton and his men. Were they all dead? God, she hoped not.

She shook away the thought. There was nothing she could do about it, and she didn't need the negative energy draining her resolve. She needed to focus on one thing and one thing only, and that was getting the fuck out of here. So, points in her favor . . . first, Aden would be looking for her, and second, she still had her gun. She'd learned from Dresner, that traitorous bitch, that you didn't need an actual stake to kill a vamp. That was the traditional method, but the key was not the stake itself, but the damage it caused. Do enough damage to a vamp's heart, no matter how you did it, and you could kill him. If she could somehow get close enough to Carl Pinto to shoot the gun point blank at his heart, that should do the trick.

Or rather, the trick would be getting the gun close enough and then pulling the trigger. She'd never killed anyone before, never even shot a gun at anything living, much less a person. But Pinto had not only killed Janey, he'd enslaved uncounted numbers of women, sending them to a horrible fate and sometimes death. Could she kill him, if it came down to it? She thought she could.

But what she *knew* was that she couldn't sit around and wait for Aden to show up. This wasn't a fairy tale, and she was no princess. She couldn't count on her hero riding in on a white horse, or in this case rolling up in a black SUV. Even if he showed up, he might be too late.

The heavy tread of booted feet pounded down the hallway and stopped outside the bedroom door. Some of the women cried out, hugging each other and eyeing the door as if expecting a monster to enter, which wasn't far from the truth. Sid didn't join the terrified huddle—she wasn't sure they'd have accepted her if she tried—but she played it safe, dropping into the corner and tucking her knees up against her chest, not wanting to take the slightest chance that her gun would be discovered.

There was a scrape of metal, and then what sounded like a heavy padlock falling against the doorjamb, before the door swung open. Sid had expected it to be the guards bringing food and water, but instead it was Pinto himself who stood there, his eyes gleaming red fire as he stared at her in the dim light.

"Get up, bitch," he growled.

Sid didn't move, just stared at him defiantly. She wasn't going to make this easy for him.

Pinto gave her a cruel smile, and, moving faster than her human eyes could follow, he zipped across the room and grabbed the youngest of the women, the same one who'd called him pretty. She cried out, hanging from his hard grip and whimpering softly.

"Get up," he repeated to Sid. "Or I'll drink her dry and leave the husk."

Sid tried to put all the hatred she felt into her stare as she stood, keeping her back against the wall. "Leave her alone," she demanded. "You want me. I'm here."

"How touching," Pinto sneered. But he opened his fingers, releasing the teenager. She dropped to the floor with a clatter of chains, then crawled over to rejoin the knot of terrified captives.

"Come then, Sidonie Reid. Let's find out why a cold bastard like Aden would find you so irresistible."

Sidonie walked slowly, steeling herself to make a break for it when she hit the doorway. But she never got there. A deafening noise suddenly rocked the house, a loud crack of wood followed by a hard slam of something heavy and flat crashing to the floor. Like the heavy front door. Her heart soared as she realized Aden must have found her, that rescue was at hand, not just for her but for the other women. She opened her mouth to scream, to let Aden know where she was, but before she could so much as draw a breath, Pinto was on her. One of his hands gripped her waist, pinning her to his side, the other covered her mouth as he dragged her away from the living room to the opposite end of the hallway which opened to the kitchen.

It sounded like war had broken out behind them, with the steady sound of gunfire and men shouting coming from the living room. Sid knew a moment of fear for Aden before she was jerked back to her own danger as Pinto slammed her against the hallway wall hard enough to knock her breath away. He flattened himself against her, his hand over her mouth, and they hung there a long moment as Pinto seemed to listen intently to something in the kitchen. And then just as abruptly, they were moving again.

Sid fought as much as she could, but Pinto was a vampire. His strength far exceeded hers, and he didn't mind hurting her. She strained to hear what was going on in the living room. With one exception, Pinto's henchmen were human. If that was Aden out there, and her gut told her it was, Pinto's human gangbangers didn't stand a chance.

He wrenched her to a stop one more time, holding her just short of the doorless opening between the kitchen and living room. He froze, filthy fingers over her mouth, his arm around her ribs so tightly that she could barely breathe. She thought she knew why he was waiting. The door to the driveway was on the other side of the kitchen, and Pinto would have to pass right in front of the living room opening to get there. Even at vampire speeds, they would be in full view of the living room for a few precious seconds.

Pinto held her in place, muttering almost silently, trying to persuade himself to make a break for it, insisting no one would notice and cursing Aden in the same breath. Sid twisted and turned, trying to make noise, to knock something over and give away their position, but Pinto had her crushed face first up against the open shelves of a pantry cabinet, the edges digging into her cheek, her breasts, her thighs. Cold air from the wide-open door to the outside brushed over her face, and if she rolled her eyes sideways she could see the opening.

Pinto's muscles tightened. His muttering became more urgent, and Sid knew he was steeling himself for the final dash to freedom. This was her moment of truth. She either acted now, or she surrendered her freedom and maybe her life.

Her left arm was trapped awkwardly by the steel band of Pinto's grip and the shelf that was jammed against her chest. But her right arm was free from her elbow down. Gritting her teeth, praying Pinto was too busy with his own worries to pay attention to what she was doing, Sidonie slid her right hand down over her belly. She moved slowly, curling her fingers into claws and gathering up the double layer of her hoodie and T-shirt, sliding beneath it until she met the tight edge of her bellyband. She paused then, testing his reaction. But he seemed so focused on the dangerous invaders in his living room that he'd already disregarded his human hostage as a threat.

Leaving her hand flattened over her belly, she waited until he made his move, until he dragged her past the cracked porcelain sink, moving vampire-fast as they popped into full view of the living room and then past it. He hesitated once more, just long enough to lean forward and sniff the air outside the driveway door, and Sid made a move of her own.

Shoving her hand under the bellyband, she curled shaking fingers around the grip of the small 9mm. It felt solid in her hand, heavy, as she inched it out of the holster, as she sucked in a deep breath of courage. And then with an effort that was more awkward than graceful, she bent her elbow, twisted the gun until it was jammed it against Pinto's chest, and pulled the trigger over and over until the slide locked back and there was nothing left to fire.

ADEN DIDN'T WASTE any time on elaborate strategies. According to Elias, whom they'd met up with as scheduled, Pinto had only one vampire left from the crew that Aden had decimated only days before. The rest were human, mostly gangbangers who were happy to act as guards and enforcers. The pay was good and the risk was low. Or it had been before tonight. Tonight, hell itself was going to descend on them in the form of one pissed-off vampire lord.

The target house was in a far worse neighborhood than the previous one. Pinto probably felt safer here. The authorities rarely ventured down these streets, usually only in response to overt violence, and there was nothing about *this* house to draw unwanted attention.

Aden's vamps had parked their SUVs halfway down the block, flashing their fangs blatantly as they climbed out, so there'd be no question of whom potential thieves were dealing with. And just to be sure, Aden had sent out a very clear don't-fuck-with-me message on a wave of power that even the dullest human would understand. They'd brought three vehicles in case there were captives who needed transport, and he didn't want to come back to find all of them stripped for parts.

They walked the short distance to the house, pausing while Aden sent out a tight thread of power, scanning the house and its occupants. Sidonie was definitely inside, definitely still alive, though he couldn't tell if she was hurt. He needed to get in there.

"One outside guard," he observed tightly to Bastien, who stood next to him. "Human, right side of the house."

Bastien nodded. "There's a side door there. Probably means no back door."

"I expected more," Aden commented, searching the dark spaces on either side of the house, using his power to scan the house and yard, looking for more guards.

"Pinto might be short on people. They lost a lot of manpower at the slave house," Bastien suggested.

Aden didn't trust possibilities, but he trusted what his own senses could tell him.

"All right. Kage, you go ahead and take out that guard. When you hear us come through the front door, you join us."

"Sire," Kage acknowledged and took off, gliding across the street like a shadow over the moon. He didn't bother asking how he'd know when Aden and the others got inside. He knew as well as any of them that there would be nothing subtle about Aden's entry.

"The rest of us go in the front, quick and dirty," Aden said, stating the obvious. "The door goes down, we go in. There's Pinto and one other vamp, but a dozen or more humans. Some of those might be slaves, so kill everything that moves unless it's female. We'll sort out the rest later."

"And Pinto, my lord?" That was Freddy. Always up for a fight, and the real fight here tonight would be Carl Pinto.

"Pinto is mine," Aden said, one side of his mouth lifting in a half grin. "You can have the other one. Let's do this."

Aden crossed the street without waiting for the others, striding up the broken concrete walkway, taking the three steps to the porch in a single bound. As his foot hit the wide porch, he gathered his power into a battering ram of pure energy and shoved it front of him. The heavy door with its metal sheeting and reinforced hinges cracked down the middle like a piece of rotted wood. Freddy stepped in front of Aden and, turning sideways, kicked the shattered door inward where it fell with a loud, booming, slap of noise.

Gunfire erupted from the human guards clustered in the front room, increasing as those who'd been knocked off their feet by the original entry found their wits and their weapons and began fighting for their lives. Freddy went down under a spray of bullets from a submachine gun. Aden caught the rich scent of his blood and sent a shaft of healing energy to his vampire child, pausing to grip his shoulder as he went past. Lifting his gaze to the human who'd fired the weapon, Aden grabbed him by the throat with one hand, cupped his other hand under the man's chin, and twisted, breaking his neck with a speed and strength no human could hope to match.

He caught movement in the hallway and turned just as one of the guards herded several terrified women ahead of him into the front room. A quick glance told him his vampires had the other guards well in hand, so he turned his attention to the coward who would use slaves as a shield for his own worthless life.

"Let me go, or I'll kill 'em all," the man shouted, his voice cracking with fear. He had his arm hooked beneath the jaw of a teenaged girl, the barrel of his weapon jabbed against her neck.

Aden eyed the man with the kind of hatred he saved for those who would enslave others, who abused them for money or pleasure. "Go to hell," he growled.

The man glared back at him, his eyes too bright, his heartbeat loud in Aden's ears. He was high as a kite, his chest puffed up with overblown arrogance. "I ain't goin' nowhere, asshole. Now, get the fuck out of my way, or they all die, starting with this one." He shoved his gun into the girl's neck, and she cried out as it sliced into her skin, drawing blood.

Aden's gaze went hooded as he studied the man. "That bit about going to hell?" he drawled, then snapped out a hand and wrenched the weapon from the man's grip, seizing him around the neck with the other. "It wasn't a suggestion."

Gun shots sounded from somewhere else in the house, and the women all screamed and ran for the front door, only to find their way blocked by Freddy's bulk. Not realizing he was there to help them, they cowered away, backing into a corner and clinging to each other, crying. Their terror was a palpable thing to Aden, like a bad taste in his mouth. They didn't know if they were being rescued, or if something even worse had befallen them. But Aden didn't have time to reassure them.

Meeting the terrified gaze of the human in his grip, he said, "Hell's too good for you." Squeezing so tightly he could feel the pressure of his own fingers meeting through the man's flesh, he snapped the human's spinal cord, then reached out with a thought and exploded his heart in his chest.

He dropped the piece of empty flesh, then turned to search the faces of the trembling women, confirming what his instincts had already told him. Sidonie wasn't among them.

He'd taken the first step down the hallway when he heard her voice behind him.

"Aden?"

He spun around. She was leaning against the open door jamb of the kitchen. And she was covered in blood.

CARL PINTO DIDN'T cry out or even groan when Sid shot him. He gave her a shocked look, shuddered so hard he shook her with the force of it, and collapsed to the kitchen floor. He would have dragged her down with him, but Sid shoved away from him at the last minute, eyeing him warily as she backed away. She stood there for a moment, staring, waiting for him to go poof the way she'd always heard vampires did when they died. But he remained stubbornly corporeal, lying there on the floor, blood soaking his shirt, twitching like a man having a really bad dream.

Sid didn't know what that meant. Would he be dead soon? Or would he suddenly rise like some movie villain to grab her ankle just when she thought she was free of him? She only knew he was down for now, and she intended to make sure he stayed that way. Her hands were shaking so badly she was barely able to press the magazine release on her Glock, and she nearly fumbled the empty mag when it dropped out of the grip. Drawing a deep breath, she forced herself to concentrate and shoved the empty mag into the pocket on the bellyband. It took her three tries before she managed to get her fingers around the backup magazine and slammed it into place. But by the time she was working the slide to chamber a round, she was feeling more confident, the hours of practice she'd put in on the gun range finally kicking in.

She started to lower the gun, intending to empty another ten rounds into Carl Pinto, when she heard women screaming behind her. The slaves! She'd left them in the bedroom, had hoped when she heard the fighting break out that they'd stay there until it was over.

Sid hurried to the open archway in time to see one of Pinto's henchman with a gun pressed to the neck of one of the teenagers who'd been trapped in the room with her. And facing the gunman, his back to Sidonie, was the most welcome sight she'd ever seen. Aden. Her heart swelled with such relief, such complete confidence that she was safe, that she finally understood why all of those fairy tale princesses collapsed in tears at the sight of their heroes.

And what a hero he was. She gasped as Aden used his vampire speed to grab the slaver's gun, seizing him by the throat and freeing the captive girl. Aden waited until all of the women were huddled in the corner, then . . . Ew. Okay, that was pretty gruesome, but it did the trick. The slaver collapsed like a puppet whose strings had been cut and, since he was human, leaving him quite dead.

Aden was about to start down the hallway to the bedrooms when she called out to him.

"Aden."

He spun at the sound of her voice, his eyes flaring blue with power as he took in her blood-soaked clothes, her battered condition. She lifted a hand to her face self-consciously, but before she could say anything, he was there, wrapping her in his arms, holding her against his broad chest, and whispering things she couldn't understand in her ear.

Sid let the tears come then, let all the fear and stress of the last few hours fall away as she held on to him. She would be strong again in a few minutes, but for now she let herself be the rescued maiden and cried with relief.

Aden pulled back until he could see her face. "Did he hurt you?" he asked, cupping her face in one big hand, rubbing a careful thumb over her tear-stained cheek. "Did he—" He drew a breath, searching her eyes, and she knew what he was asking.

"He didn't touch me," she said quickly. "Not like that."

"The blood—"

"It's mostly his," she said turning to indicate Pinto who didn't seem to have moved, but who still wasn't dead, damn it.

A deep growl rumbled out of Aden's chest as he stared at the fallen vampire.

"I shot him in the heart a bunch of times," she said in exasperation. "But he won't die."

Aden grinned and ran a hand over her tangled hair. "Do your parents know you're this bloody-minded?" He laughed when she swatted his arm and added, "You'll do nicely."

His expression turned grim when he switched his attention back to Pinto who, Sid was startled to see, was beginning to stir.

"He'll recover if we don't kill him," Aden said. "But he's your kill. Do you want the honor?"

"No," she said immediately, patting his broad chest. She could live without that particular *honor.* "I did my part. He's all yours now."

"Good," he said, and there was such malice in that one word, such cutting satisfaction, that Sid shivered, even though it wasn't aimed at her. "Watch," Aden murmured.

And Sid watched.

His gaze fixed on Pinto where he lay on the floor, twitching, Aden lifted his hand, palm up, almost like an invitation. But then his fingers closed slowly, and suddenly Pinto wasn't only twitching anymore. His eyes flashed open, and he squealed like a pig as he tried to shove himself up from the floor, tried to roll onto his belly and crawl toward the open door, bent on escape. Aden's fingers clenched into a tight fist, and Pinto's back bowed as he screamed in agony, begging, sobbing, before collapsing like a rag doll, his cries becoming high-pitched and mindless, all semblance of rationality gone.

It took a few minutes, while Sid stared in mingled horror and satisfaction, but Pinto finally, *finally,* died, becoming nothing more than a pile of dust on the cracked linoleum floor.

Aden's arms came around her, pulling her away from the mess that had been Pinto, hustling her through the destroyed living room. "The women will be taken care of," he assured her, seeming to understand that their welfare would be her first concern. "But I'm getting you out of here."

Sid nodded, sensing he was riding the sharp edge of violence, that as much as he *wanted* to see her safe, he *needed* it even more. For all his tough guy, female-hating image, Aden had a protective streak a mile wide. He needed to protect the people he cared about. He cared about those women, because he hated slavery of any kind. He cared about his vampire children. Sid had seen the way he looked at them, heard the respect in his voice when he spoke to them. And he cared about her. She'd seen the relief on his face when he'd realized she was alive and more or less unharmed, the pride when he'd offered her the honor of killing Pinto. He cared, and he needed to see her safe.

So she let him hustle her out the door and down the sidewalk. They were moving fast, with Bastien a few steps ahead of them. The others had stayed behind, presumably to take care of the captive women and clean up any evidence that they'd been there. She'd gotten the impression that vamps were very big on cleanup, leaving no footprints for anyone to follow. No wonder so few people knew anything about them.

It reminded her of the nightmare at Aden's office.

"Is everyone dead?" she asked, nearly stumbling to a stop as the thought hit her.

Aden didn't even slow down, just looped an arm around her waist and kept going. "Is who dead?" he asked absently, and Sid noticed for the first time that he'd grown more tense, not less, since they left the house, that he was scanning the street, as if expecting trouble.

"Is someone—" she started, but she never finished her sentence, because he suddenly wrapped both of his arms around her and spun away from the SUV.

"Bastien, down!" he roared, the end of his words lost as all three of the SUVs they were heading for suddenly blew up in a maelstrom of fire and debris. Sid screamed as the explosion rocked the night, blowing them off their feet and sending them sailing through the air. They hit the ground hard, Aden's arms still around her, cushioning her fall, as pieces of burning metal and molten glass rained down around them.

"SIDONIE, STOP," Aden growled. Realizing she couldn't hear him over her own screams, he put a gentle hand over her mouth. Her eyes were huge and terrified as they finally focused on him, but she nodded convulsively and sucked in the last of her cries with a gulping breath when he lifted his hand.

"Are you all right?" he asked her.

More frantic nodding, her fingers digging into his arm.

Aden held her tightly. She was trembling. She'd survived Carl Pinto, had nearly taken the damn vampire out herself, and this was her reward. They couldn't even walk down the street without some asshole trying to blow them up.

Aden stood, taking Sidonie with him. They couldn't stay here in the open. Instinct already had him searching the night, his power reaching out to find his latest would-be assassin. He would be nearby. He'd have wanted to witness Aden's demise for himself, either to claim the kill in the challenge, or to report to whatever coward he worked for.

Aden heard Sidonie whimper, realized he was squeezing her too tightly, and consciously relaxed his grip. He was beyond furious.

"God damn it," he muttered viciously. He looked up and found all four of his vampires surrounding him, the three he'd left in the house having rushed out at the sound of the explosion.

"Bastien!" he called. His lieutenant limped over to his side, and Aden glanced down to see blood soaking his pant leg.

"It's minor, my lord," Bastien assured him. "What can I do?"

"Take care of her," Aden said, transferring Sidonie into his care.

Sidonie rebelled briefly, twisting to look up at him. "Aden?"

He cupped her cheek, the gentleness an effort in the midst of his anger. "I'll be right back," he assured her. "You stay here with Bastien." He forced himself to speak softly, to let none of the rage that was boiling his blood leak into his words. It didn't fool Bastien, of course.

"Sire?"

He met Bastien's gaze over Sidonie's head. "Enough is enough," he said grimly. And with that, he reached out with his power and tunneled through the shadows like a serpent until he found the assassin. Human, he was hugging the wall of an empty house, shivering in the face of his failure, too terrified of discovery to run, too stupid to realize he couldn't hide from a vampire as powerful as Aden.

Aden dragged the coward into the light of the burning SUV, using his power like a hook dug into the man's chest, making it as painful as possible.

"I know you," he growled, recognizing the human Balderas. He'd been Silas's daytime security chief, but he was also the one who'd tried to abduct Sidonie in the train station.

"Fuck you, vampire," the human managed to gasp, pawing at his chest as if the hook digging into him was something physical he could remove. When he looked up, his eyes were filled with tears, but not with pain, or rather not that kind of pain. "You killed her!" he screamed accusingly.

"That's what this is about?" Aden questioned in disbelief. "You want revenge for that stupid bitch Silas?"

"Don't you—" Balderas's words cut off, replaced by a guttural scream of agony as Aden twisted the hook of his power down into the man's gut.

"This is how the game is played, human," Aden hissed, reeling his power in, dragging Balderas with it until he was within arm's reach.

"I loved her," the human whimpered.

"Then you can join her."

The hook became a poker as Aden rammed it up behind the man's rib cage and into his heart, burning white-hot while the human shrieked in pain, until he had no air left with which to scream, until his heart was nothing but a piece of shriveled meat.

Aden let the body fall to the street. But he wasn't finished yet. His head swung slowly from side to side, brow lowered, eyelids heavy over his searching gaze. But he wasn't seeing the neighborhood he stood in, with its neglected homes and old cars, the cracked sidewalks and dried lawns. His gaze went far beyond that. Pure, raw power was driving this search, spreading out into the city, seeking out and finding every damn vampire in the greater Chicago area, moving beyond even that to the thousands of vampires in the Midwest, their lives gleaming in his sight, some bright, some bare pinpricks of light.

"This ends now," he snarled. Gathering every ounce of power he possessed, sucking power from every vampire life he encountered, he sent out a raging tidal wave of command, claiming the Midwest as his own and daring any vampire to challenge him here and now, to wrest the power from him if they could, and to submit or die if they could not.

Throwing back his head, eyes closed, Aden stood with outstretched arms, hands open and palms up as he drew in the lives of the territory, one after another, first a trickle and then a flood. His power thundered as vampires surrendered, falling to their knees, to their faces, recognizing the new Lord of the Midwest.

SID DIDN'T KNOW what was happening. One minute they were hurrying to the SUV, and the next the world exploded. She knew Aden had saved her, that he'd protected her with his body. She didn't even think he was aware of the blood soaking the back of his shirt, of the rips and tears in his flesh. She didn't think he was aware of much, because he'd gone into some sort of Zen state that had even Bastien backing away and taking her with him.

"Bastien," she said, confused. "What—"

"Shh," he silenced her quickly. "Wait. Don't distract him."

She frowned. Distract him? Aden? He didn't look very distractible right now. In fact—Her thoughts cut off as a human suddenly came into view, looking like he was being reeled in like a fish, and just as reluctantly. She squinted. He looked familiar. The clothes were different, but . . .

"That's the guy," she whispered. Bastien's hand tightened on her arm in renewed warning, but he nodded.

"What will—"

"Sid," Bastien whispered urgently, turning her to face him. "Please. You need to be quiet."

Sid's lips flattened in frustration, but she figured Bastien knew what was going on far better than she did, and she didn't want to do anything that might jeopardize Aden's safety. She spun around, staring in shock when the guy suddenly shrieked as if someone was ripping his skin off, then felt slightly sick when Aden dropped the man's limp body to the street like a piece of forgotten trash.

Not that she blamed Aden for being angry. The guy had just tried to kill them all. But she'd seen enough violence and death in the last forty-eight hours to last the rest of her life.

She drew a deep breath, thinking it was finally over, but then Aden snarled a few words, and the world went even crazier. Her lungs strained to breathe as all the oxygen in the air seemed to disappear at once, as the few winter-bare trees around them began rattling like dried bones, bending and creaking beneath a powerful storm with Aden at its center. Thunder rumbled, but it wasn't the weather. It was coming from beneath their feet, an earthquake of sound, shaking the ground until she clung to Bastien, her feet braced as the street rippled like a sheet in the wind.

And still Aden stood, unmoving, immovable. His arms were stretched out as if he was calling down the power of the gods upon his enemies and bathing in its glow. Except the glow was the blue of his eyes, burning brighter than the flames of the wreckage, twin lasers of brilliant blue sapphire.

Suddenly Aden threw his head back and howled, his hands clenching into fists as if holding on to something. He stood that way for a long time, and then his arms fell to his sides, his eyes opened, and his head swiveled to pin her in the blue laser gleam of his gaze.

"Let go of her," he growled.

Bastien released her at once, his fingers flying open as if she'd suddenly become red-hot.

"Come here, Sidonie," Aden crooned.

She froze for the space of a heartbeat, knowing something more was going on than what her simple human senses could detect. But this was Aden, and she knew he'd never hurt her.

She closed the distance between them, going into his arms without hesitation.

He seemed larger somehow, and that was saying something, because he was a big guy to begin with. But at the same time, there was something weary in his expression, as if he had taken on a heavy burden in the last few minutes, something she couldn't see, except in his eyes.

"Are you okay?" she asked, touching her hand to his cheek and noticing that his eyes had begun to lose their laser-like glow and return to their usual midnight blue.

He blinked, seeming surprised that she'd ask. And then he smiled. "I will be. Let's go home, and I'll tell you all about it."

Chapter Twenty

ADEN USHERED Sidonie out of the elevator and into his private quarters. Elias had been summoned, and they'd used his vehicle to drive away from the bombing scene. The explosion had been too dramatic for even that neighborhood, and the scene was now crawling with human police. There was nothing to tie Aden to the destroyed vehicles, so there was no concern there. And Elias, intent on proving himself to his new lord, had remained behind at Pinto's place, calling in a team to see the women to safety and to do a thorough cleanup on the house. Aden didn't fully trust Elias, but he judged the vampire to be smart enough to see that his future depended on making Aden happy. With vampires, self-interest was always the best motivator.

"You'll probably want a shower," Aden told Sidonie as he hustled her through the sitting room and straight into the bedroom.

"Are you saying I stink?" Her response was playful enough, but she didn't quite pull it off. She had to be exhausted. She did need a shower, but not because she smelled. She was covered in blood, her clothes stiff, her skin sticky, with bits of grime from the explosion still clinging everywhere.

But Aden didn't tell her any of that. Slipping his arms around her, he pulled her close and said, "I'm saying you've had a rough couple of days, and a hot shower will help you sleep."

She sighed and leaned her forehead against his chest, her hands resting to either side of his waist. The gesture was so unaffected and spoke of such trust. He gazed down at her bent head and felt his heart clench with rare emotion.

"You're right," she said, then raised her head to meet his eyes with a wicked look that belied her exhaustion. "Will you join me?"

He gave a low laugh and let one hand slide down to rest on the curve of her sweet ass. "I have a phone call to make first. And I need to check with Bastien and the others. But it won't take long."

"Okay," she said, standing on tiptoes to give him a quick kiss. "But don't blame me if you miss all the fun."

Aden waited until she'd disappeared into the bathroom, pulling the door shut behind her, then he strode quickly back through his quarters and down the hall to his office.

Bastien and the others were waiting for him, but he raised a hand to put off any questions. "I need to call Lucas."

He didn't bother closing the door. Vampire hearing made such barriers useless. Besides, these four vampires were his closest advisers, his inner circle as he undertook to rule the Midwest. He'd have very few secrets from them.

Picking up the phone, he hit a speed dial number and listened to it ring. He didn't have to wait long. The call was answered on the second ring.

"I heard rumors of an earthquake in Chicago," a familiar voice said. "The vampire grapevine is humming tonight."

Aden grimaced. "I'm sorry about that, Lucas. It's not the way I wanted it to go, but the damn minions wouldn't stop coming. They blew up three fucking vehicles tonight, and Sidonie was with me. She could have been killed."

"Sidonie?" Lucas's voice sharpened with interest, and Aden realized he'd said more than he intended.

"A friend. Look, I'll be there tomorrow night to do it properly. I just wanted to touch bases."

"Consider the bases touched, and congratulations, my friend," Lucas said cheerfully. "I'll see you tomorrow. And bring Sidonie with you!" he added. He was still laughing when he hung up.

"Fuck," Aden swore softly. Lucas was never going to let him live this one down. Not that the other vampire had any ground to stand on. He was fully tethered to his new FBI girlfriend and looked to stay that way for a while.

Aden threw the phone onto the desk and joined Bastien and the others in the outer office.

"All right," he said. "As you heard, we're going to South Dakota tomorrow night. In and out. We'll be back here by dawn. Once that's taken care of, our first order of business is building a solid core of fighters. Bastien, I want you to put out a call for recruits. Priority goes to the vampires we worked with in Kansas, and then pretty much anyone from Lucas's or Raphael's territory. You know the drill. The four of you can do the initial screening, but I'll want a list for final review. No one, and I mean *not one*, of Klemens's brood gets in on this round. Maybe in the future, when things have settled down—don't close the door on the possibility, it'll only cause resentment. But right now, I don't trust any of them.

"I have to figure out how far Klemens's rot has spread and take out any of his former allies who have a lingering loyalty to the old guard. I don't want to have to worry about where the next fucking bomb is coming from. They'll say it's not fair, but fuck fair. We're vampires, not children.

"Next, we need a new place to live and use as a headquarters. Yesterday's attack showed how vulnerable this place is. Right now, I'm more interested in the acreage than the house. We can always build more house, but I want some space between me and the city. Put Hamilton on it. He can screen properties from a security standpoint, and he can also work with a realtor during the day. Once he has a few possibilities, I'll take a look, but I want it within the next week."

"What about Klemens's estate on the Gold Coast?" Bastien asked.

"My inclination is to burn it to the ground and sell the lot, but that might draw too much attention. Freddy, you know who handles this sort of thing. We need to make sure there are no secrets inside, no hidden passages or cubbies, nothing that can come back on us. I want it emptied to bare walls and naked floors. I want every closet emptied, every window opened. I want sunlight in every crevice and corner."

"Yes, my lord."

"Okay," Aden said, more than ready to call it a night. "Anything else?"

His vampires shared glances, shaking their heads in unison. "Nothing, Sire," Bastien said for all of them.

Aden grinned. "Then get some sleep. And congratulations, gentlemen. We did it."

SIDONIE LEFT ALL of her clothes in a pile on the floor of the bathroom, not sure if any of it was salvageable and not really caring. The only thing she took proper care with was her gun and bellyband. Folding the holster carefully, she stepped outside the bathroom and laid it on the dresser top, placing the gun on top of that and patting it fondly. It was probably silly, and not at all consistent with a tough girl image, but this was the first time she'd used the gun in a life-or-death situation. She felt proud and a little proprietary about the whole thing.

Smiling at herself, she gave the gun a final pat and went back to her shower, leaning into the stall to turn on the hot water and let it run. Guilt stabbed her about the wasted water. She was generally very conservation-minded. But sometimes a girl needed steam, and this was one of those times. Her pores needed opening. She wanted every trace of Carl Pinto and his hell house gone. Not to mention the fucking *explosion* afterward. She figured she'd pretty much used up her life's supply of adrenaline in the last two days.

While waiting for the bathroom to become foggy, she leaned toward the mirror and used her hand to rub away a clear space so she could study the damage.

"Oh my God," she muttered, horrified. This was so much worse than she'd thought. It was a wonder Aden hadn't walked away and left her on the street. Her hair was a rat's nest, and she was wearing a couple of days' worth of running mascara, but okay, that was expected. What she hadn't anticipated, although she probably should have, given her throbbing headache, was the red and purple bruising that covered half her face. She didn't know how much of it was from Pinto and how much from the explosion and didn't care. It all came together to create the nightmare image that was staring back at her. She literally looked like a refugee from a horror movie.

She closed her eyes and turned away, not wanting to see any more. The bathroom was steamy and warm, and she drew a deep, calming breath. The steam felt good on her sinuses, which were swollen nearly shut, but she'd forgotten about the injury to her side where Pinto had kicked her and had to swallow a cry of pain. She frowned and pressed the damaged ribs tenderly, checking for breaks. Not that she was sure she'd know the difference, but they didn't *feel* broken. Nothing squished when she pushed on it, no knife-sharp pain. Just really sore.

She sighed, wishing she could go back to that house, back to the moment when Aden had asked if she wanted to have the honor of finishing off Pinto herself. She wouldn't pass it up a second time. She'd blow that fucker's head off, but not before kicking him a few times so he'd know what it felt like to be tied up and helpless.

It was funny, in a not-funny-at-all way, that the worst of her injuries had come from her short time with Pinto and not the gigantic explosion later. That was because Aden had protected her, cushioning her fall and taking most of the damage himself.

She stepped into the shower, standing with her eyes closed and her head bent, letting the hot water pummel her back and neck, washing away the dirt and grime . . . and blood. Most of the blood was Pinto's, but not all of it. Needing to be clean, she turned around and reached for the shampoo. Her hair was a tangled mess, but the dirt had to come out first. She washed it quickly and thoroughly, then again, and finally massaged in about twice as much conditioner as she'd normally use. She was rinsing the last of that away, her eyes closed, her head tilted forward under the hot spray, when the shower door clicked open behind her.

She smiled without opening her eyes.

"I was wondering when you'd get here."

Aden's strong arms surrounded her, one hand going low on her belly as he nudged her back against his chest, his erection a hard length against her butt.

"I told you it wouldn't take long," he murmured. Reaching over her shoulder for the soap, he lathered it between his big hands and began to rub it over her skin with exquisite care, his touch far gentler than she would have thought him capable of.

Aden was a man of such contrasts. Not a man at all, according to him. He'd have her believe he'd left behind his humanity long ago when he'd been enslaved, treated like a thing. But that didn't explain his concern for the captured women, his kindness in making certain they were not just cared for, but safe and on their way home. The careful way he'd protected *her*. He was so powerful, and yet his touch when he examined her bruises was so tender, so full of . . .

She wanted to say love, but she didn't know if that was true. It felt like love, but maybe she was projecting her own feelings onto him. Because she was definitely falling and falling hard. She'd been teetering on the edge ever since the first night she'd met him. As rude and irritating as he'd been, there'd been an undeniable spark between them. She'd initially dismissed it as nothing more than sexual attraction. After all, the guy was sex on a stick. Any woman still breathing would want him. But the truth had crept in, growing with every hour they spent together, every tiny bit of himself that he revealed to her, until she could no longer deny it. She even knew the precise moment when she'd reached the point of no return. It was the look in his eyes when he'd seen her standing in that kitchen doorway tonight. His relief at seeing her alive, and his rage when he'd seen what Pinto had done to her.

She knew he cared, but she didn't know if he loved her.

"Turn around," he murmured against her ear, and she shivered at the rumble of his deep voice.

She obeyed, turning around to face him, lifting her gaze from his thickly-muscled chest to his wonderful, broad shoulders, past the strong column of his throat to his sensuous lips which curved slightly with amusement, before she finally met his dark eyes.

"I look awful," she lamented.

"You look beautiful. You're alive, and that's all that matters to me."

Sid sighed and rested her forehead against his chest. "I knew you'd come," she told him.

"But you didn't wait anyway."

She rolled her head from side to side. "I decided I was no fairy tale princess."

"Whatever that means," he growled. "He could have killed you. You should have waited for me."

"I couldn't. I didn't know what he would do to those women."

"I would have taken care of them. You know that."

"I did know, and I knew you'd come after us, but I was worried you'd be too late. Pinto was getting ready to move, and I was afraid he'd have us all packed up and gone before you got there."

"Then, I'd have tracked you down," he said implacably. "I *am* a vampire lord, Sidonie. I have resources."

"But you're not infallible. And I couldn't take that chance. Besides, I am woman, hear me roar."

"Again, whatever the fuck that means. Do I need to check your head for bumps?"

Sid laughed. "Poor old vampire. I'll explain it all to you later."

"Old?" His soap-slick hands slid down her back to cup her ass and lift her against his fully aroused shaft.

"Well, you *are* old," she said breathlessly, then hissed when her sore ribs were crushed against his chest.

Aden cursed and released her. "You're hurt. Let me heal—"

But Sid didn't let him finish. Standing on her tiptoes, she hooked her arms around his neck and pulled his face down to hers. She kissed him hungrily, twisting her tongue around his until he groaned. Wrapping both arms around her carefully, he took the kiss deeper, one hand tangling in her long hair, tugging her head back as his lips trailed past her mouth to her neck, kissing her softly there, letting her feel the sweep of his tongue before lifting his head with another curse.

Sidonie voiced a wordless protest. She didn't want to be pampered, she wanted to be fucked. Lifting her mouth to his, she teased his lips open with her tongue, and then she bit his lip hard enough to draw blood. He growled, but only squeezed her ass in warning.

She grinned against his lips and bit down harder, swallowing the tiny bit of his blood, feeling the rush, feeling every inch of her skin, every nerve ending tingle with awareness of him.

"You want to play?" he snarled finally. "We'll play." He lifted her higher, spinning them both around until her back was against the opposite wall of the shower, her legs around his waist.

His mouth went to her neck, and she shivered in anticipation. He sucked hard enough that she knew she'd have an old-fashioned hickey, but he didn't let her feel even the *edge* of his sharp teeth.

"Aden," she wheedled, flexing her hips against his belly.

"What do you want, *habibi?*"

"Not fair," she complained.

"I don't play fair."

"But—" She gasped as his hand slid down her back, over the curve of her thigh and into the aching emptiness between her legs, filling her with his fingers.

"You're so wet. Is that for me, Sidonie?"

"Yes," she breathed.

"Only for me?"

"Yes," she repeated urgently.

"Hmm." He pumped his fingers a few times in and out, lingered to dip briefly into her nether opening. Muscles bunched as he held her against the wall, as he reached between them to grip his cock and position it at the opening to her pussy.

"Scream for me, Sidonie," he murmured and slammed his full length inside her with a single powerful thrust, his hands gripping her ass, holding her wide open, so he could go deeper still.

And Sid screamed, but it was a cry of pure sensuous pleasure, her nails digging into his shoulders, her head thrown back against the wet tile as he pumped again and again, his hips slapping against hers, his butt flexing beneath her crossed ankles.

"Open your eyes," he commanded, and she did, eyeing him through a haze of desire, his handsome face so stern and focused, his dark eyes limned in the blue glow of his power.

"I want you to know who you're fucking," he snarled.

She gave him a languorous smile, her entire body suffused with desire, teetering on the edge of a climax that she fought to hold off, because it felt so damn good to ride this edge with him.

"I know who you are," she murmured, her words slurred with sensuality. "There's no one like you in the world. No one but you."

He growled, his eyes lighting up like lasers as his fingers dug into her ass. He leaned in, pressing his hard chest against her breasts, covering her mouth with a searingly hot kiss, his lips sealed against hers, his tongue stabbing between her teeth and tangling with her tongue. She was breathless when he finally released her, her heart racing, every nerve she possessed trembling in anticipation as he lowered his head to her neck. She felt the sweep of his tongue, rough against her hot skin, the scrape of his fangs, tormenting her, letting her feel their sharp points, but not breaking the skin, not yet.

"Aden," she pled, choking on a sob as she gasped for air, her body so ready to climax that her skin felt too tight, ready to explode from all the feelings, all the sensations roaring along her nerves, tightening her muscles.

"Sidonie," he whispered, like a prayer, and then his fangs sliced into her neck and punctured her vein, and she was lost.

She didn't scream as the climax took her, her throat seized up and she bucked in his arms, the orgasm pouring through her veins like hot liquid, feeling it in every inch of her body, from her fingers scraping over his scalp to her feet digging into the firm muscles of his ass, to the exquisite bundle of sensation in her clit, that oh-so-sensitive tiny nub. Pulses of overwhelming pleasure roared through her, waves of ecstasy so strong that she'd have been lost if not for Aden, holding her in his arms, keeping her safe.

I love you, she thought, but didn't say, as he lifted his head and met her gaze.

"Stay with me, Sidonie," he murmured.

She smiled. He couldn't say it either. "I will," she whispered. "As long as you want me."

SID CAME OUT of the bathroom to find Aden stretched out on the bed, gloriously naked, propped up against the headboard with one muscled arm behind his head. He held an iPad in his other hand, his expression very intent as he read whatever it was displaying. She stood for a moment, admiring him.

"Like what you see?" he asked, without lifting his gaze from the iPad.

She laughed, crossing the room to climb onto the bed with him. "Fishing for compliments, vampire?"

He snorted. "Like I need to."

"Oh my God! You are so vain."

He cut his gaze to look at her. "Are you saying you don't like what you see?"

Sid huffed out a dismissive breath. "Right. So, tell me something."

"Anything in particular?"

She slapped his thigh. It was like slapping solid steel, and she paused for a moment to appreciate it, stroking her hand back and forth.

"Sidonie?"

Her gaze shot up, and her cheeks heated. Jesus, she was pathetic. "Yeah," she said, covering, "I was just thinking. At that challenge gathering, when I met you the first time—"

"I remember it well."

She flushed with pleasure at the heat in his eyes, the rumble of lust in his voice. "Um, right," she said, trying to gather her thoughts under the onslaught of erotic images he conjured up without even touching her.

"How did you become a vampire?" she blurted out. She was pretty sure that wasn't what she'd been meaning to ask, but it was the first thing that came to her mind.

Aden put the iPad aside and studied her in puzzled amusement.

"I mean, I've always wondered," Sid continued. "Most of you, the few I've met anyway, seem"—she frowned, as if looking for the right word—"*happy*," she said, surprised at her own choice of words. "I've read lots of books, and they always talk about how the vamp was turned against his will, and he's a monster and he hates it. But every vampire I've ever met seems really happy to be one. Is that because you've just accepted it? Did you have a choice about the whole thing?"

ADEN EYED SIDONIE curiously. She was the most inquisitive woman he'd ever met. Or maybe it was simply that she was the only woman whose questions he'd ever been inclined to answer.

"Every vampire has his own story," he said, knowing that such a trite response would never satisfy her.

"But what's *your* story?" she persisted, right on cue.

He considered blowing her off, distracting her with more sex, which they'd both enjoy. But if he wanted to spend some time with Sidonie—and he did, a very *long* time—then he was going to have to answer her questions. Because she'd only keep asking.

"My Mistress," he told her, "that is, the vampire who made me, did offer me a choice. But it was one she knew I would accept. I was in a dire situation, albeit of my own making, and she gave me an out. A way to escape into what she said would be a better life."

"And was it?"

"Oh, yes."

Morocco, 1778

ADEN ROSE LATE in the day. It was the first week of the holy month, and business was light. Not even the wealthy would dare the wrath of their god during this time. He thought of it as *their* god because he no longer believed in god, not theirs or anyone else's. Certainly not the god of his father, who'd sold him like an animal, or even the god of his mother, who discarded him to secure her own comfort. No god had ever done Aden any favors.

But he was grateful for this one time of the year when he wasn't forced to play the prostitute, or, even worse, the whipping boy of that fat turd who continued to beat him bloody whenever the mood struck him, and all with his mistress's blessing. How could he ever have thought she cared for him? She'd replaced him in her bed long ago, buying a new young slave to train just as she had him. But he'd thought some affection still lingered between them. Her willingness to sell him so cruelly had killed any such illusions, her betrayal far greater than the simple brutality of the fat man.

He rolled off the bed slowly, feeling twice his age as every inch of scar tissue, every fresh wound made itself known. He had scars on top of scars. And when he wasn't being whipped, he was expected to service the women who continued to ask for him, though he derived only the most perverse pleasure from fucking them. He'd fooled himself in the past into thinking they desired him, even cared for him. But no longer. He was a whore, and they used him like one.

"Aden?" It was young Sana, tapping lightly on the frame of his doorway. "Can I oil your back for you?"

The child felt responsible, as if she'd somehow asked to be whipped bloody that day he'd gone to her rescue.

"Not today, *asal.*"

"Are you sure? Because we're not busy."

"Not today," he repeated.

"Very well, but if you change your mind . . ."

Aden remained silent until he heard the sound of her bare feet padding softly away. Sometimes he let her rub the oils in, because it did help, softening the scar tissue and keeping it as flexible as it was ever going to be.

But he didn't trust himself tonight. He was filled with such rage. It was a hot coal in his belly, burning him from the inside out. Was this to be the rest of his life? What would happen when he grew too old to service the women, too old for even the fat man to enjoy beating? Would his mistress turn him out on the streets to beg?

He began to pace, his long legs needing no more than three strides to travel the length of the room. With every step he took, his anger grew. What purpose was there in continuing this farce? Why not end it? He knew the herbs, a simple cup of tea, sweetened with honey to blunt the taste. One of his ladies had brought him a gift of tiny date cakes, baked with cinnamon and sesame, prepared by her cook who was a slave like him. But they would taste all the better for that, and he could eat them all with his final cup of tea. There would be no point in saving them any longer, no point in hoarding them like the only treasures of his miserable life.

He paced some more, back and forth, nursing his rage, his feelings of betrayal, until an idea began to take shape. Yes, he would end this wretched existence, but he wouldn't go alone.

Crossing to the cheap wooden box where he stored his few possessions, he dug down until he unearthed yet another gift from a customer, this one far more useful than a few date cakes. It was a blade, forbidden for one such as he to possess. But the lady had given it to him not because it was a weapon, but because it was beautiful. It was meant to be a woman's table knife, small and adorned with jewels. When she'd given it to him, it had been as dull as a child's toy, but no longer. He'd sharpened it over time, hiding it by day and working late at night, until the edge now gleamed in the low light. He pressed it gently against his fingertip and watched a line of blood well up.

He smiled. It would do.

He didn't bother dressing for the occasion. None of his clothes were any better than the loose trousers he was wearing. And it didn't matter anyway.

Palming the blade, he pulled open the flimsy door which was for his clients' privacy, not his own, and strode down the short hallway to the stairs, ascending swiftly to the third floor, with its cool, tiled hallway, where his mistress lived in far greater splendor that any of the slaves who made such opulence possible. He glanced through the small window near her door and saw that night had descended. He could hear the crowds outside, the devout whose fast ended with the setting sun, and who would now gorge themselves in anticipation of doing it all over again tomorrow.

He didn't bother knocking on his mistress's door. He knew she'd be breaking her own fast, sitting down to a finer meal than anyone else in the house would enjoy. Once upon a time, he'd have been dining with her, but she no longer invited him.

It didn't matter. Tonight, he was inviting himself.

He shoved the door open, ignoring her squawk of surprise. "How dare—" Her outraged protest was cut off, quite literally, by his blade against her throat.

She stared up at him in shock, her dark gaze wet with fear. "Aden," she gasped. "Please."

Aden watched her with hooded eyes, feeling nothing but grim satisfaction as she begged for her life.

"I love you," she whispered.

Disgust turned to rage, a cold fury that drew the gleaming edge of the sharp knife across her throat, slicing through skin and tendons, releasing a fountain of blood as she went to her death staring up at him in disbelief.

He twisted his fingers in her long hair, watching the hot blood pump out of her neck, disappointed that she hadn't lingered, that her death had been far too swift.

"You made it too easy."

Aden spun at the sound of a woman's low, sensuous voice behind him. He stared at the newcomer, the bloody blade still gripped in one hand, his other hand opening to let his dead mistress's body fall to the floor, forgotten.

The woman smiled. "If you sever the neck here . . ." She drew a finger across the front of her own throat. "It's satisfying, but the blood spills too quickly. If you want them to linger, you must cut here." She indicated the side of her throat. "They will still die, but it will be slow, and they will know every moment of their death."

Aden stared silently. He didn't know this woman, had never seen her before in this house. She wasn't veiled and didn't seem bothered by it, or by the fact that she was facing a strange, armed and half-naked male. She also didn't seem overly troubled that he'd just murdered his mistress in front of her.

"Aden, isn't it?" she said, taking a step closer.

He thought about using the knife on her before she could run screaming to report his crime. But something stopped him. She hadn't done so yet, and besides, what did it matter if this woman reported him? He couldn't remain here anyway, and he'd be long gone before anyone arrived.

She stretched out a hand, stroking it down his arm, the look in her eyes one he'd seen often enough to recognize it. Women found him attractive, beautiful even. They admired his face, his size, and the strength of his body.

"Sweet child," she whispered, urging him to turn around. "Let me see."

He turned, letting her see the ruin of his back, even as he scowled at his own complacency, his obedience. He was hardly the child she'd called him, but it was as if her voice was inside his head, replacing his own thoughts, telling his body what to do.

"She's nearly ruined you, hasn't she?" He felt cool fingers gliding over the lumpy scar tissue. "What a waste," she murmured. "But we can fix that," she added, speaking normally. "Look at me, child."

He did, wondering again why she was calling him *child* when they were surely very near the same age.

"Would you like to go with me, Aden? To leave this place, this *life*, forever?"

He stared at her in confusion. "I don't—" he started, his voice a croak of sound. "I don't understand," he said, trying again. "Where would we go?"

"Anywhere we want," she said, with a mysterious smile. "I can give you freedom you've only dreamed of. We can go anywhere, do anything."

"How?"

Her smile broadened, until it was a slash of white against her olive skin. He watched in amazement as some of her teeth began to grow, until they became . . . fangs. Like a serpent's. Two smooth, sharp fangs that split her upper gums and pressed against the lush fullness of her lower lip.

Somewhere in the back of his brain a voice was mewling in terror, urging him to run away from this monstrous female. But the rest of him felt . . . content. As if after twenty-seven years of wandering, he'd finally found the one place he truly belonged. He lifted his hand, wanting to stroke the woman's cheek which would be smooth and soft, to touch the diamond hardness of her fangs. But the blood of his mistress still dripped from his fingers, and it made him hesitate. The woman saw his hesitation and smiled, and then she did something that shocked him to his core. Taking his hand in hers, she kissed it, her tongue lapping out to taste the blood.

Aden's eyes grew wide. "Vampire," he whispered. He'd heard tales of such things, but had thought them only that, children's stories meant to frighten.

The woman smiled up at him, proudly, as if he'd done something clever, something marvelous.

"I am Vampire," she agreed. "And it is wondrous. I would share it with you, Aden, if you will have it."

"What would it mean?"

"You and I would go far away. We would want for nothing."

Aden looked around the opulence of his dead mistress's rooms, the silk and gold, the fine porcelain dishes. And he thought of his own tiny room, with its cheap wooden box hiding his few treasures, the dim light concealing the threadbare state of his linens, the gaudy gifts his women brought him as if he was an animal to be blinded by their shiny surface and too stupid to know their true value.

He thought of little Sana and the others. He would miss them. He would have given his life to protect them. But he discovered he would not sacrifice this future for them.

"What is your name, mistress?" he asked.

The woman's smile grew. "I am Leticia."

Aden repeated the strange syllables silently, tasting them on his tongue. "Leticia," he said out loud. "I will go with you."

Chicago, IL, present day

"WHAT HAPPENED after that?"

Sidonie's voice jerked Aden back to the present, to the elegant rooms of his Chicago headquarters and the warm woman lying naked next to him and smelling of sex. He rolled her beneath him, savoring her easy surrender, the way she spread her legs to accommodate him, her silky thighs cradling his hips.

"We traveled the world," he said, answering her question.

"Did you . . . I mean . . . were you a couple?"

Aden raised an inquisitive eyebrow. "You mean did we have sex?"

Sidonie scowled up at him, and he leaned down to kiss her soft lips, smoothing away the frown.

"Of course we did. She was my Mistress. She made me a vampire. We were lovers for half a century."

"Why'd you stop?"

He shrugged one shoulder dismissively. "One night I saved her life, and she released me."

"Did you . . ." Sidonie drew a deep breath, as if gathering her courage. "Did you love her?"

He stroked his fingers gently over her forehead, along her cheekbones, memorizing her face. "A vampire always loves the one who turns him," he said thoughtfully. "It's as if our blood cells recognize where we came from, who created us." He held her gaze, wanting her to understand. "But I never loved her the way you mean. She was a willing lover and an intelligent woman. I enjoyed her."

"But why would she send you away when you'd saved her life?"

"She had other vampire children by that time, and I'd grown too powerful. She was afraid of me. She called it a gift when she released me, but really, she was just sending me away. I was alone for half a century after that. I had no one until I found Bastien and made him my own."

"But how could you be lovers if she was afraid of you?"

"Sex between us had grown infrequent by then. She said I was cold. That while I knew where to touch, where to put my tongue, how to deliver pleasure, there was no passion in my lovemaking. When she released me, she kissed me good-bye and said she hoped I'd find my passion someday."

"And did you?"

Aden looked down at Sidonie, at her crystal blue eyes gazing up at him with such honesty, at the wild copper curls tangled on the pillow beneath her. He brushed a length of hair away from her bruised cheek, marveling at the contrast between them—his hands seeming so big and rough next to her delicate features, so dark against her pale skin.

"You tell me, Sidonie. Am I cold?"

She blinked up at him for a puzzled instant, then her arms looped around his neck, and her fingers stroked his nape. "No," she whispered. "You're the sapphire heart of the hottest flame. When I'm with you, I feel like the sexiest woman in the whole world. I feel cherished and safe." She swallowed. "I feel loved."

Aden froze. Did he love Sidonie? Had more than two and half centuries of life brought him to this place and time so that he could finally know what it meant to love someone? To love *this* woman? He kissed her again, a tender brush of his lips that became a lingering kiss, a seduction of her mouth. Sidonie met his kiss with eager passion, her mouth opening beneath his, her tongue darting out to taste him, to weave around his until he felt the hunger rising in him, the need to possess her again, to claim her as his own.

He lifted his hips, letting his already-hard shaft drag in the wetness between her thighs. Sidonie made a greedy little noise and spread her legs wider, thrusting against him.

"Am I cold, Sidonie?" he whispered again.

"No," she insisted fiercely. She reached between their bodies, taking his cock in her slender fingers and stroking him lovingly before tightening her grip and placing his tip between the swollen folds of her sex, letting him feel her heat.

There was nothing cold about his Sidonie, he thought as he as plunged deep into her silky warmth, her sheath clasping and releasing his cock as he drove in and out. He groaned at the satin slickness of her pussy, at the sensual fullness of her breasts, the hard pearls of her nipples.

The slow seduction became a demand as his pace quickened. He slammed his hips between her thighs, his cock burying itself deep inside her, then pulling out and doing it again. Her sheath squeezed him with every thrust, a thousand fingers caressing his length, stroking him, urging him to come, to go over that edge with her, to tumble into the unknown of ecstasy, to take the chance.

"I love you," she whispered against the sweat-slick skin of his neck, her fingers digging into the muscles of his back, her legs crossed over his back, trapping him inside her. "You're *my* passion, Aden. I love you."

A rush of emotion answered her whispered vow, a fire that spread to every inch of his body, lighting up his nerves and warming his cold heart until it slammed against his ribs, feeling as if it was beating willingly for the first time in two centuries. As if until now, this moment, it had pumped only because it had to, because it kept him alive. He felt it pounding in his chest, felt Sidonie's heat surrounding him, welcoming him, loving him.

The climax came from nowhere, roaring over his body, every muscle taut with desire, every nerve thrumming with electricity. His balls tightened and his cock swelled, growing harder and thicker inside Sidonie, filling her so completely he could barely move. She moaned, a sound full of heat and desire, and it was *his* name on her lips.

"Aden." She repeated it like a prayer, her head thrown back, her nails digging into his shoulders.

Aden growled, his fangs splitting his gums eagerly, hungry for her blood, for the fever that was Sidonie. *His* Sidonie.

He lowered his mouth to her neck, slicing through her velvet skin, piercing the thin wall of her vein and drinking down the smooth, honeyed flow of her blood, feeling it speeding to every cell of his body, giving him life, giving him *her.*

She bucked beneath him, crying out as his bite brought euphoria instead of pain, her mouth closing on his shoulder as she tried to muffle her scream. He felt his skin tear beneath her teeth, felt the pull as she swallowed his blood. He tightened his grip, lowering his full weight onto her body, holding her in place as she thrashed against the double assault of his bite and his blood. She'd never tasted that much of his blood before, never had that connection. Aden knew what could be forged if she drank more, if he permitted her to do it again in the future. A powerful link would be created, the kind of link humans could only try to replicate with their vows and their protestations of love.

If asked, he'd have said he didn't want such a link with *anyone.* So he couldn't explain why he pressed her face against his shoulder, while he urged her to bite harder, to drink more. Why his cock stirred anew when she complied, why he joined her as she moaned against his skin, as a final orgasm rolled through them both, leaving her shuddering and limp in his arms.

Aden gathered Sidonie close, holding her tightly as he rolled over and pulled the comforter back on the bed, then slid them both into the warmth beneath the covers.

"You're staying with me today," he said fiercely. "No more roaming around the office for you."

She didn't even stir, only cuddled deeper into his embrace and went to sleep. He smiled down at her, marveling at the feelings tightening his chest. He didn't know if it was in his nature to take a mate in the vampire way, to bind someone to him forever. What he felt for Sidonie was love, but forever was a long time. She might grow tired of him, of the life he led. Maybe she wanted children and grandchildren, and he could give her none of those.

But for now, she was his. And he intended to keep her for a very long time.

"Sleep, *nuur il-'en.* We have a busy night tomorrow."

Chapter Twenty-One

SID WOKE WITH a smile as a muscled arm looped around her waist and pulled her in, sliding her across the sheets and tucking her underneath his heavy body as if she weighed nothing. She opened her eyes to find Aden staring down at her, looking like a man who'd been waiting impatiently for her to wake up.

"Is it nighttime again?" she asked sleepily, reaching up to brush a thick lock of black hair out of his eyes.

"How are you feeling?" he asked instead, his gaze so intent that it made her wonder if she should be feeling worse than she did.

"Um. A little sore?" she ventured. "You're a big guy and—"

"Not that, Sidonie," he said, though he couldn't stop the smug smile that curved his lips.

"Oh!" she said, then frowned, as if just remembering the beating she'd taken at the hands of that creep Carl Pinto, remembering the explosion and fire afterwards. "Surprisingly well, actually." Her frown deepened as she realized just how good she really *did* feel. She drew a deep, testing breath, and there wasn't even a twinge from her ribs. She touched her face cautiously. Her cheekbone had been so swollen that she could see it without a mirror. But it seemed completely healed, not tender and no longer swollen. And she felt rested in a way she hadn't in weeks, although that could be explained by the rigors of the previous night. She blushed hotly, remembering exactly what some of those *rigors* had entailed.

Aden caught the blush, of course, and grinned, as if he knew what she was thinking about.

"Can you read my mind?" she asked accusingly.

"Only if I try."

"Well, don't."

"Unless it's necessary for your safety."

She pursed her lips, thinking about that one. He laughed and bent his head to kiss her, coaxing her lips with soft caresses, until her mouth opened to him.

When he lifted his head again, she was breathless . . . but still in possession of a brain, so she asked, "How long did I sleep?" thinking that perhaps she'd been unconscious for days, and that's why her various injuries were healing already.

"Through the day, a little longer. Sunset was an hour ago."

"But just one day?"

"You're wondering why your injuries have healed," he guessed.

She nodded.

"Do you remember biting me?" He nodded his chin at his left shoulder where she could just make out the imprint of a human bite mark. Her bite?

"Oh my God! I'm so sorry!" she said instantly. "I don't—"

He kissed her again, stopping the flow of words. "Don't apologize, *habibi*. It was a good thing."

"Did it hurt?"

He didn't answer her directly, saying instead, "My blood healed you."

She gave him a puzzled look. "Professor Dresner, that bitch," she added, when his eyes narrowed at the name. "She told me the reason you all were so good-looking—"

"Not *all* of us."

Sid rolled her eyes. "The reason so many of you are good-looking is because once you become a vampire, your blood heals everything that was wrong, all the defects."

"And some of us were *born* looking this good."

She laughed and cupped her hand to his chiseled cheek. "And some of you are way more than just good-looking. But," she continued, "now you're telling me that the healing abilities of your blood can be extended to anyone who drinks it?"

"That's our deepest secret. If you tell anyone—"

"I know, you'll have to kill me."

"Not I. They'll have to go through me to get to you. But eventually, the Council would kill us both."

She blinked up at him. "You're serious."

"I'm serious. Although the major concern is that it not become public knowledge, and you *are* a journalist. That brings you extra scrutiny."

"Whew! Okay. My lips are sealed. What happens if I bite you again? Do I become a vampire?"

"No, it's little more complicated than that, and I like you the way you are. But . . ." He grew far too serious all over again. "If you continue to drink my blood, it will bind us together."

She met his solemn gaze. "Like forever?"

"For as long as we choose to continue," he amended. "But it will link your life to mine in a very direct way. The longer we're together, the stronger the link, but even with what we've taken from each other already, I could find you almost anywhere. I knew you were at Pinto's last night, because we got a tip. But once there, I could sense that you were alive and in that house. Now that my blood is inside you, I would no longer need help finding the house. I could track you from anywhere in the city."

"So, we're like, going steady?"

He laughed, and she reached up again to touch his cheek. "You should do that more often," she said.

"Do what?"

"Laugh. It's a good look on you."

"I'll keep that in mind, but, Sidonie, this is serious. The more you drink my blood, the tighter it binds you to me. In the way of Vampire, we will be mated."

She shrugged. "Okay. I'd rather have a diamond ring, but super healing is good, too."

ADEN STUDIED Sidonie as she gave him a sweet smile, as if he hadn't just told her she was chaining herself to him in the most visceral way imaginable. Their bodies would be linked. This wasn't some romantic human ceremony with promises of love and devotion, this was blood calling to blood. If she stayed with him long enough, their very lives would be bound together. She would remain young as long as she drank his blood, but, by the same token, if he died . . .

Sid pushed against his weight, and he let her roll them over until she was lying on top of him. Propping her hands on his chest, she stretched up and began kissing his face all over, light touches of her lips on his mouth, his cheeks and forehead, his lowered eyelids one at a time.

"I love you, Aden," she whispered, and his heart clenched as his arms closed around her. But she wasn't finished. She slid from his embrace, dropping kisses along his jaw and neck, letting him feel the heat between her thighs as she slid downward. She kissed the pads of muscle over his chest, closing her mouth over one flat, male nipple and sucking it to hardness, then locking her teeth over it and biting gently.

His cock flexed hungrily at the feel of her mouth on him, but his gut tightened and he fought the urge to take control, to obey the hard-earned instinct screaming at him to throw her over and fuck her until she begged for release. He liked, he *needed*, to dominate his lovers.

"Aden." Sidonie's whisper cut into his thoughts, and he looked up to find her eyes wide with emotion and filled with tears. "I know what they did to you, baby, but it doesn't have to be that way. Let me love you. Let me do this for you."

Aden stared at her. He knew he was twisted, that his years as a slave had warped his sexual desires by forcing him to play the submissive when dominance had been bred into his DNA. Not even his vampire Mistress had ever forced him to submit like that. He hadn't surrendered control over his body to anyone since the day he'd left Zaahira's whorehouse in Morocco, and he wasn't going to start now.

Except. This was Sidonie. She was *his*. And somehow he had also become *hers*.

Aden forced himself to relax, consciously releasing one muscle at a time. Tangling his fingers in the silky strands of Sidonie's hair, he watched as she bent to her task once more, licking the skin over his abdomen and belly, her succulent mouth leaving soft, sucking kisses in a trail to his groin and lower. And there she paused, slender fingers wrapping around his straining cock, holding it like a thick stick of delicious candy as she stroked her tongue up one side and down the other, rolling her gaze up to be sure he was watching when she took only the tip of him into her mouth, working it like she would a kiss, her tongue twisting and dipping into the slit at its head.

Aden's snarled demand for more became a groan of pleasure when she finally took him fully into her mouth, his erection stiffening even further as her lips closed around him, as her head dipped lower with every slow suck, until finally the tip of his cock hit the back of her throat. She hummed with pleasure, and the sound vibrated along the taut skin of his shaft like a tuning fork. It was everything he could do not to grab her head and fuck her delicious mouth, not to slam deep into her throat until he came hard and she was forced to swallow every drop. But more even than that, he wanted the hot, wet glove of her pussy. He wanted her legs around his waist, he wanted her bucking beneath him where she belonged.

"I want your pussy," he growled and fisted his hand in her hair, forcing her to look at him.

She gave his cock a final, firm suck, then lifted her head slowly, her tongue gliding all the way up his shaft until she released him, her warm breath blowing across the wet head of his dick while her eyes met his. She licked her lips, savoring the taste of him with a wicked grin.

Aden reached for her, intending to roll her over and slam between her thighs until she screamed his name. But instead of submitting like a good girl, she braced her hands on his abs and slid up his body to straddle him once more, her pussy so hot it was like a fire against his groin. She raised herself enough to wrap her fingers around his cock, to position it between the swollen lips of her sex, and then she lowered herself slowly, surrounding his cock in the heat of her body, fucking him, *mounting* him.

Aden stiffened again, every muscle turned to steel, his fingers digging into her hips. But then Sidonie closed her eyes and began to rock her hips above him, swaying gently, his cock sliding in and out of her silky, wet pussy with every movement.

His fingers loosened their grip, one hand traveling up her smooth back and pulling her down until their mouths met in a slow, passionate kiss. He released her mouth gently, his teeth closing over her lower lip in a lingering bite as she struggled to catch her breath.

"Love you, *habibi*," he murmured. Her blue eyes opened in surprise and filled with crystal tears.

"I love you, too," she whispered. Then she sat up and began riding him harder, her hips flexing and rolling, full breasts swaying tantalizingly close before her hands came up to cup them and squeeze. Aden growled a protest at that, substituting his own fingers for hers, caressing the soft globes, pinching her nipples between thumb and forefinger, feeling a fierce satisfaction when her pussy clenched around his cock in response, when she cried out and her thighs clamped around his hips.

She raised her arms to cradle her head as she sought comfort for her growing hunger, as her moans grew in volume, becoming whimpers of need until Aden finally reached between her thighs and pressed his fingers against the swollen nub of her clit.

Her eyes flashed open, unseeing as she gave a wordless cry. Her movements became frantic, her fingers coming down to cover his as if to prevent him from lifting his hand, the swell of her breasts so enticingly erotic that Aden flexed his abs and sat up enough to take one tender globe into his mouth. Sucking until her nipple plumped like a ripe cherry, he bit down and drank in the honeyed taste of her blood, while her pussy spasmed around him, grabbing his cock like a hard fist.

Sidonie screamed as she came, leaning forward to dig her nails into his chest, her twisting hips grinding her sex against him until he could feel every convulsion of her pussy as her climax rippled along his cock. He rode out her orgasm, gritting his teeth, holding her as she shuddered in the aftermath, as she collapsed on top of him, her breasts crushed against his chest, her nipples rigid points that scraped his skin with every breath. And then he stroked a hand down her back and his fingers dipped into her tight, little asshole. He began thrusting up against her, fucking her with his cock as his fingers filled her ass, hearing her exhausted moans turn into blissful shouts as he slammed into her still-trembling pussy. Aden groaned as her sheath tightened around him yet again, as his own orgasm seized his body, his release roaring down his cock in a rush of heat, filling Sidonie as she writhed beneath him, her screams of climax meeting his roar of satisfaction as they fell together into ecstasy.

Aden wrapped his arms around Sidonie's trembling body as he fell back onto the bed. His heart was slamming against his ribs, or maybe the pounding heart was hers. She was plastered against him so tightly, their sweaty bodies so close that even he couldn't tell where one began and the other ended. Her breath was hot on his skin, her fingers stroking his chest lightly where they were trapped between them.

She sighed as he rolled her slightly to the side, permitting her to stretch her legs out from where they'd been wrapped around his hips. Aden glided a calming hand over her neck and shoulder, then pulled the sheet up to cover her before she could get chilled.

Sidonie made a soft noise and burrowed closer. And Aden felt . . . content. It was such a foreign emotion that he stopped to examine it. Sidonie had done this. Aden had believed himself free of the bonds of slavery long ago, but he'd been wrong. One last chain had remained, dug in so deeply that he hadn't known it was there, warping him, keeping him a slave to their twisted desires.

He hugged her close, touching his lips to her tousled hair. Sidonie's mouth curved into a smile that he felt against the bare skin of his chest, her body limp as she drifted half asleep.

He was wishing she could stay that way when his cell phone rang, vibrating across the side table like some over-caffeinated alien.

He reached out a long arm and snagged it. "Bastien? Give us an hour."

Sidonie stirred enough to mumble, "What's in an hour?"

"Sorry, *habibi*. That's how long we have to shower and join the others. Come on." He put his arms around her and climbed out of bed, setting her in front of him and making sure she was steady on her feet, before propelling her toward the bathroom with a possessive hand on her ass.

She wiggled her butt away from his hand and frowned over her shoulder, her eyes still cloudy with sleep. "Where are we going?" she asked grumpily.

"South Dakota. I'm about to become an official vampire lord."

Chapter Twenty-Two

South Dakota

SIDONIE FELT LIKE she was in a movie. One of those shadowy, film noir kind of movies, where all of the action takes place in the middle of the night, usually when it's raining. So far, her night had all the hallmarks. They'd flown out of a dark, private airport outside Chicago, with no one around except for them and their flight crew. They'd landed in Rapid City and rolled away from the brightly-lit main concourse to a small, dark hangar on the side, where two SUVs had been waiting for them. The SUVs had drivers, but consistent with the night's air of secrecy, they'd both gone in one of the vehicles with Kage and Freddy, while Travis took the wheel of the other and drove her and Aden, with Bastien riding shotgun.

There was no rain here in South Dakota, but there *was* snow. After a fairly mild early winter of nothing but snow showers, the real season was finally upon them. The snow was coming down heavy and hard, but the weather didn't seem to bother anyone but her. Maybe because everyone else was an indestructible vampire who didn't have to worry about car crashes. She leaned forward to peer between the front seats and out through the windshield of the SUV. Apparently, indestructible wasn't the only thing vampires were. They could also see in the dark, because she didn't see any gleam of headlights out there.

She sat back, her fingers finding Aden's hand and squeezing—for her own reassurance rather than his. One would have thought becoming a vampire lord was a big enough deal to warrant some nerves, but Aden was completely relaxed. He leaned over and kissed the top of her head but didn't say anything.

Sid didn't know where they were going. Oh, Aden had told her they were going to visit Lucas Donlon, who was a vampire lord himself and currently ruling what was called the Plains Territory. It seemed Aden had worked for Lucas for, oh, about a *century*. A century! She felt like a toddler. Hell, her *grandparents* hadn't even been born yet when the two vampires met. This was going to take some getting used to.

She stole a furtive glance at Aden, his profile clear in the glow of the dash lights. Yeah, that would take some getting used to, but he was worth it.

Anyway, Lucas had taken over all the vampires when Klemens, the bastard, was killed. In fact, she'd overheard a conversation between Kage and Travis that made her think Lucas had been the one to kill him. But whether that was true or not—and this part was difficult to understand—he held the lives of the Midwestern vamps as well as his own. Sid was still learning how vampire lords did their thing, but one thing she did know was that the connection between the lords and their vampires was very direct and very personal.

"Is it dangerous?" she whispered to Aden.

"What?"

"What Lucas is going to do to you tonight. Is it dangerous?"

He freed his hand from hers and put his arm around her instead, pulling her against his side. "Not at all. Tonight's mostly a formality. You already saw the hard part."

"You mean when you caused the earthquake," she said confidently.

Aden huffed a laugh. "I told you, that wasn't an earthquake. It was more of a concussive wave, like what happens with a pile driver."

"Still made the earth move."

"But, *habibi*," he murmured in her ear, "I do that *every* night."

Sid gave a surprised laugh, then covered her mouth with a guilty glance at the two vampires in the front seat. She didn't argue the point, though. He certainly made *her* earth move.

The SUV made a wide, curving turn, and there was finally something other than darkness outside the windows. There were lights and . . . a barn? With horses?

Aden caught her puzzled frown and said, "Lucas likes horses. He breeds them."

"Huh."

"Here we are."

The SUV slowed in front of a lovely and expansive house, all lit up with landscape lights that gave off a soft golden glow. Pretty. The front door of the house opened to reveal yet another incredibly handsome vampire.

Aden turned to Sid and hugged her close. "Remember, Sidonie, Lucas is a friend. No matter what you see tonight, no matter how bad it looks, I'm in no danger."

Sid pulled back so she could look into his face, searching his eyes in the dim light. She had a thousand questions she needed to ask, but before she could ask even one, Bastien pulled open the truck door, and Aden was sliding across the seat and taking her with him. Almost immediately, they were surrounded by a whole bunch of vampires she didn't know then hustled up the stairs and into the house.

"ADEN!" LUCAS'S greeting was predictably enthusiastic, though the Irish vamp had learned long ago not to try the hugging thing on Aden. They did a shoulder bump instead, gripping each other's hands in a crushing hold, their shoulders slamming into each other hard enough to move a small house.

"Lucas," Aden greeted him. "Let me introduce you—"

"And you must be Sidonie," Lucas said before Aden could finish. He all but shoved Aden out of the way as he took Sidonie's hand in his, holding it with studied care and bringing it to his lips for a gentle kiss. "I'm Lucas," he purred, gazing at her over the pale curve of her fingers. "And I am *thrilled* to meet you."

Sidonie gave Lucas a doubtful look, eyes narrowed and her chin tucked down. Her eyes cut to Aden with a look that said, *What do I do now?*

"Down, boy," Aden growled and extricated Sidonie's fingers from Lucas's hold, before tucking her against his side.

Lucas's eyes widened. "I never thought I'd see the day."

"That goes for both of us. Where *is* Kathryn anyway?"

"My lovely *mate* is on the phone as always," Lucas said, and Aden didn't miss the emphasis on the word *mate*, which was a new development. "The FBI never rests," Lucas continued. "But she'll be joining us soon. Come on back to the office. We'll get this business out of the way first."

They started down the hall and were quickly joined by Lucas's lieutenant, Nicholas.

"Congratulations, *Lord* Aden," Nick said with a grin, offering the same kind of handshake as Lucas, albeit with less macho posturing.

As they strolled into the office, Aden leaned over and whispered in Sidonie's ear, "Remember what I said." He nodded to Bastien, who stepped up and slipped an arm around Sidonie's shoulders, pulling her away to one side where they stopped in front of a wall of black and white photographs.

Aden gave her a final reassuring look, then mirrored Lucas's move to the center of the room. There was a cluttered desk to his left, and a big leather couch to his right with a battered coffee table pushed off to one side.

Lucas stopped and turned to face Aden. "There's no need to stand on ceremony," he said in a rare moment of seriousness. "You know what to expect?"

"More or less," Aden agreed. "I got a pretty good taste the other night."

Lucas's lips flattened into a wry smile. "It ain't all roses and candy, but it's a good gig."

Aden shook his head, amused by his friend's description. "Better than the alternative."

"That's true," Lucas granted. "So, let's do this."

He offered his hand, just as he had earlier. Aden took it, gripping hard as they went into the usual alpha male contest, but then without any warning there was suddenly nothing *usual* about their meeting.

Aden's gaze flashed up to meet Lucas's as their hands seemed to fuse together, making it impossible to break their hold. Lucas's eyes had taken on a golden gleam, getting brighter with every second, and Aden could feel his own power rising to meet him. The whole situation felt damn close to a challenge, and he fought to remind himself that Lucas was his friend, and that this was a willing transfer of power.

The air around them grew electric. Papers flew from Lucas's desk, and pictures rattled on the walls. And still they clenched each other's hands, their gleaming eyes meeting in a test of wills that neither of them was willing to concede. Lucas's lips peeled back in a snarl as his fangs split his gums. Aden bared his teeth in a grinning response, his gums aching until his own fangs slid out with a growl.

Arm muscles bulging, their grip tightened, drawing them together until they were nearly chest to chest. Aden was a fraction taller than his former master, and far bulkier, but then, physical strength wasn't what mattered here. This was about raw power, pure and simple, and the two of them had power to spare. The walls began to groan from the pressure, and Lucas hissed his displeasure.

His fingers squeezed Aden's until they were both bleeding, until they crashed to the floor, kneeling together, hands still clasped before them.

"Aden, damn it," Lucas finally growled. "Let. Me. In."

Aden grinned, pleased to have made his friend ask, because hadn't that been the entire point of this little display? Lucas was a friend, but he was also a rival vampire lord. Because when it came to vampire lords, there was no other kind. Lucas had clearly hoped to use his knowledge of Aden, and the loyalty between them, as a weak spot, a door to slip into Aden's mind and force the transfer.

But he'd had to ask nicely instead.

With that thought, Aden opened his mind. The transfer started as a trickle, but soon became a flood, as the lives of thousands of vampires, every single bloodsucker living in the Midwest, roared into Aden's soul. The onslaught was a far greater burden than he'd ever thought to bear, far greater even than he'd expected after seizing power the other night. But he took them willingly, soothing their fears as, for the second time in months, they found themselves with a new master. He welcomed them all, the ones who greeted his arrival with joy and the holdovers from Klemens, even the ones who would miss the dead lord's depravity and utter lack of decency.

Aden absorbed their lives, their histories, until he thought he'd burst, until he thought he could bear no more, and still they came. And then finally, with a long relieved breath, Lucas's gaze broke, and his chin dropped to his chest. His grip loosened as his hand slipped away from Aden's to fall limply to his side.

With matching groans of relief, they both sat back on their heels, chests heaving with effort. The level of vampiric power thundering around the room dropped abruptly. Papers and pictures settled, albeit not in precisely the same places, and the walls ceased their groaning with only a few cracks to show for it.

Aden remained kneeling on the floor as he struggled to make sense of all the new feelings and needs filling every corner of his self. It hurt his soul to have them there. There was a constant tug of war inside him, between the person who was Aden and the vampire who was now Lord of the Midwest. He sighed tiredly and felt a gentle hand on the back of his neck.

"Aden?" Sidonie knelt next to him, her arm around his back as if offering him her strength and support, her cheek resting on his shoulder. "Are you okay?"

His arm reached out automatically, circling her waist and pulling her against him. He raised his head and met her concerned gaze, and he wondered anew that this woman loved him.

He touched his lips to hers. "I'm fine," he murmured against her lips. "Better now that you're here."

She blushed hotly, her gaze cutting sideways to where Lucas still knelt far too close.

"Don't mind Lucas," Aden assured her. "I've tuckered him all out."

"Fuck that," Lucas growled right on cue and surged to his feet, as if ready to do it all over again.

But Aden had anticipated his friend. He grabbed Sidonie and stood just as quickly, taking two steps back to put some distance between them.

Lucas stared at Aden for a long moment, then huffed a laugh. "This definitely calls for a drink." He looked around the office, which was somewhat worse for the wear. "Maybe we should have done this outside." He shrugged. "Too late now, but let's go down the hall. The booze is better, and, if I'm not mistaken, my Katie is waiting for me."

Sidonie closed her fingers over Aden's arm when they stepped out of the office, holding him back as the others crossed the main entrance hall and continued into the opposite wing, turning into a room about halfway down.

Aden gave Sidonie a questioning look.

"Is that the last of it?" she asked softly, touching his bleeding fingers. She lifted her head, and there was a sheen of tears in her eyes. For him? "Does it hurt?"

He had to admit his hand ached like a son of a bitch, like every finger bone had been cracked to the edge of breaking. But he couldn't tell her that.

"It hurts," he admitted, "but not too bad. Lucas is probably feeling much worse." He could only hope, he thought privately.

Sidonie shook her head, her lips flattened reprovingly. "You guys are like children in a schoolyard. Are you finished now? No more tests, no more earthquakes?"

They started walking down the hall to where the others could be heard talking.

"No more tests," Aden agreed. "As for the other, time is short. I'll need to consolidate the territory under my authority as quickly as possible."

She frowned in concentration. "You mean some of Klemens's

people might try to take it back from you?"

"They might try, but they won't succeed," Aden said, shaking his head. "I can't let them. There's a far greater danger to all of us looming on the horizon, and I'll tell you all about it . . . tomorrow," he added quickly. "I just became Lord of the Midwest, and damn it, I'm taking one night and forgetting everything else. No worrying about the territory or a war that might not come. Tonight, you and I are going to celebrate. All of that other crap will still be waiting for us tomorrow."

Epilogue

Chicago, IL

SIDONIE HURRIED into Aden's office suite in the new house. They'd moved in two weeks ago, after the shortest escrow she'd ever heard of. Vampires really must be magical, she thought, if they could purchase a property this big and expensive with a thirty-day escrow. It helped that the house had been empty for a while. The sellers had been what *their* agent called "highly motivated" and what *Aden's* agent called "desperate." They'd been more than happy to let the vamps begin renovating the property for their specific needs even before the purchase went through. Renovating in this case mostly meant installing extensive security measures, including a new front gate and sensors all over the grounds that were worthy of the White House. In fact, she was pretty sure the White House didn't have this level of sophistication, it being the peoples' house and all.

The new house was huge, three levels in two wings, including a basement which had been completely retrofitted to provide secure accommodations for lots of vampires. There were new vamps joining Aden's security detail every day, and Bastien had told her there would be many more. It was more than simple security. It was an army, and they were already training like one.

She and Aden had a private basement suite of their own, well removed from the others. Doors had been installed on all basement entrances that more closely resembled the kind on big bank vaults, and there were redundancies on redundancies.

Sidonie had gotten used to the security and to living mostly at night. Although being human, she still needed sunlight, and being female, she needed to have her hair and nails done and to indulge in the occasional shopping spree or lunch with friends.

Like today, when she'd discovered a whole new crop of friends who truly *did* get where she was coming from. Tonight was the official welcoming for Aden as Lord of the Midwest and member of the North

American Vampire Council. All of the other vampire lords were in town, and Sid had been delighted to discover that most of them had mates and they'd brought them along.

The mates had all gone shopping today, a field trip organized by Cyn, who was the woman Sid had seen across the room talking to Aden that very first night at the gala. Cyn had seemed to take it as her personal mission in life to get them all into as much trouble as possible. Fortunately, cooler heads had prevailed, and they'd settled for a wine-fueled lunch, with shopping afterward.

Sid glanced down at her arm and had to stifle a laugh. Well, cooler heads had *mostly* prevailed. She was feeling far more wicked than cool right now. But then Aden loved it when she was wicked, and Sid loved it when he taught her the error of her ways. She grinned happily, just thinking about it.

Kage was lounging on the big leather couch in the outermost room of the office suite, his muscular arms mostly bare in a short-sleeved shirt that showed off his tattoos, his piercings glinting in the low light. He grinned at her.

"How's things, Sid? You ladies have a good time today?"

"We did, yes, and look—" She pushed up the sleeve of her sweater. "I got a tattoo!"

Kage's smile froze on his face. He came off the couch in a single, smooth movement, his gaze fixed on the delicate feathered quill sketched on her right forearm.

As if drawn by Kage's reaction, Bastien, Travis, and Freddy suddenly appeared and gathered around, all of them staring at the tattoo as if expecting it to leap off her arm and go for their throats.

"Sidonie." Aden's deep voice had all four of his vampires jerking in surprise, which was a surprise in itself. She'd never seen them react that way before. They always knew where he was.

"Hey," she turned around with a smile. She didn't know what the vamps' problem was, but she was feeling good and was happy to see her lover. She crossed the room and raised her arms automatically for a welcoming hug and kiss. She was used to waking up with him and had missed him today.

But like the others, Aden's gaze was riveted to her forearm, with its new artwork.

His brow lowered, and he seemed to swell with anger, his eyes shifting to glare at his vampires.

"Who the fuck—" he started.

But Kage quickly interrupted, another first in Sid's experience. "I would never, my lord. Not any of us. But I'm not sure—"

Sid had had enough. She stomped her foot to get their attention, but directed her anger at Aden. "What's the big deal. It's my arm. If I want—"

"You let someone touch you, let them bleed you?" Aden demanded.

She opened her mouth to respond, then abruptly realized the significance of what she'd done. If she'd learned nothing else in her time with Aden, it was that vampire lords were territorial about *everything*, including, no, *especially*, when it came to their mates. They were the alpha of all alphas. They made Tarzan look like a piker. And a tattoo? What had she been thinking? Blood was the ultimate prize to a vampire. She might as well have opened a vein and let another male take a lick.

"I didn't," she said urgently. "Look . . ." She rushed over to the desk and opened a drawer, grabbing the package of hand wipes that was inside. Ripping it open, she rubbed the wipe over her pretty feather quill. "It's temporary," she told him. "It comes right off."

Aden gave her a level look, then glanced over her head at his vamps. "I'll see you at the conference room." With murmurs of "Sire" and "my lord," they all filed out of the office, closing the door behind them.

"Come here, Sidonie."

Sid thought about how wicked she'd been feeling, and how she'd looked forward to her time alone with Aden. But this was not what she'd anticipated.

She finished cleaning off her new "ink," then walked over to gaze up at him, her hands resting on his narrow hips.

"I'm sorry," Aden said, surprising her yet again. This whole evening was turning out to be one giant surprise.

Her face must have registered her shock, because he laughed and pulled her into his arms. "I may have overreacted. This time. If I'd paid attention to my nose instead of my eyes, I'd have known there was no blood and that the tattoo couldn't be real. But let's be clear about one thing. Your body is mine. No one writes on it, but me. And sure as hell no one pierces it but me." He punctuated this last with a press of his growing erection against her belly.

Sid drew a relieved breath, feeling as if the crisis was over. "What about if—"

"If you want a tattoo, Kage will do it, and I'll supervise. But I love your skin just the way it is."

"It was only temporary," she reminded him woefully. "We all got them. Different ones, but we all got something."

"Who's we?"

"All of the mates, even Colin."

"Who the *fuck* is Colin?"

"He's mated to Sophia, she's Lord of—"

"I know who Sophia is. I didn't know she was mated."

"He used to be a Navy SEAL. I think he and Cyn know each other."

"Cyn," he repeated drily. "I bet this was her idea."

Sid nodded. "When she found out I was mated to you, she couldn't believe it. She said you were a cold son of a bitch, and that you owed her money."

"Did she? She's just a sore loser. We hunted the same prey not long ago."

"Who won?"

"Depends on your point of view. Cyn located the prey, but I did the killing." He grinned. "She sent me a huge fucking bill for services rendered. What'd you do when she said that about me?" he asked curiously.

"I told her to keep her fucking opinion to herself, and besides, you were the sweetest man I've ever known."

"Sweet?"

"Sweet," she said firmly.

"Hmmm. Let me see your arm," he said, switching subjects.

He took her arm in his big hand and examined it carefully. The skin was red and irritated where she'd rubbed the tattoo off. It was especially noticeable, given her pale complexion, and she sighed.

Pulling her closer, Aden kissed her arm with a tenderness that she knew would surprise everyone but her. But then, as if to remind her of that fact, he immediately dropped his big hand to her butt and palmed both cheeks possessively. "I think we need to establish some ground rules, *habibi*. But, later." He patted her butt lightly. Sid took this as a warning of things to come and felt a zing of anticipation that quickly speared down between her thighs in a rush of wet heat.

"Okay," she said breathlessly.

He laughed. "That's my Sidonie. Come on, I don't want to be late for my first Council meeting."

ON THE OTHER side of the big house, Raphael stood silently on the mezzanine at the top of the stairs. His fellow vampire lords were gathering below, outside the conference room where they would soon meet as the North American Vampire Council to confirm Aden's addition to their ranks. The lords arrived in twos and threes, talking and joking with each other for the most part, shaking hands and clapping Aden on the back in congratulations. Even Sophia joined in the greetings, her big SEAL of a mate standing with her, daring anyone to get too close. Not so long ago, these meetings had been hostile affairs, the individual lords arriving late and leaving early, the eight of them sitting around a huge table, barely speaking.

Raphael had worked hard over the last two years to change that, doing whatever was necessary to put vampires on the Council who could, and *would*, work together. He had understood when no one else had that the vampires of North America would need a united Council, that an invasion from Europe was only a matter of time.

Down below, only one Council member still remained apart, his lip curled in disdain as he skirted the boisterous group and went directly into the conference room, his lieutenant behind him. Enrique Fernandez del Solar had ruled over Mexico for more than two hundred years and seemed determined to stay there for another two hundred. He was the only remaining member of the old guard on this Council, other than Raphael himself. But Raphael saw the future, while Enrique was more likely to dwell in the past. And that made him a potential breaking point for the entire continent. He would never agree to work with the others, and so he had to go.

Raphael knew things about Enrique's territory that he doubted even the old vampire lord knew, not least of which was that the loyalty of his lieutenant, Vincent, was no longer as staunch as it should be. Vincent had been lieutenant nearly as long as Enrique had been lord. But the Mexican vampires were increasingly frustrated by Enrique's iron rule, by his unwillingness to change, and Vincent was the focal point for that restlessness.

Unfortunately for Enrique, Vincent was about to discover a truth that would push his loyalty to the very brink. In fact, Raphael was betting the discovery would tip Vincent right over the edge, and that Enrique's lies would finally be his downfall.

"Are you going to tell them about the letter?"

Raphael's mouth curved into an automatic smile at the sound of Cyn's voice behind him. She stepped up to his side, and he slipped an arm around her waist, leaning down to breathe in the scent that was hers alone.

"Not yet," he murmured, answering her question.

"You don't trust them?"

"Not all of them."

Cyn studied the group as he had, her gaze sharpening when she caught a glimpse of Enrique through the open doors as he settled into a chair against the far wall.

"Enrique?" she whispered.

Raphael nodded.

"Anything we can do about it?"

He smiled in amusement and hugged her closely. "Even I can't control everything, my Cyn. But there are events moving even now that I suspect will see a new Council member joining us soon."

"My lord?" Jared's deep voice drew Raphael's attention to the fact that all of the other lords had disappeared into the conference room and taken their seats.

Raphael bent to brush his lips against Cyn's. This meeting was for the lords and their lieutenants only. One lord, one lieutenant. He could have taken Cyn instead of Jared. No one would have questioned him. But Jared needed to know that Raphael trusted him, and so did the others. Jared had a role to play before this was over, and he would need all of his confidence if they were to survive.

So, he kissed Cyn and said, "I'll see you shortly." He let his hand slide down her back and over the curve of her hip as he stepped away.

She nodded, seeming to understand, and he thanked whatever fate had brought her to his side. They would all need people they could rely on in the coming months, people who would stand by them and not flinch in the face of danger.

But he would need Cyn more than ever.

To be continued . . .
in VINCENT

Acknowledgments

This book is dedicated to Linda Kichline, the heart and soul of ImaJinn Books, who left us well before her time on earth should have been over. It was Linda who looked at my Vampires and saw what they could be. When every other editor was telling me my vamps were too violent or that the story didn't follow some mythical formula, Linda read the first few chapters and said, "I love it!" From the beginning, it was her skill and generosity that made my books possible. She was my friend, and I will miss her.

I want to thank Debra Dixon and everyone at both BelleBooks, Inc. and ImaJinn Books who stepped in to get Aden's story out to my readers on time, and to Patricia Lazarus for bringing Aden to life on his cover.

A very special note of thanks to Karen Roma for her generous contribution to Brenda Novak's Auction for Diabetes Research and for lending me her wonderful son Kristopher, a.k.a. Kage, so that he could not only fight at Aden's side, but also create such beautiful art on Aden and all of his vamps.

As always, I owe sincere gratitude to my friends and critique partners, Steve McHugh and Michelle Muto, for their help in making everything I write sound (and read) better. They're both wonderful writers, and I'm lucky to have them in my corner—check out their books on Amazon, you won't be sorry you did. Thanks also to everyone in the Misfit-Rebel Alliance for keeping me sane when the yard gremlins wrecked my sprinklers and flooded half my house. Rebel love all around.

More thanks to John Gorski, my go-to source for everything I need to know about guns and sharp pointy things. Thank you to Zainab Mulla (and her sister-in-law) for their help with Arabic, as well as to the anonymous participants in the several online forums where we discussed the variety and appropriateness of the many different Arabic endearments.

Endless thanks to all of my readers who make it possible for me to tell my stories and do what I love. And finally thank you to my Darling Husband and my very big family for all of their love and support in everything I do. I love you all.

Made in the USA
San Bernardino, CA
02 January 2014